# SPLASH

### Volume 1

**Jake Lewis**

Copyright © 2025. All rights Reserved.

SPLASH

## Copyrights

All rights reserved. No portion of this book may be reproduced in any form without written permission from the publisher or author, except as permitted by U.S. copyright law.

# CONTENTS

DEDICATION ............................................................................................ i
ABOUT THE AUTHOR ........................................................................... ii
CHAPTER 1 .............................................................................................. 1
CHAPTER 2 ............................................................................................ 14
CHAPTER 3 ............................................................................................ 27
CHAPTER 4 ............................................................................................ 31
CHAPTER 5 ............................................................................................ 42
CHAPTER 6 ............................................................................................ 71
CHAPTER 7 ............................................................................................ 87
CHAPTER 8 ............................................................................................ 96
CHAPTER 9 .......................................................................................... 101
CHAPTER 10 ........................................................................................ 117
CHAPTER 11 ........................................................................................ 147
CHAPTER 12 ........................................................................................ 166
CHAPTER 13 ........................................................................................ 178
CHAPTER 14 ........................................................................................ 185
CHAPTER 15 ........................................................................................ 193
CHAPTER 16 ........................................................................................ 214
CHAPTER 17 ........................................................................................ 242
CHAPTER 18 ........................................................................................ 257
CHAPTER 19 ........................................................................................ 284
CHAPTER 20 ........................................................................................ 301

CHAPTER 21 ................................................................................................ 308
CHAPTER 22 ................................................................................................ 336
CHAPTER 23 ................................................................................................ 351
CHAPTER 24 ................................................................................................ 359

# DEDICATION

For the younger me, who dared to dream.

For the love of my life, who dared me to keep dreaming.

For my Father, who sacrificed everything for me to have the freedom to dream.

# ABOUT THE AUTHOR

American novelist Jake Lewis writes fiction and non-fiction books, and sometimes finds a thin line to connect the two worlds. He is a masterful graphic designer that loves to recreate other companies' logos for fun, to practice. His passion for aquatics comes from his days lifeguarding in the blazing hot summers of Las Vegas, where he spent a crucial 22 years of his life, where he met the love of his life and developed his entrepreneurial spirit alongside his brothers.

That is also where he found his love for martial arts, obtaining a first-degree black belt in Tae Kwon Do, which he still practices today. He now resides in Washington as a publisher, author, designer, and speaker. He is accompanied by his fiancée and their dog, Murphy, where they enjoy gloomy weather and the best coffee on earth. Let's face it—with all of Jake's passions and adventures in his life, there will be plenty more stories to dive into.

Follow his Journey here: instagram/theelegendjake

# CHAPTER 1

*"Clear the pool! Everyone out of the pool now!"*

Every single soul froze still as the lifeguard blew his whistle and jumped off the guard stand located near the pool's edge.

*"Steven, grab the board, he's going down! STEVEN!"*

The lifeguard yelled as he sprinted vigorously toward the end of the pool.

*"Everyone out of the pool, All M-O-D's and Directors to the pool deck immediately!"*

Reported Steven over the radio. Racing down the deck. He grabbed a bright orange bag labeled "A-E-D" off of a hook located near the front pool entrance and continued his sprint toward the lifeguard. Just as Steven grabbed the board, the lifeguard jumped off of one leg into the pool, creating a ginormous splash that echoed through the pool deck with an eerie sound. **SPLASH.**

***

*"Jay, are you up? Jay!"*

A voice said from behind the closed door of Jay's room. Not understanding if the loud knocking was being delivered from his door or his dream, initially, he didn't respond until reality set in.

*"I'm up,"* mumbled Jay.

He realized that the loud obnoxious knocking was in fact coming from his bedroom door.

*"Last day of school, you don't wanna be late, you've already wasted half of this school year, the least you can do is show up on time for the last day. I have some eggs and sausage cookin' on the stove, I'll make you a plate!"* the voice said again

*"Ok!"* Jay mumbled again as he rolled out of bed.

As he sat at the edge of his bed and put his feet on the floor, an enormous sigh of relief came over him since this was the last time that he would have to put his school uniform on. The God awful ugly, untasteful, dreadful feeling of waking up putting on the uniform that two-hundred other students were wearing as well. Repetition seemed to bore Jay, especially when it came to appearances.

He stood up and limped into his closet, put his shoes on and slowly walked into the bathroom, brushed his teeth, brushed his hair, after he was finished he bent over the sink, turned on the cold water and rinsed his face and took a deep breath. *"Last day, let's do this"* he said quietly to himself as he put both of his hands on the sink counter looking straight forward.

Looking in the mirror back at him was a tan young man, 17 years of age with a mini beard and a bald fade. He had a build of an NFL wide receiver minus the height. He was 5'8. But Jay had no interest in football, matter of fact, the only thing he had an interest in at the moment was to pass the four final exams at school today. *"One... more day"* he said again as he dried his face. When he did he felt his hand start to shake uncontrollably, examining his hand he realized his hand appeared to be a shade of blue, none like he had never seen before.

Standing there shivering ice cold, he quickly hurried and put his sweater on. Still looking at his shaking hand, curiosity struck him until the clock on his wall caught his attention. It read 7:15 AM.

Jay grabbed his book bag and proceeded to walk downstairs, where his father and cousin were waiting for him at the table. Jay dropped his book bag in the living room on the way to the dining table. *"Good morning,"* Jay said to the two.

*"Morning"* they both said back in unison.

*"You ready for the last day?"* his Father asked as he was looking at Jay and his cousin. Jay sat down at the table

*"Absolutely*, I am very glad that it's here," Jay said.

*"Same here"* Jay's cousin Zeke commented.

They blessed the food and began to eat. Breakfast that morning in the Cruz household was a quiet but relaxing meal. It usually always was until Jay decided to mention his uncle which was the case this particular morning.

*"Hey Dad?"* Jay asked, looking across the table at his father. Mr. Cruz sat there with a stale drained look on his face. He looked at his son but said nothing.

*"Did you talk to Uncle yet?"* Jay asked.

Mr. Cruz took a deep sigh similar to Dragon's nostrils.

*"Young man, how many times must I tell you? Stop asking about your Uncle, he is gone, he's not here for all I'm concerned he could be halfway across the world right now."*

There was a brief silence in the room.

**\*SMACK\*** Mr. Cruz took is fist and slammed it on the table creating a loud thumping sound that startled the two boys. Jay glanced up at his Father with fear in his eyes as he flinched his head back from hearing the sound.

*"Jameson, boy, listen to me and listen to me clearly. The next time you bring him up, you can kiss your little camp trip goodbye. Go ahead, try me. Just because he wrote you a letter does NOT mean that we need him around. He made his choice, I don't not know where he is and I don't care. I am a private contractor, not an investigator. Eat your food, boy."*

The relaxation at the table vanished as there was now a tense feeling in the air. Jay continued eating his food in silence as it seemed that was his only option in moments like these.

Soon after breakfast, Jay, Zeke, and his father hopped in the family car and drove to the school in which Jay attended. He attended a school located in the middle of Los Aqui. It was a small city just on the outskirts of Las Vegas. Los Aqui had a place to call home for the Cruz family for as long as Jay could remember.

A hidden town to most of the world, outsiders never really considered anything much of Los Aqui. Despite its neglectors, Los Aqui had everything a regular city had. From the surface it was a city of normalcy.

As for the beings who formed this city they were the only ones truly aware that the city was not what it seemed under the surface.

Unlike some of the other teens that he grew up with, Jay had the opportunity to attend a prestigious Legion Leadership Academy. There were only three leadership schools in the whole city. Zeke however did not gain this prestigious opportunity. Never driving tension between them, they were happy in their separate schools.

With Mr. Cruz's Jeep strolling into the parking lot the three of them could see the sign in bright red letters that read **Legion Academy of Leadership and Excellence.**

The vehicle entered the parking lot and came to a screeching stop in front of two big and narrow gates. Their Father looked at Jay and said, *"Alright, last day of school, go make it happen."*

*"Thanks Dad, have a good day."* Jay said.

In just a matter of a few short seconds Jay looked at his cousin who stayed in the car. His cousin returned the look, their nonverbal communication skills worked for times like these, after all. It was obvious to both of them what the facial glares meant. If you live in the Cruz household, you ignore the elephant in the room. That's just the way it is.

*"Have a good day,"* Zeke said.

*"Alright, you too, I'll see you later".*

Jay hopped out of the jeep and closed the door. The vehicle sped off, revealing what was behind it. Legion, the school where Jay had spent the last four years trying to achieve his own version of academic success. In the days when Jay was younger he had dreamed of attending this school. Now that it had become such a formality, he was used to any criticism he would receive from his friends back in his neighborhood.

They would slander names at him such as **"privileged"**, or **"lucky"**, and even go far enough to make statements like **"he thinks he is too good for us"**.

While unfair, this didn't penetrate Jay much. He believed in the definition of success which he searched for while in preparation for a research paper he wrote at the beginning of the school year: **"The accomplishment of an aim or purpose."** There are two definitions of the word success, there is the first one which Jay believed in and the second which is: **"A person or thing that achieves desired aims or prosperity."**

Jay always believed that society focused on the second definition. He thought about this as he walked up to the gates of the school. Before he entered the gates, he had stopped his stroll to look at his hand. Relieved that his hand had returned to his normal skin color he smiled and continued walking into school.

As the bell rang, Jay immediately went inside the long hallway near the basketball court where he would go every morning to catch up with his friends. The bell rang exactly at 8:10 AM every morning. Jay proceeded to class. As Jay's first period began the class walked into room 202, in this particular room there were posters with motivational quotes plastered along the adjacent walls of the room.

In the front of the classroom was a big poster of Muhammad Ali standing right over Sonny Liston after he knocked him down on May 25th 1965. The knock down declared Ali the victor by knockout at 1:00 into the very first round.

Anyone in the world of boxing knows that this is not just any poster. This poster speaks more than just words, it delivers a sense of pride. For Jay, it resembled the notion of greatness and a relentless spirit.

It made him embody a sense of the mindset **"When life hits you, you HIT back."** It gave him chills every time he saw it because it forced him to think of his own struggle and how he always felt as if he was making a comeback.

# SPLASH

Below this poster sat a 43-year-old man with glasses, Jay's Science teacher.

Mr. Siege began to speak: *"Alright class, today is the last day of school.... You know, I hear students all the time say ...Why do I need to learn this? How is this going to help me in my future? That is the silliest thing to me, can someone please explain this notion to me?"* asked the instructor.

*"YES, Kye"* the instructor said loudly as he pointed to a student in the back of the class. The student began, *"Well a lot of the things we learn don't really correlate to the real world, we should be learning how to be a young adult, chase our career etcetera you know?"*

Mr. Siege took a second then began again. *"Not true, you must have surely paid attention to the speech I gave in the beginning of the year about how we correlate chemistry problem solving to real world situations did you not? As many of you know, I come from Mexico, where I'm from there is one school in my entire village. Growing up I had a couple of choices. My first choice was to go school, the school that was built in my village was about the size of two of these classrooms here at Legion High..."*

The students gasped

*".. There were 4 subjects, math, science, reading, and history. There were about 40-60 students in a class depending on the subject, school hours were held from 10AM - 6PM. It was first come, first serve. That's it. Because of this, some students weren't able to attend, forcing them to move to another part of Mexico or stay at home and work. My other choice was to stay at home and clean and work with no chance of getting a formal education. I chose to go school. I stand before you today because I made the RIGHT decision. I became a teacher because I plan to re-visit my village to build 1 school that has 15 different branches across Mexico, so I can ensure that every student has the opportunity to*

go to school. School is a privilege, not a RIGHT, with that being said... none of you, not a single person in this room has any reason for not being successful. If you did not learn a single thing from my class, please remember this. What you must realize is that the REASON you do what you do is more important than whatever you do in this life. The WHY behind your actions determines your outcome, your results determine your legacy. We are Legion, we do NOT settle, I challenge all of you to raise your standards.... Right here, right now."*

As Mr. Siege walked back to his desk the class was silent, the class was filled with deep thought. *"Alright this is the last test of the year"* Mr. Siege said as he passed out the test and answer sheets. *"The test is 50 questions, 40 multiple choice, and 10 written responses. You have one hour and a half to complete the exam. Does everybody have a test?"* Mr. Siege asked. The class nodded. Mr. Siege cleared his throat again *"OK, lets pray"* the class bowed their heads.

*"Heavenly father, thank you for your presence this year in our classroom. Thank you for blessing these students to learn and grow through these last few months and as we come to the end of this school year, let these students take what they have learned to remembrance. I pray for this test and for these students to apply what they have learned. Thank you for glory and grace. In Jesus' name, we pray. AMEN."*

**"Amen"**. The class repeated.

It was now time for the moment that Jay had been anxious for. He had stayed up all night studying for this test. The tests were out and the class was quiet.

Jay wrote his name on the top and proceeded to answer the test questions. 25 minutes had gone by and Jay had finished the last question. Very quick considering everyone had finished their test around the 1 hour mark. Jay stood up making all of the awkward noises the desk made in a quiet class room and walked to the front of the classroom and placed his test on Mr. Siege's desk.

Mr. Siege glanced at Jay, nodded then reverted his eyes back to his computer screen. Jay then walked back to his desk and returned sitting. While waiting for the class to end Jay began studying for his other classes that he had exams for: Math, Writing, and Geography.

An hour had almost gone by when Mr. Sidious broke the silence. *"Alright! Start finishing up, you all have 5 minutes left."* For Jay, those five minutes flew by faster than a Corvette going from 0-60 in six seconds. Supposedly similar to most people, time flew by a lot faster when preparation wasn't involved. He was completely unprepared for his math Final.

Before Jay knew it, those five minutes were up.

*"Class, thank you for an amazing school year. I wish you all the best. Have a good summer!"* Mr. Siege said.

The sound of the school bell made Jay's stomach drop more than give a feeling of sorrow because he was leaving his favorite teacher for the last time. The end of the school year in Mr. Siege's class ended surprisingly well, considering how it started, horrible but of course that was a thought for another time.

At this moment in time Jay was only focused on this dreadful test that was approaching like a line-backer trying to tackle him to win the game in the very… Last… Fourth… QUARTER.

The class left the room and flooded the halls to blend in with the rest of the school forming a merge of students commuting to class. By the time Jay arrived down the hall and around the corner to the math classroom the class was still testing, he joined his friend Kye and waited outside.

# SPLASH

Standing there waiting for Jay was a boy the same height as Jay with blonde spiky hair with brown eyes. Kye Nacksworth. As Jay walked up to him, he saw the improved version of Kye, the one that he was proud of.

Despite their differences in goals and a few outlooks they had remained partners, wingmen, batman and robin. Jay thought about how his friend would break the big news to his Mother today.

It seemed as though Ms. Nacksworth tried almost every alternative to give her son the drive to want to attend college, any college. One time she even tried bringing him along to her job, she worked as a marine biologist for the only true competitor of the **MAGIC** aquarium.

The Magic Aquarium was home to some of the world's largest sea animals. On the front doors to the entrance was a sign that read **"Magic Aquarium where there is one of every kind of animal that has been discovered by man."** The aquarium often got in trouble for this approach because while it was very unique and intriguing to have one of every sea animal it stirred up waves with the government.

Since Los Aqui was a water city or a city surrounded by water, it seemed only natural.

All that one would have some fascinating creatures to look at in an aquarium but the issue came from the scarcity of these rare animals that they would find.

This speculation eventually spun erratically into quite the case: Magic vs. The United States. At the start of the trial the United states argued that there were only a few of these rare animals and in many cases only one so in taking them, the aquarium would limit chances of reproduction and harm the natural flow of the sea.

# SPLASH

This was why the states were charging the aquarium. Now, of course this is one of many viewpoints chosen by the states but this was their strongest point. Magic responded with the notion that they clearly had the means to create reproduction and better growth to create more of these animals.

This played right into the hands of the states as they were naturally shocked to see an argument that was brought to them so easily. After all, Magic was one of the biggest aquariums in Los Aqui so one would think that they would not lose in trial. But even with the best litigation lawyer in Aqui, it was almost impossible to defeat the states.

Part of the rules of the United were that you were not allowed to use another lawyer from any other city, they had to be from your city. Weeks later as the trial continued, the states finally responded with a statement that shocked the world. Naturally since this was everyone's favorite aquarium the trial drawed tons of attention. People's eyes were glued to the television when the trial would air.

The states specifically stated that it would be unsafe to conduct unnatural reproduction in an unequipped hostile environment with unknown sources. Magic later on responded stating that they were fully prepared to undergo complete reproduction using enhanced features to better create a unique animal to aid humanity. Sokki remembers watching the heated debate on television. As does the whole nation remember staring at their TV set in shock... It played back in Kye's head.

*"Enhanced features such as?"* the attorney of the states responded.

*"We have no further comment on that at the moment."* Magic responded.

*"And where do you plan on getting this technology, why do you have it... HOW do you have it?"* The state's attorney asked. *"Well, that... is*

*one question for you, you and YOU!"* the Magic attorney said pointing at the Judge, and two members of the offense team.

*"Should ask yourselves, oh well why is that? You might ask? Well we have this technology from Area 9. And you, the United Government approved it, with that being said, you can thank your commanding officer and chief"* Said the Magic Attorney.

*"Are you referring to area 9 from Reno Nevada?"* Asked the United States attorney.

*"Yes"* The Attorney from magic replied.

*"Is this true your honor?"* The plaintiff asked the judge.

*"Yes, this is correct"* judge Hellerson responded.

*"No further questions your honor"* The Plaintiff responded.

Kye remembers the whole debate from start to finish, especially since he and Jay had to write a five page report on it. Kye had aided Jay on the paper since he was the one that watched it the most.

**PALA: Perspective Aquarium Of Los Aqui.** The aquarium was built shortly after MAGIC came into its massive existence. The two aquariums were similar, minus the fact that **PALA** featured top biologists from around the world with an expert research and dive team. Which is a factor to why Ms. Nacksworth brought her son to the aquarium last year when the schools were out for a training day.

Kye had always had an interest in the Marine animals. His mother used opportunities such as that day to hope to present an idea in his head that he could work and be around these animals if he studies and attends college. She never knew if these ideas were forming any solid thoughts in Kye's head but it was always worth a try. Ms. Nacksworth had earned a Ph.D. in Biology so for her, education was a must.

She was from a small town where everyone including her family all went to college. It became not only a family tradition but a life long tradition, so it was completely normal for her to speculate over this in every way imaginable. She began to formulate a possible path of how this was possible, she thought about Jay and about how her worry began when Kye and Jay went to a college fair in the summer of the freshmen year.

Ms. Nacksworth was so excited for her son's first college fair, she made sure he had a suit and tie with his hair cut **"the whole 9 yards"** as she would say. When he got back from school that day of the fair he walked in the house and when his mother asked him about the fair his response was *"I don't know, it was ok, I guess. They all seem the same to me, yeah, I'm not sure about college."*

He went upstairs to his room before she could even respond. That day she sat there in the living room staring at the carpet. At this time, she only thought about how Jay must have been a positive influence on her son's life. Ever since the two met in their freshman year, they seemed to have always connected which was a huge relief for her considering the fact that she thought there might have been the slight possibility that Kye would have a little trouble making friends.

This wasn't the case at all, midway through his first year of high school, he was frequently trying to bargain with his mother to allow him to bring friends over but the only friends that ever came in were Jay and Sokki.

# CHAPTER 2

"Did you study?" asked Kye as he nudged Jay out of his day dreaming zone. "Man, you ok? I think you were literally just daydreaming."

"Huh? Yes," he said hesitantly.

"I was thinking about this weird dream last night" whispered Jay.

"Umm Jay, you always have weird dreams" said his friend

"I know... but this one was different". Replied Jay.

"How so?" Kye asked.

"Well, I was on a pool deck"

"Really? Huh you haven't swam in ages, that IS weird." Said Kye quickly,

"I know right, yeah I was jumping into the water to SAVE someone" said Jay.

"Wait! A lifeguard?"

"Yes, keep your voice down please" Jay said

"Ok-ok, sorry, I know this is random but did you tell your Dad about your hand tingling yet?"

"It sounds weird when you say it like that and no, i didn't tell him yet im not ready"

"Maybe we should whisper.... INSIDE the CLASSROOM!" Mrs. Noble said with a slight smirk

Jay and Kye realized at the moment that they were the only two in the hallway.

*"Oh, wow I didn't even hear the bell"*. Jay said startlingly,

*"Me neither, sorry Mrs. Noble"* said Kye.

As they walked inside behind Mrs. Noble, Jay continued to whisper to Kye.

*"But to answer your question nope! I didn't study…. It's ok though, I'll tell you one thing, I am sure ready for this speech we are doing in English".* Jay said as he was looking at a quote that was posted on the wall of the hallway right next to the class.

The quote on the wall read: **"Success is a lot of little things done great day after day".** - **Ray Lewis.**

An odd reality rose in Jay at a very young age, most children his age that he grew up with didn't take interest in most subjects especially subjects like English and history.

With Jay, it was different. He loved writing essays and short stories and his favorite subject was history. Another firm belief that it was our liberal duty to learn our history so that it does not repeat itself. He was taught that history always has a funny way of repeating itself….even in our daily lives.

Throughout the day, there was a feeling of comradery amongst his fellow peers but in the same instance there was a warm feeling of relief, due to Jay's first two years of high school being the farthest from smooth as possible. Of course one, not even Jay's family could not perceive this harsh reality from the outside looking in. From the outside perception it simply appeared that he was a privileged kid that went to a very expensive school and got whatever he wanted, or course this wasn't reality.

An hour and a half had gone by. After, it almost seemed as if he had just come out of war, like a hard fought battle. After period two was finished, the bell rang for lunch.

Jay and Kye left Ms. Noble's classroom and walked to put their backpack with their belongings inside their locker then proceeded down the long walkway just outside the main building that led to the gymnasium which was also the cafeteria. This was no ordinary cafeteria, inside there were tables set amongst the side of the bleachers for the students to sit and eat.

A full basketball court with a weight room in the back through the doors next to the kitchen. Not your ideal cafeteria, especially for a leadership school that cost something near $20,000 to attend, but nevertheless, the school was resourceful. Everyday, lunch time was a time to relax but today was different. Jay was on a mission, had a speech to give, he had given three speeches this school year but this one was completely different.

He wanted this one to be the best. Ever since Jay's class was assigned this particular speech he had been preparing for it. The assignment was given half way through the year and Jay started working on it immediately.

The instructions were to give a speech based on one of three types:

1. Informative,
2. Persuasive or
3. Motivational.

It was very difficult for Jay to choose a type, Jay loved to teach, from that standpoint the decision to choose a speech type appeared to be an easy one. Not quite, ever since Jay was 14 he wanted to be a lawyer, he had such nache for arguing, while it was used in a negative connotation when he was younger he always knew it would turn into a learning lesson and something positive.

If one thing Jay knew how to do, it was argue. His peers could possibly answer the question of whether or not he was persuasive. The last choice was motivational, this seemed like the last choice that he would pick.

*"You're thinking about that speech, aren't you?"* Kye said as they were sitting down at the table waiting for lunch to be served.

*"Yep!"* Jay replied.

*"Dude, you're fine."*

*"I hope so,"* Jay replied laughing.

About 45 minutes went by after the pizza was delivered to Jay's table, then the bell rang..

*"Well! Time to go to class!"* One of Jay's classmates blurted out from down the table he was sitting at.

Jay and Kye grabbed their bags and headed back down the pathway that led them to the building where their class was located immediately on the left through the double doors. Jay and Kye walked inside and took a seat. They usually always sat next to each other in class when possible, especially during English.

*"Alright class, hurry, hurry, take your seats, we have a lot to get done and not that much time to do it…… quiet please, we will start in one second."* Ms. Till said sharply.

She closed the door to the classroom and walked to the front of the classroom to start organizing her papers she would be using to grade. Ms. Till is the 11th grade English and performing arts teacher. She has a Ph.D. in English studies and a Masters in communication. Somehow, her English was perfect. She had long brown hair, wore glasses with a long black dress to class almost everyday.

"I swear black must be her favorite color" said Kye as he chuckled in a low tone of voice.

"Yes, something like that since she always wears it." replied Jay.

"Hey, are we meeting Sokki after school today to plan this trip?" asked Kye.

"Yeah she is meeting us by the band room after school."

***BANG!*** Jay jumped as he looked at Ms. Till, he could see she just a textbook on the table. The whole entire class turned and stared at Jay and slammed Kye as they saw Ms. Till glaring at them.

"Oh, I'm sorry, did that STARTLE you gentlemen? Maybe you two should focus more on class and less on your little side conversations…. Kye!" Ms. Till said, raising her voice as she was looking in Kye's direction.

"Yes ma'am." Kye answered.

"How long is our class today?" Ms. Till asked rapidly after Kye spoke.

"Ummmmm, An hour and a half" Kye stated proudly knowing the answer.

*Jay could already tell where this outburst was going…*

"How many students are there in this class?" Ms. Till asked quickly again.

Kye began to speak slowly "Hoooow aaaam I suuuuuppo…"

"How many?!" Ms. Till said as her voice sharpened.

"Ummmm…. 1, 2… 3, 4, 5, 6… There are 17" Kye replied after counting the rest in his head.

"Correct, now, how long is the assigned speech?" Ms. Till asked in a calmer voice as she tapped her pen on the desk repeatedly.

As she was standing up leaning on her desk at the front of the classroom with one hand, with one leg crossed in front of the other, she waited for Kye to respond. The whole class was sitting quietly, but Jay had a sense in the air that the class was enjoying this little mini dialogue between the two, mostly because students at Legion love to stall when it comes to taking a test. Especially when they are not prepared. It made Jay think of Ms. Till's favorite quote of all time. **"Failure to plan is planning to fail"**.

"*5 minutes,*" Said Kye.

"*17 students' times five minutes is what?*" Asked Ms. Till

"*85 minutes,*" Kye responded.

"*Now, you out of anyone should understand that we do not have a lot of time, especially for someone who has the best scores in Math this year in the entire school. So please, be quiet!*" Ms. Till said as she sat down at her desk.

Somehow Ms. Till had a way of giving a little embarrassment to create a humble learning-teaching moment while raising students up at the same time as well.

"*Your number one in math? I didn't know that, congrats man!*" Jay whispered to Kye as he gave him a fist pump.

"*Thanks man*" Kye said as he smirked

"*It's definitely not you!*" said a student who heard Jay's comment from across the room.

"*Quiet Kevin*" Ms. Till said in a sharp tone again.

Jay was quiet, as he looked to the back of the classroom, Jay noticed that the door was slightly cracked open, ***Knock, Knock***

"Oh come on, you have got to be kidding me!" Ms.Till said under her breath but loud enough for most of the class to hear.

"Come in!" Ms. Till said.

"Hey Ms. Till? Mr. Siege asked me to give this to you".

The student entered and began walking to the front of the classroom carrying a long orange envelope. She had long red hair with dark brown eyes wearing square glasses with rounded edges. She approached Ms. Till and handed her the envelope. As Ms. Till grabbed the envelope, she opened it and pulled out a stack of documents. A stern look came over her face.

"Thank you Sokki, You may return to class now" Ms. Till said softly with a smile on her face.

"You're welcome," Sokki said. As she walked towards the door she stopped and turned towards Kevin.

"Oh, and Kevin... It's okay because Jay has the number one score in English this year out of the whole school... Just letting you know." Sokki said as she turned and winked at Jay.

The class began to make sound effects "*ooooooo*" said some of Jay's peers. She turned toward Jay and Kye sitting in the corner.

"I'll meet you guys after school by the band room" whispered Sokki.

Kye gave a thumbs up and smiled.

"We will see if that spot holds after the speech" Mumbled Ms. Till under her breath.

Jay was still quiet, this angered him a little. Jay hated the feeling of doubt, but nevertheless he viewed it as a huge motivating factor. His whole life he felt he had to prove people wrong because he believes everyone doubts him, so when someone is giving him credit and believes in him, he is shocked. At this moment and time the classroom was completely silent with the exception of Mrs. Till clicking away at her computer.

*"One sec, class"* Ms. Till said as she looked at the door and jumped out of her seat abruptly. She walked towards the door and poked her head out the door...

*"Is this what I think it is? Does this mean we are canceling it?"* Ms.Till asked someone outside her classroom.

*"No, we will just have to be very careful with the students"* whispered the voice back.

*"We can not afford to lose any more,"* Ms. Till said.

*"I... know, I know,"* said the voice back. Ms.Till closed the classroom door and began to head to the front of the classroom again.

*"Was that Mr. Sidious?"* Kye asked, looking over at Jay.

*"I believe so, I couldn't hear his voice"* Jay said quietly because he didn't want to let Ms. Till hear them talking. Jay paid less attention to the voice behind the door and more to the time when he met his friend Sokki.

In their freshman year, a teacher that they had for Biology for Beginners, took them on a field trip to the Magic Aquarium. On their lunch break, Sokki had wandered off to the jellyfishes. These were highly sensitive jelly fish so one could actually see their tentacles light up with shock waves. Jay had wandered away from the group as well, he ended up by the jellyfish section with Sokki, when he saw her he said

"*Aren't you supposed to be with the rest of the class*" in a deep voice pretending to be their biology teacher. She turned around quick,

"*You scared me! ...I thought you were Mr. Wiler.... Wait, aren't you supposed to be with the rest of class?*" she said.

"*I am sent to come find you! They sent out a search team*" Jay said, sipping his soda. Sokki had a shocked look on her face.

"*Oh no!*" she yelled.

"*I'm KIDDING, lower your voice... I highly doubt that he realizes that we are gone.......soooooo whatcha lookin at?*" Jay asked as he saw Sokki glaring at the glass. Where there were jelly fishes floating around in the bright blue water

"*They are so cool, you can see the electromagnetic waves jumping back and forth from their tentacles to their frontal corporole,*" she said.

"*I can't see that... and their what to their what?*" Jay asked.

"*Everytime they move in a direction the brain or frontal cortex which is the decision making part of the brain... it adjusts the amount of electromagnetic pulses or waves it distributes to different parts of the body.... Watch*" she said. She put her hand up to the glass and pressed against it. The Jellyfish placed its tentacle up against the glass. The tentacle seemed to glow bright blue and the electric pulses raced faster and faster through its tentacle.

"*That's pretty... Rejuvenating, it's as if almost I can feel their pulses... As if... We are connected*" she said, staring at the Jellyfish.

"*That's crazy...I'm Jay by the way,*"

"*Im Sokki, nice to meet you*"

"*Oh yeah, you moved from....*" Jay started,

"*Hungary,*" Sokki said.

"*Yes,*" Jay said, relieved that she finished his sentence.

"*Yep, that's me,*" She said.

"*Well, nice to meet you as well,* " he said to her.

***

From that odd interaction they kind of naturally just always bonded with each other, hanging out at school and they became really good friends over the course of two years. That moment when they met was the first and only time that they would go to the Magic aquarium. The students, unaware at the time of the future of the aquarium, the most talked about place in the whole city for its lack of immoral standards. The aquarium, currently involved in a nationwide court case.

The sound of Ms. Till's voice pulled Jay out of his day dreaming mode.

"*Alright, let's begin. Kye pass these out pleas*e" Ms. Till said as she gave a stack of paper to Kye.

"*Yes Ma'am,*" Kye said.

As Kye began to hand out the stack, Mrs. Till began to explain.

"*On the paper you are being given, you will see that this is the order in which we will go in.*" She said,

"*Remember, all students must be quiet during speeches, your speech will be five minutes long, you will be graded on all of the concepts we have been studying this year. Sentence structure, pronunciation, creating a visual, story creating, and deliverance*" Ms. Till said.

Kye had finished handing out all of the papers to the entire class.

*"I'm second, what are you?"* Kye asked Jay.

*"Last! Ha! That's funny"*

*"LOL,"* Kye said.

Jay looked at him fast *"Did you just say LOL? That is only when your texting"*

*"Whatever"* Kye said as he chuckled.

*"Is something funny Mr. Cruz?"* Ms.Till asked, raising an eyebrow at Jay from the front of the classroom.

*"No ma'am"* Jay replied

*"Alright then, Samantha, you're up!"* Ms. Till said sharply

Samantha was the Valedictorian of the school finishing out this year with a 4.35. In Los Aqui, the grading system was different. The top students had a 5.0+ in their school system. Jay never did get to meet Samantha until their junior year. In a way, he looked up to her. Similar to the Muhammad Ali poster, she seemed to have that drive for school. Jay believed you could apply that drive to anything. With all the gifts that Jay had been blessed with, he loved to speak almost the most out of anything.

Samantha began to speak to the class.

*"While most young adults at this stage in their life found themselves asking the question: What am I going to do after I graduate? I have been asking myself what I WANT to do? Because after all, there is a difference. What's my calling? And I have decided, I want to become a doctor. I feel there is no better calling than saving lives every single day, that is what I want to do. Let's take a look at the medical field..."*

Jay had always known that Samantha wanted to be a doctor. This is the first time she openly expressed it to everyone. He was glad to see her finally announce it. Samantha continued to speak and before he knew it, it would be time for him to deliver his speech. Nervous, yes, but overwhelmed, not quite.

When Samantha finished, the whole class clapped, as it was mandatory to do so once a speaker finished speaking.

Next was Kye. For Jay, this was like icing on the cake. Jay had already heard this speech from Kye about a half a dozen times. He had been practicing it for a very long time. Jay would go over to Kye's house, listen to him give a speech, and correct it. Give him pointers, correct, give suggestions.

Kye was giving a speech on social media, it was an informative speech but he was also defending it. Kye believed that social media was one of the best things that has happened to the world and that we should use it to our benefit. Jay found it ironic that Kye chose that topic because Jay felt strongly about the topic as well. Jay thought about this through the duration of Kye's speech.

… *"So after all of that, two people that haven't talked in over 10 years are now friends again, through facebook…. So the next time you see one of the little white ghosts, or the blue F, or the blue bird…. All I want you to do is take a step back and think about what exactly they symbolize and what would our country be without it"*

Kye stated as he finished his speech standing still as he was staring at the class. The class began to clap. Kye walked back to his seat. Jay gave him a fist bump.

*"Good job!!"* Jay said as Kye sat down.

*"Thanks for all your help,"* Kye said to Jay.

*"Oh, no problem,"* Jay responded. Jay's notion was correct, it only seemed like a few minutes flew by and it was already his turn. Sitting

there at his desk, nervous he looked at his hand, it was a vibrant shade blue yet again.

# CHAPTER 3

*"Jay, you're up"* demanded Ms. Till.

Jay got up out of his seat hesitantly and walked towards the front of the cricket quiet class room with a smirk on his face. He turned and faced the class and began to speak

His voice trembled as he started to speak.

*"So I'm sitting in the back of the classroom, listening to everyone talk about some of the things they love and what they want to do in life, but I haven't heard anyone talk about what it takes to get there. Let me tell you a story. There was once this 12 year old boy. The boy and his dad walked into a martial arts school and when they got inside, the martial arts school was empty. Standing behind the counter they saw a middle aged man with a beard. "The dad looked at the man and said,"* Are you the master?" "Why Yes I am. Go ahead! Take a look around, please be my guest".

So the boy began to step on the mat.

*"Take your shoes off before stepping on the mat,"* the instructor said.

*"How come?"* The boy asked.

*"Because where you are standing is sacred ground, when something is sacred, you respect it".*

*"Yes sir"* the boy said.

The boy stepped on the mat and all of a sudden chills rippled through the boy's body. He had never had anything like this happen in his life before. The boy began to walk forward, with each step the boy started to feel lighter. He walked up to the kicking bag sitting in the corner.

*"Go on. Give it a kick"* the master said.

The boy stepped back, raised his right leg and kicked the bag. And as he kicked the bag chills rippled through the boy's body. A smile came over the boy's face. The instructor looked over at the boy's dad and asked; *"would you like him to join?"*

*"Yes sir!"* said the boy before his father could get a word out. Over the next year and a half the boy had got halfway to his black belt. He already had a sprained ankle and a cyst in his right hand from hitting the bag too hard. The boy didn't quit.

The boy's best friend died when he was 13 years old. The boy fought and sparred with the master's son and received a black eye from a spinning back kick that landed on the boy's right eye. The boy didn't give up, he kept going.

Another year and a half went by and it was time for the boy to test for his black belt. At the beginning of the test. The master lit a candle and placed it on a kicking bag and said *"blow the fire out with a kick without hitting the bag or the candle."* If you don't blow it out, you must run one lap around the mat once and try again.

*"Yes sir,"* replied the boy. The boy threw his hardest kick, the fire only wavered. He ran around the mat. He tried again. Same result. He tried again, over and over and over but nothing happened. The fire only wavered.

*"You can quit if you want,"* said the master as the boy was sweating profusely.

*"No sir,"* the boy said. He spent 2 hours kicking this fire from this candle.

*"Since you can't get it, we will move on."*

After that, the master had brung a board with spikes on it out from the closet. The master wrapped a blindfold over the boy's eyes.

*"I want you to punch this board of spikes".* The master said.

*"But won't I hurt my hand?"* The boy asked.

*"Who told you that you were going to hurt your hand? What are you afraid of?! Face your fears!"* the master said.

*"I c... I can't"* said the boy back. *"Punch it!"* the master said.

The boy clinched his teeth and threw the hardest punch he could. The master turned the board around to the flat wood surface and the boy's fist shattered the board in two. The master took the blindfold off. The master looked at the boy and said, *"Your fears are only your fears because you let them be. They aren't real. What's real is this"* he put his fist on the boy's heart. *"Do you feel that? That's real! Don't ever be afraid of an illusion. You must have faith. Trust your instinct, trust yourself."* The master walked to the front of the classroom. *"What have you lost since you joined my school three years ago young man?"* asked the master.

*"I've lost a lot. I have no more friends, my best friend passed away, I have a cyst on my hand, I have sprained my ankle three times."* The boy said

*"Yes, you have endured a great deal. Therefore I tell you, there is no success without sacrifice."* Two weeks later the Master conducted the boy's black belt ceremony. His family and friends were there.

***RING!*** The bell at Legion rang for the 3rd period to end. Ms. Till and the class didn't even flinch. It was an unspoken rule that Legion students don't leave until the teacher dismisses them. The class was completely silent including Ms. Till. Jay continued.

*"His final task was to break 3 boards. The boards were spaced apart being held by three different people. The boy kicked two of the boards in half. He ran to the 3rd one jumped, turned sideways in air and extended his leg and he cracked the board wide open with his heel!"*

He hit the board so hard that one of the pieces flew into the crowd and almost hit someone. There was a celebration and after, his heel was in pain and the pain stayed with the boy for the rest of his life. The pain was to remind him of his sacrifice. The boy finally understood the term **"no success without sacrifice."**

"SO," Jay said as he stared at the class taking one step forward.

"I am sitting in a room full of dreamers and the walls are crawling with aspirations. But I ask you this: **What are you willing to sacrifice for your success?** Thanks, that's my time." Jay said. As the class stood up, they roared in applause.

"Jay, that was…. That was beautiful Mr. Cruz". Mrs. Till said as she had the biggest smile on her face that Jay has ever seen.

"Class, you are dismissed. Have a great summer!" Mrs. Till said smiling at the class

"Yeah man that was awesome! Good job" another student said as he was walking out of the classroom. Jay glanced down at the orange envelope on Ms. Till's desk the words **"CAMP CHOICE VOIDED - DNE"** Jay smiled as he walked back to his desk to grab his things. When he walked out of the classroom Kye was standing there waiting for him.

"Dude, what was that? That was phenomenal, look! I still have goosebumps!" Kye said as he pointed to his arm. It was covered in goosebumps and the hair on his arm raised up.

"Do I get to keep my number spot in English?" Jay asked looking back at Ms. Till as he was the last one to leave the classroom. Ms. Till smiled again,

"It appears that way, have a good summer Jay"

"You too."

# CHAPTER 4

Jay and Kye began to walk to their last and final period of the day. *"That's crazy, do you see WHY I was so nervous now?"* Jay said, still smiling.

*"Umm yes?? Of course……. Wow."* said Kye, still looking at his arm. Kye had goosebumps from the speech….

*"Please, please tell me you studied for THIS test."* Kye asked.

They were now standing on the side of Mr. Worthy's classroom. Room 98.

*"Yes, I did. This class is always so peaceful".* Jay said.

***RING!*** The bell sounded, the students that were waiting on the side of the various classrooms went inside the classroom and took their seats. Mr. Worthy was an 11th grade professional development teacher. He had a Masters in communication and a Ph.D. in Psychology, something that Jay never understood in a clear way.

He viewed it as a type of a Jedi mind trick to play with people's minds. In Jay's mind it was kind of scary to think that they train people how to do that and then give them a degree afterwards. In 1996, they were a dying breed.

All of a sudden they appeared again more masterfully than ever. Mr. Worthy was about 5'2 with a long white beard and always wore a tan-like sweater. When the students walked in, Mr. Worthy was standing at the front of the classroom with his hands behind his back as if he was about to perform a magic trick. It was a huge hint to why the students call him a wizard.

*"Ladies and gentlemen. Let's face it, you are not boys and girls anymore so I will not treat you like it. Mr. Worthy will treat you like the young adults you are. That is why we are not taking a test, or a final*

exam. We are simply going to watch a video. If you watch the video, you get 100% on the final exam" Mr. Worthy said as he raised two fingers on each hand, bending them twice to signify quotations.

"Haha!" chuckles came from the class.

"Awesome," some students whispered. There was chatter among the class and they began to celebrate.

"OOOOOR we can just take a 100 question test about the fundamental principles of how to develop self confidence with the 250 terms we learned this year". Mr. Worthy said with a serious face. The class became deathly silent.

"Well alright then, I need you quiet while I figure out this video" Jay looked over at Kye sitting next to him and mouthed the words "and to think I really studied for this test." Kye chuckled under his breath.

"Ah hah! Here we go!" Mr. Worthy said.

"Ok, please put everything under your desk," Mr. Worthy said. The video began to play. To Jay's surprise the video had interviews from famous people that are very successful. After the video was over the screen went blank.

Mr. Worthy stood up out of his chair and asked the class "So what did you think?" Most students in the class expressed that they liked the video.

"Which interview did you like the best? Mr. Worthy asked.

"Kobe's" Jay blurted out.

"How come?" Mr. Worthy asked as he turned quickly, pointing at Jay.

"Well because, since we all know him as Kobe, He is so great with so much talent. He really was strategic in his work but I like how he embodied such a powerful work ethic. He was relentless in working hard to become the best. You can see that 2nd place was not an option for him. Koby Bryant makes the people around him better and I think that we can all take that and apply it to our everyday lives. IF... only IF we work hard enough to be the best then, and only then can we achieve it. Hard work beats talent when talent doesn't work hard".

"Exactly! Very good Jay. How many rings does he have?" Mr. Worthy asked Jay.

"5" responded Jay.

"Yup, one less than..." Mr. Worthy paused.

"Micheal Jordan" Jay responded.

"Oooook, so let me ask you this, Kobe Bryant has 5 rings and Micheal Jordan has 6 rings, six championships correct?" Jay nodded. Mr. Worthy continued

"Ok, we all know that Micheal Jordan is the best basketball player of all time so why is Kobe considered to be the best player of all time in discussions when Kobe only has five rings and Jordan has six?....Anyone can answer this question" My. Worthy said softly.

"Well because he worked harder," A student said in the classroom.

"Nope!" Mr. Worthy said quickly" There was a short pause...

"Because he played longer," Another student said.

"Who said that? Emily? Nope, valid but that is not what i'm looking for. Anyone else?" Mr. Worthy asked again.

"He had more points than Jordan right?" A third student asked.

"That may be true but that is not the answer I'm looking for. Guys, the reason that Kobe is said to be the best is because of the quality of his work. The quality in which he plays basketball. His standard of quality is VERY high. I know you have all heard Mr. Siege tell you to raise your standards..."

"*He told us today!*" a student interrupted. Mr. Worthy paused for a moment...

"*Why do you think that is?*" Mr. Worthy asked curiously as he looked up at the clock on the wall in the back of his classroom. The door to the classroom opened. Sokki entered the room and sat down. Mr. Worthy stopped pacing back and forth and paused to put his hand on his hip as he raised one eyebrow staring at Sokki.

"*Mrs. Till let us out early,*" Sokki said, responding to Mr. Worthy's stare.

"*Very well,*" Mr. Worthy said as he turned his attention back to the student he was previously talking to. "So *John, why does Mr. Siege tell you to raise your standards?*"

"*So we can improve the quality of our work?*" John replied.

"*YES! Thank you, so that you can improve the quality of your work, ladies and gentlemen, once you begin to raise your standards and improve the quality of your work you begin to reach a new level and get the things you want out of life.*" Mr. Worthy said. There was a long pause and the class was silent. Mr. Worthy stepped forward, crossed his arms and put one hand up to his chin to hold his head.

"*Always remember this in life.....It is in the moment of your greatest struggles and triumphs that you will discover who you really are.*" Mr. Worthy said, scanning the classroom ending as he caught Jay's eye.

*RING!* The bell had interrupted the silence.

"*Have a good summer!*" He said trying to speak over the bell. The class became noisy as students grabbed their bags and flooded the halls with their chatter.

"Jay, let me talk to you for a second," Mr. Worthy said as the last of the students left the classroom.

The class was now empty, Jay wasn't really hesitant, maybe he would have been if this wasn't the last day of school. The only possibly negative conversation that could occur right now was for Mr. Worthy to tell him that he failed his class which Jay knew wasn't the case. Personal development was one of his best grades. Jay ran this process of elimination in his mind while approaching Mr. Worthy very slowly.

"Jay, what do you want to do with your life? What is your dream job per say, or do you have one?" Mr. Worthy asked.

"I want to be a motivational speaker, I want to travel the world. And motivate and inspire people everywhere to chase their passion." Jay said. What he released to Mr. Worthy, he hadn't spoken of with anyone. Not his father, not Kye, not Sokki. Not a single soul. This was his ultimate dream.

"That is pretty awesome, that is inspiring within itself. You will get there, I know that for sure. You are a very talented individual. I want to see some leadership out of you young man because I know it is in there. I feel that there is something more in store for you as well… I'll tell you what, come speak to me on the very first day of the next school year." Mr. Worthy said as he was sitting back in his chair behind his desk making direct eye contact with Jay.

"You're not coming to camp?" Jay asked.

Mr. Worthy leaned forward and tilted his glasses slightly off his nose *"Did I say that? I don't think I mentioned anything about camp did I? Come see me on the very first day of school and we will talk."*

"Yes sir" Jay said.

"Ok, on you go, I have a meeting to catch," Mr. Worthy stated.

"Have a good summer," Jay said as he left the classroom.

After Jay walked out of Mr. Worthy's classroom he checked his phone for any missed messages. To his surprise, he didn't have any missed calls or messages, unusual for the end of a school day. As he looked up the hallway that was still flooded, students talking and laughing, smiles were everywhere, Jay felt like he was at a parade, he felt a sense of relief.

The final bell had rung and school was over. He made his way down the hall to where the band room was located. Along the way he saw his fellow students running and hugging each other, as he walked past room 56 he saw that the door was cracked open slightly. When he turned his head and glanced in he saw Mrs. Till, Mr. Sidious, Mr. Worthy and Mrs. Noble inside standing around a table talking with plenty of hand gestures.

From his perception, something was terribly wrong. Jay saw that Mrs. Till was frantic, he knew this body language too well especially since it resembled the same body language she would present when she was angry with a student. He knew something wasn't right. *"Well what do we do about this??"* Jay faintly heard Mrs. Till say in distraught. Jay paused, he walked closer to the door to peek inside from a slight distance, as he peeked in he could see Mrs. Till pointing to the orange envelope he had seen in her classroom.

The same one that Sokki brought in earlier. Mr. Siege turned his head to the door. At that moment, sensing that he was at risk of getting discovered, panicking, Jay immediately backed away from the door bumping into a student and almost knocking him over. *"Sorry!"* Jay said to the student. Jay quickly turned around and walked down the hallway to the band room at a rapid pace with sweat racing each other down the side of his face.

While walking, he continued to look over his shoulder to check and see if any of the four teachers came out of the classroom. As he turned his head back in the direction he was walking he became startled as he felt a body jump on him with their legs wrapped around his waist and their arms wrapped around his neck giving him a hug. *"Hi Jay!!"* The voice said. Jay realized it was Sokki.

*"Hiiiiii Sokki,"* Jay said back with a smile. As Sokki got off of Jay he saw Kye standing right next to her leaning against the wall.

*"Sorry, Mr. Worthy had to talk to me."* Jay said.

*"About what?"* Kye, and Sokki both asked simultaneously.

*"Oh….. It's irrelevant"* Jay said hesitantly.

*"You're so secretive sometimes!"* Sokki said.

*"And you are so sassy! Secretive, I'll tell you two everything!"* Jay retorted sarcastically.

*"That's true, I guess we can't argue with that,"* Sokki said, glancing at Jay's watch, *"You scratched it? What time is it?"*

The excitement grew dull after Sokki began to take a closer look at his hand which caused Kye to do the right thing. Standing there, the three of them were silent all staring at Jay's hand. It was shaking out of control, to change the focus of attention, Jay placed his hand back in his pocket. Sokki decided to break the silence in typical Sokki fashion.

*"3:30, ahhhh! Let's go."* Sokki blurted out, she began to walk down the hallway that led to the outdoor basketball courts, the same place they came in for school.

*"You ok?"* Kye asked as he looked at Jay.

*"Yeah, I'll tell you two later,"* Jay said. As they continued down the stuffed hallway rummaging their way through clusters of students, Jay frequently glanced over to the right side of the hall to try and peek in room 56 but the door was closed shut and the lights were off. Despite the fact that Jay found this extremely mysterious.

He averted his attention forward, on his friends. On the way to the front of the school, they stopped by Jay's locker as the students began to clear out and walk outside to be picked up Jay, Kye and Sokki walked outside to the side of the basketball courts and stood by the entrance gate to the school

"So are you guys packed?" Sokki asked, crossing her arms, staring at the both of them.

"Haha" Kye laughed.

"Halfway," Kye said.

"I have not even started," Jay said with a smirk on his face.

"Guys!! We leave on monday!" Sokki said, throwing her arms up in the air.

"'I'm going to blow up your phone with messages reminding you to pack,"

"Yes, send it to the group message," Kye laughed. Sokki took the bag off of her back and swung it at Kye.

"OUCH!" Kye said sarcastically.

"What are we doing tonight by the way?" asked Sokki.

"I have no idea," Jay replied

"Kye, what are you thinking?" Jay asked looking at Kye

"Treehouse?" responded Kye.

"Ooooo yes!" said Sokki.

"So what time do you want to meet? Eight?" Asked Jay.

*"Maybe around ten because of dinner?"* Sokki responded.

*"Perfect,"* Kye said.

*"Alright bye guys! My ride is here"* Sokki yelled as she was walking out of the gate.

*"Bye"* they said back.

*So what has been on your mind brother?"* Kye said to Jay….. There was silence

*"Hey! Earth to Jay??"* he said again, this time leaning towards Jay's direction.

*"Huh? I'm sorry, what did you ask?"* Jay said as he unfocused his eyes on the double doors to the hallway while rubbing his eyes.

*"What time did you wake up this morning?"* Kye asked with a chuckle.

*"Regular time I guess, well I woke up at 5am at first then fell back asleep"* Jay said.

*"Fooooor?? Is there some worm you are trying to catch?"*

*"I already caught it"* he replied in a low voice

*"And which worm is that?"* Kye asked smirking

*"The speech? Our finals…I was studying"* Jay replied this time putting his head into his hands in distress.

Kye sighed, *"Yep, it is official, you need sleep"*

*"I should be fine"* Jay began to rub his eyes again.

*"See, look there is proof right there, and plus we are going to the treehouse tonight. You can't be all tired."*

Jay delivered his famous silent no verbal agreement in response to Kye's comment.

*"Look, I'm just sayin' you know you're my boy, I'm just tryin' to see you get some rest man, you feel me?"* Jay nodded.

A few brief moments went by before Kye began to leave Jay and went towards the gate out to the front of the school. *"Alright, see you tonight, my mom is here to pick me up"* Kye said, giving Jay a fist bump.

*"Alright, see ya"* Jay replied.

Jay began to walk around the basketball courts to look around for any friends he could talk to before his sister came to pick him up. While looking around for peers to say bye to, his phone began vibrating vigorously. He took his phone out of his pocket and answered it.

*"Hello?"*

*"Hey im here"* said the voice on the other end of the phone.

*"Ok, I'll be right there,"* said Jay.

Jay hung up the phone. Jay walked towards the gate and headed to the front of the school. He walked up to Jay's sister's car who drove a Nissan Racer and hopped in the car only to find Zeke in the back seat looking out of the window missing all the exciting thrills that normally come with the last day of school.

*"Hey Letty!"* Jay said.

*"Hey! How was school?"* she asked with excitement.

"It was very interesting, Zee what's up cuz how was school?" Jay asked with his best Robert De Niro impersonation while looking in the back seat.

The gesture made his sister laugh out of confusion. Nevertheless all Zeke said was *"what's up?*

Jay looked at his sister and mouthed the words *"what's wrong with him?"*

She returned a similar look for a brief moment then looked straight out of the front window and sighed.

*"Elephants Jay, elephants."*

# CHAPTER 5

It was a relaxing drive home as Jay almost fell asleep in the passenger seat. She drove back to the Cruz household. When they arrived, the garage was open and Mr. Cruz was standing just outside the garage talking to the next door neighbors.

*"Are those the Uptons?"* Zeke asked Jay under his breath.

*"Yep oh gosh save me NOW. I swear these people are like ghosts, yeah dry ghosts that don't have any emotion. I wonder if we can sneak past, Letty keep driving"* Jay remarked.

*"¡Seré un buen chico!"* Letty said.

*"Fine, you ready?"* Jay asked looking at Zeke,

*"Ready"*

*"Ok, Bye Letty"* Said Jay.

*"Hey Letty"* Jay's Dad said as they were getting out of the car

*"How are the boys?"* He asked.

*"They are good, I'm going to go pick them up right now!"* she responded.

*"Alright tell them we said hi, thanks for picking Jay and Zeke up."* Mr. Cruz Said.

*"No problem will do!"* Letty said. Jay and Zeke walked up the driveway towards the garage.

*"Hey Jay and Zeke,"* said Mr. and Mrs. Upton as they walked up to the top of the driveway.

*"Hey,"* the boys said.

*"Guess what? You won't believe this"* Mr. Cruz said.

*"What?"* Zeke said,

*"Try me, wait…..They got it??"* Jay asked in shock.

*"Haha, Yep".* Mr. Cruz said, laughing.

*"Got what?"* Zeke said

*"Yeah right, really?"* Jay asked, looking at the Uptons.

*"Got what?"* Zeke asked, assuming that no one heard him the first time. Mr. Cruz turned towards Zeke, acknowledging that he heard him ask his question.

*"We decided we wanted a whale a while ago and we finally bought it today"* Said Mr. Upton.

*"I'm sorry, did you say a well, like an underground one? What is wrong with your sink?"* Asked Zeke

*"We decided we wanted to live a little less… modern….. I'm kidding, we mean a whale silly. You know? Like an animal."* Mrs. Upton said.

*"Oh, that kind of whale. Are you kidding or are you serious?"* Zeke asked.

*"We are serious, do you want to see?* Mrs. Upton asked.

*"Sure,"* Jay said.

Mr. Upton nudged his wife too subtle for anyone to catch on.

"Uh, honey are you sure?" He said smiling without moving his mouth practicing his ventriloquist skills. The two of them turned from the group and walked away towards their front door.

"Yah, it will be fine. Can you please not be so obvious?" His wife replied.

"Jay, do you have your key?" Mr. Cruz said, looking at Jay.

"Yeah I have it," Jay answered.

"Ok, I am going to close the garage, come through the front when you are finished" Mr. Cruz said.

"Ok"

Jay and Zeke followed Mr. And Mrs. Upton inside into their house. The Upton's had a big sign above their door that said **"Everyone is Welcome".** Jay found this strange, as most people would.

"Why not just have a sign that said WELCOME. Do they discriminate?" Jay said, walking along his cousin behind the Uptons. His cousin didn't respond.

When they walked inside they walked past the living room and into the kitchen where they saw what looked like a fish tank next to the sink. There was only a small shining light that leaked through the blinds of the backyard.

"This house is a graveyard, have you ever heard of let there be light?" Jay nudged his cousin for the ridiculous extremely accurate comment.

"This is it!" Mrs. Upton said in excitement pointing to the tank. Completely ignoring Zeke's question. Mr. and Mrs. Upton took a step back from the tank and let the two boys admire the tank.

"Whaaaaat in the world?" Zeke said. In the tank, there was a whale the size of a ketchup bottle. A baby whale, but this didn't appear like a normal whale, it had a rounded nose and its eyes were bigger than normal. It was navy blue and had white eyes. Zeke leaned in close, glared at the glass and slowly put his finger on it. The tiny whale swam up to the glass and stared at Zeke's finger. *"That's cool!"* Said Zeke removing his finger from the glass.

The whale swam away from the glass and into a log behind some seaweed that was placed in the tank by the Uptons. Jay put his finger on the glass and the whale seemed to notice, but this time the whale swam up to the glass faster, the whale looked at Jay through the glass, his eyes began to anger while focusing on Jay. The whale began to nudge his nose against the glass repeatedly. The Upton's stood a slight distance away from Jay and Zeke.

*"What is he doing?"* whispered Mrs. Upton to her husband. The whale continued to ram the glass with his nose, each time with more aggression than the last.

*"I guess he likes you,"* Mr. Upton said laughing nervously.

*"I told you this was a bad idea!"* Mrs. Upton whispered loudly.

*"YOOOOOOU told me? You are insane!"* Mr. Upton replied glaring at his wife angrily, a similar look as the whale.

*"Or he doesnt"* Zeke said quickly. Mrs. Upton leaned back and tilted her head towards her husband. *"It's ok, the guy said that glass was bulletproof"* she said in a very low voice. The whale swam around in a circle, this time charging full speed at the glass ***CRACK!!...*** a sound came from the glass. Mr. Upton started to speak.

*"Did he just..."*

*"Yep!"* Mrs. Upton interrupted,

*"He just cracked the glass".* She said,

"Woah, I am so sorry, I did not know that he could do that." Jay said apologetically.

"It's not your fault, maybe he just wanted to play," Mrs. Upton hesitantly said.

"I'll call the guy for the glass," Mr. Upton said to his wife.

"So we were right," Mrs. Upton said with a shaky hesitant voice, making direct eye contact with her husband.

"This means...." Mrs. Upton interrupted.

"Yes, it does," she said, cutting him off again while she took a hard swallow. Mr. Upton crossed his arms and took a step back. He looked like he was in deep thought.

"You were right about what?" Jay asked softly.

"Oh, nothing," Mrs. Upton said. There was a quick pause before Mrs. Upton snapped out of the daze she was in, staring at the ground next to Jay's feet. She had a concerned look on her face. Her body looked frozen as if she had seen a ghost.

"Ummmmmm alright boys, off you go, I'm sure your father is probably waiting for you" Mrs. Upton said, glancing down at Jay and Zeke her demeanor had shifted dramatically after the glass had cracked.

"Ok, I am SO sorry about your glass!" Jay said.

"Tell your Dad we said have a good evening, close the door behind you as well." Mrs Upton said.

"We will," Jay said.

Jay and Zeke headed for the door. As they left, the awkward feeling left Jay. They started to walk back inside across the street to their house.

"That was weird," Jay said to Zeke.

"Yeah, absolutely it was". Said Zeke.

When they got inside a feeling of relief came, that glorious feeling of not spending all night trying to finish homework that could as well as be classwork. As Jay walked in, he dropped his backpack next to the door and walked past the living room into the kitchen. The floor plan of Jay's house was similar to Upton's house.

Every house in the neighborhood had a similar floor plan, when they first moved into the neighborhood there were no houses. Jay and his family were one of the first families to move into the neighborhood.

"Something smells good!" Jay said.

"Yep, I'm making shrimp fried rice," Mr. Cruz said.

"Nice speech by the way!" Mr. Cruz said, looking at Jay as he was reaching back to grab a spatula.

"Wait what? What speech?" Jay said with a confused look on his face.

"Your speech, didnt you have a speech today at school for your test?" Mr. Cruz said as he was stirring the rice in the pot.

"Oh, my speech, thank you, I practiced all week long for those five minutes.... Wait, how did you know it was good?" Jay asked, quickly glancing back and forth at Zeke.

"You know my friend from work? Johnny? His daughter goes to your school, ummm" Mr. Cruz paused.

"Rachel?" Jay said.

"Yeah, I guess someone recorded it and Johnny sent me the link on youtube or whatever that thing is. I guess your video is on there" Mr. Cruz said.

"Wait what? Youtube?" Jay said in shock. Jay reached in his pocket and pulled out his phone and pushed the button to power it on.

"That's crazy!" Jay said as he was waiting for his phone to power on due to it being dead from the trip home.

"What's that?" Mr. Cruz asked.

"That's on youtube, I didn't even know anyone was recording" Jay said, still staring at his phone.

"When I watched it I was like wow I didn't know you could speak like that" Jay's dad said. Jay's phone turned on and began to vibrate and ring intensively.

"Is that your phone?" His father asked.

"Yeah, sorry, I'm getting a whole bunch of notifications". Jay said.

Jay was staring at his phone in confusion. "What in the world," he mumbled to himself under his breath. He saw that he had received messages from almost everybody on his phone from school. Scrolling down the messages he saw that the majority of them said

"Check youtube!" He scrolled all the way to the top where he had messages from Sokki and Kye. He opened Kyes message

-"Hey Jay have you checked your facebook or your youtube?" Jay had seen that Kye had sent him a link to youtube.

"Here it is, I guess," Mr. Cruz put down the spatula and headed towards Jay, who was standing by the dinner table. Zeke came around the corner from the living room. Jay opened the link, and the video began to load.

The screen appeared with Jay standing in front of Mrs. Till's classroom. Yep, this must be it. The video began to play, the video was taken from the back of the classroom. Jay was holding the phone up as Zeke and his father were shoulder to shoulder to him peering at the screen. *"So I'm sitting in the back of the class..."* The video continued. It was silent in the house. After the video stopped, Zeke and Mr. Cruz began to clap along with the class in the video.

*"Good job!"* Zeke said.

*"Yeah that was like top of the line!"* Their father said this time with extra enthusiasm in his voice.

*"Thanks, I appreciate it,"* Jay said.

*"Jay!"* Zeke yelled.

*"What's up?"* Jay said as he poked his head around the corner to look at Zeke sitting on the floor by the game console and TV.

*"Your video already has 10,239 views. It's only been up for three hours".*

*"Wow, this is crazy!"* Jay said.

*"What time is it someone?* Mr. Cruz asked.

*"5:17"* Jay said.

*"Ok, dinner will be ready at about eight. I still have to cook this fish"* Mr. Cruz said.

*"Alright,"* Jay said as he began to walk up the stairs.

When he walked past the living room he saw Zeke playing the game system. *"Scoot back a little from the TV a little, you're gonna go blind"* Jay said to Zeke.

Zeke moved back from the TV still focusing on the game he was playing. Jay picked his backpack up from the front door and headed upstairs. He walked into his room, threw his bag next to his bed and plopped down on his bed. He laid back and put his head on the pillow. Another feeling of relief set in.

It seemed to have come in waves through the last day of school. He closed his eyes for a second, he felt fatigue set in. He was tired since he spent all of last night studying and preparing for his speech, now that it was over it began to set in. Somehow he managed to stay awake, he knew if he kept his eyes closed for any longer then he would be completely sleepy for a long while.

As he opened his eyes he sighed and grabbed his phone which was sitting right next to him. He opened it up and checked his messages. He still had 48 messages that weren't open. He was so extensively tired that he forgot he was a star on YouTube by the time he reached his bed. He did not have the patience nor the energy to look through all those messages and read every last one of them. So instead he opened up the group instant message he was in with Sokki and Kye.

- Jay: *"Hey guys". 5:25 pm.*

Jay typed to the group but he got no response. Jay Put his phone down and closed his eyes. His body started to fall into a daze. Jay felt his phone vibrate. He picked it up and opened the notification, the phone opened up to the group message.

- Sokki: *"Hey Superstar!" 5:30 pm*

- Sokki: *"Like, ummmm can I have your autograph?? LOL"*

- Jay: *"Lol, I'm trying to picture you saying that"*

- Kye: *"Congrats"*

- Jay: *"Thank you? I think LOL"*

- Kye: *"You better remember us when you get famous"*

- Jay: *"Of course, How could I forget?"*

- Sokki: *"Hey, I call the secretary!"*

- Kye: *"Wow, in that case, i'm bodyguard*

- Sokki: *"Oh wait....*

- Kye: *"What? Lol*

- Sokki: *You can't...*

- Kye: *"And why is that?"*

- Sokki: *"I better be the bodyguard, maybe you can be secretary, we wouldn't want Mr. Jay Cruz getting robbed".*

- Jay: *"Uh oh".*

- Kye: *"What does that mean?"* Lol

- Sokki: *"I feel like we would have a hostage situation where Mr. Jay gets threatened, gets mugged or something and you are just sitting there eating tacos.*

- Jay: *"!!!!"*

- Sokki: *"Then poof! There goes the #1 motivational speaker in the world gone... all because of you and your obsession with tacos".*

- Jay: *"HAHAHAHA, you just made my stomach hurt, I'm about to roll off my bed. I was sleepy, but I am WIDE awake now. HAHA"*

- Kye: *"I'm going to throw something at you Sokki."*

- Sokki: *"What... tacos??*

- Kye: *"Jay, get your friend"*

- Jay: *"Nope, because I don't want to be next and she is your friend too."* LOL

- Jay: *"What are you two doing right now?"*

- Sokki: *"You mean at the moment?"*

- Sokki: *"Cleaning"*

- Kye: *"Sitting on my porch".*

- Sokki: *"Eating tacos"*

- Jay: *"My goodness"*

- Kye: *"What did I do to you?"*

- Sokki: *"Nothing, love ya!*

- Jay: *"Hey, treehouse tonight right?"*

- Sokki: *"Yes! What time, I'm fine with anytime.*

- Kye: *"Absolutely, same here."*

- Jay: *"I'm going to eat around 8..*

- Jay: *"How about 10?"*

- Sokki: *"Yup!"*

- Kye: *"Perfect."*

Jay put his phone down and closed his eyes again. He began to fall asleep. Usually around the time Jay got out of school, he felt a little fatigued, but not like this. This was a different kind of tiredness. His room always had a peaceful feel to it.

As the sounds of rice sizzling in the pot and his brother smashing away at the video game controller, this didn't bother him. But nevertheless Jay woke up out of his sleep, got out of his bed, closed his bedroom door then jumped back in bed and finally fell asleep.

Soon, dinner was ready. *"JAY, dinner is ready"* Mr. Cruz said from outside of Jay's room in a muffled voice beating at his door in his own version of knocking.

*"Ok, I'm coming"* Jay said as he woke up from his sleep stretching his arms underneath the covers. Jay arose out of the bed, and walked down stairs, he still had his school uniform on. He did not mind, he wouldn't be wearing this uniform for three months when he went back to school. He walked down the stairs. The video game was paused. As Jay walked down the stairs the aroma of fresh seasonings and fish covered his nostrils and made him smile.

That feeling he got when knowing he was about to eat one of his favorite meals always made Jay smile. *"Ok, wash your hands, grab a plate"*. Mr. Cruz said as he was grabbing a plate of his own. Jay went into the bathroom that was next to the garage across from the kitchen. As he was washing his hands he looked in the mirror and felt the feeling of being tired but with good energy. He stared at the bags under his eyes through the mirror. He realized that he was really tired. He dried his hands and as he walked out into the kitchen he looked at his phone and saw the messages.

- Sokki: *"Jay, so what happened earlier?"*

- Kye: *"I think he fell asleep"*

\*\*\*

Jay grabbed his plate, a knife and a cup and began to put together his dinner.

"This looks really good," Jay said, looking at his Dad.

"Thanks, I tried a new recipe, I figured since you're leaving on Monday I thought that we could have a nice dinner before you go".

"Yep, I'm excited," Jay said. Jay, Zeke and Jay's father sat down at the dinner table.

"Heavenly Father, Thank you for this meal, we appreciate every meal you bring our way. We thank you for the little things we have in our life and the blessings that come our way, even the ones we don't see. We are grateful for the big and small. Lord, as Jay gets ready to embark on his journey we ask that you protect him, bring him back home safe and that he can find a career path that you can bless him with. Thank you Jesus, in your name, we pray, AMEN." Mr. Cruz said.

"AMEN" Jay and Zeke said together.

"Can you pass me the salt?" Mr. Cruz asked Zeke. Everynight for dinner, they always sat at the same place. Jay sat at one end of the table, opposite to his father and his cousin sat in the middle perimeter of the table.

"So Jay, are you excited?" Mr. Cruz as he glanced at Jay across the table while he took a fork full of asparagus to his mouth.

"Yes, I can't wait, I know it is going to be really good!"

"Have you decided what skill you wanted to choose yet?" Mr. Cruz asked Jay.

"I have not". Jay said shocked, he had forgotten all about the fact that he needed to choose a career.

"So I was thinking and I think that you should go for lifeguarding, I think that would really be good for you". Mr. Cruz said.

"Lifeguarding? You know better than anyone that I can't swim" said Jay.

"Yeah, he swims like a frog," Zeke said.

"Well you can learn, won't they teach you?" Mr. Cruz said as he took a sip of his orange drink out of his glass.

"Yeah, I'll think about it," Jay said, wanting to end the conversation.

"What about you? Do you have any plans for the summer?" Mr. Cruz said, looking at Zeke as he took a sip of his orange drink.

"I am not sure, I was looking at maybe going to a frisbee camp" Zeke said.

"Frisbee?" Jay asked.

"Yeah, professional frisby is so fun! You gotta try it" Zeke said with a big smile on his face.

"Frisbee huh, who is it ran through?" Mr. Cruz asked.

"The NFA, the National Frisby association," Zeke said. There was a pause, Zeke took a fork full of his food and chewed it. The three were quiet, when Zeke finished chewing he said *"The NFA has plans for frisby, they want to make it a national pastime."* Soon, they were finished eating. Afterwards, they all put their food plates in the sink.

"Alright, I am going to bed," Mr. Cruz said.

"Goodnight," Jay and Zeke said.

It was now an empty kitchen with just the two boys. As they heard Mr. Cruz go upstairs to his room they sighed in a full stomach of relief.

Jay began to wash the dishes in the sink and Zeke began putting away the food. "*That was good,*" said Zeke.

"*Yeah, I'm stuffed, that hit the spot,*" Jay said.

"*What are you doing tonight?*" Zeke asked as he was wrapping the plastic pan of fish in foil.

"*I am going to the tree house tonight,*" Jay said. He felt his phone vibrate. He stopped washing dishes to check it but he paused and realized that he didn't want soap on his phone. From the dish water he made so he stuck his hands back in the water, pulled out a silver plate from the water and continued to wash dishes.

"*That's too bad, I wanted you to play the telly with me,*" Zeke said.

"*Maybe next time buddy, we have an important meeting tonight, but maybe tomorrow,*" Jay said.

"*Ok, but you have to promise,*" Zeke said. Looking at Jay while he is still washing dishes.

"*I promise,*" said Jay.

"*Cool,*" Zeke said. After Zeke was finished putting all of the food away into the containers he went into the living room to go back to his game that he had been playing earlier. As Jay heard the game system turn on he felt another vibration from his phone. He assumed it was Sokki and Kye. As he finished washing up the last pot he felt his phone vibrate a few more times. He grabbed a wash rag from under the sink and began wiping the counters and table. After he wiped everything down he put the rag back under the sink and washed his hands.

"*Alright, I'm going to head out for a little bit,*" Jay said to Zeke as he walked past the living room where he was playing a video game. Jay's Father had bought a Telly system for Zeke and Jay about 3 years ago. Before its arrival Jay wanted one really bad, the telly was a virtual reality game system that came with a headset that you wrap around the back of your head. The front looked like an oversized pair of goggles. It reminded Jay of the superhero cyclops from the popular comic x-men. Cyclops was a mutant that was blind and whenever he opened his eyes he red lasers shot from his eyes. As time went on Jay fell out of his love of the Telly, most of his attention drifted towards school.

*"Ok, i'll see you later"* Zeke said, never taking the vision goggles off. Jay threw a sweater on, headed out the door, locking it behind him and proceeded down his driveway. It was dark outside. As Jay started to walk out of his neighborhood he looked up at the vibrant sky and noticed that it was grey, due to the clouds. Cloudy nights were Jay's favorite type of nights.

They were very common in Los Aqui, He continued walking towards the tree house which was located right outside Jay's Neighborhood not a great distance from the school. Jay pulled out his phone, there were five missed notifications. His phone read:

- *Sokki: "Jay, are you done eating yet?"* **9:32**

- *Kye: "When are you gonna head to the point Sokki?"* **9:34**

- *Sokki: "In a few..."* **9:34**

- *Kye: "Same here, just finishing folding clothes"* **9:35**

- *Sokki: "I swear you are always folding"* **9:41**

*Jay decided to join the conversation, so he started texting.*

***

- Jay: *"Hey sorry! I was cleaning ...I am walking to the Point now. Are you two there already?"* **9:56**

- Sokki: *"I was waiting on you! I thought you fell asleep or something"* **9:58**

- Jay: *"Sorry, lol"* **9:58.**

- Sokki: *"You're fine, I was just watching TV with my Mom."* **9:59**

- Sokki: *"I'm leaving the house now."* **9:59**

- Jay: *"Ok."* **9:59**

- Kye: *"I am halfway there."* **10:00**

- Jay: *"Perfect, same here."* **10:01**

Jay walked along the sidewalk that led around to the back of the school. There was a field about two blocks away from the school. It was located behind the school, and the field had about a dozen trees in it. Jay walked along the sidewalk and eventually reached where the sidewalk ended and he turned towards the field, looked around to see if anyone was watching then he walked towards the field. He walked up to the first row of six trees.

There was a giant gust of wind that passed. He stopped, staring at all of the trash that was racing through the gust. He continued to walk towards the trees. We approached the third tree from the left. He stared at the 52 foot tall tree up and down. At the bottom right at the height of the grass the writing J.S.K was carved out of the bark.

It was underlined three times with a circle around it. Jay kicked it twice with his right foot. He stared at the top. He began to walk up the carved stairs. One foot at a time, he got to the top. When he reached the top he stood on a platform. When Jay, Kye and Sokki built this tree house they made the platform with just enough space where the three of them could stand on it. At the entrance to the tree house, there was a door with three metal bars on it and a lever on the side of the door. The lever was hidden underneath a panel that was camouflaged with the bark of the tree that required a key to open it.

Jay slid the first metal bar to the right, he moved his hand down to the second lever and pulled it slid to the left. He then slid his hand down to the third bar and moved it to the left, finally he pulled out a mini blue key from his pocket, stuck it in the keyhole in the panel and twisted it. *CLING* the door was unlocked. Jay grabbed the handle to the door and pulled it open, the aroma of fresh wood brushed across his nose.

There were three tiny steps that were at the entrance to the tree house. Jay walked up the steps. He reached his right hand and flicked on the light switch that was mounted on the entrance wall. The room lit up, Jay stepped on the main floor. The floor was wooden with a long black mat that sat at the entrance when you walked in. The mat read **"WELCOME"**. As if anyone beside Jay, Kye, or Sokki ever occupied the space. The inside of the treehouse was about half the space of Mr. Worthys classroom.

There were 3 bean bags on the floor that had one letter on each bag. It had 3 initials to represent their names. They were all black with the white letters. On it were handwritten words that covered half of the wall on the left side. The writing consisted of ideas and notes that the three had come up with. They would brainstorm and write their dreams on the wall. It was known to the three of them as **"the wall"**. Jay looked at his bean bag sitting on the floor with the letter J on it.

A swift thought came across his mind, that of which he wanted to plop down on the bean bag. He turned away towards the window. And looked out the glassy window. He then saw Kye coming from a distance as he walked from behind a bush. He closed the curtain to the window, turned around and plopped down on his bean bag with a J on it. **\*Shift, shift, shift\*.** Jay heard the latches on the door being shifted three times. The door then opened.

"What's up man?" said Kye.

"What's up?" Jay said back.

*"How was dinner? What did you have?"* Kye asked.

*"Good, fried rice and fish,"* Jay responded. ***Shift, shift, shift.*** The door opened. Sokki walked in. *"Oh! I didn't see you out there when I looked"* Jay said.

*"Yeah, I was trying to creep up on Kye to scare him"*. Sokki said with a smirk on her face.

*"Well, you're too slow!* Kye said. Kye and Sokki both plopped down on their bean bags

*"Can you believe that we are all going to be seniors next year?"* Jay said looking at them both,

*"I know that is unbelievable!"* Kye said back. Sokki nodded

*"Are you two ready?"* She asked.

*"I am,"* Jay shrugged confidently.

*"Whether we are or not, it's coming,"* Kye said. Kye often removed his feelings from situations because he knew that he would have to deal with the situation regardless of how he felt. It was a characteristic trait that he retrieved from his mom.

*"Wait, pause, Jay, what did you need to tell us earlier?"* Kye said as he looked over at Jay.

*"You have that exact same face from earlier. What are you thinking about? What's on your mind?"* Kye asked. Sokki stood up, moved her bean bag to the middle to form a triangle between the three.

*"Jay…. Hey!"* Kye said, raising his voice a little to try and snap Jay out of his trance.

*"Oh, sorry"* Jay said startled

"He had the same look earlier," Kye said, glancing at Sokki.

"So what's up, tell us!" Sokki said.

"Ok, Sokki, what did you take to Mrs. Till in class today?" Jay asked, staring at Sokki.

"When? I was running a lot of errands today..."

"As you always do," Kye said under his breath.

"The teachers usually trust me to run errands to other classrooms usually. But I am trying to remember, when did I go to Mrs... Oh! The envelope??" Sokki asked as she looked back at Jay.

"Yes, the envelope" Jay said as goosebumps appeared along with the hairs that rose on his arms.

"Oh, I don't know, Mr. Sidious didn't tell me what it was. He just asked me to take it to Mrs. Till.

"Why what's up?" asked Sokki.

"You have absolutely no idea what that was inside?" Jay asked again.

"No, I don't," Sokki said again.

"Hey, tell us what's going on?" Sokki said as she sat straight up in her bean bag.

"So you guys know the speech I gave in Mrs. TIll's class earlier today?" Jay asked.

"Yes, the one that is all over the internet. Of course" Kye said.

"What about it?" Sokki asked.

"Well after I finished my speech I happened to glance down and see the words CAMP CHOICE VOIDED. DNE on the envelope. I don't think Mrs. Till knows that I saw it. Jay said.

"Wait what do you mean voided? Like not valid?" Kye asked with big eyes.

"I DON'T know… That's all i saw" Jay said looking at the floor.

"Um, that's creepy, DNE? What does that mean?" Sokki said with a confused look on her face.

"I am not sure… I mean the ONLY thing that i can think of is Do not exceed. You know the term we use in science where it says l like DNE then it will have a number after it? Something like that" Jay said, looking at Kye.

The three stood up out of their bean Bags almost simultaneously. There was a short pause.

"Oh! You're talking about Tri-sets aren't you?" Kye said, leaning against the wall.

"Yes! Those equations we had to learn right before finals. Those were fun" Jay said, pacing around the room.

"Yeah, once I showed you how to do it step by step" Sokki said as she was looking down at her phone.

"Hey I wasn't…"

"Hold on, shhhhhhh! I think I got it," Sokki said, looking at her phone intensely…

"Let me see… I found some acronyms for DNE on a site. . Does not exceed, no we just talked about that… hmm Do not explain, Do not enable. Nooo. UH OH!!" Sokki paused and her eyes got big.

"Whaaaaaat?" Kye and Jay said at the same time.

"Why do we keep doing that?" Jay said, looking at Kye.

"Saying things at the same time?" Kye said.

"Yes haha" Jay replied.

"Guys, uhh i think I found what it means…. DO NOT ENTER… it's the only thing that would make sense".

"Yep I bet that's it!" Jay said.

"Wait, why don't they want us to enter camp?" Kye said, putting his finger next to his mouth with his arms crossed.

"Maybe it has to do with Los and the Aqui" Jay smirked

"Stop, are you kidding me?" Sokki replied

"Yeah bro, you know that's not real, it's just a myth," Kye added.

"Well, I'm just saying, you never know it could be real" Jay spoke under his breath this time, feeling less confident in what he was saying.

"So you're telling me that you really believe that there are creepy people who magically have the incredible power to turn into sea creature's everytime they go into the water?" Sokki asked.

"Absolutely," Jay replied.

"Yeah, then you're crazier than I thought," she replied.

"That's why this is REALLY creepy," Kye said.

"Well, we leave Monday and we still haven't been emailed or called. Then again I don't know if our parents checked their email yet. Have you checked the VC yet guys?" Sokki asked.

"I'll check it," Kye said.

"Yeah, I can't. My phone battery is at 5 points." Jay said, looking at his phone quickly.

"You never charge your phone," Sokki said.

**"WELCOME TO VIRTUAL CLASSROOM"** *a voice said coming from Kye's phone.*

"I hate that sound every time it powers on." Sokki said.

"Nope! No emails have been received. The last one the school sent was about finals a few days ago" Kye said.

"This is weird. What do you think they are waiting for?" Jay asked.

"A better question would be what's in that envelope..." Sokki said. There was a pause and silence in the room.

"So today when I was walking to meet you two after School I saw Mr. Worthy. Mrs. Till, Mr. Sidious and Ms. Noble inside classroom 56 talking, standing in a circle. They all looked really kinda angry. Mrs. Till was waving around that exact envelope saying "What are we going to do about this?" Jay said.

"Are you sure it was that envelope?" Sokki asked.

"Oh I'm positive, I remember seeing the red stamp on it. That said VOID CAMP CHOICE DNE" Jay replied.

"And they didn't see you looking at them?" Kye asked.

"No, the crack in the door was too small," Jay said.

"*Wait, who teaches in that classroom?*" Kye asked as they were all pacing nervously around the room.

"*I have no idea,*" Jay said. Sokki stopped pacing and stood still.

"*So all day I have been asking myself what could possibly be inside that envelope… and now my other question is why dont they want us to enter camp?*" Jay asked.

"*This is freaking me out,*" Kye said.

"*Same here*" Sokki said while she looked at her arm for goosebumps.

She then looked at Jay… "*No, nope. Not happening*" Sokki said with a straight face, making direct eye contact with Jay.

"*What?*" Jay said.

"*Forget about it,*" Sokki said once more.

"*Hey, do you two remember Ms. Spear?*" Jay asked.

"*Stop Jay!*" Sokki said with a louder tone this time.

"*From 8th grade?*" Kye asked.

"*Yes! Do you remember how she had that broken window that the school never fixed all year? Then do you remember when we went to visit her last year and the window was still broken?*" Jay asked. Sokki was quiet while staring at Jay with a harsh glow. Jay could tell that she wanted him to look at her. He avoided eye contact.

"*You mean the one that is lifted up a little bit in the corner?*" Kye asked.

"*Yep!*" Jay said with a slight smirk on his face.

"I really want to know what's inside that envelope... and even more I want to know why we can't enter camp choice" Jay said as he stopped and crossed his arms.

"No, Jay, I've seen that look too many times. I know exactly what that means" Sokki said.

"What is she talking about?" Kye asked Jay.

"I have no idea" Jay said as he turned around as if he was distracted about something and began reading old notes on **"The wall"**.

"He wants to sneak into the school to find out what's the secret envelope," Sokki said, giving Jay a strange look.

"And you know this because..." Kye said with a sarcastic tone waving his hands back and forth waiting for Sokki to answer.

"Look at him, look at that face," Sokki replied, looking back and forth between the two.

"Ha, I see it.... Well Jay?" Kye said, smiling.

"Guys c'mon, getting to that envelope is the only way to find out why we are not supposed to go into camp choice. The school is hiding something..." Jay said, staring at Sokki and Kye.

"I knew it!" Sokki said.

"You do realize that you will get a mark against your record if you get caught. Not to mention your scholarship, are you willing to throw that all away for what? Some STUPID envelope that has very little to do with you??" Sokki said, interrupting with a raised tone in her voice.

"I just... I have a feeling" Jay said

"You will be labeled CRI" Kye said with a more serious look on his face.

"CRI?" Jay said with a strange look?

"Yes, do you know how our justice system works?" Kye asked.

"A little," Sokki replied.

Jay knew that this was going to be a very long explanation of the system so he sat back down in his bean bag. Sokki followed and did the same thing. Kye cleared his throat and began pacing around the room. His inner professor lecture skills were preparing to arise like a phoenix

"So in our justice system we have three chances"

"Like the city Los Sala?" Sokki asked.

"Not quite," Kye said.

"So in our justice system we have three chances. The very first time you are charged with anything, whether it is a murder, theft, arson, ANYTHING... You are marked as CRI, this serves as your first warning pretty much. You get sent away to another country and serve time over there. Depending on what the offense was, that determines how long you will be over there in other countries' jail. If you are charged with another offense then you get marked with MIN. Leaving you CRI-MIN. This is your second warning... and your last. You now will still get sent across seas BUT here is the catch. For example, if someone in Los Aqui, our city, robbed a bank and let's say they were charged with: theft from a public property and damages on three levels and they were charged with two years. Of course that stays on their file but if this person gets charged with a second offense. They take the previous number they were charged with, and multiply it by six."

"Why six?" Jay asked.

"Because they count the letters. C-R-I-M-I-N-A-L. That is six letters. They take that and add it to your current charge. SO If this person robbed a bank, got charged 2 years. Later IF this person... I don't know, let's say robbed a mini grocery store and got charged one year for his second crime. It is now twelve PLUS one year. Two times six is twelve and add a year for the new offense. This person is now serving 13 years. This is really the last warning because the next time you are charged you are officially marked and labeled as CRI-MIN-AL. AL of course being your third offense. They stop counting, the officials send you away"

"Where?" Sokki asked.

"Guess," Kye said, leaning against the wall.

"Oh no, don't tell me." Jay said softly, looking slowly at Sokki.

"Yep!" Kye said, nodding his head up and down.

"Reno?" Jay asked with a drenched look on his face.

"Exactly, and you do not come back, well... You are not welcomed back to Los Aqui. After you finish your massive sentence you are not allowed to step foot in Los Aqui ever again. I have not met one person that is in favor of this justice system. Vegas is different, that is why everyone wants to move there." Kye said.

"Reno? That's scary, I hear they have ice dinosaurs up there.... How do you know so much about the justice system?" Sokki asked, staring at the ground.

"Well, when your cousin works for the DA's office. You learn a thing or two, and what in the world is ice... Nevermind...... Jay, are you really going through with this man or not?" Kye asked.

"I am, you know, a lot of things I am indecisive about, but not this. I am going" Jay said.

He began to walk towards the door.

"So I'll see you at my house later?" Jay asked.

"Jay, as your close friend, I can not let you do this...." Kye said.

"Thank you Kye," Sokki said with a satisfied look on her face.

"ALONE... I'm coming with you" Kye said.

"Thanks Kye," Jay said. He stared at Sokki for a few seconds.

"FINE!! I'll come. We better not get caught." Sokki said, stomping her feet towards the door.

"Matter of fact, if I lose my scholarship your happy self will go get a job and pay for my scholarship. DO YOU UN-DER-STAND?" I've worked too hard for it, you better be right about this..." Sokki said, looking Jay in the eye.

Jay nodded.

"Wait, so what is the plan?" Kye asked. The three of them huddled around the entrance door of the tree house.

"So we will have to enter from the back of the school. That's where Ms. Spears' classroom is. Since the school is shaped like an L we will look at it as we are entering from behind the L shape. Once we are inside. We will have to get to Principal ReLouf's office, get the master key and get to classroom 56. I know the envelope is in there. I have a feeling."

"That better be a pretty strong feeling" Sokki said under her breath low enough for Jay not to hear.

"Hands in," Jay said. They all gathered around in a huddle and put their hands in the middle, creating a pile.

"One, two ..." wait, wait, wait, wait... You've been planning this all day huh?" Kye asked.

SPLASH

*"Kinda, one… two… three… "US!"* they all said in unison.

# CHAPTER 6

Jay, Sokki and Kye exited the treehouse. When they got outside, the sky was completely dark, with black clouds. Los Aqui is known to have the darkest sky amongst all the major cities. Jay moved all three latches back in their original locked position and pulled the lever on the side back up to its original position. They climbed all the way down the treehouse and hid behind a bush. The air was still with not a single tree blowing.

*"It's so dark, I can't see ANYTHING!"* Sokki said in a louder voice

*"Shhhhh! I know, that's why we have to stay close, alright follow my lead"* Jay said. They began to push their way through the bushes until they reached the edge of the sidewalk. Jay began to get really nervous. As he glanced over at Sokki and Jay and saw they reciprocated, his feeling began to intensify. They looked around in each direction and proceeded to the school which was about two football field's length away from them.

They continued rummaging through bushes until they reached the Legion. The three ran silently to the front of the school. Leaning against the walls. They scooted along the edges of the building to the back of the school.

*"Where is it?"* Kye whispered, tapping Jay on the shoulder from behind.

*"I'm looking"* Jay whispered as they were walking in a crouched position looking at every window they passed. Jay knew that her window faced the playground.

*"Hey Jay, wait, where is Sokki?!"* Kye said.

Both boys turned around with confusion. *"I thought she was right behind us??"* Jay said with a panicked look on his face. The boys began to look around with more intensity…

"*Hey! Get over here!*" a voice whispered from behind them. Frightened, they jumped up and turned around. They saw Sokki poking her head out of an open window.

"*I found it!*" she said.

"*Yeah we can see that,*" Kye said. Sokki backed away from the window. Jay crawled in the window, after Kye followed and the three were in Ms. Spears' classroom. The room was dark and quiet.

"*You scared me, I thought we lost you!*" Jay said to Sokki

"*Yeah me too,*" Kye said.

"*Sorry guys,*" she whispered back. The nervous feeling Jay had felt now doubled.

"*We shouldn't be here guys,*" Sokki said to the boys.

"*We will reach the envelope and get out I promise….. Alright, let's head to Principal ReLouf's office*" Jay said.

They left the classroom and walked into the hallway without a sound detected. They began to make their way down around the corner and down the hallway to the main office. As they approached the office, looking down the long hallway, it was pitch black. The only light that was shining was that of the light poles of the basketball court which shone through the window and halfway up the lobby.

The main office consisted of the front desk where they would answer calls, and guide students who were lost. Behind the desk there was a big sign that read **"Live as if there was no guarantee of tomorrow because there isn't"**. Beside the office were the back offices where the faculty stayed and conducted their administrative responsibility under the direction of Principal ReLouf, who had been Legions principal for 20 years.

# SPLASH

There had been talk of him retiring after the upcoming school year. Sad to hear, but for Jay, Kye and Sokki, they would be granted the privilege of having him as principal for their last year of high school. *"It's locked!"* Jay said as he jiggled the door knob.

Sokki turned on the flashlight on her phone and shined it on the door where Jay was trying to open it. *"Do you have your... Oh there it goes"* Sokki said. Kye stepped in front of Jayy, reached in his pocket and pulled out his City ID and stuck it in the door wedge where the handle and lock were located.

*"So I'll push this down while you try to jiggle the door to open"* Kye said looking back over at Jay next to him. Jay began to jiggle the door and click, the door opened.

*"What? Don't look at me like that, I used it to get into my parents room one time"* Kye said to Jay and Sokki that both had a telling appearance on their faces. When the three stepped inside, an undeniable wall of cold air breached the inside and greeted them at the door. As the cold air brushed the three, Jay got goosebumps immediately almost as if the air carried them with it. Chills started to arise.

*"One of you stay out here to make sure no one is coming"* Whispered Jay.

*"I'll stay,"* Sokki said. At that moment, she handed her phone to Kye to use for a flashlight.

*"Can you come inside with me and help me look for the keys?"* Jay asked Kye.

Kye nodded, *"Yeah, let's go!"* They two boys walked around the corner where Mr. ReLouf's office was. It sat at the front of the office hallway. As they looked left before walking in the office to his room to the right, they noticed that there was a fan on in the very back of the hallway.

"It's just the fan," Kye said to Jay as he saw him staring at it with suspicion and intensity. Kye began to shine a light in a few different directions looking for keys.

"Check the drawers," he said to Jay. Jay walked around the wooden desk and opened the very first drawer on the right side.

"Found em" Jay said as he pulled out a keychain with a mirage of keys on it.

"Let's go", Jay said. Jay and Kye left the office.

"We're clear so far," Sokki said as the boys approached her.

"Where is room 56?" Sokki whispered. It should be just down this hallway. They turned around back to the hallway in which they came and started walking towards it, still crouching, with each classroom they passed they looked at black panel next to each door knob and read the number...

"34, 36... we have to keep going, it's going to be on the left hand side" Jay said. They continued to tiptoe down the hallway. Jay stopped and stared at a panel next to a door knob.

"What happened?" Sokki said,

"This is it.... Room 56" Jay said as he gulped."

"It's ok, we have your back Jay. We're all going in together". Kye said. Jay entered one key from the rings that they retrieved from Mr. ReLouf's office. The key didn't fit. He tried another key, but this key didn't work either. He took a look around behind him to take a peek down the hallway. Goosebumps began to breach his body and a scary sense of chills continued to take full control over Jay's body.

Jay tried two more keys before he came across a key that was longer than all the rest. Intuition led him to believe that this was the right key. He inserted the key and twisted it to the left click! The door unlocked, Jay swallowed again, as he swallowed he looked down the long, dark hallway once more, then glancing at Kye and Sokki. The three stared at each other. He turned his attention back to the door.

He twisted the handle downward and pushed the door forward slowly, as the door opened, another cold wall of air leaked out of the room. ***SCREEEEEECH.*** The door made a loud noise as it opened. The room was completely dark, black was an understatement. Jay took two steps into the room, Kye followed in next.

Kye reached his hand to the light switch that was next to him on the right entrance of the door. He flicked it on with his middle finger. The room remained dark. *"That's weird,"* Kye said. He flicked the light switch down again and then the room lit up. When the light turned on they noticed that there were fish tanks filled with water all over the room. Each tank had something different in it.

*"That's too bright, we have to turn it off!"* Sokki said. Kye quickly flicked the light switch back up.

*"That's so weird,"* Kye said again.

*"Turn on your flashlight from your phone"* Jay whispered softly. Kye and Sokki pulled their phones out of their pockets and turned on the flashlight. When they did, they saw that Jay was already near the desk which he had seen the teachers talking about earlier. Jay continued to rummage around the desk looking for the folder.

Kye shined his flashlight on the tanks filled with water to the right of the room. As he shined his light on the tank he noticed that there was an eight legged creature in the tank.

***SMACK!*** The eight tentacled creature turned its body, swam towards the glass and smacked its head against the glass glaring at Kye, somehow this octopus appeared to be angry.

*"Ah!"* Kye yelled as he jumped back bumping into a desk.

"What happened?!" Sokki asked.

"This octopus would have attacked me if it could!!" Kye said.

"SHH!" Jay said, shining his flashlight on the glass on the tank from the front of the room.

"Octopus?" Sokki glaired from the opposite room of Kye.

"There is a weird lizard looking thing over here" She said, flashing her light towards Kye's direction. Kye turned away and walked across the room to Sokki.

"A lizard?" Kye asked, walking up next to Sokki.

"I thought lizards don't swim," Kye said.

"What's in that one?" He asked Sokki, looking to the right.

"I don't know, let's look," Sokki said.

"Is that a …. "Stingray?" Kye asked.

"No, ummmm ….. Electric eel" Sokki said.

"This is really weird," Kye said. They walked closer to the front of the classroom looking at another tank. When they approached it, they saw a sharp tale, a long body white on the bottom and dark blue on the top.

"Woah" Sokki said as she covered her mouth.

"What the…." Kye said right after her.

"Jay, why is there a SHARK in here??" Kye asked as he flashed his light towards Jay who was still looking all around for the envelope.

"SHHHH, remember we need to be quiet". Jay said quietly.

"Kye, come here, you have to see this...." Sokki said.

"What's up?" Kye said walking up next to her this time closer to the front of the classroom.

"How in the....but I thought they would.... That doesn't make any sense." Kye said. The hairs on his skin rose as he and Sokki glared at the last tank in the front of the classroom.

"I don't see how that is even possible" Sokki said she took her hand and moved it from the front of her head to the back pushing her long hair to the back.

"I found it!" Jay said. Kye and Sokki walked over to Jay, who was standing over the desk in the front right part of the classroom. They all shined their lights on the envelope sitting on the desk.

"Wait," Jay said.

"What?" Sokki asked.

"Did you say shark?" Jay responded looking at both of them.

"Yes!" Kye said

"We need to get out of here, that's way too creepy, those tanks were not here earlier," Jay said, staring at the tank that had the shark in it.

"Let's open this really quickly," Jay said.

"Good, it's already opened," He said. Jay grabbed the envelope with one hand and pulled out a thick stack of papers that were stapled together. Wrapped around the bottom of the papers was an old newspaper.

Jay set the packet of papers down on the desk and he began to open up the newspaper wide. Sokki moved the stack of papers out of the way. Jay laid the newspaper down on the desk. Sokki and Kye walked around to the other side of the teacher's desk where Jay was. They stopped as they read the headline of the newspaper out loud. **"JOHNNY SILVER DROWNS AT CAMP CHOICE, TEACHERS MAY BE IN QUESTION"** -Published on August 1992.

*"OH my goodness!! Who is Johnny Silver??"* Sokki Asked.

*"I don't know, I've never heard of him,"* Jay said. There was a big picture underneath the headline.

*"That must be camp choice,"* Kye said, pointing to the picture.

*"It says here... Mr. Smith in question with four other teachers...* Jay skimmed the page... *five Legion teachers face trial in two weeks"* He read out loud.

*"There is a corner that is ripped off,"* Jay said.

*"I wonder what's on that piece,"* Kye said.

*"Who would rip it off?"* Sokki asked

*"That's a scary question,"* Jay said. They were all standing over the teacher's desk shining their flashlights on the newspaper. Jay went to the next page of the newspaper and there was another heading: *"STUDENT CAMPER DROWNS AT CAMP CHOICE"* -Published on August 2001.

*"That's crazy..."* Jay said. He flipped to the next page...

*"Please don't tell me,"* Kye mumbled. The headline for the page read.

**"ANOTHER STUDENT DROWNING AT CAMP CHOICE."**

*"That's awful...."* Kye said. Jay flipped to the other pages and saw that there were more similar headlines. He opened one particular page that read:

# SPLASH

**"A FATAL DROWNING OCCURED AT CAMP CHOICE CAUSING CITY TO SHUT DOWN CAMP"** - *Published on September 2005*

"Looks like there was a gap because they shut down. I don't see anymore". Jay said.

"But I wonder what is causing all of these drownings" Sokki said,

"It's creeping me out, I have goosebumps like crazy." Sokki said, rubbing her arms.

"It's really strange," Kye said.

***SMACK!!*** *A loud sound came from the room*

"What was that?!" Kye said jumping and looking around.

"Calm down, it was just the flow of the air conditioning to lift the blinds on the front door then it drops. It happens in these rooms sometimes." Jay said

"I have never heard of that," Sokki said. Jay folded the newspaper up back in its original position and set it back in the envelope. He then grabbed the stack of stapled paper that Sokki had set aside and placed it in the middle of the table.

On the front of the packet read the words **"CAMP CHOICE, DNE. NO."**

"NO?" Sokki said. Jay flipped to the second page and there was a black and grey picture of a young adult. He had whiter skin. He had hair that was gelled up, pushed to the side and had the build of an Olympic swimmer. He had his hands on a gate with his fingers poking through and he was looking down where the picture didn't capture. In the background there was a big building with two C's on top facing away from each other back to back with a circle around the two letters.

"Who is this????" Jay said with confusion.

*"Wait, the picture is time dated... what does that say? November 5, 2009 5:22:00 PM"* Kye said. Jay flipped the page. On the next page there was another picture. This time it was an octopus.

*"Ok, this is creepy... Jay, we need to get out of here like now!"* Sokki said, frantically as she nudged Jay on the shoulder.

*"What's wrong?"* Jay asked, his nerves increased from Sokki's worrisome mood.

*"Someone was just here..."* Sokki said in a startled voice.

*"What?? What do you mean? How do you know?"* Jay asked,

*"Because I just know I can just feel it,"* Sokki said. We are going to leave soon. There was a pause, the three listened for any sounds...

*"There is an Octopus over there, in that tank,"* Kye said. They all shined their flashlights in the tank to the right of the classroom. Jay flipped the next page and was a lizard.

*"Ewwwww What is that?!!"* Sokki said

*"Shhh,"* Jay said.

*"Oops, sorry"* Sokki reverted back to whispering. Jay flipped another page and there was a picture of an electric eel, next page there was a shark....

*"Ummm what was that?"* Sokki said. She walked toward the door.

*"I hear keys,"* she said as she grabbed the door handle. She slowly opened it avoiding sound. As she poked her head around the door and looked to the right down the long hallway, she could see a white light flickering as it seemed to be approaching closer.

*"We have to go now! Someone is coming!!!"*

Jay immediately put the white packet into the folder, turned off his flashlight and ran towards the front door with Kye.

Sokki began to count *"One, two, three"* The three rushed out of the classroom to the left and sprinted down the hallway. They could see that the light was shining on them, neither of them looked back. The source of the light remained quiet.

After they reached a curve in the hallway they stopped and looked around vigorously... *"Here!!!"* Sokki said, pointing as she rushed towards a door that read EXIT directly above it. Sokki pushed the door open with full force, Jay and Kye followed. They ran around the right following the trail that led to the back of the school.

*"To my house!"* Jay said yelling loud enough for just those three to hear. They ran until they reached the trees that lead to Jay's neighborhood. They stayed low in the bushes.

*"We can't take any chances, c'mon"* Jay said as he began to run again. They followed. When they reached the first house in the neighborhood, they slowed down and began to walk. Jay's house was three houses away.

*"Who was that??"* Kye asked painting out of breath

*"I don't know! I couldn't see who it was... I really hope that wasn't the police"* Sokki responded.

*"I think if it were the police then they would have chased us and they would have been yelling"* Kye said.

*"Night security?"* Sokki said

*"Still would have yelled or SOMETHING, I find it weird how they were quiet"* Kye said. They approached Jay's driveway and walked up to the front door.

"We have to be quiet because I think everyone is asleep". Jay said. He reached in his left pant pocket and pulled out his house keys. He inserted a key from the key ring, twisted it and opened the door to his house

*"Front door"* The voice said from inside. Jay's house was equipped with an alarm system that alerted every time an entry door was opened. It was completely dark in the house.

*"Upstairs,"* Jay said.

The three all walked upstairs to Jay's room.

*"I'll get the sleeping bags,"* Jay said. They waited in Jay's room until he brought them sleeping bags. Jay tiptoed across the living room into the cabinet, pulled out two sleeping bags and carried them to the living room dropping one along the way. He picked it up and went into his room. When he got inside Kye and Sokki were sitting on the floor. Jay closed the door until it was cracked where it barely opened.

*"Sokki, you can take the bed. Kye, and I will sleep on the floor with the sleeping bags"* Jay said.

*"Thanks,"* Sokki said with a half smile on her face.

*"No problem,"* Jay said. Sokki climbed on top of the bed, put her head on the pillow and put the covers over her. Jay and Kye laid the sleeping bags out on the floor. Jay layed two sleeping bags down, one next to the closet and one across the room next to the dresser. Jay climbed in the sleeping bag next to the dresser then handed Kye a pillow he had in the corner of the room.

*"Do you have one?"* Kye asked Jay.

*"Yeah,"* Jay said, reaching for a pillow on the other side of his dresser. Kye unzipped the sleeping bag laying next to the closet across the room and got inside.

"Goodnight y'all," Jay said.

"Goodnight man," Kye said.

"Is she asleep?" Jay asked, referring to Sokki.

"I think so… Sokki??" Kye said.

"Geesh that was quick!" Jay said.

"Yeah she must have been tired," Kye said, trying to speak through the middle of his yawn.

"What do you think all that stuff was?" Kye asked with his eyes closed.

"I am not sure, but I know something is not right" Jay said with his eyes wide open staring at the ceiling.

"We will sleep on it…… but that is crazy," Jay said.

"Yeeeeeah" Kye said, yawning again.

"Well alright, I'm going to close my eyes, try to get some sleep, I am exhausted. Probably because of all those finals" Kye said.

"Are you sure it's not because of sneaking through Legion all night? Haha" Jay asked.

"Heehee, yeah, or that," Kye said laughing.

"Alright man, goodnight" Jay said.

"Night," Kye said. There was now silence in the room, Jay layed on the floor inside his cold sleeping bag on his back staring at the ceiling. He didn't try closing his eyes. Flashbacks of what he saw in room 56 kept appearing in his head. He began to get goosebumps again. He could not stop thinking of the black and white picture of the young adult in the packet he found.

*WIIIIIIIISH WOOOO HOOOOO*. The wind began to blow the tree outside against Jay's window. Since Jay's room faced the front of the house he could see everything that was going on outside if the tree permitted the view which in most cases it was willing. He could hear the leaves and branches beat against the widow like a marching band whose sound kept being paused every few seconds.

Jay laid there staring at the ceiling wondering about camp choice, what it would be like and if the school was going to cancel. Thoughts came and left his head similar to a crowd at a train station. Soon, Jay began to fall into a deep sleep with the continuous sound of wind blowing the trees back and forth. The night continued on orchestrating the sound of the wind, whistling and blowing, conducting the music of the Los Aui unpredictable weather.

Soon, dawn came to introduce the morning. The birds outside of Jay's window began to chirp and light began to shine through the window. *KNOCK, KNOCK, KNOCK!!* There was banging at the front door of the Cruz household house. The house was still, there was a long pause. *KNOCK, KNOCK, KNOCK, KNOCK!!* A door opened from upstairs in the house, Mr. Cruz opened his bedroom door and came fastly walking down the stairs, placed his head in front of the window at the bottom of the stairs next to the front door. He opened the blinds slightly. He saw two gentlemen standing at the door in uniform.

"*LOS AQUI POLICE DEPARTMENT*" A voice stated from behind the door. Mr. Cruz unlocked the bottom lock then unlocks the top lock and opened up the door wide. The sun's greatest asset being the light shined through and lit up the entire house. Mr. Cruz looked quickly, glanced and saw the black patrol car with a fin on top that resembled a shark then he looked at the officers in front of them.

There were two officers standing there with a clipboard in their hand. They wore a shiny black peaked cap along with a black button up shirt, with slacks, belt and a cape. Mr. Cruz knew that the easiest way to distinguish Vegas PD versus Aqui PD was the uniform. Vegas PD wore all red. Aqui PD wore all black.

"Hello officer, good morning," Mr. Cruz said, looking at the officer.

"Hello sir, good morning, I am Officer Haun and this is Officer Johnson. We would like to speak with you about some trouble going on in our community. We are visiting different houses in the neighborhood. Are your kid's home?" The officer asked.

"Uh, um yes, is there a problem?"

"Could you have them come here?" asked the officer

"They are not in any kind of trouble, we just want to ask them a few questions"

"KIDS, JAY, ZEKE. .......JAY!!" Mr. Cruz yelled looking back towards the upstairs part of the house. Jay awoke from hearing the yelling, he slowly opened his eyes.

"COMING!" Jay yelled, answering.

"They will be down in a little bit," Mr. Cruz said. Meanwhile upstairs, in Jay's room, Jay was just awakening in the morning. He rubbed his eyes really quick then jumped up on his feet. He put his hand on Sokki's shoulder who was still sleeping and shook her until he saw movement.

"Huuuuh?" Sokki said.

"We need to go downstairs now," Jay said. Jay walked over to where Kye was laying in his sleeping bag and Jay began to shake him.

"I'm up," Kye mumbled.

"We need to go downstairs like now" Jay said with a great deal of urgency in his voice. Kye and Sokki stood up, stretched and followed Jay out of the room. Jay knocked, walked over the door down the hall on the right and knocked on it. ***KNOCK, KNOCK, KNOCK!***

"Yeeeeah?" a voice said from inside the room.

"We need to go downstairs now." Jay responded.

"Ok, coming" the voice said.

"Is that your cousin?" Kye asked while rubbing his eyes.

"Yep" The three walked to the edge of the stairs. Zeke walked out of his room. He walked up to the three, the four of them proceeded down the stairs. When they reached the bottom they walked around the door to where they could see outside.

"Good morning kids, The reason we are here Mr. Cruz is because there was a break in at the school down the road last night around midnight, the school has been robbed" The officer said.

# CHAPTER 7

The birds that were outside that morning seemed to stop chirping their morning songs as there appeared to be an uncomfortable feeling knocking on the Cruz's front door that morning.

*"A robbery? What did they take?"* Mr. Cruz asked

*"Last night, or this morning I should say, at about 1:30AM documents and other assets were stolen from a classroom inside of the school. Do your children attend Legion?"* The Officer asked.

*"Yes, they do….. And you're asking this becaaaaaaause"* Mr. Cruz said slowly.

The officer cleared his throat and looked at the three young adults standing in the doorway.

*"Would any of you happen to know anything about what happened last night down at the school?"* The officer asked while holding a pen to a notepad anticipating a response.

*"No, we had no idea. That's crazy"* Jay replied. Sokki and Kye agreed.

*"Did you hear anything last night?"* the officer asked, looking back and forth between Mr. Cruz, Jay, Sokki, Kye, and Zeke.

*"1:30 this morning? I was sleep"* Mr. Cruz said, making eye contact with the officer.

*"Same here,"* Zeke said. There was a short silence,

*"Did you question the teaching staff? Maybe one of them took something home to work on"* Sokki said.

*"You do know that yesterday was the last day of school right?"* The officer asked, looking at Sokki.

"Yes," Sokki said. The officer didn't expect such a short response. Sokki had an intriguing way of answering a question how someone would least expect it. In this particular case it surprised Jay that she answered the same way to an officer.

"We have already contacted all of our faculty staff and the last teacher was there at 12:30 AM finishing up some paperwork," the officer said. Jay glanced at Sokki, he remembered what she had a strong hunch about last night. The officer took a deep breath in.

"So....wait were you three?" The officer asked the three looking directly at Jay, Sokki and Kye.

"I'm sorry?" Jay said.

"He asked where you were last night," Mr. Cruz said with a serious tone in his voice.

"We were at the treehouse," Jay said looking at his Dad.

"I didn't know that," Mr. Cruz said under his breath.

"Treehouse??" The officer asked.

"Yes, it's a treehouse that we built a few years ago," Sokki said.

"Where is this treehouse?" the officer asked.

"Umm." Sokki started to speak. There was another short pause. The group never ever gave up the hidden location of the treehouse

"It's been our thing so we haven't really told anyone where it is," Sokki finished.

"Ok, fair enough. I think we are done here" the officer said, leaning forward to shake Mr. Cruz's hand. Mr. Cruz just stared at the officer, deciding not to shake his hand. There was a tense silence.

"Ok..... We're done here" Officer Haun said whispering to his partner. The officer turned and walked away. When he reached his car, he then stopped and turned back towards the front door of Cruz's house. Looking at the group staring from the doorway, still standing by the passenger side of his officer car he said *"And by the way, I am required to let you know that any assessment of a crime automatically makes you guilty by association. I would hate to see you children get your first strike and be labeled CRI so early. You haven't even started your career..... Let alone graduated SO, if you know anything at ALL that might aid us in this case then you are required to report it to us immediately. If you don't..... Well, you are smart. I'm sure you could figure it out."* Heck, I am looking at three top students, I believe. The officer pretended like he was squinting, he continued

*"I believe that is Sokki Sioso, number one student in science from Legion... Right?? Kye Nacksworth, number one student in math. And is that Jay Cruz??? Top student in English out of the entire Legion Academy. Not to mention a future motivational speaker. WOW, there is a lot of talent and smarts just standing in that doorway alone. Such a shame.... Well, Let us know if you hear or see anything at all. Have a good day".* He got in the passenger seat of the car door. The car was still, after a few seconds. It sped down the street.

"That was weird," Sokki said. Everyone went back inside the house. Jay's dad closed the front door.

*"Alright, kids, I'm only going to ask you one single time.... Do you know ANYTHING about what he was talking about?"* Mr. Cruz said, staring at the three of them. All four, including Zeke, shook their heads signaling **"NO"**. Ironically enough, as strange as it sounded. They were telling the truth. They heard nothing about a robbery and nothing to do with one.

*"Ok, good, that stuff is pretty serious, if you know anything you better say somethin'. You two might wanna text your parents and let them know what is going on, maybe they might have heard something, or I don't know"* Mr. Cruz said.

"Ok we will," Kye said.

"Ok, its seven AM, I'm going back to bed, I have to work in a little bit, Jay"

"Yeah?"

"Please finish packing. Like today." Mr. Cruz said.

"Alright, will do." Jay said. Mr. Cruz walked upstairs, went into his room and closed his bedroom door.

"I'm going back upstairs, I'm tired," Zeke said. The four began to walk upstairs, when they reached the top of the stairs, Zeke went down the hall to his room, went inside and closed the door. Jay, Sokki and Kye walked right and went into Jay's room.

As the three walked inside Jay's room, Jay closed the door behind him. Sokki jumped on Jay's bed, Kye sat down on the sleeping bag he was using. Jay sat down in his chair that he had at his desk that was in front of the window.

"That was a close one," Jay said.

"Yeah, that was really weird," Kye said.

"Yeah a little too strange" Sokki said sitting up with her legs crossed looking at Jay and Kye.

"Why do you say that?" Jay said, looking at them both.

"Because, well do you remember how there was a light yesterday from someone coming down the hallway?" Sokki said

"Yes," Jay answered.

"What if that was the thief?!" Sokki said, waving her hand up in the air.

"That is a very good point," Kye said.

"That would make sense why he didn't say anything to us when he saw us…Wait a second! Guys, what was the first thing the officer asked my dad when we got to the door??" Jay asked the two.

"Have we heard about anything?" Sokki said.

"No, before that" Jay said……. Jay stood up.

"I heard him when I was half asleep. He specifically asked my Dad if we currently attend Legion" Jay said.

"Ok…. and?" Kye said.

"Well what was the little smart remark he made before he left? He pointed out that we were the number students in Math, English and Science… and he is correct by all means but how… on this God given green earth did he know that?? And why did he have the audacity to ask if we attended legion when he already knew? That doesn't make any sense." Jay said as he was leaning against the wall next to the window.

"Something is very fishy" Sokki said,

"Yeah literally" Kye said with a smirk on his face.

"Yeah, especially since there were all of those animals in that room yesterday, that confused me.. What was there? Wasn't there an octopus?" Sokki asked.

"SHhh! Yes, that thing was veeeeery creepy….. And a shark" Kye said

"Sooooo… Sharky?" Jay said.

"LOL" Kye said,

"You have to stop doing that, that's for texting only," Jay said.

"Something was up with that cop," Sokki said while she checked her phone for any missed calls. "I'm surprised my mom hasn't called yet. I'll probably leave in a little bit." she said. Jay looked at the clock behind him that was on the wall above the desk.

"Oh yeah!! Do you remember last night when you said someone was JUST in that classroom last night?? How did you know that?" Jay asked as he sat sitting back down in his chair.

"Yeah, that was crazy that you said that because that cop said that a teacher was JUST there at 12:30 last night" said Kye.

"Yeah, that's why I looked at you when he said that," Jay said, looking at Sokki.

"I don't know… it was weird almost as if it just came over me. Very strange, I have never felt anything like that before. I can't explain it. It was just weird" Sokki said.

"So it just all of a sudden came over you?" Kye said.

"Yeah, I guess. Like I said, it was weird". Sokki replied.

"See, my thing is if the school has had so many drownings then why in the world are we going back there?" Jay asked the two still leaning back in his chair against the wall.

"Well apparently the school hasn't been back there in quite a long time. That's why this year Mr. ReLouf is pushing it so much to the juniors" said Sokki.

"I'm pretty excited," Kye said.

"Have you decided what you want to do?" Jay asked.

"You mean for camp or like in general?" Sokki asked.

"For camp," Jay replied.

"You two know I'm going to go swimming. From there I would like to start teaching children how to swim" Kye said.

"Yeah that backstroke of yours is on point!" Jay said. ***DING, DING!*** A noise came from Sokki's phone.

"Hold on guys," Sokki said. Sokki began to scroll her thumb on her phone screen, she started to type away. **\*TICK, TICK.....TICK, TICK,TICK,TICK\***

"Sorry, it's my Mom, she texted me. I have to go" Sokki said as she jumped up out of Jay's bed and put her shoes on. After she had both shoes on she headed for the door. She opened Jay's room door.

"*Are we doing anything tonight?*" she asked, looking back and forth at the two".

"*I am not sure, we'll text you*" Jay said walking towards the door. Kye and Jay stood up and together they all walked downstairs. Jay opened the front door and the same shine from a few minutes ago came rushing in blinding him in his sight.

"*I probably better get home too, my Mom is probably worried,*" Kye said. Kye and Sokki began to walk outside.

"*Alright guys*" Jay said.

"*Alright, we will see you later*". Sokki said.

"*Alright man,*" Kye said. Jay began to close the door

"*Jay!*" Sokki yelled. Jay opened the door wide again.

"*Don't forget to pack, like TODAY*" She said, uttering the same words to her Dad just a few minutes ago.

"*Don't worry, I will,*" Jay said, responding with a big smirk on his face. Just before the door closed, Sokki ran up to the door and stopped it. Jay opened the door up wide again, this time using Sokki as a shield for the beaming sun rays. She extended her arms big and wrapped them around Jay delivering a warm hug. When their bodies connected a vibrating shock rippled through Sokki and hit Jay.

"Ouch! That was weird. You didn't feel that?" Jay asked, looking at her with a diranged expression. He let go of his friend and started feeling his chest as if he just got shot with a bullet.

"Oh no! I definitely did, that was weird. It didn't hurt though, that is literally the second time it's happened today! I'm sorry, are you ok?"

"Yeah, but what was the hug for?"

"Life is too short, I may not see you tomorrow, I dunno, something may happen to me, or you, or Kye or any of us. I'm just sayin, alright bye forreal this time," she said.

Jay chuckled and closed the door, **BAM!** Just like that, the picture of the young man he had seen the night before had appeared in his thoughts again. He let out a big sigh and put his head in his hands. He walked upstairs to his room and began cleaning his room. He made his bed, rolled the sleeping bags and threw them in the closet down the hall. He grabbed the red vacuum from the closet and rolled down the hallway and into his room.

He then unwrapped the cord from the back and took the end and plugged it into an outlet near his closet. He flicked the switch that was on the handle of the vacuum and began moving it back and forth, letting the vacuum suck up all of the lint and random small pieces of paper on the floor. He closed the door to quiet out the noise from the rest of the house. After he was finished, he turned off the noisy machine and unplugged the cord.

He wrapped the cord around the back, opened his door and began rolling it across the hallway to the closet where it belonged. Jay didn't always favor cleaning but when he started it was very hard for him to stop. His stomach began to growl, so Jay walked down his flight of 14 steps and walked onto the kitchen where he would find a bowl, cereal and milk. He poured some cereal into a big white bowl and sat down at the table to eat.

Ever since he was younger he could always remember that he loved cereal. He always ate it. He liked the other foods for breakfast but he just always favored cereal, ESPECIALLY if it was PBCA. The popular cereal Peanut Butter and Chocolate Attack. In Los Aqui, there is a breakfast called Azey. It was a very soft toasted bread marinated in milk and eggs with cinnamon chunks on top. He tried to have it whenever he could. Jay sat there at the table this Saturday morning, enjoying his breakfast in silence thinking about the events from last night and this morning.

# CHAPTER 8

Meanwhile, Sokki was just arriving home. When Sokki arrived, she entered through her front door. Standing next to the couch, in the living room was a tall woman with red fluffy hair with brown eyes, light skin complexion and glasses with black frames dressed in business attire. It was Sokki's mother. Since they lived in the same neighborhood. Jay's house and Sokki's house had a similar floor plan. The only difference was that Sokki's house was smaller, the house didn't have two stories like Jay's did.

*"Young lady, where on earth have you been? Do you know what time it is?"* Sokki's mother asked with wide eyes staring down at her from a couple feet away leaning against the couch.

*"8:27... AM... Sorry mom, we stayed at Jay's house last night after the tree house"* Sokki said again.

*"Who is we?"* Soki's mom asked.

*"Me, and Kye."* She said,

*"Aaaaand you couldn't send me a text? To be as smart as you are... you have the communication skills of a whale"* Sokki's mom said standing still.

*"You know, whales actually have very good communication, when they send signals, it reaches over 1,000 miles"*. Sokki said. Her mom glared at her with a straight face

*"Sorry,"* Sokki said.

*"I'm serious, you are getting ready to be a senior next year then in college soon, I need you to be a little sharper around the edges."* Her mom said.

*"But mom, I have straight A's,"* Sokki said.

"I am not just talking about in school, I am talking about life. There are just some things that I am going to need you to straighten up.... Oh, and did you talk to Mr. Relouf about the spectrums in his office?" Sokki's mom asked.

"No, I forgot". Sokki responded.

"See that's what I'm talking about, it's fine, I will call him tomorrow" Sokki's Mom said. Sokki put her head down for a brief moment staring at the ground then raised it. There was a pause, the two women were standing at the front door face to face.

Sokki's mother never believed in walking away when someone is talking, when she really wanted to have a conversation with someone she would stand there with no distractions. She knew this although she never studied communication. Sokki was literally a carbon copy of her mother, very intelligent with electric personalities.

Mrs. Siaso broke the silence "So......Aqui officers came to the door today, they said that they were looking for information on a robbery last night at the school, did you happen to hear anything about that?" she said.

"Yeah, they came to Jay's door too, but no... it surprised me," Sokki said.

"Yeah," he said that they were going around in the neighborhood asking everyone. He wanted to know if you were home, he wanted to speak to any students that attended the Legion to see if they had heard any students maybe talking about breaking in the school" Ms. Sioso said.

"Did he say anything else?" Sokki asked.

"He said that quite a few things were taken from a classroom but there was no sign of forced entry or a break in point. And they still have yet to review the security cameras."

"If they have no sign of forced entry and no break in point how are they possibly calling this a robbery? What if someone missed placed these items? And they are being very vague on what these so-called items are. Why can't they just tell us? I swear the officers in this city are so secretive" Sokki said, shaking their head.

"Don't they kind of have to be? That is their job, here they protect the public from danger" Mrs. Sioso said.

"Yeah, and the truth," Sokki said.

"And I'm sure that they have already searched the school," Ms. Siaso said.

"Yeah, I suppose," Sokki said.

"Hey well anyway, I have a client to catch, I will see you a little later. Lock this door." Her mother said. "Alright. Have a good day" Sokki said.

"Alright you too, see you a little later" Her mother said.

Ms. Sioso walked past Sokki, opened up the front door and walked out of the house. Sokki closed the door then locked it. ***VROOOOOOOOM*** Unlike the previous house they had lived in, Sokki could always hear the sound of the car starting up from the driveway.

Since it was just her and her mom she knew usually that there would only be one other person leaving, and one other person coming in. That is why her guards were up anytime she heard something when she knew her mother was at work.

Usually, Sokki embodied the definition of the word **"productive"**. When she came home from school she would immediately complete her homework and then study, clean and still have time to go for a run in the late evenings. If her studying and homework did not permit her to go for her evening midnight run then she would go in the early mornings before school started.

## SPLASH

This morning was a different case. She took off her shoes and placed them near the door, walked in the living room to the right and plopped down on the couch. She put her feet on the couch so she could lay down. She turned on her back so she could stare at the ceiling. She was exhausted. As she began to doze off she envisioned herself in her own dorm room in college, walking around campus.

From birth, her mother had raised her to be very independent doing unusual practices like having her grab her own binky. She was just a couple weeks old to now , letting her cook her own meals, wash clothes, and even save money in a secret fund that no one knew about. For her, living on her own in a dorm wasn't a scary thought. Like most kids her age, fret the idea of leaving their comfortability at home and living on their own.

Although Sokki's Mother was around all of her life and raised her from a baby, Ms. Sioso created such independence in her that it almost felt as if she was a regular adult. Sokki always felt older than she was. Ms. Sioso often found herself saying things like "Sometimes I forget how young you really are because you are so much older in maturity."

Jay, Sokki and Kye were all 17, turning 18 in the following year. Somehow, their birthdays lined up perfectly in the first three months of the year. Jay's birthday was January 1st. Sokki's birthday was February 1st and Kye's birthday was miracally March 1st. Sokki thought about all of this as her eyes were closed, she laid there on her couch drifting off to sleep. About five minutes passed and she was now resting.

It's raining outside, the sun has just gone down...

*"Hey Sokki come on,"* a voice said from afar.

*"I'm coming, one second. I'm just going to put this stuff away, then text my mom"*. She grabbed the two bright yellow balls that were sitting on the pool deck. And placed them in the shack near the building.

She walked back to the pool deck. Unplugged the time clock that was sitting on the edge of the pool deck, walked over to the edge of the deck and picked it up. She pulled out her phone and began texting her mother. *"Hey Mom, the first few..."* At that moment she felt two hands on each of my shoulders and all of a sudden she started to tilt, she lost her balance and fell into the water. ***SLASH!!!***

\*\*\*

*"AHH*!!" Sokki yelled as she sat up from the couch. She had been dreaming, sweat was running down her face, her heart was beating fast. She was relieved to know it was just a dream.

# CHAPTER 9

The noon sun beat down at the Cruz's house and the birds had sung their last song and had now reverted to flying around the neighborhood making their rounds in circles until night time.

"*Are those sirens?*" Jay's father asked as he paused the TV and glanced at Zeke who was sitting in the living room on the couch next to the window.

"*They sound like they are coming this way,*" Mr. Cruz said.

"*Yeah, they kinda do*," Zeke said. Mr. Cruz stood up and walked to the living room window above the couch that Zeke was sitting at. He slightly opened the blinds and squinted peering out of the window. The sirens became louder. As Mr. Cruz stared out of the window he saw two fin cars drive up in front of his house and park.

"*Again? What do they want now?*" Mr. Cruz said under his breath, Mr. Cruz then reverted his attention now to the window at the bottom of the stairs. By the time he had poked his head through the window. He saw two officers walking with steps of intensity towards the front door. He noticed it was the same two officers from earlier. Before they could reach the door Mr. Cruz opened the front door, stepped outside and closed the door.

"*Hi officers, ca... Can I help you?*" Mr. Cruz said, stuttering.

"*Yes. Is Jay here?*" officer Haun asked.

"*I'm sorry, what is this about?*" Mr. Cruz asked with a serious tone that rippled through his voice.

"*My humblest apologies, we have information that may link your son Jay directly to the crime committed last night at the school*" The officer said.

*"What do you mean, like what?"* Mr. Cruz said.

*"Mr. Cruz…. I am going to need Jay to come outside if he is present"*. The officer said,

*"One sec"* Mr. Cruz opened up the door, poked his head inside and yelled towards the upstairs

*"JAY, DOWN HERE NOW!"* he yelled. Jay heard his father's request, he appeared from his room and walked downstairs. From the sound in his father's voice left Jay feeling a little nervous. Jay reached the bottom of the stairs and walked outside the front door.

*"Jay, can you explain this image? It was a screenshot taken from the video of you on youtube presenting your speech at school yesterday"* The officer asked as he pulled out a picture from his pocket.

Shaking, Jay grabbed the picture from the officer. In his mind he immediately assumed that it was a picture of him and his friends sneaking through the school but Jay was incorrect. When he looked at the picture he saw him standing in front of the classroom staring down at the teacher's desk in the front of the classroom. Jay continued to shake

*"Um yeah, I had just given the speech in Mrs. Till's class"* Jay with a confused tone.

*"What were you looking at?"* Officer Haun asked. There was a short pause as Jay looked at the picture for a longer time.

*"I don't remember,"* Jay said.

*"Well let me help you out, do the words: CAMP CHOICE DNE sound familiar to you?"* The officer said,

*"No, Well…. I mean, I happened to see that when I glanced down looking at the packet"* Jay said.

*"So you just happened to be staring at it??"* Said the officer as he put his hands on his hips. He glanced once at Jay's father then reverted his attention back to Jay.

*"Yes,"* Jay said.

*"Well, that is the packet that was stolen from the school last night.... So I am going to ask you again, and you might want to re-consider changing your story. Where were you last night?"* the officer asked. Chills rippled through Jay's body, he cleared his throat, looked at his dad quickly then at the ground, then stared back at the officer.

*"I was at our treehouse,"* Jay said. The officer took a deep sigh. The officer looked at Jay's father.

*"Mr. Cruz.... I am terribly sorry about this but I gave you a chance"* He said looking down at Jay.

*"Jay Cruz, please turn around and put your hands behind your back"* said the officer.

*"WHAT?!! No! This is not happening, what in the Hell do you think you're doing?!"* Mr. Cruz asked, approaching the officer. The officer stepped back and reached his hand behind his back

*"Step back now!"* Officer Johnson yelled.

*"Please don't make this harder than it already is"* said Officer Haun.

Mr. Cruz realized that he was approaching an officer that was equipped with a lethal weapon, he slowly stepped back and yelled *"YOU CAN'T TAKE HIM!"*

*"Unfortunately we must, Mr. Cruz, he is a possible suspect in the crime at the school, we will need to hold him until we find further evidence"* the officer said. Mr. Cruz took one step forward again and looked the officer in the eye.

*"I am not a man of many promises but I am a man of my word. You will be hearing from my lawyer and if anything even comes close to happening to him. I will do nothing else until your badge is provoked and you are thrown in jail and everything you love is stripped from you like a bandaid from a fresh wound…. THAT, you stormtrooper is a promise and a guarantee"* The officer broke eye contact with Mr. Cruz and looked over half of his left shoulder at his partner that was standing behind him who had his hand on his gun holster. Officer Haun then looked over at Officer Johnson as well.

*"If I were you, I would step back,"* Officer Haun said whispering in a soft voice.

*"Just remember what I said."* Mr. Cruz said. Glancing back at officer Haun as he stepped back he pulled out his phone.

*"Jay, please put your hands behind your back"* Jay turned around and put his hands behind his back.

*"You have the right to remain silent. Anything you say can and will be used against you in a court of law. You have the right to speak to an attorney, and to have an attorney present during any questioning if you cannot afford an attorney, one will be provided for you. Do you understand these rights as I have read them to you?"* Officer Haun said. ***CLICK*** the final latch of the handcuffs were around Jay's wrist.

Jay thought about Miranda rights, he thought that it was state law that they must tell you what you are being arrested for, this part, Jay didn't understand clearly but nevertheless he remained quiet.

*" Jay, do you understand these rights as I have read them to you?"* The officer said again with a higher tone interrupting Jay's thought process.

*"Uh yes,"* Jay said.

# SPLASH

"*Let's go,*" Officer Haun said to Officer Johnson. Officer Haun put his right hand on Jay's right shoulder and began escorting him to the fin car.

"*Don't worry Dad, I'll be fine. I know I'm innocent*" Jay said looking back at his father. Mr. Cruz did not respond as he was in shock. He couldn't put two words together.

"*Tell Sokki and Kye where I am,*" Jay said as they finally reached the fin car. The officer opened the back door of his fin car and put his head on Jay's head to prepare for him sitting down in the back seat. Jay looked at his father who was standing on the porch one last time. Mr. Cruz stared at his son.

He nodded to Jay, Jay nodded back. The officer then slowly pushed his head down and Jay got in the car. ***DOOM*.** The slam of the door closing gave Mr. Cruz a very sick feeling in his stomach. Almost as if the door had closed in slow motion. For Mr. Cruz, it felt as if someone had walked straight up to him and stuck a long sharp knife through his stomach and there was absolutely nothing he could do about it.

Mr. Cruz stood there and stared as his son was taken away from his sight and the fin car drove off around the corner and out of the neighborhood. Mr. Cruz looked at the floor beneath him for a while. He always told his sons how he would be so proud if they go through life with no marks against them. In times like these Mr. Cruz seemed to jump to conclusions at a rapid pace. He soon then raised his head and walked inside his house. When he got inside he closed the door very slowly.

"*You ok? Where's Jay?*" Zeke asked, standing in the middle of the living room.

"*The fins took him,*" Mr. Cruz said.

"*What do you mean they took him?!*" Zeke asked.

"They think he might be connected to what happened at the school last night," Mr. Cruz said.

"Are you serious? How would he be connected!?" Zeke said, crossing his arms.

"At the end of his video he was looking down at the envelope that was stolen last night," Mr. Cruz said, leaning against the couch.

"Just for looking at a stupid piece of paper?! That is so STUPID!!" Zeke said with anger.

"Hey, it should be ok. They will find the truth and he should be released soon. I know my son and you know your brother. I know it's not our normal version of comfort but we gotta try and relax, I am going to get on the phone with our attorney" Mr. Cruz said.

"Ok……. That is crazy, hey you know the uptons were poking their head through their window the entire time" Zeke said

"Really? Well, Im sure they will call me later"

Zeke ignored the random comment, looking down at the carpet. Mr. Cruz walked upstairs slowly and closed his bedroom door. Zeke then walked upstairs and went to his room and closed his door. It was now quiet again in the Cruz's house with no birds making songs, just pure quiet silence.

***

***VOOM, VOOM*** Sokki's phone vibrated on the couch next to her. Sokki was sitting on her couch inside her quiet house with her head in her hands. She sat there, trying to clear the dream that she had out of her head so she could start cleaning her house. She soon got up and went to room and decided to attack the pile of clothes that had been sitting there for some weeks.

# SPLASH

Towards the end of the school year she had been so busy with studying and end of the year tasks that she didn't have the time to be really tidy around the house. MOST kids her age would have just laid there on that couch and slept all day. Not Sokki, somehow she always had a productive mentality. She felt that she always had to be doing SOMETHING. Whether she realises it or not, that is how she and Jay met.

It all started in the 2022 school year when Sokki moved to Los Aqui as a transfer student from hungaria. She was born there, her mom decided to move when her husband was attacked by two tigers. He was a famous photographer that was traveling through a small savana when he decided to get out of his truck to capture footage for a documentary he was working on.

The documentary was going to feature life in the Savanna from an unlikely part of the world. He saw two tigers from a distance under a small tree, he parked and got out of his vehicle. He began to get closer to the tigers. As he crouched down on one knee one of the tigers noticed him, the tiger stood up and started sprinting towards him. He was so far away that he did not think the tigers were sprinting towards him.

He thought sure enough they were after a gazelle or something. Soon enough, the tigers were close. It was HIM that they were after. As he started to retreat, he felt something sharp around his ankle holding his foot in place. When he looked down he saw that his foot was in the mouth of a baby cub. As he bent down to push the cub off, he remembered that he had always carried a long sharp knife with a wooden handle on him for protection. He reached around to his carry bag and yelled and screamed for help but there was no one around because he took this voyage by himself.

Normally, he would have a partner but that particular time he was by himself. He knew he had a gun in his travel vehicle but couldn't reach it in time so he settled for his knife. As he continued struggling for his knife he heard a loud roar and galloping. As soon as he looked up he saw the mother lion in mid air lunging towards him. She pounced on him and bit his neck. The doctors weren't able to revive him from all of the blood that was lost. He passed away the next day.

No one knows to this day how he was able to get back to the hospital or who took him there.

Although the incident was two and a half years ago it was still a fresh penetrating scar in Sokki's family. One would never have the capability to know if something this tragic happened to Sokki because of her positive outlook and personality. She has always had an electric personality but Jay was always able to tell on days where it would bother her more than most, he somehow just knew when she needed to be left alone.

For the two years that Sokki knew Jay, she had always played the role of the energizer, she helped when she could and always seemed to stay positive. To Jay's knowledge she had a past tendency to dedicate herself to being extremely organized and very punctual.

While she kept the punctuality, other strong qualities seemed to fade after her dad had passed away. Jay was always able to tell when Sokki had her moments where the passing of her father would really haunt her. For six months, she would wake up and have the exact same dream. In her dream she was in a huge grassy field with just only one really tall tree.

It was her and her father, she would look at him and say, *"Are you ready to climb it?"* and he would say *"Of course!"* They would run towards the tree in a full sprint and when she reached the tree she would climb up the bark of the tree as fast as she could. When she reached the top she would look down and see her father at the bottom.

Two tigers came out of what seemed like thin air and chased him. Sokki had to watch all of this from 50 feet up in the air hanging from a long branch from the tree. *"DADDY! LOOK!"* She would yell, as he turned back the lions jumped towards him and everytime it would get to that moment she would awake sweating.

Sokki's mother became familiar with calming her down after she would have the recurring nightmare. Sokki, Jay and Kye had this saying they would say when one or maybe all three of them needed to hear it. *"Make it a great day or not but the choice is yours"*. Sitting alone in her house she began to feel sleepy again, she knew she wasn't ready to lay back down so she sat back on the couch and turned on a rosaic instrumental composed by her band teacher Mr. Ricky.

He was a famous composer that was generous enough to instruct music at the high school level. It was times like this, with nothing going on. No teachers yelling, no loud noises, no trouble, no pressing assignments that reminded her of a simpler time back in Hungary, but for now, she was here. In Los Aqui, she loved Aqui, she enjoyed this moment because it reminded her of home.

***

\***BARK! BARK! BARK!**\* *"Shhhhhh!"* Kye said.

*"Hey son,"* Kye's mother said from afar.

*"Hey mom,"* Kye said as he walked into the kitchen. He stood there, in the middle of the floor.

*"Is everything alright dear?"* His mom asked.

*"Uh, yes, just a little tired, long night,"* Kye said.

*"Wait what?"* His mother asked.

*"Hey I am sorry, I know I said I was going to be here for breakfast,"* Kye said, hurrying past the fact that he just mentioned he had a long night. In some odd fashion, Kye was a master at changing the subject, being around Jay for all three years had all to do with it. Jay was

originally the master at changing the subject and everything around it. Meaning, he would always be able to divert away from any question he didn't want to answer.

It was at the top of the list of the aspects that people in Jay's life were bothered by. The fact that he never finished a sentence always struck a nerve in whoever he was conversing with at the moment. He did it so much that he didn't even know he was doing it.

*"It's ok, I didn't get to see you yesterday. How was the last day of school?"* Ms. Nacksworth asked, staring at her son and walking into the living room. She walked right past him and sat down.

"It wasn't so good, I barely failed all my final exams," Kye said looking at the floor.

"You did what?!?" Ms. Nacksworth said.

"I'm kidding! I know I passed everything... with flying colors" Kye said with a smile on his face.

"Well sir, that's what I like to hear," his mother said.

"Hey do you have a moment?" Ms. Nacksworth asked her son.

"Yeah what's up?" Kye asked. His mother walked and sat down at the dining table. He also sat in the chair on the side of the table. Ms. Nacksworth laced her fingers with each other and placed them on the table in front of her.

"Have you given any thought about college lately son?" Ms. Nacksworth asked.

"You know... I have..." Kye said with a smirk on his face.

"Aaand?" his mother asked as she leaned forward and turned her head slightly

"I have decided that I am going to go," Kye said, nodding his head up and down.

"You are?" His mother asked.

"Yeah, you know I have given a lot of thought and I realize that I have nothing to lose and everything to gain," he said. His mother began to smile.

"It really hit me when Mr. Worthy's brother came to speak to the class the other day. He has a Ph.D. in business. He came and spoke to the class about the importance of building something, something that's yours and something that will become a tool. Then after class I saw him and Worthy and a few other teachers talking towards the end of class and they just had this style to them... Like... Flow. They had a certain flow to them. I don't know exactly what that flow was. I just know I want it" Kye said.

His mother didn't like when he used the word flow, from her point of view it was the strangest thing. In Las Vegas the language was different, they used words like swagg instead of flow but Ms. Nacksworth wasn't focused on the word flow right now, she was more focused that her son just said that he wants to attend college for the first time ever.

All throughout his childhood Kye never expressed interest in college. In Los Aqui, it was common for a child to express ideas about their future very early on. Within the culture, it was almost expected that one was supposed to know what they were going to do in life. In Kye's upbringing, he was never entirely sure what he wanted to do, it was because of this that he and his mother would have a multitude of conversations about the importance of college and the severity of what would happen if he didn't attend college. Kye agreed but he would also have his alternative opinion of what he could possibly achieve in his life.

Then Kye's mother would respond with the popular saying in Los Aqui which was that education was the key. It was a town that was focused on education, in the same instance they were ranked 150, last of the cities of the United. This is what Kye didn't understand, not only did he not understand it but he didn't like it either. He viewed it as a town that was very focused on education but had some of the worst schools from the United.

Kye wasn't against college, he just never knew his final decision until now. Hearing this news sparked an urge in Ms. Nacksworth's head to write a letter to Mr. Worthy, thanking him for bringing his brother to the school that day. All of the counselling, the conferences and calls to try and encourage her son to go to college all brought her back to this time as she was staring at son with tears in her eyes

*"Son, I am very... very happy to hear you say that, I am so proud of you"* Ms. Nacksworth said sitting there at the table with her son. A tear started to come down her face on the side of her cheek, then another tear followed that one.

*"Awe, mother, don't cry,"* Kye said. He stood up out of the chair, walked around to the front of the table and wrapped his arms around her. She sat still and embraced her son for a moment. When her son let go she smiled as she tried to wipe the tears away from her face but more kept falling from her eyes.

*"So what school are you going to?"* His mother asked, still smiling with her eyes still watery.

*"I don't know where exactly but I know that I am going. Most likely somewhere with a good business program. I was hoping that maybe you can help me too?"* Kye asked with a smirk.

*"Of course! There are so many to choose from, I'm so happy for you"* Ms. Nacksworth said. She stood up and gave her son another hug.

*"Uhhhhhh I am exhausted, I have worked 12 hours for the past three straight days, I need some rest"* Ms. Nacksworth said.

# SPLASH

"*Ok mom, get some rest*". Kye said. She walked upstairs and went to her room and closed the door. Kye felt a sense of relief that he had not felt before in a long time, he loved to see his mother happy. It was redeeming for him considering him and his mother didn't always see eye to eye on everything. Kye opened the door leading to the backyard and walked to the corner of the yard where a hammock was hanging.

This was one of his favorite places to go in his down time. He would lay in the hammock all day if he could. He would read books, eat candy and simply relax. Life in Los Aqui could be extremely busy so when students had a chance to relax, they took full advantage of it. For all of his life, Kye chose the simple route, he could never be explained as a complicated person. So quiet time with nothing going on fit right up his alley. He stared at the hammock for a second then got on it. With no book, no fruit to eat, he laid on the hammock, turned to his side and closed his eyes. This was his medicine for the time being.

\*\*\*

"Wake up! "Hey... Are you sleeping?? Wake up!!" Officer Haun said. He looked in the back seat of the fin car and shook Jay on the leg.

"Kid??.... JAY!" Officer Haun yelled again. Jay began to open his eyes slowly when he opened his eyes fully, he looked around and realized it was dark, he had fallen asleep in the car ride hoping that this was all just a nightmare or a scary dream.

He began to rub his eyes. "*Alright let's go!*" Office Haun said getting out of the car. He closed the passenger door in which he was sitting and then opened the back door. Jay began to scoot closer to the edge of his seat towards the door, he put his right leg out of the door, Officer Haun grabbed him by his arm and lifted him up.

"*I'm going to fill out this paperwork, see you inside?*" Officer Johnson said to Officer Haun from the other side of the fin car.

"*Sounds like a plan, partner*" Officer Haun said.

*"Alright, let's walk"* He said looking at Jay. Jay took a moment, looked around and realized that he was at a police site, or at least this is what he suspected. Looking around him it was dark, there were fin cars parked in rows along a long grey building that read "Holdings" on the side of the building. It almost seemed too quiet in the air at the moment.

He had never seen a police base before, he had heard about it on TV but that was the furthest of his knowledge of any police base. Where Los Aqui differed from a lot of other states was that the fin officers had bases, not stations. It was known to feel like a criminal lock down when one was on a base.

*"I said let's go,"* Officer Haun said. Jay began to walk forward. Officer Haun led him to an all grey building located east of the fin car they had rode in. While Jay was walking, a thought came to his head, curious to know how long exactly they were on that long car ride to the station, he knew it must have been a while.

For about an hour, he hesitated asking officer Haun because he didn't want to ask the wrong thing. Growing up, he was taught that the only two answers you should always give to an officer are either yes sir, no sir, yes ma'am, no ma'am. That's it, no attitude, no smart remarks just yes sir, no sir, yes, ma'am no ma'am. That's it. This should be a common reality in all teachings to children in Aqui, after all, it was one of the most sensitive towns when it came to law enforcement. When they reached the front door of the grey building officer Haun knocked on the door.

*"It's me, H5"* he said, while staring at the door. A brief moment went by, Jay still thought about asking about the lengthy car ride. He chose to remain silent. Soon the door to the grey building opened up.

A tall Asian officer opened up the door. He stood in the door steps, *"Last one for the night?"* The officer said to Haun,

*"Ohhh Yes!" I ... am... done!"* Haun said.

# SPLASH

*"Alright, bring him in,"* the officer said.

*"Yeah right, get outta here, you brought HIM here? Well look who it is, Mr. Motivational speaker huh… wow, my daughter is in LOVE with your video, you go to legion right?"* The officer asked. Jay nodded.

*"Well that's a shame, you were probably a potential role model for her and many other students too, but it looks like you blew it…. Hey when you said you had someone regarding the missing documents this is the LAST person I thought you would bring here. Come inside, we have a place for him"* Jay and officer Haun walked inside the building and closed the door behind them. When Jay walked inside the building he realized where he was, as he looked down the long dark hallway he saw a number of cells with bars that were laced with spikes. He heard some chatter down the hallway.

*"Go ahead and stick 'em in 56"* The officer said.

*"Move,"* Officer Haun said to Jay as he nudged him on the shoulder. Jay began to walk, as he walked by each cell he could see a person in each cell, laying on the bed, some were awake but most of them were asleep. In the hallway there were overhead lights adjacent to each cell. Jay wasn't even looking at the numbers of each cell. His skin began to crawl with the uncertainty that lay ahead. He didn't belong here.

They had finally come to a stop. *"Alright"* officer haun said as he pointed to a cell. Written on the wall in white what looked like chalk read 56A. Officer Haun pulled some keys out from his belt and opened the cell gate. Jay took a deep breath in, then he exhaled slowly, still holding some breathe in. He walked in slowly. He felt his cuffs become unlocked. He stretched his arms, twisting back and forth slowly.

*"You know…"* Jay said, starting to speak before Haun cut him off.

*"Quiet Jay, what you did….. You know, that is just plain unacceptable, you are well aware that in this city you are guilty until proven innocent, this isn't Vegas"* officer Haun said while he was fumbling with some

keys. Jay looked around, he saw a sink, a bed, and a towel. He sat down on the floor with his legs crossed.

*"You know there is a bed right there"* Officer Haun said to Jay looking down on him. A rush came over Jay's body, for all his life he was only taught to say yes sir or no sir to an officer. But in this instance he thought about speaking his mind. He paused for a moment,

*"I never get comfortable in a place that I won't be staying at"*. Jay said, His heart was pumping fast and his arms were shaking, he wasn't sure if his remark would cause repercussions. Officer Haun looked at him, stared for a brief moment then looked away. Jay was nervously waiting for an angry response but it never came. Haun was silent. Officer Haun grabbed one bar and pushed the gate closed. ***CLANK*** the cell door closed.

For Jay, when he saw the cell door close he stumbled upon the realization that this was now a very real scenario, it wasn't a dream, nor was this something that he was watching on TV, this was the real deal. He was in it. He was alone, all by himself in that cold empty cell.

# CHAPTER 10

A00A55: *"Hey guys, did you hear about my cousin?"*

Sokki: *"I'm sorry, who is this?"*

Kye: *"Yeah, I'm sorry, I don't have this number saved in my phone."*

A00A55: *"I'm sorry, this is Zeke..."*

Sokki: *"Oh! Sorry! Hey! How are you? Wait, your cousin? Jay?? What's up?"*

Kye: *"???"*

\*\*\*

Sokki: *"Zeke??"*

A00A55: *"Sorry guys, I was talking to my pops."*

A00A55: *"So yesterday Aqui officers came by earlier."*

A00A55: *"They took Jay..."*

Sokki: *"Wait.... WHAT??! WHY???"*

Kye: *"Nooooooo."*

A00A55: *"My dad spoke to the officers, he said that they suspected that he was involved in the case of the missing documents because he was staring at them when he finished his speech in that video."*

Kye: *"You're kidding right? Just because he was looking at the documents? That is BEYOND ridiculous."*

Sokki: *"Only in Aqui I freakin swear..."*

A00A55: "Yeah… It's pretty wack, I'm just trying to relax before I flip out."

Sokki: "We're sorry…."

Kye: "Yeah…. We really are, hey if you need anything at all please call. We got you."

Sokki: "Definitely!"

A00A55: "Thanks guys, I have to run."

Sokki: "Alright, thanks for letting us know…"

 Zeke put his phone down on his bed and put his hands behind his head and laid back against the bed. He sat there exhausted and he closed his eyes.

***

Sokki: "This is crazy."

Kye: "Beyond."

Kye: "I wonder if there is a way we could get our hands on those security cameras…"

Sokki: "You're crazy, you would really…"

Kye: "The thing is I want to see if we are really on the cameras and if we are not we could use that to free Jay."

Sokki: "Pleeeease, for the sake of your own common sense please tell me that you are not thinking about going BACK to the school and breaking in again."

Kye: "How else are we supposed to look at the footage?"

Sokki: "…"

Sokki: "That's digging a deeper hole for us than we want right now. You do realize that we are very close to going to Jail right?"

Kye: "Don't talk like that…"

Kye: "Wait…. Aren't you supposed to be the positive one???"

Sokki: "I am……It's just I'm kinda nervous. I have never done anything like that before."

Kye: "You're very fine then lol."

Sokki: "This is not funny…"

Kye: "I'm laughing with you not against you."

Sokki: "I'm not laughing."

Sokki: "Hold on one second…"

***

Sokki: "Hey! Sorry, I have an idea!"

Kye: "As you always do… Thank goodness, I'm Listening."

Sokki: "Can you meet me at the park by Jay's house?"

Kye: "Oooooooh, I think I know what you're thinking."

Kye: "Yeah, I'll meet you by the park."

Sokki: "I'm walking there now so come on…. STAT."

Kye: "LOL k… I'll see you in a minute."

Sokki's personality mirrored a fast pace race car who never stopped racing around a track, she was quick. It was just her personality. She preferred to move at a faster rate to get things done faster. Often she was aiming to hurry Jay and Kye up. So in this case she wasn't really walking to the park yet, but she knew that is what she had to say if she wanted Kye to hurry. She knew that he didn't like to make anyone wait.

Matter of fact, Sokki was laying down on the same couch she had that haunting dream earlier. She was scrolling through all her missed notifications on her phone. When school was in, Sokki was in a trance, she often ignored messages, didn't answer calls due to her studying, she was relentless when it came to her education. If school was a sport, she'd be a star athlete. Or that's how Jay and Kye viewed it anyhow. It was very easy to relate anything to sports when tier is an edge or competition.

The humorous irony soared right over the head of three of the smartest students in Legion. The reason contributing to that idea was that they didn't realize it but school felt like a competition at times. You have your top students and eventually, if one was invested in their education then they probably have tried to compete. If ten students in the school all have a 4.0, someone has to edge out to that 4.1 to strive to top.

Sokki wanted to be that one, everyone believed that she was. But she was in the middle of a comeback, after her father passed, her grades truffled a little bit only delivered to the verity that she wasn't going to school for a short period of time. Sokki finally stood up, stretched and walked to her front door. When she walked out of the house it was dark outside already.

She locked the door and walked down the driveway and began walking right to start her path to the park. She walked past the houses in her neighborhood. She continued to stroll on getting closer to Jay's house.

When Sokki finally reached the park she didn't see anyone, not a single soul, however she did see a little animal that resembled a squirrel scurry passed the playground.

"*You look so creepy walking in the middle of the dark like that*" a voice said. Sokki jumped,

"*You freakin scared me!!*" She said looking at Kye walking into the playground area from the opposite direction in which she came from. Kye laughed.

"*I didn't even see you! Where did you come from?!*" Sokki asked.

"*That way*" Kye said as he gave her a hug from her side.

"*How's your mom?*" He asked

"*Good, working like crazy… and your mom?*" She asked.

"*Good! I finally told her that I am going to colleg*e" Kye said proudly

"*Really? That's awesome, I bet she was super happy*" Sokki said smiling.

"*Yeah, she cried,*" Kye said as he grabbed a monkey bar.

"*That's because she is proud… and you should be too,*" Sokki said.

"*Yeah, definitely,*" Kye said. There was a pause. But there were many of these between Sokki and Kye, while they were really close friends, both of them were really close to Jay. Naturally, Sokki and Kye argued quite a bit. It was a simple typical brother sister relationship.

Like all good friendships, they went through struggles, some fights far worse than others but nevertheless nothing ended. So the times when they actually had a decent conversation with no disagreements was nice.

Kye broke the silence *"Yeah, that's crazy what happened to Jay!"* He said,

*"Yes, I know. We have to figure this out"* Sokki said, staring directly at the ground.

*"Like I was sitting in my room and I really thought it was a joke. Jay is the last person that I thought this would happen to"*. He said,

*"I'm having a hard time with it to be completely honest"* Sokki said. She sat down on a platform of the playground that led up the slide. Kye sat down on the platform parallel to her.

*"Yeah, so what's your plan? What were you thinking?"* He asked her. She stared at him for a second.

*"What?"* Kye asked

*"Why am I always the one that has to come up with the plan? Sokki, Can you figure this out, Sokki, what do you think about this? Sokki, we need help with this…. Sometimes, I just don't know. I am tired of pretending like I do!! "*

*"I'm sorry, I thought you had a plan. That's why we came here, right?"* Kye said, sitting directly across from her staring at her as she was sitting down with her head in her hands. It went silent….

*"I'm sorry, you're right…. I'm sorry, I have a lot on my mind"* Sokki said.

*"It's ok, don't apologize,"* Kye said… another pause went by before Sokki finally lifted her head. She stared back at Kye, *"Do you remember Mr. Skies?"* She asked….

*"From"*…..

*"Mirage"* Sokki said.

"Your Moms friend…. Oh yeah! Are they still dating?"

"Yes, unfortunately" Sokki said, sighing at the same time.

"Yeah, well what about him?" Kye asked.

"Well….He is the executive principle for mirage, which of course is our sister school. A while back I was talking to my mom and she was telling me that she was going on a date one night.. She was upset because he cancelled because he said he had to go into work. Legion needed him to be part of a meeting where they would be discussing the new curriculum programs at the five schools" Sokki said.

"I'm sorry, I still don't understand where exactly this is going," Kye said confused.

"Well since he is the executive principle do you think he would have permission to view footage at Legion?" She asked him.

"I highly doubt it, yeah he is the principal but I mean he is at an entirely different school" Kye said.

"Well, it's worth a try… Should I text him?" Sokki asked?

"Yeah, you're right. You probably should:", Kye said.

"Ok, i'll text him now, doubt he's up but it's worth a try" Sokki said.

Sokki began to type away on her phone.

"How do you think you did on the finals?" Kye asked.

"Good" Sokki said,

"I'm sure you aced everything," Kye said. Sokki smiled at his comment while she was still looking down at her phone typing.

"And you?" Sokki asked.

"Me wha? Oh! I think I did alright. What's funny is that we know that you passed science, we know I passed math, and we know for sure that Jay passed English" Kye said.

"Kye….." Soki said, smirking.

"Hm," Kye said.

"I'm not trying to be cocky or rude but I pass everything," Sokki said.

"You know…. this is true"…

"There, I said. Hello! It's Sokki here. Sorry to bother you so late. But I have a little bit of an urgent question. It's regarding Jay Cruz, my friend from legion. It's a school related matter that I think only you can help us with. We need your expertise. Get back to me when you can. Thanks!" What do you think?" Sokki asked.

"It sounds good."

"Man, this isn't good. I bet they took him to Reno holdings" Kye said, putting his down for a moment.

"Which means what?" Sokki asked.

"Which means that they are going to hold him there until they take him to Reno. And once he is In Reno, well you know what that means."

"Do you really think that they will take him to Reno? For something that they are not completely sure that he did. Because after all they have no real evidence" Sokki asked. *BEEP! BEEP!*

"Well, you know this city just as well as I do, I know you haven't been here long but what you've seen from our fin department is not by accident, I Hate it because it's how this city is. I'm not tryna be negative but I don't think that they will take him to Reno just yet but once they think that he did it, he will be out of here in a heartbeat". Kye said

*"That's weird... "* Sokki said.

*"What?"* Kye said,

*"My mom just texted me".* Sokki said while looking at her phone with various faces of confusion.

*"Why is that weird? You and your mom text more than anyone I know"* Kye asked. Sokki gave him a look.

*"What? I'm just saying. You do?"*

"It's weird because she texted me "is everything ok?" I find that strange because I just texted Me. Skies" Sokki said. Her fingers were hovering over the keyboard on her screen trying to think about what to text back.

*"Maybe he let her know that you texted him?"* Kye said

"Yeah but why?" Sokki said. It doesn't make any sense. ***BEEP! BEEP!**** The same noise came from Sokki's phone again. Sokki stared at her phone intensely.

*"You have got to change your ringtone."* Kye said to Sokki.

"You were right, she texted me back she said I am with Seth right now….. You texted him?? I thought we had an agreement." Kye looked at her with a funny look on her face.

"What agreement?" he asked.

"So when he and my mom started dating she sat down and talked to me…. Because like, I mean my mom, she is very… hmmm how to say this… PROTECTIVE of me" Sokki said with a big sarcastic smile on her face.

"I see," Kye said.

"You know, all of my life she has made sure to try and protect me from getting hurt, and I get it but sometimes she doesn't realize that I can protect myself BUT anyhow that is a story for a different time. So when they met we had a talk... She was saying that it's new for her to be in a new relationship, and she wanted to kind of keep my distance from him. She wants to be sure about the relationship first, you know?" Sokki said.

"I get it, I'm sorry, that must be tough," Kye said.

"No, no it's ok I'm doing better than I thought I would be doing with it, it's weird but I'm doing ok with it" Sokki replied. ***BEEP, BEEP*!***

"Let me see... she just said... Where are you, I'm at the house……. At the park…. With…Kye" Sokki said as she was typing.

"She must have just got there because I literally just left the house," Sokki said.

"That's weird she normally never invites him over, especially not this late". "I'm on my way back, can kye come?" she replied back to her mom.

"Alright let's start heading to my house, can you come over for a little bit?" Sokki said, looking up away from her phone and towards Kye.

"What if she says no?" Kye asked with a smirk on his face.

"She won't," Sokki said.

"She really likes you and Jay" Sokki said.

"That's good," Kye said. ***BEEP, BEEP*!*** Sokki's phone vibrated once more.

"Yep, she said yes" Sokki said as she began to walk back towards the direction of her house.

"Man, that is crazy!!" Kye said.

"*What is?*" Sokki asked.

"*The whole thing is, Jay... that's crazy. What if they don't let him out? Then we lose our best friend for a very long time?*" Kye asked.

"*Sokki, we can't let that happen... c'mon. We have got this, we have been through worse*" Sokki said.

"*Well I mean... Mmm kinda, I guess..... Yeah you're right*" Kye said.

As he was walking alongside Sokki he kicked a rock down the street towards the direction that they were walking. When they reached the house, Sokki walked up to her front door, got her keys out and began to unlock the front door. Kye began to back up in front of the door. Sokki noticed and looked back at him,

"*Whaaaat?*" Sokki said with a bizarre look on her face.

"*Wait! Are your dogs out??*" Kye asked, now backing away from the door even further.

"*Really? No, they are not, there in the backyard*" Sokki said with an annoyed look on her face.

"*Are you sure?*" Kye asked again as he approached the door. Sokki was quiet. Sokki open the door to her house,

"*Hey so,*" Mrs. Siaso said as she walked in.

"*Hey Mom,*" she replied back. Sokki looked down at Kye's feet.

"*Take off your shoes*" Sokki whispered to Kye,

"*Remember, it's disrespectful to keep them on*" Sokki said once more.

"*Sorry!*" Kye whispered back. When Sokki and Kye were fully in the house Mrs. Siaso cleared her throat very loudly and intentionally. For a quick moment, sokki was lost, wondering why her mom made such an obvious remark. Her mom's style of sarcasm was inimitable. Sokki knew this to be true… "*Hi Mr. Skies, this is…*"

"*Kye Nacksworth…. Ahh yes I know very well who this young man is. I keep track of all of the top students at our sister school*" Mr. Skies said, cutting her off.

"*Yeah, that's true. I should have guessed that you would have already known. Silly me*" Sokki said as she looked at Kye from the corner of her eye. Kye knew this look. He tried not to smile.

"*It's an honor Mr. Nacksworth,*" Mr. Skies said.

"*Thanks,*" Kye replied

"*Geesh*" Mrs. Sioso said, shaking her head,

"*I'm surprised you kids aren't asleep. I remember when I was your age…*" she looked at Mr. Skies.

"*Remember? When school got out we just wanted to relax and we would sleep in too!*"

"*Well… we can't, or I DOUBT we will be able to actually sleep well right now with what's going on*" Sokki blurted out.

"What do you mean? What's going on?" Her mom asked. Sokki looked down at the ground in response to her mother's question. There was quite a pause in the downstairs living room.

"*The fins took Jay…*" Kye said. He preferred to say that versus stating that Jay was in jail.

"*What do you mean they took him?*" Sokki's mother asked.

"*The case you were talking about earlier, they think that he might have something to do with it*" Sokki said.

*"What case?"* Sokki's mother asked.

*"The school, the robbery?"* Sokki replied.

*"OHHHHH, that case, wait, why do they think that he would be involved?!"* Ms. Sioso asked.

*"Ok, so we had this speech in English that was due this morning for the final….*

*"That's weird, we were JUST talking about that. Mr. Skies showed me a video"* Ms. Sioso said, cutting Kye off. Kye nodded then continued…

*"Yep, so we have been working on it for about half of the school year. Or at least that's when it was assigned. So, Jay and I have been kind of practicing back and forth which is good because I really needed help because I do not like public speaking. It's a five minute speech where we could either be persuasive, educative or motivational. So I'm assuming you know which one Jay chose. So the speech was finally today, Jay goes up and gives his speech. You have already seen the video, at the END of the video, he looked down as the camera was getting ready to stop which is weird because I didn't see anyone taking a video. And I remember looking around the room too. Did you… Oh wait, you weren't there. I keep forgetting you don't have that class with us"* Kye said, looking at Sokki.

*"Nope,"* Sokki said.

*"So anyhow, he gives the speech then the video shows him looking down. The Fins came down to his house and told him that they were going to take him because at the end of the video, he looked down at the same envelope that happened to be stolen that same night"* Kye said

*"Geesh, I know that this city is a little dramatic when it comes to law enforcement but that is a little excessive"* Mrs. Sioso said.

"A little? No, that is very excessive, especially for someone who is even 25 yet". Sokki said. She stood there, crossing her arms, staring rigorously at the ground.

"Why 25? That was a random number" Kye said.

"That is the age in Aqui where you are legally considered an adult, you should know this Mr. Law"

There was an odd silence in the room. "*Soooooooo we were wondering, umm… we have a question. My friend Samantha from Legion told me that the school is not able to get the camera system working correctly, do you know why that is Mr. Skies?*" Sokki asked, now looking up at the 6 foot adult that stood there in her mom's dining room with a concerned look on his face.

"It's not? That's strange, I thought it was working fine" Mr. Blank said. In this curious instance, an alarm went off in Sokki's head.

"So you didn't know anything about it?" Sokki asked him.

"No," Mr. Blank said straightforwardly.

"Should I?" He asked.

"Yeah, weren't you…?"

"Well, we need your help!" Sokki said, cutting Kye off from his sentence.

"Yeah because you…."

"We need your help," Sokki said, cutting Kye off again and this time giving him a look out of the corner of her eye.

"My help…. I'd be happy to help, what exactly is it that you need my help with?" Mr. Skies asked.

"This should be good," Ms. Sioso said as she took a sip of her red wine from her glass. She saw Kye deliver her a look out of the corner of her eye.

"Oh no hun it's just wine. I'm not a drinker, it's just wine" Mrs. Sioso said. Mr. Skies smiled then spoke,

"Yeah... she prefers the sangria red wine from italy! ..... You know, as the story goes the local citizens, in their quest for refreshment, and alcoholic enjoyment, created fruit punches from the red wines they were now enjoying. They called these drinks sangria. For they were the color of blood, and packed a punch because they were often fortified with a 'punch' of brandy. And also..."

"Uh honey that's ok, we don't want to bore the poor children with wine stories" Ms. Sioso said smiling nervously.

"That's ok, Ms. Sioso, I was actually enjoying it," Kye said with a smirk on his face.

"And plus, it is a special occasion... hunny you want to tell them or should I?" Ms. Sioso said in progressive excitement. In the instance, Sokki's heart began to get heavy like it was carrying a 2 ton wait, her palms began to get sweaty. She became extremely nervous.

"We are celebrating our 6-month anniversary!!" Mrs. Sioso said. Sokki let out a big sigh of relief.

"Anyhow, what did you say you kids need?" Mrs. Sioso said.

"Umm, oh yes! We were wondering if you could take a trip to the school with us tonight" Sokki asked, raising her shoulders in discomfort anticipating a negative response.

"Fooooor what?!" her mom asked, standing there with her hand on her hip.

"You see Mrs. Sioso, we know that Jay is innocent, if we can get those cameras to work down at the school. We can PROVE it" Kye said. Ms. Sioso's disposition started changing a little.

"Prove it??" she said.

"Yes," Kye said.

"Well this is something that would have to happen during the day when the faculty is at the school right" Mrs. Sioso said.

"Schools out mom" Sokki said

"And we would have to do it tonight because we leave for camp Monday morning" Kye said,

"I'm sorry kids but absolutely not, this is entirely too risky" Sokki's mom stated, glaring at her daughter.

"You know kids... I know what it's like to want to prove someone's innocence and not have the resources to do it. Before I started working in the school district, I worked for the DA's office. But those are stories for another time.... And Sokki your mom's right, but with that being said... I'M in, I'll drive" Mr. Skies said.

"Wait, I am not going over there," Ms. Sioso said, standing there with one hand on her hip and the other hand on the table. Mr. Skies looked back at her,

"Honey, it's for the kids," he said.

"Ughhh! Fine, i guess I'M coming TOO!" Sokki's mom said as she turned towards the dining table and put her glass down.

"I will see you later, i'm so sorry, i'll be back I promise!" she whispered to the half glass of wine that was sitting there.

"Mom, c'mon!" Sokki said as she was leaving the front door.

# SPLASH

"*Ok, hold your horses young lady, I'm comin'*" her mom said back to her as she stumbled towards the front door rummaging in her purse for car keys.

"*Hey... babe? Do you know where my car keys are?*" Mrs. Sioso asked Mr. Skies.

"*It's ok, I'll drive, we can take my car,*" he said as they both approached the front door. There was some reason all the houses in the neighborhood all had connecting walkways from the front door to the kitchen/dining area.

"*I still need my keys to lock the door,*" she said.

"*I'll lock it!*" Sokki yelled from outside the door. As the adults left the house Sokki was standing there next to the door waiting to lock it. As she locked the door she yelled "*shotgun*" and ran to the door of Mr. Skies Stallion that was parked in front of the house of Ms. Sioso.

"*Yeah right in your dreams*" Mrs. Sioso said, giving her daughter a strange look.

"*Ahh well, I tried,*" Sokki said. The car's headlight Flashed as Mr. Skies pressed the unlock button on his remote. The lights on the front and back of the car flashed once. Then he walked around to the driver side of the car to get in.

"*I wish for once a man would open my door for me*" Ms. Sioso said under her breath as she sighed and jumped in the car.

"*Alright, everyone buckle up!*" Mr. Skies said once everyone was in the vehicle, the car roared as he turned the key in the ignition.

"*This thing just LOOKS fast. I have never been inside one*" Kye said as he looked around the interior of the car's design.

"*Oh well sweetie then you haven't lived!*" Mrs. Sioso said.

"*What year is this?*" Kye asked,

"*2024*" Mr. Skies said as he began to put the car in drive, he made a u-turn and drove down the street.

"*When Mr. Ford announced that he would be making a variation of this car. I actually was pretty fond of the car. I liked the idea*" Skies said.

"*I see why, this is awesome!*" Kye said.

"*You know Kye wants to build his own car one day?*" Sokki's mom said as she looked over at Mr. Skies with her head against the headrest.

"*Yeah? Well, I will have to show some things on my 2015 that I have. It's old and I don't use it. And of course once you are ready to start on that dream of yours, I can get you connected with some well known people in that line of work*" Mr. Skies said.

"*Really? Thank you, I appreciate that!!*" Kye said with excitement. Mr. Skies smirked as he looked up in the rear view mirror.

"*You know, let me be the first to say that I am not a fan that Vegas has to seperate us when it comes to everything, but I will take the cars. I am sorry but the mustang is ugly*" Sokki said.

"*You know, one of my old buddies has one. I remember when he came I went to visit him in Vegas. The two cars just don't feel the same*" Mrs. Sioso said. Sokki looked at Mr. Skies face to see if he had any reaction. To her surprise, there was none, she thought maybe in his mind there was but he did a very good job of not showing it.

The jealousy bug had spared Mr. Skies

It was completely normal for two conversations to be conducted at once in the same car. Mr. Skies turned the radio on and turned the volume down really low. Ms. Sioso began to ask something to Mr. Skies, no one heard what she asked except for Mr. Skies. The two continued their conversation in the front of the car while Sokki and Kye were in the back.

As the trip went on the group became more and more relaxed. Kye looked over at Sokki,

"Are you sure about this?" Kye asked. There was a long paused look on Sokki's face as she stared out of her window with her hand on her chin.

"Yes, I am sure." Sokki said. No further explanation came from Sokki, that was it. Those were the only words of insurance that Kye had to go by.

Kye wanted more but he chose not to pressure the question. The car continued on towards the end of a street that only had an option to go left. Mr. Skies turned around the corner where there was a long road leading to the district of schools.

"Are you guys ready?" he said. He eased the car up a little bit, he released his foot off the pedal to where the car would only drive in neutral. There was a long road where you could see nothing but some buildings off in the distance. Jay had always called this the lonely road.

"Watch this Kye" he said as he slammed his foot on the pedal. The car began to roar with a sound of intensity. As the car began to get faster and faster Kye and Sokki put their hands up in the air.

"Wooooooooooo" Ms. Sioso screamed

Mr. Skies chuckled. Kye leaded his chin over the back edge of Mr. Skies' seat and saw that the speedometer was already at 120 miles per hour.

"That's pretty fast," Kye said to Sokki. Before they knew it, they were at the entrance of the school district. As they passed through, they noticed that a light was shining through a window. As the stallion creeped closer, they realized that the light that shone was from their school.

"That's weird, there is a light on," Kye said.

"Yeah, every school has a cleaning crew that comes by at night. Maybe one of them left it on." Mr. Skies said in a calm voice.

"Woah……" Kye said in a really low voice looking over at Sokki in the back seat.

Mr. Skies continued to drive really slowly towards the school as the loud roar of his car returned to its normal hum.

"What is it?" Sokki asked Kye.

"The cleaning crew," Kye Whispered,

"We didn't even think about that," Kye said leaning closer to Sokki.

"What?? I don't get it" Sokki said.

Kye leaned over to whisper in Sokki's ear. "The person we saw walking towards us didn't say anything. The night we were here"

"Shoot, I didn't even think about that" Sokki said with a shocked look on her face.

They felt the car turning. "I am going to park in the back," Mr. Skies said.

Once Mr. Skies arrived behind the school he parked the car in a parking spot with a blue label that read the word **"FACULTY"** When they stepped outside of the car the sky had a similar gloomy feeling to it the night Jay and his two accomplices were there. The group began to walk on the trail that led all the way around the front of the school. The two adults were walking ahead in the front of the school and Kye and Sokki were trailing in the back. Soon, they were approaching the final path to the front double doors of the main entry hallway. Kye looked over at Sokki.

"*I don't know about this, are you sure this is a good idea?*" Kye asked Sokki.

"*Yes*" she replied back.

"*But what if I, you and Jay are on that tape? I don't think you get it. Jay is in JAIL.*"

Sokki paused, she walked in front of Kye and stopped him in his tracks. She put her hand on his chest,

"*Stop, ok, everything is going to be fine, trust me ok*". Sokki said.

"*I know but....*" "*Stop it!*" Sokki whispered loudly,

"*Have I ever let you down!? HAVE I? You have known me for two years, have I ever said something and it wasn't true? Have I lied to you? When have I ever let you down Kye? You or Jay?? Please tell me when, when have I ever let you down. It's been two years*" she said, holding up two fingers.

"*Two years, it's time for you to start trusting me! We have to have faith. And oftentimes that comes at the most inconvenient times and it comes without vision*" she came closer to Kye's face glaring at him directly in the eye.

"*Are you in or are you out??*"

"*...Im..In*" Kye said after a short pause.

"*Alright, now let's go,*" Sokki said.

"*You two alright?*" Mrs. Sioso asked them standing a few feet from them holding the main entrance door open. Sokki and Kye walked inside the door and Ms. Sioso closed it behind them. Standing there were the four, Mr. Skies, sokki, Kye and Mrs. Sioso. The group stared down the long dark hallway.

"This hallway is so dark, I can't even see my hand, this is unsafe. This is crazy, can't believe you dragged me into this." Mrs. Sioso said.

"Alright, everyone phones out" Mr. Skis said.

"I need your light"

The group continued down the long dark hallway, periodically peering their light through classroom windows. This was more an act of paranoia since Legion was clearly vacant at the time. A familiar feeling approached Sokki and Kye.

"Do you have the key with you, babe?" Ms. Sokki asked.

"Yeah, hey ummm if you guys want to wait out here you can. Here, let me…"

Mr. Skies moved a few chairs around and placed them all in a row.

"Alright, I'll be back. It may be awhile, I just don't want you all to be standing the whole time"

Mr. Skies cruised through the back offices working his way to the security cameras.

"How long do you think it's going to be?" Kye asked,

"As long as it takes, he is a professional," Sokki said.

"Yeah, he's good at fixing stuff, very talented. One time I watched him fix a radiator leak on a car in like two minutes" Mrs. Sioso said.

"Really? Wow……. How'd you two meet?" asked Kye

# SPLASH

Mrs. Sioso smiled and stared at her hands in her lap twiddling her thumbs. Sokki looked at her mom in disbelief.

"It was two years ago in the summer of 22'. It was the peak season for my business, I had a client at the school he started out at. I was bringing my client a delivery. Well back then, anything the schools accepted always had to transfer throughout the front desk, it wasn't like it was now where you can just walk in and walk wherever you want to in the school. You had to have clearance which I didn't have at the time. When I walked into the school, I saw him at the desk. He was wearing blue denim jeans and a button up. I remember like it was yesterday"

Kye glanced at Sokki, hoping she wouldn't notice.

"At first all I saw was a tall man with wavy brown hair and a jawline so straight that you could cut a tomato with it". Kye chuckled

"When I walked up to him I said "Hello, I'm here to deliver this to a client. What's the name? He asked. Then I told him Mr. Johnson. He said he will make sure that he got the package. THEN he asked me for my name, then he introduced himself... the rest is history after that" She finished with a telling grin on her face.

"I wonder if that package ever got delivered," Kye said laughing.

"Ha, yeah it did, I checked!" Mrs. Sioso said.

"I bet you did," Kye said.

"You know, that's the first time I have ever told that story" She smirked

"Really? I feel special" He said

The three sat there at the front desk, quiet, staring down the adjacent hallway of the main entrance. The sound of the double doors opening rippled through the hallway with an uncomfortable echo.

"What was that?!" whispered Sokki.

Ms. Sioso stood up from her seat and peaked around the corner, she saw a flashlight waving back and forth coming closer to the front desk.

"Should we hide??"

"No, no".

Anticipation sat still and pretty waiting for the attention of the three. It left once they realized who it was around the corner.

"Ma'am, what are you doing here?" The security guard said.

"I'm so sorry officer, I hope we didn't startle you. Mr. Skies is working a little late tonight, we are family." Mrs. Sioso said to the guard.

The guard walked toward the door of the offices, it was propped fully open.

"Skies, you in there?" He asked. The officer turned and looked back at Ms. Sioso who was standing at the entrance of the front desk near the little barn door used in most places.

"SKIES!" he said again in a louder tone.

"Yeah, I'm right here, I'm coming……….. How's it going, officer?" Mr. Skies asked as he appeared from the dark offices

"You workin' late tonight?"

"Yes sir, the school district is having a major issue with their security cameras. Ya know, tonight is family night, after we finished up some festivities I figured we would all take a drive down to the school. Late night for the kids but schools out ya know?"

# SPLASH

"Ok, fine. I get it, do your thing. When I saw some lights up down here I thought ah shoot! Cause we've been getting some calls about kids running around the school and when I saw the lights on i thought ah shoot, time to bust some kids"

"All good here, but we will definitely let you know if we hear or see anything," Mr. Skies said.

"Thanks, you know, I really appreciate that" The officer said.

The officer looked at his phone "ah shoot, it's the inner city again, so bad over there. Every single night" the officer said as he was walking to the side exit next to them.

"Alright well, you all have a good night. Just make sure you lock the place up when you leave"

"You too, have a good night," the group said.

"Hey guys, you might wanna come check this out" Mr. Skies said. As he looked to make sure the security guard had already left. Walking back to the office doors. The three of them all came from behind the desk and followed Mr. Skies into the office.

"I've never been inside here," said Kye.

"I have, once," said Sokki. They walked down the hallway following Mr. Skies into the back of the office. They walked through a door labeled security. Inside there was one big monitor and 3 other little monitors on each side. Mr. Skies, clicked the mouse. A video on the big monitor began to play. It was a video of the hallway right outside the front doors.

Kye looked down at his arm, he began to get goose bumps. Mr. Skies forwarded the video. "*Right here, watch,*" he said. A man with a hoodie comes walking across the screen, across the front desk and turns the hallway heading to the lower grade classrooms near the band room. Just as he heads off of the camera's view he pulls something out of his pocket. Mr. Skies rewound the video

"*He pulled something out of his pocket, did you see?*"

"Yeah, what was that?" Ms. Sioso said in curiosity. Sokki looked at the ground and took a deep breath. Kye tapped her on the shoulder.

When she looked up at him he mouthed the words are you ok? She shook her head up and down.

"*But that's it, that's the only thing on this entire video*". Said Mr. Skies.

"*Um guys… we should go,*" Sokki said.

"*We will be fine, I have to get clearance to be here*" Mr. Skies said.

"*No, hunny I think she is saying that she doesn't feel right*"

"*We need to go like now,*" Sokki said again, looking behind her shoulder.

"*Ok, let me eject this tape*". Said Mr. Skies

Sokki began to walk towards the door, she peered out of the window looking to see if she could see anybody. "*Anybody there?*" she asked her mom.

"*No but we need to leave*". She said, Mr. Skies and Kye all headed for the door, to escape the office area. Sokki opened the door and walked out into the hallway. "Ghost is clear out here!" she whispered loudly.

"*Let's go, we will go this way. I parked out here,*" They ran out the exit door next to them, Mr. Skies locked the door behind him and started walking towards his car. They all got inside the stallion and the car drove away from the school.

"Sokki, hunny, you ok?" Her mom asked.

"Yeah, I'm ok. I just didn't feel right, like something felt off" she said.

"Like we were doing the wrong thing?" Mr. Skies asked with his voice really, really low.

"Well, no... I felt as if almost like we were uh, being watched."

"That's strange, like who?" Ms. Sioso asked

"I don't know, I just don't like that feeling" She said

Ms. Sioso looked over to Mr. Skies and reached to tap him on the elbow.

"She has been having some sort of crazy apprehension mixed with psychic abilities, I have no idea. Don't ask. These kids and their phases, who really knows" Ms. Sioso whispered.

"Well, at least the tape is working now" Her mom said out loud.

"True!" Kye said from the back of the car.

"So I will have that on your principal's desk first thing in the morning," Mr. Skies said.

"Thank you, we really appreciate that and i'm sure Jay will too" Kye Said

"... Then at the stop sign you can make a left," Kye said. After the car stopped, it turned left on a street titled arrow point.

"Then it is going to be the last house on the left". Kye said

"That's so creepy, it's because of that movie why I don't watch scary movies anymore, never again" Sokki said leaning against the door on her side of the car.

The car came to a park. *"Alright, Ma'am, thank you Mr. Skies,"* Kye said as he opened his car door.

*"Hold on, I'll come around and give you a hug,"* said Sokki. She closed her door then walked around the car and extended her arms out above his shoulders and gave him a hug. He wrapped his arms around her.

*"I really hope this works,"* Kye whispered in her ear.

*"It will, remember what i said, alright"*

*"Alright, have a good night"* He said

*"Ok, I will, you too. Text me in the morning please,"* She said.

*"What time is it?"* Kye asked, he pulled out his phone and read 2:09AM.

*"I might not not wake up for a little bit"* he said.

*"Alright, have a good night,"* said Sokki. She opened the car door, got in and the car drove away from Kye's house. Sokki layed down across the entire back seat.

*"Young lady, sit up and put your seatbelt on"* Ms. Sioso said,

*"Mom, we are around the corner from the house"*

*"That does not matter, most accidents happen within a mile from the home. "*

Sokki obeyed her mom's request. The car drove around the corner down the street into the other development of homes in which Sokki lived. The car made a stop at the gated entrance to the neighborhood.

*"DRIVER OR PASSENGER?"* a woman's robotic voice said coming from the screen.

"*Passenger,*" said Mr. Skies. A long stiff skinny pole with a laser extended from underneath the screen and traveled into the car and stopped right in front of Ms. Sioso's face. She opened her eyes wide. The laser began to scan her eye "***ACCESS GRANTED***" said the robotic voice. The laser retracted and the gate opened up wide. Mr. Skies drove into the neighborhood and parked on the first house on the right into the neighborhood.

"*Oh wow, she's asleep. That was a two minute car ride. I don't know how she falls asleep so fast*" Ms. Sioso said. As she glanced back and forth between the back of the car and Mr. Skies.

"*I was like that when I was younger,*" Mr. Skies said.

"*Sok' hun... Wake up. We're here*" Ms. Sioso said. She began shaking her leg.

"*We're here*" Sokki awoke but was quiet. She opened the door.

"*Good night Mr. Skies*" She mumbled.

"*Good night,*" he said. She stumbled up her pathway into the house. When she touched her front door, her hand began to vibrate intensely, it began turning blue.

"*Ouch!*" She said,

"*Sokki hun you ok?*" Her Mother yelled from the car. Sokki said nothing, walked inside and closed the door. When inside she began examining her hand while preparing to crash on the house.

Mr. Skies and Ms. Sioso sat in the car thinking for a brief moment. Ms. Sioso put her purse on her lap.

"*Thank you for what you did for the kids tonight, you know Jay is a really good kid*" she said.

"No problem, it was the least I can do. I'll make sure to get the tape to ReLouf in the morning. It'll get it to his desk…. I was thinking, since I have to be at a conference in the morning… Do you think I could come in and get some rest?"

"Seth, are you asking to spend the night? You know the rules, no spending the night or moving in until we are married". Mrs. Sioso said.

"You're right…. I'm sorry I asked"

"Have a good night and thank you again, seriously". She said, Ms. Sioso closed the door of the car and went inside her home. Mr. Skies drove off into the blue moonlight of Los Aqui, and there wasn't a single car insight.

# CHAPTER 11

The cold air blew through Los Aqui, quiet throughout the night with an eerie silence, just chilled air blowing cooler from any other city at this point in the year. Students of Los Aqui anticipated air like this, warm all day outside and eventually cooling down in the evening. After all, the city was preparing to embark on the warmest part of the year. Where the scorching summer would have its own party of dehydration, frustrations, mood swings, and dead car batteries.

Located in the front of the Legion school was a leaf that was swept up like a feather, this feather began to float as if it were on an imaginary boat on the ocean cruising its sails to a better land. However, the land that this leaf was sailing towards had not presented any light that perceived to be better than any of the surrounding lands around it.

As the leaf floats towards the land, the blade of the leaf begins to get lighter and lighter as a sense of warmth is felt among its veins and the leaf begins to descend. Along with the night time to introduce the morning. The Leaf gently floated down in front of two large gates with the words **"JAIL OF LOS AQUI"**.

*"There is a folk tale that is told in Los Aqui, the story of the two brothers. You ever heard of it?"* The elderly man asked

*"No"* Jay replied

*"As it goes, the story is about two brothers and their father. The Sky and the two stars. The two stars were constantly in disagreement with each other, always arguing. Every day the brothers would go around, chasing and playing with different stars then return to their place in the sky. One morning, the older star asked the Sky "Father, how do we become something else?" asked the younger star. "Well, why would you want to become something else?" asked the sky.*

"You are great as a star," the Sky replied to his son.

"But I want to be something else. Something bigger. Something unstoppable."

"Ok, you must go to the North Star and find out how to change. Ask him, he will tell you. But be careful what you ask for because once you change, you can not change back" The father warned the son.

"Ok, father, I will," said the son.

The elderly man continued, "Well, the next morning the younger brother went to his father and said. "Father, how do we become something else?" "Well why would you want to become something else?" Asked the Sky.

"You are great as a star," the Sky said to his son.

"But I want to be something else. Something brighter. Something that can help people."

"Ok, you must go to the North Star and find how to change. Ask him, he will tell you. But be careful what you ask for because once you change, you can not change back" The father warned the son.

"Ok father, I will." The star said.

"So the next morning, the younger star flew a long distance up in the sky to visit the North Star. When he got there he saw his older brother with the North Star."

"I want to learn how to be something big and unstoppable and I wish to never see my younger brother again" The older star said.

"I want to learn how to be something bright and helpful. I wish to never see my older brother again" the younger star said.

The North Star told them how to become wanted. Both of the stars went back among the sky and did what the North Star said.

"It's not working," the brothers said.

As the night came along. The stars went to sleep, frustrated. The next morning the stars woke up. I'm really big and hot!" the older star said.

"I am really bright and cold" the younger star said

The sky saw this and said, "My older star, you are big and give the people heat I shall call you Sun. My younger star, you are bright and give the people a light in the darkness, I shall call you Moon. You two are dividing the light. Half of the people have light and half the people have darkness. You two must separate."

"But father, what shall I do when I get tired?" The older star asked.

"Your brother will come and shine his moonlight." The father said,

"So I can never see my brother again?" asked the younger star sadly.

"Remember, I told you to be careful what you wish for because you can never change back. No, you two will never see each other again. At the same time it's balanced, you can not have one without the other. The moon flew away. When his brother began to get tired and lose his sunlight the moon would fly back to the people and shed his moonlight and leaves would fly in with the moon to present itself and it repeated forever and ever. "

"Why leafs? What do they have to do with anything?" Jay asked

"Leafs represent return and freedom, when you see a leaf fly and land it often means that something or someone is free. Or, they have returned" the elderly man replied

*"So what does the story mean?"* asked Jay. The elderly man peered through the bars of the cell across from him.

*"That is for you to figure out, young man. You will figure out what the story means when you are supposed to"* The elderly man said. As the two heard footsteps coming down the hall the elderly man wrapped his cover around his body covering his mouth and scooted back in the corner of his cell, leaving Jay to his own thoughts.

*"34, 35, ah..... 45..... 51..... 56"* a voice said coming down the halls.

*"Jay Millie Cruz, get up, you're going home"* An officer said standing in front of Jay's cell. Jay stood up slowly as the gate of the cell slid across. As Jay stepped out of his cell and looked into the cell of the elderly man.

*"Who are you?"* said Jay. The elderly man took a quick glance at Jay.

*"You already know that kid,"* he said.

*"Lets go"* The officer said as he escorted Jay to the entrance and exit of the holding facility.

*"Kid, you're innocent, the camera system footage came in. We reviewed the footage, we now have zero evidence to hold you here, you are free to go..... "* Officer Haun said. Jay didn't speak, he was completely still.

*"You don't have any parents to come pick you up, friends?"* He opened the door and walked outside. When he stepped outside, he realized it was already morning time. He looked to his left, saw the big entrance gates and walked up the gate. The officer at the gate approached him.

*"A squad car will be waiting for you outside to take you to your house since you do not have a ride. Do you have all of your belongings?"* The officer asked. Jay nodded.

The officer opened up the gate, once the gate opened all Jay saw was the blank emptiness of the Los Aqui dessert welcoming him. As Jay approached the squad car, he noticed a leaf on the ground next to him. He got in the car and the vehicle drove away.

"*Where to?*" The driver asked.

"*1859 Sea swallow Avenue*" Jay said. He found it strange that the driver didn't input the address into the system the entire ride, he thought maybe this was just an experienced driver that had been in that area before. After all, Los Aqui is a small city. It is made up of a lot of empty spaces with sections of buildings so Jay thought maybe this driver is the designated driver for the jail system and he has been driving for them for years.

Somehow, throughout the entire 2 hour trip back home, Jay managed to stay awake. He listened to music on his phone, he didn't bother trying to message his dad, or his friends. He knew there was no service through the desert he was traveling in. On the contrary, he wanted his return to be a surprise for his dad, cousin and friends. With the passive controversy stirring around him.

Jay managed to clear his head, oddly enough, this was the clearest his mind had been in a long time. He was just able to relax, with no distractions.

When Jay arrived at home, he thanked the driver. "*Yeah, no problem*" The driver said, then drove off. When Jay got inside the house, his little cousin threw down the remote, rushed up to him and gave him a hug.

"*Uncle! Jay's back.*" Mr. Cruz rushed out of his room and down his stairs and embraced his son.

"*Glad to have you back son!*" He said,

Mr. Cruz began cooking right away. He started making Jay's favorite; Meatloaf. *"You're probably tired, do you want to go lay down before you eat?"* Mr. Cruz asked.

*"Umm, not sure, I think I actually may go swimming. I haven't been in the pool in awhile. I want to get un-rusty before I go to Camp Choice."* He said,

*"Does that mean you're going to do lifeguarding?"* His father asked.

*"I think so"* Jay said with a smile.

*"Ok well, how are you getting there?"* Mr. Cruz asked.

*"I think I will walk, I could use the fresh air. It's not that far"* he said.

*"Alright, we'll be safe, and watch your back".*

Jay went upstairs, grabbed stuff and headed out the door.

*"Text me when you make it there, i'll give you a call when dinner is ready,"* Jay's dad told him as he was walking out the door.

*"Alright, I will,"* Jay said. He walked around the corner and towards the railroad tracks that were behind his neighborhood. He exited the gate and to the gym circle, when he got to the gym he entered and scanned his ID and proceeded to the locker rooms and changed into his swimming trunks that were black, red and silver. The colors resembled some basketball team in a professional basketball team in Portland. As he was walking to the entry to the pool, he stopped once he crossed a mirror that was plastered next to the lockers. He walked backwards and stared in the mirror. He shook his head with a slight smirk, when he reached the pool, it was empty. He placed his duffle bag on a hook hanging next to the pool's edge. He sat at the edge of the pool with his feet dangling in the water.

His skin raced with goosebumps. He sat there, staring into the water, the blue clear water. A variety of thoughts bursting into his head appeared in and out like a fast paced game of whack-a-mole but instead of trying to grab these thoughts to catch them, he couldn't because everytime he did his mind got distracted and another one popped up. All of this, after school is out. School for most children in los Aqui was their main occupation.

Oftentimes certain parents wouldn't even allow their children to commit to extra curricular activities because it was **"extra"** and too impeding on their academic performance. He continued to stare at the water, his main thought was about his departure from his one day stay-cation. He truly just wanted to know how he got away with breaking and entering. I'm a criminal, I wonder if this will make it on the first 48.

This was a question that he never fully asked. A few minutes went by, then he made the conscious decision to freeze himself. As if the air in the city wasn't cool enough, his mission now was to go full sub zero. When his feet emerged, they froze into icicles. There is no season for warmth with the water of Aqui, only the cold. Anyone who lives in the city of Los Aqui knows that the water in Aqui is always cold. No matter what.

When Jay eased into the water his skin began to freeze along with his viens which had now colored themselves blue. Halfway frozen, his body desired more. He hesitated, put his goggles on and slowly dropped under water. He stayed down there for a couple of seconds then he popped his head back up. He walked to the edge of the pool, moved his shoulders around and tilted his head from side to side like some famous legendary swimmer. He looked up at the clock on the wall, submerged himself, pushed off the wall. He swam from end to end, struggling in an unconventional, unorthodox way. But he didn't care. He just needed the water. After a few long laps, he would stop and breathe and think. Then he would go again and again. Soon after, his workout was now over and it was time for him to head back. Returning, Jay didn't think about much at all. Just about his trip, what will it be like? Will I get nervous? He thought.

When he arrived at his house the smell of the fresh aroma of different seasonings rushed him. The Cruz's were finally able to sit down and eat as a family again, just the three. Zeke, Jay and Mr. Cruz.

"So how was it in there?" Zeke asked as they were all sitting at the table eating dinner.

"Horrible" Jay sighed.

"It was….. I had to try really hard to not think about the fact that I was in there, good thing I wont be marked CRI" he said as he looked down at his plate and stared at the fork of mashed potatoes he was about to stuff in his mouth, he focused on the little green onions that appeared to be throughout the potatoes.

"But you know, it will still be on your record, these sorts of things don't just go away" Mr. Cruz said.

"Well… is there any way to remove it?" Jay said.

"No, that is why I just said it does not go away, how'd you get involved in this mess anyway?" Mr. Cruz asked with a dull expression on his face.

"You know as much as I do, someone, I don't know who, recorded me outta nowhere and I just so happened to be looking at an envelope that was stolen that I have absolutely nothing to do with. So like I said, you know as much as I do". Jay said

"You better watch your tone, you hear me?! We aren't the ones getting caught up in some mess, you don't see me in and out of jail do you? You don't see Zeke your cousin in jail". Mr. Cruz said. Staring hard at Jay directly in his eye staring across the table.

"But how is this my fault? I did absolutely nothing wrong!" I didn't put myself in jail did I?? The fin at the station said that they have no evidence to hold me there so how can you tell me again, how is this my *fault?"* Jay said. His right hand was shaking, he had stopped eating his food. Mr. Cruz put his fork down, and raised his head.

*"Who are you talk'n to? Huh? I sure know it's not me.... Like I said, you better change your little attitude, or you can forget about your trip".* Mr. Cruz said, glaring at Jay. The dinner table became tense and everyone was quiet. Zeke glanced at Jay multiple times. After a while, the kitchen became still.

*"Alright, I'm going to bed, goodnight. Jay, what time are you leaving in the morning? What time does the bus leave?"* Mr. Cruz asked, standing by the stairs.

*"T*he *bus leaves at three, Sokki and Kye were going to meet me here around one forty five, and we were going to leave from here, I'm going to pack right now, then maybe try and get some rest".* Jay said very monotone.

*"Ok, i'll be up at that time"* said Mr. Cruz then we walked upstairs.

Jay and his cousin stared at each other again with no words. Zeke shrugged his shoulders but didn't speak one word about the topic.

*"Hey, if I'm not up, can you wake me up?"* Zeke asked his older cousin.

*"Yeah."* Jay said. Jay put his dishes in the sink, and walked towards the stairs.

*"Alright, I'll see you later"* He said to his cousin. To Jay's surprise, Zeke didn't jump on the telly like expected. Instead, he followed Jay up the staircase and he started to open his bedroom door, he stopped when he reached the door. He was in front of his door, Jay was in front of his.

*"Glad you back man,"* Zeke said.

*"Thanks, I'm glad to be back,"* Jay said.

Zeke went to his room along with the elephant that refused to be discussed. Oftentimes it came from his Father's wild and random mood swings. However, there were bigger elephants in the house that Jay knew nothing about.

He went into his room and closed his door. One day had felt like an eternity and an eternity felt like a lifetime for Jay being in a place he didn't want to be. When Jay opened his bedroom door, the sense of familiar comfort met him at his door. His room was just the way he had left it. He gave a smirk then walked out of his room, down the hall and grabbed a big red bag out of the closet and went back into his room and closed his door.

When he realized and remembered that he was going to go for the majority of the summer he went back into the hallway and grabbed another black bag from the closet. He went through his drawers, looking for outfits. Of course he packed his swimming attire first, that was the easiest because he only had one pair of swimming trucks. And his clear goggles that his father had bought him. *"Let's see,"* He said to himself. *"How many weeks, one, two, three, four, five, six, seven, eight, nine, ten"*.

He packed his bag accordingly counting on being able to wash his clothes because he didn't have nine weeks of outfits. When he did the math that came out to 48 outfits. Jay's closet space and dresser wasn't that of a large size. He soon became distracted and began scanning through his phone. To his surprise, he had many text messages, most of them from Sokki and Kye, wondering if he was back home.

*"Are you ok?"*

*"I don't know if you're getting this but I really miss you and I hope you return home safe, we need you on this trip"*

*"Let us know when you make it"*

Jay called Sokki and the phone began ringing

"*...HELLO??!*" Sokki said over the phone.

"*HEY!!*" He responded once Sokki answered.

"*OH MY GOODNESS YOU'RE BACK*!!" She screeched

"*Yes, finally, hold on, let me call Kye,*" Jay said as he took the phone away from his ear and started looking through his phone contacts. He called Kye and the phone began to ring again.

"*Hello!?*" Kye answered.

"*Hey man!*"

"*He's back!*" Sokki said.

"*Woah, what's up!!? Glad your back man!*" Kye yelled

"*So you're going on the trip right?*" Sokki asked.

"*Yes, I barely made it back in time*" Jay said

"*Yeah, that was a close one,*" Kye said.

"*Yeah it was, you ok? What happened there?*" Sokki asked.

"*I'll have to tell you guys on the bus,*" Jay said.

"*Yeah, well we have something to tell you as well*".

"*Ok, hey are you two already packed?*" Jay asked

"*Yeah,*" Kye said.

"*You know I'm already packed,*" Sokki said.

"*I'm packing right now…. Hey are you two still going to come meet me at my house at one forty five?*"

"*Yes!*" Sokki said.

"*Ok, well you two should probably get to sleep, I'm going to finish packing,*" Jay said.

"*…..Ok, hey wait, are you just getting out like right now?*" Sokki asked.

"*No, they released me earlier, it was a LOOOONG drive home then I went swimming when I got home, but for some odd reason, I am not tired*". Jay said.

"*Probably because you have a lot on your mind,*" Sokki said.

"*Yeah I have a feeling that I am not going to get much sleep,*" Jay said.

"*You almost finished packing?*" Kye asked.

"*Yeah, almost*".

"*Hey we will call you when we are on our way, I guess…. I will go to Kye's house then we will walk over to your house from there*" Sokki said.

"*Sounds good, alright, get some sleep, we have a big day tomorrow! I'm so excited! Worst case scenario I can sleep on the bus*" Jay Said.

"*K, goodnight guys. See you in a few hours haha*" Kye said laughing.

"*Goodnight y'all,*" Sokki said.

"*Alright guys*" Jay said.

Jay continued sorting through clothes to put in his packing bag. When he finished he quickly shoved the extra clothes in his drawer and soon made friends with his bed and his phone. As the friendship quickly faded, he charged his phone only to return to the bed. His all time best friends, Sokki and Kye had no chance against the beloved mattress and two pillows, his comfort level was much higher with his bed. Laying there was much better than lying in jail. Throughout this wacky blank stare expression Jay had on his face his mental attention focused towards the future, life after this night.

***

"OK, for our first race we have the 10,000 freeflow swim. For this race we have: JY, GR, ST, and KN."

*All racers swimming please step up! All swimmers take your mark, Get set...* ***BLEEP!*** All the swimmers bent down, crouched and leaned forward. **"GO!!"** The swimmers jumped off of the long starting block. He dove into the pool, as he approached the surface of the water the pool seemed to open up, the water began to get darker, and darker. The water began to split to the side.

*"AHHHHHHHHHHHHHHHHHHH!"* Kye awoke with his head ringing and his room was swinging in circles. He was experiencing an extremely sharp migraine along with seeing double. He rose up scratching his head, looking around his room realizing he was dreaming. He put his head back down and closed his eyes.

***

Half asleep, Jay heard his phone vibrating in the corner of his room *"uhh, Hello?"* Jay answered.

*"Wake up! Haha"* Sokki chuckled

*"Oh shoot! What time is it?"* Jay shockingly. He jumped up out of his bed and looked at his alarm clock, the time on the clock read 1:35AM. In his mind he knew it wasn't past 1:45am because Sokki was involved.

*"Ok, I'm getting dressed right now... are you two on your way over?"* Jay asked.

"Yeah, I'm on my way to Kye's house then we will head over to your house after that, I suppose we should have re-thought this walking thing through a little bit because of our bags" Sokki said painting out of breath.

"Oh yeah huh, is it a struggle?" Jay asked.

"Yes, but I think we can manage, how many bags are you bringing?" Sokki asked

"Three," Jay said.

"Geesh woman!" Sokki laughed

"I know right, well it's because I don't have a really huge bag, I wish I did" Jay said.

"Ahh, I see. And my apparel is smaller than yours". Sokki said. Jay chuckled.

"I'll umm, see you when you get here." Jay said, trying to avoid Sokki's comment.

The awkward avoidance of the comment made Sokki laugh *"Yes Jay, I'll call you".* She said,

"Ok, i'll see you in a little bit," Jay said.

"Ok, see you," Sokki said back. She smiled then hung up the phone.

Jay quickly got dressed then dragged his bag downstairs and out into the middle of the living room floor then traveled back up his stairs ***KNOCK, KNOCK, KNOCK*** Jay knocked on Zek's door.

*"I'm up... I'll umm ... be up in a second"* Mumbled Zeke.

Jay continued rummaging through his bag looking and double checking for items to make sure he wasn't forgetting anything. He wasn't sure what not to bring so when this happened he just decided to pack his room, his whole room and nothing but the room. If he could fit his dresser in his bag, he would. While Jay was scanning his drawer for items, he heard what sounded like a bedroom door opening. When he walked out, he expected to see Kye but as he looked down the hall, he realized it was his father.

"Goodmorning," his father said.

"Goodmorning" Jay said,

"Are you all packed?" His father asked

"Yeah, I am, just trying to make sure I have everything". Jay said. Mr. Cruz walked back into his room and came out with a beanie,

"Here, take this, I know it might get a little cold out there. Do you have some jackets with you?" Mr. Cruz asked.

"Yes, I have a couple" Jay said as he was examining the beanie, he read the words: "Organization 56. Thanks Dad this is pretty cool, it's from your old company huh?" Jay asked.

"Yeah, I figured it might be a little cold out there, so I figured that might help." He said. Jay put the beanie in his bag. Zeke came strolling out of his room stretching with a look of exhaustion on his face.

"I'm going to head down stairs, I think Kye and Sokki should be here in a little bit." Jay said, the three of them walked down the stairs into the living room.

"Alright well, let's say a prayer". Mr. Cruz said. The three of them huddled in a circle.

"Heavenly Father, we come to you this morning to say thank you, thank you for allowing Jay to go on this trip, we pray that he has a safe and eventful summer. We ask that you open up his mind to blessings to discover his true passion and the career path that you have laid out for him. We thank you for keeping this family safe and we ask that you bring Jay home safely. In Jesus' name we pray. AMEN."

"*AMEN*" Zeke and Jay said.

"*Are you excited?*" Mr. Cruz said, patting Jay on his back.

"*Yeah, I'm READY!!*" Jay said with excitement.

"*Yeah man, you got this*" Zeke said.

***

***KNOCK, KNOCK, KNOCK, KNOCK.*** 

"*I think that is them,*" Mr. Cruz said. He opened up the door and Sokki and Kye were standing right there on the porch. Jay grabbed his bags and headed out the door, as he did, his dad gave him a hug, along with his cousin. The three stood there, on the porch.

"*Alright you all have a good time*" His father said. Jay's dad closed the door. The sky was as dark as the night before, when the door closed Sokki and Kye rushed him and hugged him. It was silent, not a word was said. Just the language of embrace as the three friends enjoyed this moment together.

"*Alright, let's walk,*" Sokki said. The three began walking towards the exit of the Jays Neighborhood. When they reached the exit, Jay slowed down his stroll he had been on.

"*Do you guys want to take the long road or do you want to curve around?*"

"*That long road when you're not in a vehicle is kinda creepy...*"

"*Yeah and we are right here so we might as well just curve around*" The group continued to walk along the curve to get to the school.

When they arrived at the entrance to the school, they saw everyone in a line. *"Are we late?"* Jay said

*"We can't be late, it's only 2:15,"* Sokki said.

*"It only took us longer because we have all of this luggage"* Kye said to Mrs. Till who was looking at him with a goofy curious face.

*"Mr. Nacksworth, did I mention anything about your arrival time?"* Mrs. Till asked Kye.

*"No ma'am"* Kye said, not even bothering by her tone.

*"I was just curious as to why all of you are walking with tons of bags, Literally."* Mrs. Till said standing in front of the three students looking down on them shrugging her shoulders.

*"That's her favorite word,"* Jay said under her breath.

*"And Cruz, I'm surprised to see you here, I thought you would be locked in chains somewhere... but that is neither here nor there, or anywhere for that matter, back to my question, why are you three walking? Three of the smartest students in school, I would just think that you have a little more common sense than that"* Ms. Till said, taking a step back.

*"Well, did you know that common sense isn't always common?"* Kye and Jay chuckled

*"Oh, and we decided to walk because studies show that people tend to sleep 30% more on car, bus and train rides if they have some form of exercise before they travel, I hope our bus driver didn't walk here or go and play some late night zumba on his telly. Oh, and Jay had no reason to be in there in the first place, that's why he was in there less than 48 hours"* sokki said as she continued smiling

Mrs. Till had a blank expression on her face. Jay could tell that she was trying to contemplate responding in durastic fashion. *"Very well then, get in line"* Mrs. Till said.

*"Umm remind me NEVER to wake you up at 1AM GEESH!"* Kye said, looking at Sokki as they were traveling to the back of the line.

*"I know, what was that? Where did that come from"* Jay said laughing.

*"She clearly has no chill! Not even a little bit, for crying out loud it's 1 in the morning and she is coming at us all sideways"* Sokki said, throwing her bag around her shoulder. They finally made it to the back of the line.

*"ALRIGHT LISTEN UP! We do not particularly care where or who you sit next to. What we do care about is if our students are not obeying the rules of this bus, Vegas was kind enough to let us borrow the bus so you need to respect it. We shouldn't have to discuss the rules of the bus to you, no getting up, no loud yelling, music fighting etcetera. You all are juniors, you should all know the rules by now. If you don't then well maybe you don't need to be on this trip after all. It's simple common sense, but maybe common sense isn't always that common"* Sokki looked at Mrs. Till with glare and the three friends laughed.

*"Do I make myself clear?"* Mr. Worthy said.

*""YES!""* the class said.

*"ALRIGHT, everyone on the bus"* Noise began to chatter among the line again as the line moved closer and closer to the front. When Sokki walked up the steps to get to the inside of the bus she walked down the bus finding a seat right in the middle of the bus.

*"We got lucky, it's a three seater"* She said looking back at Kye and Jay. The three placed their bags in the top compartment above the seats that were used for storage. Sokki got closer to the window, next

to Kye, then Jay. Once everyone was seated a muscular gentleman with sweats and hoodie came on the bus.

"Alright listen up!" as he waited for the bus to become quiet the students stared at the gentleman with confusion.

"My name is Coach Hines, I will be your life skills trainer. Legion has brought me on this trip to help you choose a career field, you all are juniors now, this trip is supposed to be fun, but you will also be learning a lot. My expectations during this summer will be very high, higher than you ever saw this summer. I suggest you all get some rest, we start when we arrive. We will be making a few stops along the way. Other than that, you all enjoy this trip and be ready when you get off the bus. WHO ARE WE?!!" He yelled.

*"WE ARE LEGION, WE DON'T QUIT, WE NOT SETTLE!"* The students yelled back in unison

"Alright driver, let's go!" Hines said.

# CHAPTER 12

The bus was still no more, the 18 wheels began to roll away with the certainty of meeting its destiny.

The roads in Aqui differed from any city imaginable. For example, if one wanted to travel to the stores district where you can find grocery and clothing stores. One specific road would get them there. These roads all branched out from what is called the main town. Main town was where you would enter Los Aqui, from another city. Main town was located right in the middle of Aqui, some say it's the heart and soul of the "Los".

*"It's crazy how little of the city we see sometimes, like the other day when I was getting transported out, I had seen stuff that I have never seen before, like for example our main town is HUGE, I have been down there before but the other day, we drove straight through the entire thing. It was as if I was in another city, seriously"* Jay said, looking at Kye and Sokki.

*"When I was younger I used to always have to go down there during the summer since my mother works down there, we used to always get pas from the store down there, Mmm, so good!"* Sokki said while she licked her lips.

*"Oh, I know where you're talking about - That one little place on the corner there huh?"* Kye said.

*"Yeah,"* she said.

*"I've never been there, is it good?"* Jay asked.

*"Oh yes, It's sly"* Sokki said, the bus continued along the bumpy road back and forth occasionally swaying the students on the bus left and right.

*"That's weird..."* Jay said.

*"What is?"* Kye said

*"We went this same way when they captured me"*.

*"Captured... What do you mean capu--Ahh, ok? Gotcha. Well Well this is this way that leads towards the other side of town-- By the way, what did they say when they released you?"* Sokki asked Jay to lean forward. She glanced at Kye.

*"They didn't say anything at all. All they said was that they didn't have anything to hold me there anymore. Per evidence"* Jay said, holding up two fingers making quotation fingers.

*"Did they mention anything about camera footage?"*

*"SHHHHH! I know that it's very loud here but I don't think that we should broadcast this through to the entire 11th grade"* Kye said.

*"Camera... What do you mean camera foot--?"*

*"Are we slowing down?"* Sokki asked cutting Jay off, she peered out of the window. The bus began to steer towards the rocks. Getting maneuvered by the largely oddly shaped rocks laying next to the Los Aui dessert.

*"Yeah we slowed all the way down,"* Jay said, glancing back at Sokki.

*"He is probably slowing the bus all the way down to tell us down to tell us all to be quiet"* Kye said. The bus finally came to a rough hault kicking up dirt that covered the long white bus in the aqui dirt that seemed to only live in the desert of the city. Instructor Hines stood up and walked out of the bus. The students peered out of the bus, the air reflected from the sun peeking over the mountains that Los Aqui was surrounded by.

Hines walked around the bus a couple of times, then back the other way around. He stood there for a second. He began using his phone, he put it to his ear for a brief moment, he quickly took the phone away from his ear and gave a tiny smirk. He walked back on the bus and the students silenced their chatter on their own. He started whispering with the teachers in the front of the bus.

"What is he doing?" Jay asked.

"Talking to Mr.Sidious-- I think they are all talking" He said.

"ALRIGHT, EVERYONE... Off the bus. LET'S GO!" Hines yelled. The students began to slowly get up, and leave off the bus.

"LET'S GO!!" He said again. After all of the students left the bus, Instructor Hines walked off the bus and walked in front of the group of the students and cleared his throat.

"How are you guys doing? You guys awake?" He asked, the students began to chuckle,

"Alright so here is the deal. Our bus miraculously has four flat tires and my phone, or any phone for that matter does not have any service so this means that we have to change them ourselves. There are four spare tires in the back of the bus and a bus full of capable students. So go ahead and put two and two together. I am going to seperate you into four groups and we will change our tires. SO here is..."

"But it's like zero degrees out here," a student from the group.

"Are you only going to be successful when it's warm outside?" Mr. Hines said, looking at the student.

"Plus, the sun is out and shining, you will be fine. GUYS, being successful is not about being in your comfort zone, it's about being comfortable in the uncomfortable times... If you really push yourself in life, you will see what i mean... ANYHOW, like I was saying, we are going to go ahead and get you into groups, ... SO here is... 1,2,3,4,5...6,7,8,9,10. You are over here, at this back tire. This 10 on this side over her. Jay, Samantha, Mathew, Kye, Sokki, Donald, Yenny, Yammy, Keith and Kelly.

*You're over here. And the last ten, you are on the last tire over on the other. Don't move yet!"* The students became quiet again.

As he smirked, he continued. *"You are some of the smartest students in the entire school. That is why I am not going to walk you through everything, because in life, you don't always get shown how to do everything. No one is going to hold your hand through life. You need some critical thinking skills to aid you when mommy and daddy aren't there to save you. So the tools are in the back of the bus along the tires. You have your groups, you also only have 10 minutes, if your group can meet the time requirement I will have a little something for you."*

You have your first objective, change your assigned tire and get us back on the road. My self and the other teachers will be walking around to help you if you need. This is a test... We want to see where everyone is. We will have a life skills section during camp that will look a little bit like this. This is just a sneak peak. *"Alright, READY… SET……..GO!!"* He said, the four groups became noisy as they ran to the back of the bus to get their materials bumping and running into each other. Laughs and questions were heard among the noisy chatter. The teachers stood together at a slight distance from the bus. The teachers all had on shades.

*"You know, this was really a good idea."* Mr. Sidious said.

*"Yes, this is brilliant,"* Mrs. Till said, looking at Mr. Hines with a smile. Mr. Hines' face froze for a brief moment, he looked at Mrs. Till…

*"Thank you, I really appreciate input from such a brilliant scholar such as yourself".* Mrs. Till smiled, her face turned a little red. *"I really wanted to give them a really good experience, I know they all made a lot of sacrifices to come on this trip"* Instructor Hines said.

*"Yeah, he pulled this one out of the old playbook,* Mr. Worthy said.

Back at the bus, the students were all hustling to complete their task.

"Is that the right one?" Sokki asked.

"Ummm, I think so, let me see!" Jay said as he placed the big T shaped wrench on the big bolt, he turned it around again.

"Ummmm, I don't ... hold on.... Got it."

"Do you have the jack?" Sokki asked

"Wait, this one or the other one?" Yammy asked back.

"Whichever one is bigger; we are going to need it.... Hold on, don't untighten all of them yet," said Sokki.

"Shoot, I think they are almost done," Kye said, glancing back and forth at the team working on the tire next to them and looking at the back of the bus to see if Yammy was coming around the corner with the jack. Noise, circled the teens as they all rubbed their hands together and clinched the bodies towards an attempt to stay warm.

"Remember that time that one of the kids let one of our good tires roll down the road, and then it almost hit that car?" Mr. Worthy asked, smiling enormously.

"Waaaaaait what?!" Ms. Noble asked while she leaned her forward and gave Mr. Worthy a crazy look.

"Yeah! I think it was the year before you came, we had this kid umm Fable!"

"Wait, fable from..." Ms. Noble paused.

"No, he doesn't go here anymore, he went here a few years ago. So… this was the last time HR used this scenario… Fable was here, and it was funny hehe. I remember when..." Ms. Noble interrupted again

"We brought HR along?" she asked Mr. Worthy.

"Oh boy" Ms. Till injected.

"Get your life together! No! That's his nickname!" Mr. Worthy said pointing to Hines,

"Ooohh, I feel very unintelligent at the moment," Ms. Noble said.

Mr. Worthy chuckled. "Any waaaaay, so they were changing the tire, like same thing, we had groups. So he brought around a tire, he was struggling with it then he finally got it out from behind the bus. When he put it down he started rolling it, well him and his buddy thought it was a good idea to roll it back and forth to each other like a bunch of idiots. So they were rolling it back and forth then Fable rolled it to his buddy when his buddy wasn't looking and he missed the tire so the tire went rolling down the freestreet and it almost hit a car"

Mrs. Noble interrupted Mr. Worthy "Luckily we had this one couple that stopped after they had seen what was going on, they pulled over ahead of the rolling tire, because you know, it's so big, and trust me it was rolling fast! Haha, so the couple drove ahead of the tire, check this, they got outta their car and they both got into... because at first I thought that they were going to try and let the tire hit the back of their car but i guess you couldn't really do that cause then the tire would like roll up on their car and like dent it somehow. So yeah, they got into the front of their car on the back side, got into some type of warrior stance. HAHA! You know, like warrior 1 from yoga?" Mrs. Noble chuckled.

"They stood there and braced themselves and we were running down there like GET out of the way! But they didn't when the tire hit them they just stuck their arms out and leaned into it. The tire bounced a little but that was it, anyhow, I'll let you finish sorry!"

Mr. Worthy looked at Ms. Till with an amused face.

"That was it, the two boys got sent back from the trip back to the school. What is interesting is that we never saw or heard from them again. I guess they didn't want to come back"

Mr. Worthy nudged the three teachers in an attempt to step away from Mr. Hines with a gesture by nodding his head away from where the group was standing. To put away suspicions, they didn't go far. Only a few feet away from Mr. Hines.

*"Hey, So are we sure that we have the right kids?"* Worthy asked the three barely whispering.

*"Well, I'm ninety percent sure, I can feel it."* Mr. Sidious responded.

*"Ok, i'm not opposed to that but you do realize that if we made this trip in confidence from your ninety percent sure, if you are off, wrong in any way then we lose lives"*

*"I understand, and if I may ask. How do we know for sure the Silvers are still lurking around up there?"* Ms.Till interjected.

*"Shhh! Do not say that name out loud, you know our rule, and we don't know for sure that they are not. That's the issue,"* whispered Mr. Worthy loudly.

*"Hey, I think we should talk once we get back to camp, I don't want to take any risk"* Mrs. Noble whispered. There was a silent agreement between the teachers, they returned to where Mr. Hines was standing.

*"DONE!"* a group yelled from the bus

The teacher began to walk forward. *"KIDDING"* the group yelled back, laughter began to spread amongst the group. Mr. Hines stepped forward *"Alright, that little joke will cost you two minutes. You will see what I mean soon".* The groups continued to work rigorously along the bus and the wind began to blow even faster. About 45 minutes had gone by

*"Hey, Jay double check that,"* Sokki said. She walked up to the group of teachers.

*"We are done, Mr. Hines,"* she said.

"Are you? This may be the fastest time that I have ever seen someone get this done. Good job Ms. Sioso. Please tell your team, they can stand over there".

"Are you going to check it?" Sokki asked.

"Should I have to? Are you second guessing your team's work?" Mr. Hines asked

"No sir," Sokki said.

"You know, there was certainty in that response so I'm going to trust that, let's just hope that your team feels the same. Again, you're positive it's correct, yes?" Mr. Hines asked.

"Yes, sir, I am" Sokki replied.

"Then? ....Sokki, you have to learn to trust yourself before you can trust anyone else" Mr. Hines said.

"Yes sir," Sokki replied.

Shortly after, all of the groups were finished and everyone had a look of tiresome on their face.

Mr. Hines stepped forward. "As I was just telling Sokki here, I am not going to double check your work. You must hold yourself accountable for your own actions more importantly this ends our first lesson for the trip, in life you must trust yourself before anything else. That is the difference between the ones who are great versus the ones that are good. Understood?"

"Yes" some students in the class mumbled.

"Yes, what?!" Mr. Hines responded.

"Yes sir!" The class said in unison with more voices present...

"Alright, everyone on the bus, let's go! WAIT! Before I forget, you all owe me 2 minutes. Ok, here is what I want. Everyone against the bus!"

The students stood against the bus.

"Everyone put your back against the bus…. Ok, now, slide down the bus and go into a squat position."

The students had a look of confusion on their face… Nevertheless they did what was instructed by them.

"Arms out! …..Trust me, this is nothing, wait until we start adding time. Now! Here it is, in this position, you will not make a single sound, no grunting, clearing your throat, yelling, comments, questions… NOTHING unless I ask you to repeat something or unless I ask you a question. Understood?"

We will call this minute of silence or MOS.

"Yes sir!" The class responded.

"Thank you! SO…. We will call this minute of silence or MOS".

For this first set, we will have complete silence, however… During camp you will learn the code of ethics and decree of conduct.

"Ok! 2 minutes starts now!"

"But we already have been here for two minutes," the student blurted out.

Mr. Hines turned around to face his body towards the direction of the voice. "Thank you James, class, everyone say thank you James."

"THANK YOU JAMES!!!" the class yelled as they all looked at James in confusion unaware of what was happening

# SPLASH

"Congratulations, you have just earned your team another 15 seconds. Next time it will be more".

The class responded with complaints.

"Quiet please or I will add more time". The class became quiet.

Still there in the cold air the students squatted against the bus, Jay thought about the last school year and what this camp was going to be like, what things were like back home... his thoughts seemed to shift from racing around in a circle to jumping across from one mystical platform to the next.

Before he knew it the short two minutes which may have seemed like an eternity was now over, the class was now entering the bus in a less prepped mood. Once the bus finally rolled away, the relaxing air seemed to take over the bus in its entirety. Carrying through the dusty road that led out of town. The sky was the furthest shade from clear, foggy with a light breeze. Looking back in the mirror, the students realized that they would not see their beloved city until the end of summer.

The Los Aqui police station for the first time in two weeks and had been quite empty, with the exception of the drunk drivers from the weekend and a 34 year old man who was accused of setting his fish on fire, these sorts of crimes were taken to a lesser extent than expected. Ironically, it was suspicion of a crime that had Jay staring at those empty cell bars on the cold ground of Los Aqui a couple days prior.

Although oftentimes random, fin officers operated by a code of structure that trumped military operations. They embodied the real LAPD. The people of Los Aqui believed in their minds that the PD secretly had a sign behind closed doors that said something to the aspect of *"Everyone Is Guilty, We Focus on the Crime, Not the Individual"*.

**\*KNOCK, KNOCK, KNOCK\***

"Ah yes, Davidson please come in"

As the officer walked in he was blinded by the light that shone through the window from the sun beaming on the desk. A tall white thin man with a white button up shirt and blue slacks came walking in the spacious office with a cup of coffee in one hand and a stack of papers inside of a tan folder in the other.

"Chief, I have some interesting leads on the legion case," Davidson said.

"Finally, about time. What do we got?" The chief asked

"Well, I've been studying that tape that the principal turned into us.. ReLouf? I found something interesting. At the end of the tape, the suspect we found walking down the hall shines his flashlight and starts leaning his head forward and he appears to be squinting at something" Davidson said.

"That's odd! Are we missing something?" Captain Sting asked.

"Well that's just it, there's more...... I kept replaying the clip over and over again to see we were missing anything and at exactly 3 minutes and 2 seconds the video seems to skip. Check this out" Officer Davidson said as he pulled a stand with a laptop over to Capt.Stings desk.

"One sec... Uhh dah, ok! Here we go!" he said. There was silence in the room as the two were watching the content playing on the laptop. **\*CLICK\***

"Ok, right here... You see this piece of paper on the wall from the decorations? It moves in a certain direction then all of a sudden it shoots up and skips back to another pattern." Davidson said.

"That is a little strange... if someone tampered with the tape then that means we have an entirely different case and suspect on our hands. Get it over to our tech specialist and videographer in Ramport. In the meantime I'll see what I can find on Jay Cruz... Something's off" Sting said with his chin in his hand tapping a pen in his other hand on the desk.

*"Yes sir, I'm on it,"* Davidson said.

# CHAPTER 13

Los Aqui was known for its beauty but what lies outside of the city told a different tale, Las Vegas was the closest destination to matching its marvelous scenery but even Vegas couldn't be quite fair. Furthermore, what Vegas had to offer its people was far more appealing to the ones venturing to a new home.

The question of what the Vegas city has is more of a myth to the ones who didn't have the privilege to partake in its living conditions. The fascinating thing about myths is that they are often true or at least partially. Camp choice seemed to be a myth when Jay was a freshman in highschool until he realized that he will actually be partaking in the venture some day.

This is what Jay has been dreaming about all year, as he lay his head on the chair of the bus he aimed to stay awake for as long as he could to grasp some of the relaxation he aimed to partake in by himself, no conversation, no phone, just him similar to when he was in Los Aqui jail, although not a long period of time ago, Jay didn't seem to really tamper with the thought so much. At this particular moment in his life, he was focused on the now, not really looking back on the present to an extent.

Jay soon drifted away in a deep sleep along with the rest of the students on the bus. While asleep, the instructors began to whisper amongst each other with gaps of silence.

"The bumpy hills through the desert seemed to grow exponentially bigger as Jay and the rest of the gang were still fast asleep. 12 hours had gone by and the majority of the students were asleep.

***

"*Huh... where are we?*" Kye mumbled,

"Uhhhhhhh, I don't know go back to sleep Kye" Sokki said,

"No, Sokki, wake up. The bus stopped and I don't know where we are" Kye said scratching his head

"Kye, shut up, seriously... just go to..."

"SOKKI!" Kye whispered loudly

"WHAAAAAAAT!!??" Sokki said as she rose up and looked back at Kye with her eyebrows raised as her red hair whipped around her face. Staring at Kye intensely,

"What? What? What is so important that you had to wake me up from sleeping, I was REALLY enjoying my nap You PEOPLE! You must really have a thing for not letting me sleep. You, my mother. I wish for just one day just ONE day that I can get some sleep without anyone bugging me, Sokki, Sokki, sokki, Sokki. You know how hard it is to get complete oh and i mean a complete 100 percent grade percentage on everything the ENTIRE school year? Do you? To do that it requires one thing and one thing ONLY, Does anyone, I mean anyone on this bus know what that is? Huh???"

The students stared at her rubbing their eyes... "Of course not because I am the only one on this freaking bus who has got that score. If this were our senior year I would be the valedictorian... One night really, that's all I ask, not a week not two, and this IS.A.TRIP and I STILL can't get any..."

"Mrs. Sioso?" Hines said, looking at Sokki.

"Yeeeessss Mr. Hiney hines? Do yoooou have the answer to the question or would like to wake me up too?"

"Do wild animals wake you up?" Mr. Hines asked.

"I'm sorry, what?" Sokki asked with a confused tone.

Mr. Hines clicked a button and all of the lights in the bus turned off. When they did, Sokki noticed that there was a figure outside of the bus that was moving closer to the bus as she moved a student out of the way and she began to try to make the strange figure out.

"Is that a …… Oh my goodness, that's… A.. WOLF!!" A student screamed at the top of her lungs. Outside of the bus there was black wolf with a long torso and a rough tail. The tip of the tail was red and the wolf's eyes were red also. As one opened its mouth Sokki noticed a large fang about the size of a ruler.

More screams and panic from the bus started to brew as the realization of the upcoming situation dawned upon the students. The figure that Sokki saw seemed to have somehow multiplied. The figures began to ram the bus causing the bus to stray back and forth, snowling sounds were heard from one of the windows that was cracked open in the back of the bus.

Sokki turned back around to Mr. Hines, "*Whyyyy are you just standing there, you don't seem terrified at all!*" She said looking up at Mr. Hines.

Mr. Hines ignored her comment then cleared his voice so he could speak louder *"So, these are war wolves, and there is only one thing that will make them go away. Lesson number two, figure out how to survive, in other words, figure out how to make the wolves go away"* Mr. Hines said addressing the class swaying his hand gestures back and forth.

*"Lesson two, survive using teamwork and critical thinking to surpass your challenge, similar to our previous exercise. I will not hold your hand through this lesson. I will say this though, these wolves aren't from Los Aqui, so therefore they do not think like Aqui animals would typically think. Well, you have your mission now to complete your task"* Mr. Hines said as he sipped some coffee from his mug.

The class began to murmur chatter and the chaos became greater with students arguing and moving back and forth. Some began banging against the bus window as if they were fish in a fish tank. One student, James, started to snarl at the window then got frightened, jumped back and knocked another student over on their back once he realized how big the wolves' teeth were. Kye and Sokki stood still in the middle of the bus, telepathically thinking to themselves, Kye began to wonder what Sokki was thinking not about how to stop the wolves, but rather what she thought about this entire scenario, but Kye didn't bother asking as he calculated that would more likely than not anger Sokki, and plus he knew that there was no time for his ill timed joking.

*"I'm terribly sorry, I know this isn't the time for this but I have just one question. We are in the middle of the dessert.. Where on earth did you get coffee from??"* Kye asked, looking at Mr. Hines in confusion.

Mr. Hines stood there with a blank face, staring at Kye for a couple of seconds. *"Irrelevant Nacksworth,"* Mr. Hines said. Kye and Sokki began to whisper amongst each other,

*"Solve your next task and then talk to me about coffee, and why are you whispering, we are ALL on this bus, aren't we?"* Mr. Hines said, staring at the two.

*"Guys! Alright, I think I got It! Quick, everyone take out your flashlights from your bag"* Yammy said as she was coming down the aisle of the bus. Sokki grabbed both her and Kye's flashlight. The students began rummaging through their bags in search of a flashlight

*"I can't find mine!"* a student said.

*"C'mon guys hurry! Ok, ok, ok everyone pick a window I believe they are sensitive to light because if you notice it's dark out here! And where were these wolves this morning when we left? Huh?"* Yammy said, aiming to gain the classes agreement. Sokki turned around and looked at Mr. Hines, she noticed that he had a slight smirk on his face.

*"That can't be it"* Sokki whispered to Kye,

*"Really? Why not? It sounds reasonable to me"* Kye replied back

"Of course it does, but there is no way that he would have all 60 of us figure something out that simple... And plus look at his face, he doesn't look like we figured it out. Oh aaaand, when we left this morning, we weren't in the middle of nowhere" Sokki said, reverting her eyes back to Yammy as if she was listening to her the entire time.

"Ok, everyone pick a window, we are all going to shine our lights at the same time" She said. The students all went to a seperate window of the bus, all eager for anything to work at this point.

"Alright, ready... One.... two.... Three!!! Turn on your flashlight!" She yelled. The wolves did not seem to care as they continued clawing and scratching at the wheels of the bus. ***CRACK!!***

"Ahh!" "What was that!??" Someone yelled.

"Oh my goodness, one of them cracked the glass! Pleeeease get us out of here!" Yammy yelled in a frightened high pitched tone.

"They are clawing at the tires!" another student said looking out of the window.

"Well, you put them on, let's just hope you did a good job," Mr. Hine said, mumbling under his breath.

"Sokki, come here... Hurry!" Kye said. Sokki tripped over her bag as she leaned next to Kye.

"Hey what was that thing that Ms. Heller used to do to get us to be quiet? Member? I forget... Was it if you can hear me say yes?" Kye said, scratching his head.

"If you can hear me... Clap your hands once, if you can..." Sokki said

"Yes!" Kye said as he cut her off from finishing her sentence.

Kye moved his way to the front of the bus through the noisy panicked students...

"IF YOU CAN HEAR ME CLAP ONCE!" Kye yelled from the front. The class simultaneously clapped together and there was still some chatter,

"IF YOU CAN HEAR ME CLAP TWICE" Kye said a second time. The class then clapped twice. A couple whispers were still heard among the group.

"IF YOU CAN HEAR ME CLAP THREE TIMES" The class responded and clapped three times.

"GRRRRRRRR!" The sounds from the wolves seemed to quiet down. Kye moved his hand in a downward motion to tell the class to sit down in their seats with his other hand over his mouth making a shushing gesture with his finger. *"I am very shocked that it still works"* Mrs.Till said as she whispered to Mr. Hines. He said nothing as he was staring at Kye with a slightly proud look in his eye. The bus was now quiet in its entirety, there was not a single noise made across the bus. From the foggy desert a large figure began to shape out the thick Aqui Dessert fog, as it emerged, whispers jumped throughout the bus. *"What is that?" "Oh my goodness"*

The figure walked up to the side of the bus and sat there, unable to decipher the figure, the students put their head against the glass to get a better look. *"That thing is. Is. t...t...t...taller than this bus and this bus is HUGE"* Keith said with enlarged eyes

In the midst of the silence, the wolves appeared to become less aggressive, the wolves circled around the bus quietly with their red eyes piercing through the confidence of each student who looked at them. *"What if they eat us!?"* a student yelled. One wolf who heard the student yell, charged against the bus frightening the students in the back of the bus into a further troubled state. Yelling and panic began to take its place. The bus became noisy again. The wolves started pounding against the bus furthermore this time with more aggression

"SHHH!" Kye tried to quiet the bus but it was not working.

"*Sokki, my head is RINGING"* Kye said. Sokki replied nothing to his complaint. As she looked over at the mysterious figure she realized it was now gone, she looked all around the bus then her eyes froze. The figure was now on the other side of the bus sitting down. As the figure stood up, it rose almost towering over the bus, two dark glowing red lights appeared, peering directly into the bus.

"*Kye, sorry about your head. Hey I know what we need to do, we need Jay.*"

"*Oh my goodness JAY! Kye, Look at JAY!!*" Sokki said

"*How is that even possible?*" said Mr. Hines

# CHAPTER 14

The students were still in a frenzy, with multiple windows shattered on the bus the cold air from the desert seeped into the large vehicle and began to freeze the seats.

*"It's freaking freezing on this bus!"* Yammy screeched.

*"Yep, that's what I thought, that is a very, very large wolf. I can see it now... He's just SITTING there!"* Kye said

*"Kye focus! We need to wake him up!"* Sokki said as she began shaking Jay like never before.

*"JAY, BUDDY, wake up pleeeeeease, there are craaaazy wolves outside! We need that smart brain of yours"* Kye said leaning over the seat that Jay was sitting on.

*"How is that kid still asleep?"* Mr. Hines asked Ms. Till who now had a cup of coffee in her hand.

*"AHHHHH!"* another screech came from the back of the bus.

*"Kye, we have been trying for like 5 minutes, i've already checked his pulse and breathing he's fine, just in accoma apparently. BUT everyone is super loud, we need to quiet them down because for some reason, when we are quiet, they seem to stop attacking the bus!"*

Kye nodded.

The two then began to move down the bus to let all of the students know one by one to be quiet, but it didn't seem to suffice.

*"He's walking towards US!"* Yammy yelled looking out of the window trying to lean away from the direction she was looking in.

"WHAAT?" Kye asked in confusion.

"That thing!! The BIG THING" Yammy replied,

As Kye looked turned his head in the direction Yammy was pointing he saw the large figure slowly walking to the bus with its glowing red eyes and the figure got closer EVERYONE backed up against the other side of the bus, climbing on seats and standing up on them.

The wolves seemed to rally around the figure. The large figure reached the bus window, and at this point, most of them were shattered. The figure got so close that the students could smell the rough Aqui air from it. Its red beaming eyes gazing into the bus. The figure exhaled and the air from his breath rushed the students. The stench of its breath covered the bus in its entirety. The entire bus was now church quiet

"Huh... wait, where is... Everyone" a voice said

"SHHH!" someone whispered.

"Oh my goodness, it's going to eat him!" Sokki whispered, staring at Jay with a frightening gaze.

Jay was on the same side of the bus as the beast

Jay slowly began to stand up. At this moment, all the wolves behind the figure screeched as if a nail landed on their toes. They began to whine and squeal. They galloped away from the bus as fast as they could.

"Guys what is going on?" Jay asked, still rubbing his eyes.

Sokki pointed behind him and whispered *"Come here!!!"*

As Jay turned around he stopped in shock and fell down on the floor startled.

"What in the world is that!?" he yelled loudly. Jay stood up slowly, standing there, he looked at the beast in shock with the beast staring directly at him. The stare of the best seemed to become more aggressive when Jay arose. Not knowing the best plan of action, Jay felt compelled to test his theory out. He walked down the bus and the beast followed watching his every move. Then when he moved back the beast followed as well. The beast then backed away from the bus in a frightened fashion then started galloping away into the foggy mist air in the desert.

"Are they... scared of you?" Sokki asked Jay.

"I...I, I, d,don't know.. I just woke up and that thing was staring at me! ...Wait, no one tried to wake me up!?"

"Sokki and I tried Jay, I promise... But it's like you were in A COMA. We tried saying everything, from waking up to the spider on you... I was shaking you violently."

"You know what this means right?" Ms. Till asked as she leaned over to Mr. Worthy.

"Well... this is what we suspected... But now it is confirmed, the day that is upon us is inevitable now." Mr. Worthy replied back with a look of discern on his face.

"This lesson was supposed to be about self control...but I guess Mr. Cruz has different plans." Mr. Hines said, addressing the class.

In the midst of everyone trying to get back to their seats in relief that their lives wouldn't end by being eaten alive by carnivorous wolves, Mr. Hines and Kye made direct eye contact. Kye looked down at his coffee cup that he was holding in his hand. When Kye's eyes reverted back to Mr. Hines. He continued staring at Kye and said "the wolves gave it to me." then turned around and sat down in his seat.

Kye turned his head sideways in confusion. *"O-kkkkk??"* Kye said while he scratched his head.

The bus began to drive away from the dusty desert leaving nothing there but some broken pieces of glass and the heavy fog in the air. By this time the air had chilled and the sky completely black with the exception of the brightness from the moon. Los Aqui was known for its extremely dark skies in the night time where Vegas seemed to be a little bit bluer.

The term the grass is greener on the other side seemed to ring literally for the people of the Los. The bus traveled up a long mountain range with twists and turns, each one more daring than the next, headlights of the other cars seemed to be a challenging task for the bus driver due to the fact that everytime a car would come driving down towards his way he would make little comments under his breath. Not noticeable in the overall ambiance of the bus. Some students were mumbling to each other about their previous adventure, some students were looking out the window and some students went right back to sleep.

Overall, the bus was quiet with minimal interruptions of silence. 11 hours had passed by with the bus stopping once for the driver to get some sleep, as unconventional as it may have seemed, they were able to stop on the side of the road for about 4 hours to then proceed traveling. When they arrived down from the mountain range, there was a crooked sign sticking out of the ground that read **"WELCOME TO CEDORPORT - CONTINUE AT YOUR OWN RISK."** Some students observed the sign and began to comment on it. 24 hours had now passed from the time that they had left legion.

*"Very welcoming,"* Tammy said as his eyes stayed connected with the sign and the bus rumbled through the rough ground.

*"I think we are almost there,"* Sokki said loudly enough so only Jay and Kye could hear her.

Down the road, they could see past the dust kicked up from the road.

*"There is not a single person out here,"* Jay said.

*"That's because there is not supposed to be..."* Mr. Worthy replied low underneath his breath loud enough for Jay to hear. Jay thought about asking why the students were not supposed to enter Camp Choice.

Then he came to the conclusion that a question of that nature would practically remind everyone that he was supposedly the thief of the missing documents when in fact it wasn't him who stole those documents. Jay was secretly guilty by association. One would only have the sheer audacity to break into a school. View top secret documents which later just so happened to go missing all in the same instance be charged out of missed suspicion.

Get let go due to no evidence then embody the ignorance to ask a question such as this. He knew this same question was coursing through Kye and Sokki's veins but mostly, just Jay's. He was the one that decided to break into the school and look at those documents.

Through the fog ahead Jay began to squint and make out a large sign with his eyes.

*"I think that's... it,"* Jay said, peering out of the front window of the bus.

As the bus got closer to the building the fog began to disperse away. After the fog cleared, the building appeared with the famous camp logo. Two c's facing away from each other. The abandoned building was grey with multiple levels, similar to an office building.

A red sign that read **"Keep Out"** in white letters was one of the chilling indications that led to Sokki's uneasiness about the campus. Her suspicions started long before the previous sign that read **"Enter at your own risk"**. At this moment, the bus halted so Mr. Hines could unlock the gate and remove the sign.

Jay sat in the bus staring at the gate as he came to the realization that the gate looked strangely familiar. The photos from the DNE file appeared in his head in a flash. The hair on Jay's skin stood up similar to that of a porcupine. His spirit seemed to have become restless with his heart beating fast, no feeling compared except when he told Becky May freshman year that he had a crush on her, although similar, this experience was vastly different. An unspoken entity between the three friends swirled the spirits all differently.

Mr. Hines returned and the bus drove past the gate. Jay's new friend returned to shake his hand but he never stopped shaking. Jay stuck his hand in his pocket to try to hide his crazy hand shaking. Just returning from jail, the last thing he needed was his friends creating the notion that he was a psychopath.

*"Do you have any pain relievers!?"* Kye nearly yelled at the teachers near the front of the bus.

*"Dude, you ok?"* Jay asked worriedly examining Kye grab his head and swing it back and forth.

*"You ok Nacksworth? We will get you some as soon as we get inside, hang in there."* Mr. Hines replied. He reached in his bag and tossed Kye a bottle of water.

*"Thanks,"* he said as he chugged the water bottle vigorously.

Along the entrance of the property, there was a garden bed with nothing but yellow tulips on the left. Further down the students could notice the Olympic swimming pool with luxurious sparkling water. The pool had two sets of flags that ran across opposite ends of the pool. The pool resembled a brand newly built pool that was recently super cleaned and scrubbed in every inch. Oddly the beauty of the pool didn't match the rest of the facility.

As the bus started to slow down Jay noticed a tiny silver bonnet ornament on the edge of the pool. As his eyes focused on the emblem he realized it was an octopus with a skull like head. He looked down at his hand as he realized that it began to shake even more, this time it was uncontrollable. He tried to not panic but the peripheral vision of Ms. Till captured the event.

The three teachers all made silent eye contact and communicated as they all had witnessed Jay's hand shake like a plan with bad turbulence.

The bus continued driving past the emblem and Jay's shaking stopped. After the shaking stopped Jay did not pay attention to it at all. The bus had finally stopped for the last time in front of an entrance that read welcome.

*"Can you all please be quiet, I know you are really excited for one second, can you all just simmer down, it is extremely too loud!"* Sokki said.

The entire bus stopped talking and looked at her with great concern, everyone was quiet for about seconds until someone blurted out *"Don't be sad, get glad!"* The bus of students burst out into a laughing frenzy with high faves aimed at the source of the joke. While funny to the majority of the bus, Sokki did not co-sign.

*"I can't! You all are ridiculous"* She yelled. She grabbed her bags and stormed out of the bus and the class continued conversing.

*"Uh oh... looks like our three friends are waking up"* Mrs. Noble squirmed with excitement, ensuring that only the other teachers could hear her.

*"Yes, indeed they are but we still need to keep our distance."* Mr. Worthy responded.

The bus was parked and the hand shaking had finally ceased. Jay had finally made it. He was anticipating this trip since his freshman year when he heard about it from one of his junior friends that he had made during the school year. The students piled out of the bus and began unloading their bags, after the bus was unloaded. The bus then drove off speeding past the gate leaving a mountain of dust and dirt that kicked in the air. The three students stood there gazing back and forth between each other.

*"WE MADE IT!!! Wooooo!"* Jay said, chanting. Jay gave Kye and Sokki a synonyms hive five, grabbed their hands and said "Let's do this!"

The three put their hands on top of eachother in a huddle. *"1....2...3 US!"* They said in unison, with smiles and laughter and a look of relief on their face, the three walked into the building, unsure what lay ahead, that thought seemed to be secondary because they had finally reached Cederport, they had finally reached camp.

*"So adorable, I've watched them do that since they were freshman"* Ms. Till said looking at Mrs.Noble.

*"Yes... adorable, I hope they are ready for the challenge that lies ahead"* Mr. Sidious said without the slightest form of emotion on his face.

Ms. Till looked at Mr. Sidious standing off to her left *"Yes…. me too"*

*"Just remember, please keep your distance,"* Mr. Worthy said.

*"Why? It's not like they are harmful!"* Mr. Sidious remarked.

*"We don't know if they are Los or if they are Aqui."* He replied.

# CHAPTER 15

When the three ominously walked into the building along with the rest of the students, they began to stare in amazement and a little apprehension. Along the walls of the entrance, there was a silver plaque that read **"Our camp alumni heroes."** Below the plaque was all of the students who attended camp choice that eventually became successful, famous or went on to complete something of notoriety such as gaining the Los Aqui Lifetime achievement Award. There were two columns of people, same wall section but for some reason there was a line in between them. As the students began to walk down the hall Jay stood there staring in confusion,

*"Hey Mr. Worthy... Why is it split up?"* Jay curiously asked, scratching his head.

*"Come along, we need to get you situated in your room..."* Mr. Worthy responded.

Jay just stood there and looked at him.

*".... Well, everyone must stand for something"* Mr.Worthy said in a low tone of voice.

*"What is that supposed to mean?"* Jay asked.

*"In time, you will know,"* He said back.

*"... Gotcha, and the frame that is missing a picture?"* Jay asked

*"You are very observant... That is a very special someone... Questions later. Right now we need to get you unpacked into your rooms"* Mr. Worthy said as he was walking away. Jay followed him up the hall, as they began to catch up with the other students.

In the grey building, the walls were decorated with awards and accommodations for the camp. This didn't resemble anything that the three had seen in the classroom the night of the break in.

When the class had reached the end of the hall there were two separate staircases that spiraled up into different directions

*"Alright class, listen up, we are the only ones on camp premises... Which means we have the whole entire camp to ourselves, just us so you can choose a room anywhere in the facility. As long as it is only on the first or second floor. Do not go past the second floor. Do I make myself clear?"* Mr. Hines asked.

*"Yes sir!"* The class responded.

*"Good go find your rooms then meet me back down in the front courtyard in 30 minutes"* Mr. Hines said as all the students rushed up the stairs to find rooms

*"OH, and only two are allowed into a room and boys are on the second floor, and the girls are on the first. Nice try"* Hines said with a smirk on his face.

Sokki found Jay and Kye,

*"Well I guess I will see y'all in 30 minutes... I will probably be rooming with Yammy,"* she said.

When Jay and Kye finally made the trip up the stairs, they observed that the room hallway setup was similar to that of a hotel with chandeliers along the hallway and rooms spaced apart on each side. The hallway had a strange yellow looking wallpaper filled with sharks and dolphins... And more sharks. Jay walked and Kye followed *"05, let's do room room 5, you wanna do this one?"* Jay said looking at Kye

*"Yeah sure,"* Kye said. Jay twisted the door knob and opened the door. **"SCREEEEEECH"** the door made a sound as Jay pushed it open. As Jay walked in with the millions of bags he had he looked at Kye,

Kye's eyes got big then he looked back at Jay. Jay dropped his bags in shock. Kye did the same thing.

Kye stood there with his mouth wide open staring at the room.

*"Hey, why is there a bucket of water in front of each room?"* Jay asked.

Kye said nothing. *"This is pretty nice,"* Jay said.

*"Nice. No, this is luxoooooorious!"* Kye said.

Inside the room resembled something similar to a dorm and a hotel room combined. The room was spacious with a bathroom on the right of the entrance. The walls were white, straight ahead of the entrance was a large window along the wall. Further into the room, there was a TV mounted on the left and two beds lay adjacent from the TV across the room.

*"I'll take the right,"* Jay said.

*"Cool, cool i'll take the left!"* Kye said.

Jay dropped his bag near his bed and walked over to the large window overlooking the campgrounds. He opened the covers of the window, then bright light came rushing in from the beaming sun outside. The room was now extremely bright, becoming more lit than it already was previously.

Through the window, one could see practically the entire small city of CP. Cederport was a small city about 50 miles out of Los Aqui, it was a city that a lot of citizens of surrounding cities forgot about or simply looked over, seems impossible to overlook an entire city but not one that you would miss if you blinked while driving by of the interstate which was the case for Cederport.

In camp, there was an obstacle course on a blue ground, next to a big green field with statues on it. It almost resembled a giant chess board and a dirt range equipped with bow and arrows and red targets made from bushes. Although the appearance seemed normal this particular camp was far from normal.

"*Sunny Cederport. Yaaaaay*" Jay said with a sarcastic tone.

Jay walked over and jumped on his bed and lied on his back staring at the ceiling. Kye did the same thing on his side of the room.

"*I wonder what we are doing today,*" Jay said.

"*Well it looks like we are about to find out in… 20 minutes*" Kye said looking at his watch.

Meanwhile, on the first floor, things were much rowdier with the girls of the camp.

Sokki walked up to Yammy and tapped her on the shoulder. "*Hey*" She said

Yammy turned around when she saw who tapped her and she placed a look of disgust on her face.

"*Yammy, I know me and you haven't always seen eye to eye but I was wondering if me and you could room together*"

There was an odd silence between the two a silence that began many months ago

"*Yes, I was already planning on it because if I get into any trouble out here at camp which I probably will, you can use your goooooooooooood name to get me out of it. Or you can think of a clever plan to get me out of the trouble I'm in*" Yammy said in a high pitched voice, her blonde hair whipped around in traditional Yammy fashion as she turned around from Sokki with a suspicious grin on her face.

"*Now, now, come along, I choose the room!*" Yammy said walking in her high heels and leggings.

"*Hmmm, aha! Here we are, room 17!*" Yammy opened the door wide and yelled

"*AT LAST, a bed!*" Yammy kicked her high heels off, adjusted her leggings and laid down on the bed, closed her eyes and started singing a random song that she had been singing the majority of the bus ride.

"*Oh, goodness. Pleeese don't make me regret this*" Sokki said in her breath.

"*Ahehe im sorry darling, what was that? I didn't quite hear you*" Yammy said still with her eyes closed laying on her back on the bed.

"*Oh nothing, I was just saying that this was a nice room*" Sokki replied back.

Yammy continued singing. Sokki kicked off her sandals, placed her bag in front of her bed and began organizing the things in it. Then she proceeded to do the same in the bathroom, setting her items out to be prepared.

"*Ohhhhh! Sokki, Sokki, Sokki myyy dear! Why don't you sit down somewhere, you have a perfectly good bed all to yourself. You're always such a busy body. Babe, we are on VAAACATION!*" Yammy said yelling towards the bathroom while she was massaging her temple and forehead with her finger tips

"*Just reeeelax and enjoy this time*" Yammy said in a lower toned voice.

"*Well... wait, first of all did you just call me babe?*" Sokki asked from inside the bathroom

"*Darlin', I'm from Houston Texas, that's how we talks arounds those partssss*" Yammy said giggling.

"*Stop, you know I hate when you do tha*t" Sokki said

"*Doooos whats?*" Yammy asked with a big cheesy grin on her face.

"*Yammy...*"

"*Ok, I'm sorry! I'll im tryna say is that you should relax a little bit more*"

"*I'm just trying to be ready for tonight because after we do whatever Mr. Hines has for us, then I'm going to crash once we get back here, I'm more tired than usual*"

"*Well, like you said, it takes a lot to do what you did with them grades, I don't think I could've done it*" Yammy said

"*Well, when you have a mother like mine, I think anyone could do it*". Sokki said. Finally lying back on her bed and undoing her ponytail.

"*That is very optimistic of ya but... I see the way you are in class, you really have a passion for learning, you like it. Yep, you are a worm*"

"*What did you call me?*" Sokki asked while glancing over at Yammy to her side of the room.

"*A worm, ya know like a book worm? You've never heard of that before?*" Yammy asked, looking at her.

"*Ohhhh, I thought you meant it in a different way*" Sokki said as her eyes reverted back to the ceiling then eventually closed them.

The building seemed to be noisy for the next 20 minutes until a loud horn blew from out in the court yard. Some students looked outside the window, others just assumed that it was now time to arrive downstairs.

The students all flooded the house and left the hall to meet outside where Mr. Hines was standing with the four teachers. Everyone became quiet, it was becoming a standard that when Mr. Hines is presented in front of the students and quiet that meant that they should probably be quiet too.

"OK, that will be the only time that I blow the horn to let you know that it is our meeting time. Moving forward... If you are late, that will be 5 additional laps for each individual that is late. Obviously, your phones don't work on this trip so you better make yourself resourceful in telling time. If you don't know how much time you have left then being early is always an option. It's always better to be early than right on time with everything. Let me give you an example: If I am going to hire you to work for me this off-season and I am choosing between the two of you, which candidate is going to appeal better. On one hand, I have a candidate who is very talented, does every single thing I ask of them and is always either right on time or a few minutes late to work, (or school in your case). On the other hand, I have a candidate who is not really talented, still does what I ask but is always 10-15 minutes early every single day? It's rhetorical for now but we will talk about it after our PT" Mr. Hines said.

Some students began to gasp and sigh at the thought of physical training.

"I'm sorry, what. Did you think you were on vacation?" He asked the class.

Sokki looked at Yammy, Yammy didn't look back.

"So, which brings me to my next topic, every morning, we will eat breakfast then have our PT, I'll break down the flow of camp a little later. But for now, everyone will be doing PT. 50 laps around the obstacle course... Not through, like one big circle. We run together, not seperate. Alright let's go!" he yelled.

The class began to jog around the course in unison. "I will be doing the counting," Mr. Hines said. The class jogged and completed one lap around the pool, then the obstacle course that led over to the field, then curved around to the edge of the green field and back around to the starting point in front of the building. The class continued to run around the track again.

Mr. Hines turned on the loud megaphone and began to speak into it. *"Ok.... what did I say... Does anyone remember what I said being successful is about?"* he asked the class while the class was still running around the course.

The class was quiet with the exception of panting and a little heavy breathing. *"That's 10, good job 40 more to go. You're tired now, but this will build up your stamina not only physically, but by the end of this camp, my goal is for you to be mentally stronger than when you arrived. This generation IS. TOO. SOFT! Look around, does anyone see mommy and Daddy? No, that's because they are not here. I get it, family will always be family but when you get out there on your own yall have to be ready to grind! I have a passion for this generation and honestly they are talking about yall. Man! No foreal, they are... I refuse to let society bring this generation down. Together we will rise and together we will fall. Back to my question, being successful is about being...."* Mr. Hines paused, expecting the class to finish the sentence.

*".... Being comfortable in uncomfortable times."* Jay said in between his breaths while still jogging

*"Ah yes! Thank you Cruz... You would know all about that, especially now. It's a miracle that you're even here right now, but guess what he is here right now. Still smiling, look at em. Jay, I love the toughness son you're about to reach a whole new level this year... ALL of you are. That is 20 keep it up! Let's go, lets go lets go"* Mr. Hines said with a slight smirk on his face. Sweat began to drip down Mr. Hines face down from his scalp to his cheek.

*"I'm sweating, so all of you are! Sweat is good for you, it means your body is working.... Most of the time"* he said as he looked at Ms. Till. Ms. Till stared at him with a curious face and an entry of a smirk.

"Hold on, what was that??" Mrs. Noble asked, whispering to Ms. Till as she bumped her in her arm.

"Wha--, what was what?" Ms. Till said, stuttering.

'Stop! You have a thing for him don't you!" Mrs. Noble asked, whispering loudly.

"What? No, yeah right, me naw…" Ms. Till said, blushing.

"Lady! Stop, you are the top English teacher in all of Aqui and Vegas and I have never heard you use the word naw. You practically have perfect english AAAANDDD you are blushing!" Mrs Noble said grinning from ear to ear.

"First of all, it's Los Aqui… not Aqui, you know how I feel about that."

"Yeah, yeah, whatever, quit trying to change the subject" Mrs. Noble responded.

"And second of all… I use naw, plenty of times" Ms. Till responded.

"Uh huh, yeah sure and what about you blushing? You have an answer for that?" Mrs. Noble said proudly. Ms. Till said nothing and bumped her in the arm in an attempt for her to be quiet with a smirk on her face and cheeks were red.

The class continued to run around the course in a tiresome fashion. Jay was running in the middle of the group, he noticed his hand began to shake really bad after Jay completed the next lap the shaking seemed to lessen or go away. Once another lap was completed, Jay's hand began to shake again vigorously. He ignored the odd event and kept running.

"I have a headache" Kye said to Jay as he caught up to him in the group

"That's odd, did it just start?" Jay asked.

"Yeah, for some reason," Kye said.

"45! Good job! Almost done" coach Hines yelled out.

One student stopped running and immediately puked on the side of the track into a trash can.

Mr. Hines took a couple steps forward. Still a great distance away from the students. *"You ok son?? You're almost done, that is your body responding to hard work that is something that we are going to work on this summer as well. Listening to our bodies and responding appropriately, after all, we only have one body and that same body is going to stay with us for the rest of our lives, whether you like it or not"* Mr. Hines said.

The student stood up and kept running to catch up with the group.

*"I love the heart, son, keep it up"*. Hines said.

The sun appeared to be going down on the small city of Cederport. And the weather became a little cold. With a slight breeze.

*"Last one, finish strong"* Coach Hines said as he walked to the field which was now almost completely dark.

The class had finally finished their last lap. They all stopped and slowly started walking in random directions. Some sat down, some even laid down.

*"Alright, over here"* Coach Hines said, instructing the students to come over to where he was standing. The students all piled over to the benches where Mr. Hines was. The sky had gotten so dark that they could barely make out the shadow of Mr. Hines standing there not even five feet apart from them.

***WOOOOOSH!*** A big flame ignited roaring right in front of the students. SOme jumped back in surprise. Everyone could now see each other due to the bright light from the frame. They all sat there around the flame with Mr. Hines standing there in silence setting the match down on the ground that he just used to ignite the fire

"This is like survivor, and SOMEBODY is about to be voted off the island" Yenny said

"HAHAHA!" The class started to snicker and laugh, some uncontrollably.

"Yes, this is elimination time, there will be one every night. Whoever gets a question wrong is gone" Mr. Hines said as he pointed towards the entrance gate that they had embarked through earlier.

"Whoever completes their challenge first that day has immunity. Whoever does not, you will be on the chopping block. Since James, you threw up. You are the chopping block, please step forward. Here is how voting will work. Those who have immunity will be able to vote first. IF the majority votes you out, you will be sent back home out of the city. Ok, let's get started…." Mr. Hiens said, staring at the class. The class gave him blank stares

The class became quiet; gasps were heard through the group.

"Wait, what really?" someone blurted it out.

"IM KIDDING GEESH, you all should have seen the look on your faces. Priceless" Mr. Hines said.

The class was overwhelmed with relief, exhales were heard from the group.

"So he dooooes have a sense of humor" Kye said whispering to Jay

"Aaaannnny way, who has thought about my question from earlier? Which person of the two should I hire?" Mr. Hines asked with his hands behind his back.

Sokki raised her hand. "This is an open discussion," Mr. Hines said.

"Well, maybe I'm being biased, but I think you should hire the person who has average talent but always shows up early because you can always train that person to become better at job responsibilities, but you can't necessarily force them to break a bad habit that they have had for who knows how long" Sokki said.

"Very good, so let's talk about it, so if I choose the person who always shows up on time, I now have an average talented person working for me. This has its pluses and it has its minusus. What are they?" Mr. Hines asked the class.

"Well we know that they are never, well rarely going to be late and this is crucial… Because I don't know what the position entails but let's say you're meeting a client at two for lets say an extensive personal training regimine and your assistant position is to set up everything to a T while you brief the client and give customer service and all that, and if they are late, its makes you and your company look bad" Keith said

"Ok, good!" Mr. Hines said while flipping a stick in his right hand while pacing back and forth.

"On top of that, you will probably lose customers" another student piped up

"Aha! Yes, I see we have some future business majors out there, good bad perception, losing clients not customers, good I like those responses… Let's think….. Bigger picture. Ok, grreeat, I have an employee that is always on time, I mean you all didn't even ask me about their work ethic, I told you that they do whatever I ask them to do, plenty of people can do that. What separates this person from the rest? More importantly, what am I missing from this equation? If I have an average barely motivated employee that then forces me to do what? … Anyone? It forces me to train this employee. SO, all of my time is spent training when I could use this time to market and gain new clients. We must start thinking outside the box." Mr. Hines paused to connect with everyone's eye contact.

"Ok so what is the big picture when it comes to hiring an employee that is SUPER talented?" Mr. Hines asked

"Well, they are kind of unpredictable and therefore unreliable if they show up at random times for work" Mattay said

"Niiiiice Mattay, i loooooove it! I can't have an unreliable person for Mr. Hines, I'm entirely way too busy...... But give me more" Coach said

"So they are unpredictable, they don't put in much effort... In... To show up on time so" Mattay was cut off by Hines.

"Yes, dig, dig, diiiiiiig" Mr. Hines said, waving his hands and pretending like he had a shovel and he was digging.

Some students began to chuckle at the enthusiasm and excitement from the coach.

Mattay continued "If he... puts no effort into showing up on time then... he probably does the same when it comes to completing tasks on time and the amount of effort he puts into the things he does..."

"Yes! Because you didn't say he was a great worker, all you said was that he was talented. And that could mean anything, literally" Yammy said

"Just because we are talented, that doesn't mean that we use our talent" a student blurted out in the back of the group

"WOOOOOAH! Yeeeees! Now THAT is what im talking about. That is how we critically think, just because something looks a way on the surface that does not mean that it has to be what it is. Critical thinking is very crucial to your success. Don't ever forget that. Therefore, employee number two that is always on time is a better option. That is truly our first lesson of camp. Practice this skill because you are going to need it......" Mr. Hines lowered his excitement and stood straight up and looked at the class with a different look in his eye...

"This scenario I just gave you is not all fiction. I am the number one trainer in all of Los Aqui and Vegas and I am looking for assistants and individuals to manage some areas of my facilities on a special and tactical ops level. I'm looking for individuals who eventually want to become experts in their field. At the end of camp, I will choose 5 of you to work for me in the off season back in Los Aqui and Vegas. There will be no test, no special considerations... actually the entire camp is a test. I have been watching you since you all shook my hand back at the school on the bus. This summer, I demand greatness from you, I didn't say perfection I said greatness. You all have the potential to be great but we... are going to be legends. This camp will push you to limits then kick you past them. You've been gifted with the ability to simply just be here... Today. The fact that you are standing on this very ground where legends stood gives you no excuse. You have all of your fingers, hands and feet last time I checked. Anybody missing any fingers? Arms? Didn't think so. With that being said, you have all you need to succeed. There have been people that have sacrificed so much for you to be here right here. Right now. You owe it to them to not only do your best but you owe it to them and more importantly you owe it to yourself to be the greatest at your craft, and at your gift. God blessed you with your abilities. USE them, to the absolute fullest of your ability, everyday. And then you will reach greatness... Seriously, that is what it's going to take to get there, because out there... the world is too unforgiving for you to be average or mediocre, you wake up everyday and you grind, grind like your life depends on it, because it does. So you make a decision, right here. Right now.

"I want you to think about that when you all go to bed tonight. Any questions?" Mr. Hines asked

The class was quiet. "Ok, get some sleep, I will see you in the morning, make sure you are right here back at this field at 8AM sharp. No excuses. We will eat breakfast then do our morning routine. You know what happens if someone is late. Good night."

The students all stood up and started walking back to the building. Jay found Sokki and Kye.

# SPLASH

*"Quite the first day huh?"* Kye said to Sokki

*"Yeah, definitely.* Sokki said.

*"My hand keeps shaking for some odd reason. I don't why"* Jay said. As he turned his head, his eyes happened to land on the octopus mini statue at the edge of the pool, he stared at it for a while

*"Here he goes again"* Kye whispered to Sokki,

*"Jayyyy, come on!"* It's getting cold out here! "Sokki said.

*"Huh? I'm sorry, coming…. Huh what the?"* Jay said, looking at his arm.

*"What is it?"* Sokki asked?

*"Something just landed on me… It's black, like dark black. It almost looks like ink"* Jay said, staring at his arm intensely with confusion.

*"First of all, I'm going to try and act like I did not just here you say dark black."* Kye said, chuckling.

*"Kye, c'mon man you know I'm color blind, I can't really see color that well, I'm assuming it's black since it's really dark"* Jay said moving his arm closer to Sokki so she can see.

*"Oh, I see what you're saying, that ISSS really dark, what the heck is that?"* Sokki asked.

*"I'm not sure it literally just landed on me, and it's not raining but it is windy so that drop could have come from anywhere, it looks like ink"* Jay said.

*"Yep without a single pen in sight,"* Kye said looking around.

*"Well…. I don't know"* Jay said and he wiped the ink from his on to the red shirt he was wearing. The three of them began to walk inside

down the hall towards the stairs. The lights in the hallway were bright, yellow shining but still presented a comfortable feeling.

*"I wonder if this is how it's going to be. We don't really get to hang much"* Jay said, thinking out loud.

*"Well, you two do... but we aren't in the same room"* Sokki said as she looked up at Jay and their eyes connected. Jay's eyebrows lowered, they both remained still staring at each other's eyes for a complete two seconds. Sokki looked away, breaking eye contact.

*"Well... goodnight"* Sokki said.

She reached her arms around Jay's neck and leaned him closer giving him a tight hug. Jay wrapped his arms around her waist embracing her gesture. Sokki let go and turned and walked up the stairs following Yammy. Sokki looked over as she was walking up the stairs.

*"Goodnight, Kye"* she said with a grin on her face.

*"Night Sokki"* He said as he grinned back.

*"Yeeeeah, good niiiiight Kye"* Yammy said as she twirled her around her finger.

*"Girl c'mon!"* Sokki said as she nudged Yammy up the stairs. Once Sokki walked into her room and sat on her bed, a sigh of relief came over her, she stood there. Scratching her head gently. She took off her shoes and put them underneath her bed.

*"I am going to take a shower Yammy"* she said as Yammy closed the door to the room. *"Alrighty, you do that"*. Sokki walked into the bathroom and turned on the shower and closed the bathroom door. Yammy flipped on the TV and started surfing through channels. After a while, Yammy got up and went to the bathroom door

***KNOCK, KNOCK, KNOCK***

"I'm in the shower" Sokki replied,

"I know... I'm so sorry I just really have to go pee!!" Yammy said, crossing her legs outside the bathroom door.

"Im... In the shower..." Sokki said again in a slower form.

"Sokki Sioso either, you let me pee or It's going on your bed" Yammy said standing on one leg.

Sokki reached her arm out of the shower curtain and unlocked the door then quickly stuck it back in.

Yammy quickly opened the door, pulled down her leggings and sat on the toilet. *"Thank you dear!"* She said sitting there.

"For the record, I just want to tell you, so you know. You are disgusting" Sokki said from inside the shower curtain.

"Yah, Yah, Yah I think you forget sometimes that I met you in a restroom." Yammy said.

"Hey I think Kye's mom, or no wait, maybe that's the other one... Anyhow some aquarium is on the news, something must be going on," she said.

"R-r-really? I dont think it's anything" Sokki said.

"No really, it must be because the mayor is going to make some type of big speech tomorrow" Yammy said as she stood up, pulled her leggings up, flushed the toilet and then washed her hands. Yammy walked out of the bathroom and closed the door.

After a while, the shower had stopped. Sokki came out of the bathroom with pajamas on and her hair still wet. "Can I see the remote?" Sokki asked.

*'Here you go,"* Yammy said as she handed it to her then went into the bathroom and closed the door.

Sokki pressed the rewind button on the remote *"ahhh, where is it.... Aha"* She said as she jam pressed the play button. On the TV screen, a stubby brown man with a bald split stood on a podium with a microphone

*"We will make a decision soon... I promise, iF we need to intervene in the case and pull it from court I will do so myself. I am not going to delay the much needed growth of this city due to some petty, imocrable opinions of a few animal extremist... that's all i have to say, good night"*

In other news, a local store begins to raise wages for its employees...

Sokki changed the channel *"they can't pull that case they have worked too hard to get this into court"* Sokki mumbled to herself. She turned around and stared at the bed for a moment, then pulled the covers back then slowly crawled to the head of her bed.

She laid there with her eyes closed thinking about the aquarium and how that would affect this city. Almost 15 minutes had gone by when Sokki heard the shower water stop. Yammy came out of the shower with a robe on and her hair wrapped up in a towel.

*"Aaaaat lassst"* Sokki sang in a high pitch tone as she walked to the bathroom.

*"My loooove has cooome alooong"* Yammy sang continuing for Sokki in a lower tone.

*"That's not even the song I was singing, I just sang that because you took forever"* Sokki said to Yammy as yammy came strolling in the bathroom. Sokki grabbed her toothbrush and began brushing her teeth, Yammy did the same.

"Oh no, you were singing that song... About that Jay kid..." Yammy said right before she stuck her brush in her mouth and started scrubbing.

"Wait what!?" Sokki said, almost choking on her toothpaste.

Yammy looked at Sokki through the reflection in the mirror. "The Jaaaay Kid, it's obvious that you like him," Yammy said.

"He IS my best friend, but it's not like that" Sokki said

"No, no, no... I may be blonde but I wasn't born yesterday. I saw the way you gave him a hug, you IS clearly in love with that kid" Yammy said.

"In love? He is just my best friend" Sokki said

"Again girl, i ain't dumb. For how long I've known you, I have never known you to not directly answer a question and you just did it twice avoidance behavior, remember from theories of Philosophy?" Yammy said, spitting her toothpaste out in the sink. She turned on the water and began rinsing her mouth out. Sokki was quiet for a moment, just staring at herself in the mirror.

"No, I don't like him like that.... And if you're being technical, you never asked a question, you just made two assumptions, first rule of absolute truth, you must ask a question first" Sokki said before she spit out her toothpaste and started rinsing her mouth out.

"Ok, whateva you say giiiirl! I'm just sayin I think you have a thing for that kid. And plus, that friend of his... Kyeee? Kye whatever his name he is cute, now that young man right there is a looker!" Yammy said she walked out of the bathroom. Sokki stared at herself in the mirror for a second thinking about what Yammy was blabbering about and then turned off the light in the bathroom then went back to her bed. Yammy sat on her side of the room and undid her hair towel. She clicked the lamp on her side then laid on her back. The room was completely dark.

"*Are you watching this?*" Sokki asked

"*Nope*" Yammy responded

Sokki grabbed the remote and clicked the TV off.

There was now a comforting silence in the room. Sokki tucked and snuggled herself under the covers.

"*Hey Sokki?*" Yammy asked

"*Yeah?*" Sokki replied.

"*Do you remember that lady from freshman year that came to the school selling apples?*" Yammy asked quietly

"*Haha, yes, I do… then we bought all of her apples from her and sold them back to the school for double the price? Girrrrl*" Sokki said

"*Yah, the boys were the funniest because you hit them with all these scientific facts about how apples help you, immune system, digestive la la la. Then I would flirt with them until they bought the apples… ahhhh, we made a pretty good team*" Yammy said.

"*Yeah we did,*" Sokki Said.

"*Hey… Maybe I'm just exhausted from all that runnin we did earlier but what if me and you I dunno started some kinda business or somethin ya know? But one that could help people…*" Yammy said in a sleepy voice.

Sokki looked at Yammy with a look that presented insanity, one that if Yammy saw she would be offended and probably apologize for suggesting such a nonsense ideal of thought. Instead of responding how Sokki would normally respond, she rationalized with herself for a brief moment "*You know… I've never thought about that but that is definitely a possibility*" Sokki said… There was a pause of deep thought in the room.

*"Well, I'm gonna get some shut-eye... Goodnight girly"* Yammy said as she let out a big sigh

*"Good night,"* Sokki said back.

# CHAPTER 16

*"Oh boy, I'm tired,"* Jay said.

*"What really? You know what's funny, we ran longer than that when we did our 5K do you remember?"* Kye said, closing the curtains of the large window that he had opened earlier

*"Yeah but we actually trained for that race for about a month,"* Jay said.

Jay sat there for a moment and said nothing.

*"Wait, hold on."* Jay whispered. He stood up and walked towards the window.

The room was silent.

*"What is it?"* Kye asked, he was staring at Jay while he was creepily looking out the window.

*"Hey am I going crazy, come here. What do you see?"*

Kye jumped up from his bed and walked over to Jay to peek out of the curtains.

*"Right there, is that a puddle?"* Jay asked with certainty.

*"No, that's just... Well I think that is water. What is it doing on the deck? No one got in the pool today"*

*"Weird, I know. Maybe one of the teachers had to dump something out, anyways what was I saying? Oh yeah, the run yes... yes we did, it was rough.... This is going to be a tough camp"* Jay said.

*"Yeah but we are tougher right?"* Kye said as he let out a little chuckle.

"I'm glad I took that hot shower because if not I would be extremely sore... I mean, I still am, but you know what I mean" Jay said.

"Hey you think the entire camp is gonna be like this?" Kye asked Jay

"Whatchu mean?" Jay asked as he lay on his bed staring at the ceiling.

"This intense..."

"Maybe...I guess we will find out.... I'm SO SORE"

The room was quiet for a minute with both of the boys staring at the ceiling in relaxation. The day was winding down. They were so tired from running that they forgot the mind pulling events that took place prior.

"Hey bro, what time is it?" Kye asked Jay, glancing over at him.

Jay began to look at his watch and as he took it off he said "*10:35 PM*"

"Hey man, I am really tired.. I am going to get some shut eye" Jay said, rubbing his eyes. He pulled the cover over him and began to snuggle in.

"That's a good idea, I am gonna do the same, night bro" Kye said.

The two laid there in silence in the dark room. Jay could no longer hear the chatter from the other room next to him anymore, instead the soothing wind sounds breathing up against the glass of the house rocked him to sleep and danced with the rest of the students. Outside, nothing seemed to be still except for the building itself.

Wolves from the Los Aqui dessert came strolling by camp, staring into the gates. Growling at the pool from the outside similar to how they had tormented the students earlier with the same intimidation.

Midnight came and all in the house was quiet. Jay and Kye were fast asleep.

*** 

Back at the staff section of the house, the teachers befriended coffee as an ally against the sleep monsters.

"Well here's the thing, we need to figure out strengths and weaknesses," Mrs. Noble said.

"I know but it's a little too early in the game for that," Mr. Worthy said.

"True, BUT we know there's a 97.8% chance that we're not alone here… and honestly we don't know how much time we have left." Mrs. Noble said.

"Wow, you and your math.. 97.8%". Ms. Till said, making a side note mocking Mrs. Noble. She was sitting down in a blue chair facing away from the table.

"No, like I'm serious, you saw the diagnostics and report and ESPECIALLY since we don't know who, well I guess, we do… Took the documents from the school…. and I guess if we know who, then we really know why as well." Mrs. Noble said as she placed her hand on her chin. She walked away to the counter to go retrieve some coffee.

"Indeed, I understand where she is coming from. Time will be limited, but this has to stop this year.. Because the inevitable is coming unfortunately and we need to be prepared." Mr. Sidious said. He was leaning against the edge of the sofa with a black coat on, some sweats and slippers.

Mr. Sidious had relatively long hair for a male, oftentimes he would place it into a ponytail and it would present a wet, crunchy appearance. Mrs. Noble stared at his outfit for some time before resuming back to her coffee. She then reverted her eyes back to Mr. Worthy.

"I mean c'mon, it's obvious that those kids are in danger! I mean, what would you do if that was Samantha? Or Emily? YOUR OWN DAUGHTERS" Mrs. Noble said. She was staring at Mr. Worthy intensely while grabbing her coffee mug extremely tight. She had wide eyes and she waited for a response but it was delayed. The room was semi quiet, these instructors knew how to talk while saying anything verbal. Mr. Sidious's non verbal cues were at an all time high.

"I understand your concern! I do! Really I do!! But right now we are those kids' only protection, are we not??" Mr. Worthy said.

Mrs. Noble spit out her coffee in a spray towards the center of the room.

"...I'm sorry! I thought I heard you say protection... Are you serious right now? Hey you tell your students not to do drugs and substances right? Right?" Mrs. Noble said after she wiped her mouth of her coffee drippings. She placed her coffee mug on the counter and stood there with her hands on her hips staring at him.

"Yes, I..." Mr. Worthy started

"Then, you should take your own advice, cause you're... On... crack. Protection, I'm sorry, the last I checked we are ALL under cover woosh!" Mrs. Noble said as she took her hand and waved it like she was pretending to cover the room.

"And if we blow that cover then the entire city could fall. What don't you understand about that? You know this... and also, I don't know if you know this but we are not all quite what we used to be." Mrs. Noble said, looking at her hand, as it began to get red.

"Ok, let's all simmer down, we need a solution..... I will say, I am surprised that redhead has not discovered it already... as much of a smart-mouth that girl is, she is extremely intelligent" Ms. Till said.

".. So we force them, yes, that's it, how about we have HR design a scenario that will have them wake up?" Mr. Worthy said.

"If I may... that would be a brilliant idea IF we knew what would cause that but we don't. This camp is a month long, and we don't necessarily have the time to figure something like that out." Mr. Sidious said.

"The longer we take, the more these students become at risk," Mr. Worthy said.

"They are smart, after all, they are the smartest students in the school. BUT I will say I am a bit surprised that they didn't seem to be curious about the bus scenario. IF anything, that was a clear sign. But, nevertheless, they will figure it out" Ms. Till said.

"God help us all until they do," Mr. Sidious said.

*** 

Meanwhile, back in the students' corridor things were a little less complicated as the students were fast asleep.

*KNOCK, KNOCK, KNOCK!*

*KNOCK, KNOCK, KNOCK!*

"Huuuuuuuuuh... Jay. wake up. I think someone is at the door..." Kye said, rubbing his eyes. He walked over to where Jay was sleeping and shook him. He quickly thought about the crazy bus episode that occurred and how impossible it was to wake him up then. With that notion in his head he gave it a few more tries. Jay mumbled but didn't really budge an inch.

"Knock, knock Knock! Guyyys, let me in!" A voice said from outside the door

Kye began to call Jay's name louder but this didn't work. He grabbed his own pillow from his bed and began whacking Jay on the head like he was in a losey game of whack-a-mole.

*"Stop that"* Jay mumbled with his eyes still closed

*"Well then, wake up*! Kye said. Jay said nothing back, instead he rolled over to his stomach and wrapped his arms around his pillow and turned his head away from Kye. At this point, Kye had to make a big decision, whether he was to go to the door to see who it was or stay here and try to wake the sleeping shark. In times like these, Kye found it easier to make the easier of the two choices.

Sometimes he would voice his motto: *"If it isn't life or death, It aint gonna kill me".* Which to an ordinary person, would be absolute nonsense because the sentence didn't make sense. Kye sighed, he then walked to the door only to discover that there was no peep hole to view who in the wonderful big green world would be knocking at their door at 2:06 AM. So he did what any logical person would do.

*"Who is it?"* He asked. He waited for a second standing there in a completely dark room.

*"The boogie man, who do you THINK it is? It's me you idiot, now open the door!"* The voice said.

Although the comment was not appreciated the slightest bit by Kye, he still had the evidence he needed to collect to determine the mystery knocker. But that wasn't enough, he let his alter ego's extremely paranoid side take over similar to a detective but from a dissociative identity disorder vibe. Kye cleared his throat.

*"I mean you sound like her but... ok, tell me something that only she would know"* Kye said, raising an eyebrow looking at the door. The disorder was in full effect now. While this made the person on the other side crack a chuckle, Kye was still at suspicion.

"Okaaay, your name is Kye James Nacksworth, you are the number one student in science at legion leadership academy and you had Jay help you with your delivery speech for MONTHS until you gave the actual speech" The voice said.

"Ok and? A Lot of people know my middle name and they say that Jay and I are friends. As far as I'm concerned, that is public information. Sooo that doesn't prove anything!" Kye said not phased by the information given the slightest bit.

"You have a secret tree-… wait nevermind. Sometimes in the winter time, you only sleep with polka-dotted under…" The voice said pausing.

Kye opened the door quickly, "You promised we would never talk about…That." Kye said, pausing with an embarrassed face staring out into the hallway.

"Uhh, umm… Yammy? W-w-w-what are you doing here? And H-h-how did you know all of that stuff?"

"I didn't," Yammy said with a red blushing face of confusion as she let out a little giggle.

"GOTCHA!!" Sokki said as she jumped out from behind Yammy! Sokki began laughing profusely. Kye continued standing there with an embarrassed look on his face.

"Well, c'mon! Give it to me, that was great. I am the mastermind" Sokki said. She waited for feedback but didn't receive any due to the fact that Kye was staring directly into the eyes of Yammy, and Yammy was staring back. Sokki noticed this and interrupted the eye affair.

"Hey Yammy, do you know what room your brother is in?" She asked, breaking up the silence.

"Uh? No, that's actually what I'm going to find out while I'm up here" She said whispering.

"Well alright, I'm going to find him," Yammy said.

"You're just going to sneak around the halls guessing, knocking on everyone's door until you find him? How are you going to find him?" Sokki whispered back.

"Well, we have this thing, I'm not quite sure what it is, it's like we can tell when we are near each other, it's almost like we can communicate without talking, kinda like a mind thing. It's weird because we have had one since we were young. Like 5, I think, it gets stronger as we grow older" Yammy said.

"What am I thinking right now??" Sokki said, leaning her forehead towards Yammy with her eyebrows raised towards each other.

"Sokki, hunny im not telepathic darling. I just know my brother, on a... mental level I guess" Yammy said looking down on the ground.

"You know, I almost want to come with you to see how this works," Sokki said. She shifted her weight back and forth from foot to foot. With excitement.

"Nothin you can see, and besides.. I don't need both of us getting caught. Member what I told you..You're my insurance policy" Yammy said.

"Yah, yah" Sokki said.

Yammy walked away from the two wobbling down the hallway.

"Ewwww, why are you walking like that? You look drunk" Sokki whispered loudly while laughing.

Yammy stuck one finger up in the air and continued walking away from the two.

"Hey look Kye! We are number one!" Sokki said while laughing

*"Insurance policy? What the heck is she talking about?"* Kye said.

*"Dont worry about it, it's nothing. C'mon, let's go inside before a teacher comes."*

She followed Kye inside of the room and closed the door.

*"Wow, ours is nicer than yall's"* Sokki said with an accent. Her eyes gazed around the room as she paced back and forth to view the room.

*"Did you just say yalls?"* Kye asked. He tilted his head to the side while looking at her.

*"Sorry! I've been hanging with Yammy, don't look at me sideways"* Sokki said

The sound of Jay's snoring interrupted Sokki's thought process and also, her pacing back and forth came to a halt.

*"What the heck?" He's still asleep? How?"* She asked.

*"You know him, he can sleep through just about anything."* Kye replied back. He sat on his own bed staring back at Jay snoring away.

*"You know what? I have an idea..."* Sokki said. She walked over to Jay's bed and sat down on the edge of the bed. *"IS... THAT a... Whale??"* Sokki asked loudly.

Jay shot up from his lying position nervously and began to look around the room. *"A whale? Where??"* He asked, still looking back and forth between Kye and Sokki. Kye was still sitting on his bed laughing away while Jay looked for this magic whale that was non existent.

*"Jay, buddy... There is no whale. We just wanted you to wake up"* Kye said.

*"Whyyy... What's up? You know I don't like whales, one tried to attack me at my neighbor's house a few days ago"* Jay said.

Jay was so sleepy that he failed to realize that Sokki being in their room was not supposed to be occuring at the moment. He rubbed his eyes in circles with his fist clenched on both eyes. There was a quick silence in the room.

"Wait... why are you here? Did something happen?" Jay asked Sokki to clear up the confusion. In his mind, this was some kind of really odd dream, the kind you experience when you are really supposed to be asleep but you are experiencing events as if you are awake in the current time but Jay was in control of everything that he did so he quickly came to the conclusion that this was no dream. He ventured through his entire thought process in a matter of a second or two.

"I snuck over here, and no silly, nothing happened. We are the three amigos, we can't be away from each other for long." Sokki said. She picked up Kye's pillow and threw it at Kye.

"Did you get some sleep?" Jay asked.

"Yah... A little, I'll get more. Don't worry" Sokki replied. She moved her hair to the back of her head and looked at Kye *"You ok?"* She asked. Kye had one hand on his head, he reached over and grabbed a water bottle that was on the nightstand next to him.

"Yeah, I'm just glad I got rid of this crazy headache I had earlier.... It came out of nowhere and started to simmer down after we left from outside." Kye said.

"That's weird, glad you're ok..." Sokki replied. She then stood up and walked across the room, grabbed the love seat and dragged it over to the center of the two beds to form their group triangle they seem to always present when chatting.

"Yeah, I don't know what was going on earlier. Kye had a killer headache, my hand was shaking like I had Parkinson's" Jay said.

"RIP, Muhammad Ali" Kye said as he laid down plopping back on his back. The bed rumbled a little. Jay pointed at him.

"Ummmmm, that's a little odd because either I'm going crazy or I am having extreme anxiety issues" Sokki said leaning forward in her chair.

The tone in her voice made Kye sit up on his bed along with Jay on his side.

"I'm not trying to be rude or anything but you do have anxiety" Jay said hesitantly.

"Yes, Jay I know... but this... this was different. This was something I've never experienced before in my life... it's as if I was almost going to pass out from all the running we did." Sokki said.

"I mean, I think that is natural. I'm pretty sure we all were, watch I BET you, 10 more laps and somebody would've dropped." Kye said jokingly, but also serious. Looking in Jay's direction.

Jay reached over and flipped on the lamp light "I'm sorry guys I could barely see you" Jay said.

"I ran cross country last year, remember? I am still pretty conditioned, I would NEVER feel like that when I was running. I mean you remember, you two were at all of my meets." Sokki said.

"Yeah Kye, member when she had to run 100 miles without stopping around the city?" Jay asked.

"TRUE" Kye said. He was scratching his head.

"Ok, so let's get this straight, Kye you have, sorry, you had a headache which is now gone... Jay your hand was shaking and it has now stopped and my heart was beating really fast and everything inside of me just felt rushed like I was being electrocuted... But now it has stopped" Sokki said. She crossed her legs on the love seat and put her hand on her chin.

"Yeah... Very weird coincidence" Jay said

"Coincidence i think not... there is no possible way on earth that we are having all of these weird things happen to us for no reason... I dunno, something about that just doesn't sit right with me" Sokki said in disbelief.

"Guys, did you happen to see that little umm..." Sokki paused trying to remember what she wanted to say

"The octopus medal thingy on the side of the pool?" Jay asked to ensure that's what she was referring to.

"Yes!" Sokki said.

"Yeah, it was odd because it seemed like my hand began shaking more when I passed that part of the track," Jay said.

"I'm starting to get freaked out because that's what we saw in the classroom, a freakin octopus! But how is it connected to this place?" Sokki asked.

"I'm telling you, the Los and the Aqui" Jay rambled.

"Oh shut up, we've been over this already, it's not hun, sorry to burst your bubble" Sokki said, squeezing his cheeks.

"That's a very good question, and even moreso, why the cameras were just randomly weren't working, then on top of that the offer that came to the door seemed like he knew something that was..." Kye said. He paused because Jay cut him off

"Wa-wa-wa-wait, what about the cameras?" Jay asked, looking at Kye. His face read with confusion.

"Oh, that's right. Sokki, we haven't told him yet..." Kye said.

"Umm, tell me what?" Jay said.

"Nothing bad, I mean, ok so while you were in prison, we came up with an idea to get Mr. Skies to come with us into the school since he has clearance to be in the school whenever he pleases. Soooo myself, my mom and Kye all went to the school with Mr. Blank so he could fix the cameras. When the cameras were fixed, the fins related it to you because there was no clear evidence that the cameras supported so they had to let you go." Sokki said. She looked down at her nails twiddling her hands.

"Wait, you did all that for me?" Jay asked.

"Jay, you are friends, you know our A1 since day one?" Kye said.

"Wow you two, I really appreciate that. You two are truly the best, I could not even begin to ask for better friends you two.... I'm sorry but I think this calls for a group hug... C'mon!" Jay said. He jumped up out of his bed signaling for the two to join him. Sokki made a grunting noise then stood up. Kye did the same without the grunting and joined together for a group hug.

They embraced each other for a moment until Jay interrupted the fun silence.

"Wait" He said

"What? What's wrong?" Sokki said.

"You said that the cameras didn't have any evidence of us right?" Jay asked. He stepped back from the group, still standing, he remained still along with the other two.

"Yesssss, why?" Sokki asked.

"And was anything else on the video?" Jay asked

"Yeah, there was a guy walking with a flashlight. Passed the office towards the classroom" Kye said.

"Oh my goodness…. This means." Jay said then he paused and covered his mouth.

"What Jay? You're scaring me, you're making me nervous" Sokki said.

"GUYS, why am I the only one who sees what's going on right now!?" Jay asked. His eyes became big looking at the two.

"Jay, man what spit it out!" Kye yelled impatiently

"Guys, you don't get it. If the tape shows the gentleman walking by the office with a flashlight, you don't get it. We walked past the same office when we took the key then went to the classroom. Umm hello?? We should be on that tape too" Jay said, His voice getting louder.

"This means…" Kye started

"That someone cleared us from that tape!" Jay said.

"Wow… who would do that?" Sokki asked with great confusion

"And why would they want to help us?" Jay said

"KNOCK, KNOCK, KNOCK… KEEP IT DOWN, it's 3AM!" A voice said from outside.

"Was that Mr. Worthy?" Sokki asked

"I dont know!" Whispered Jay loudly. The three sat in complete silence, Sokki hid in the bathroom just in case the mystery voice attempted to make an entry. Jay quickly turned off the lamp light and Kye quickly laid down and tucked himself under his covers. The room was now in complete silence.

"Hey guys… Imma head back to my room before I get caught" Sokki whispered.

*"Ok, probably a good idea!"* Jay whispered back. Sokki quietly opened the door to the room and tiptoed down the hall and scurried down the stairs to get back to her room. When she arrived back, she realized that Yammy was fast asleep. Sokki followed and did the same.

Soon, the morning came and the sun returned to shining its rays on the lovely town of Cederport. The smell of freshly cooked breakfast rushed the halls, awakening Jay to an intriguing morning. While the delicious smell of Jay's favorite breakfast radiated throughout his nostrils, what he saw when he looked out of the main doors to the courtyard was just as intriguing. Maybe he thought his eyes were playing tricks on him but he thought he saw what appeared to be Mr. Sidious laughing with Mr. Hines setting up cones and various objects in the field.

From Sidious being caught red handed with a grin on his face to Jay miraculously being awake and alert before both Kye and Sokki considering his sleeping habits made for an odd beginning to their first morning at camp.

Soon, the entire dining hall was filled with hungry loud students. The dining hall was located towards the back of the house on the left side of the hallway behind the stairs. On the door a sign read **"dining hall"**. Inside the hall the room was furnished with a 25 yard table that stretched down the majority of the room along with a kitchen section for the chefs that were hired specially from Vegas during camp season. The hall was decorated with lamps that hung above the table and paintings from a famous artist who lived in Cedorport for 22 years. The paintings were in bronze color frames around the hall.

The rest of the instructors were all inside of the hall talking and chatting with the students but mostly each other.

At the table all of the students were busy eating and talking away.

"I am so glad we got French toast! On a side note, I slept strangely last night" Jay said. He began cutting his french toast with excitement. He was thrilled to be sitting with all of his peers eating his favorite breakfast. The sound from the chatter of the students was ecstatic, filled with laughter and a celebratory mood.

"Look, all I know is that you must be on drugs because you were up before me AND Kye.... no seriously. Are you ok?" Sokki asked looking back and forth at Kye for agreeance

. "I'm awesome! How are you?" Jay asked.

"Why darlin' Jay Cruz. I am just purely delighted that you are doin alright. And I'm just peachy" Sokki said with a southern accent. This made Jay laugh with a mouth full of French toast.

"Yammy?" Kye asked

"Woooah, she sounds too much like her!" Jay said, still chuckling a little.

The three sat there at the table along with the rest of the peers broadcasting chatter and amusement.

*"Where is she at anyway?"* Kye asked.

*"Somewhere with her brother, we room together. We DEFINITELY don't need to eat breakfast together"* Sokki said as she was in the process of stuffing food into her mouth.

*"Hi Kyyyyyye"* A group of his peers with ginger colored hair said as they walked by twirling their hair, giggling and whispering.

*"H-hi ladies"* Kye said as he barely waved with a smirk on his face.

*"Kye, Kye, Kye... Ladies man"* Jay said. Kye smirked and continued eating his eggs and bacon.

Yammy saw this from down the table, unbenounced to Kye thinking it vaguely reminded her of her previous situation with Ken Swindle; she had on a face that almost spoke of disappointment.

Yammy saw this from down the table, unbenounced to Kye. She had on a face that almost spoke disappointment. Yammy wasn't necessarily known for chasing after her prince charming, especially after her heart break in freshman year when a young lad by the name of Ken Swindle put a bad taste of the dating life in the mind of young Yammy. Ken was a tall blonde hair boy with blue eyes. She remembers it like it was yesterday.

It was the beginning of her 9th grade year when she had met this handsome looking boy in her homeroom class. She was nervous, keeping to herself and not really anxious to start any crazy conversation because she wasn't used to this new and exciting start, after she moved from Texas. She was from a small town by the name the Okies, It was about three times the size of Cederport. Although, Okies wasn't known for any seclusion, the new feeling of starting over for Yammy and her older brother Tammy was unsettling to say the least.

IN their town, everyone knew everyone so there wasn't much you could do without anyone or everyone knowing or ANYTHING for that matter. This case was true for the Okie Twins or the YamTams as the city nicknamed them that after Yammy and Tammy put on a play for their school. They played the role of two detectives that constantly finished eachothers sentences in order to bring down the crime lord in the city, a character they created called Dr. Darky.

They would set the scenes to portray the two working in two opposite locations discovering clues for a case. When one would say something, the other would finish the sentence as if they were reading each other's minds. After they solved the case they would put their backs together and say **"We are the YamTams"** In unison and the class would laugh. What their peers failed to realize through the 7-year old humor was that the two twins always seemed to do exactly that. Since they were 5 their parents knew something was unique about the two.

It all started when one day Yammy was sitting on the couch with her mother eating a banana. Yammy blurted out the words *"I want a... I want a... I want a..."*

Out of nowhere all the way from upstairs her brother yelled *"A fork!"*

Yammy smiled and pointed upstairs because her brother had finished her sentence. Their father who was upstairs at the time with Tammy didn't know why he blurted that out. *"Hunny, why do you want a fork with a banana?"* Her mom asked her.

*"I'm just silly haha, He know, he know!"* Yammy said in her cute little voice pointing upstairs to her brother who she couldn't see.

Later that night after the kids were asleep.

Mrs. Long asked her husband *"Hey, how did Tam know Yam wanted a fork earlier?"*

*"Is that why he blurted that out?"* Mr. Long said, looking at his wife. Since that day, other situations lead them to ask similar situations. Just like the situation that broke Yammy's heart when she first came to Los Aqui. About mid school year, her relationship with Ken Swindle had spiraled into Yammy developing really strong feelings for him. One day, Tammy happened to run into him before the first bell of school had started.

*"Hey Ken, What's up man!"* Tammy said

*"What's going on bro?"* Ken said back.

*"Hey, how are you and my sister?"* Tammy asked

*"Uhh, we are alright I guess"* Ken said.

"What do you mean by that?" Ken said.

"Well I got to be honest, I love your sister. I really do, but it's always been my dream to go to texas but you can only get in if you know someone sooooo I realized that im only dating her for that. I let that get in the way of our actual relationship." Ken said. Tammy was standing there, just staring at him. They were both about 6 '2. Tammy stared at him for quite some time before deciding to speak.

"Dont hurt me man, I wasn't trying to do her any harm," Ken said. Tammy took a deep breath in.

"You know, in my city we got a sayin. You either with someone or you aint, I suggest you tell her and not lead her on" Tammy said. He threw one of the straps of his backpack over his shoulder and walked inside the main building as the bell was ringing.

Later on that day, Yammy ran into her beloved boyfriend during a passing period in the midst of the crowd of Legion students, *"It's over Ken. We're done"* Yammy said. She stared at him with a stern look in her eye.

"What?? Why? Did your brother talk to you? Is this about Texas babe...I...?"

"No, this aint about Texas! And no my brother aint talk to me. It's about you, it always has been and it always will be! You're selfish and that's just the way you are. My momma said don't try and change no one, it's a full time job trying to change yourself." Yammy said. She gave him a hug, squeezed him around his torso and walked away slowly.

"Wait, you hug me? I was expecting a slap honesty" Ken said

"Well, I'm sorry to let you down darlin, that's just not how we do things where i'm from..... You know what we say back home? Kindness is like medicine, you may not always like it... but you gotta have some. Because... at the end of the day, it will make you feel better" She said holding back a tear, she quickly turned and started speed walking away from him, dodging all of the students in the hallway with her head down.... *THUMP!* Yammy realized she had run into someone "Oh, im sorry, I didn't mean to... As she looked up, she stopped her apology because she had ran into her brother. She gave him a big hug and squeezed him tight.

"*I saw what happened, Yammy, I'm so sorry,*" Tammy said.

"*When he told you that earlier, I got this really strong feeling I could literally FEEL the words coming outta his selfish mouth! You know, days like this where I wish we didn't know what each other was thinking...*" Yammy said.

And now she was here. Crushing on a boy that wasn't even aware. She couldn't decide what was worse. Crushing on a boy that was unaware or having her heart broken. She sat there at the table, stabbing her food with her fork as she thought about her past but was interrupted by her brother. "*Hey! You ok? It's time to get out on the field.*" Tammy said as he was getting up from the table. Looking across from the table.

"*Yeah, I'm ok,*" Yammy said.

All of the students began to stand up from their seats and walk outside to the field. Once everyone was outside, they began to wonder where Mr. Hines was located. "*SPLASH!!*" Water came pouring down on the group of students from above. As they all looked up they saw Mr. Worthy on the roof pouring big buckets of water on them. The students began to react in a panicked fashion. Some began to laugh and giggle.

"*Alright, everyone against the wall!*" Mr.Hines said as he walked out in front of the students. The class began walking to the field.

"*I'm sorry, all of a sudden we are walking... Seeing the energy you give me out here will accumulate to the energy you put out there! Let's go! Ruuuuun!*" Hines said. The class started jogging towards the field. When they reached the wall they all squatted down on the wall.

*"Alright, 2 MOS"* Hines said.

The class became quiet and they continued to squat against the wall. Jay, Sokki and Kye all stared across the property to that pool with the octopus emblem. Jay thought about how things were back home. His Dad was angry at him for ending up in a Los Aqui jail before he even turned 18.

Not to warrant being in jail after the age of 18 was justified but nevertheless the thoughts began to bother Jay. His mind swirled until the prefrontal cortex of his brain threw up the stop sign. During MOS, he told himself in his mind that he wanted to let MOS be a moment to clear his mind, not swarm it.

*"Alright! Let's warm up. 10 laps!"* Hines said. The students began running around the track again just like they did the previous night. Mr. Hines walked over to Ms. Noble and the group of teachers that were standing in the shade, *"C'mon get some sunlight!"* Hines said, taking Ms. Till's hand and leading her out into the sun.

*"Hey, are the pools ready? Did you test it?"* Mr. Hines asked Mr. Sidious

*"Yep! All ready to go. I'll take the covers off now."* Said Mr. Sidious. Shortly after, the students had finished laps around the pool and went over to the water fountain to get a drink near the entrance to the building. Jay walked on the side to grab a cup and get some water.

*"Hey! I was here first, and besides jail birds last!"* Mikay said, nudging Jay to the side.

*"Jail bird, ok angry bird!"* Jay said, nudging him back. Some students who overheard these comments began to laugh.

*"Well, at least this angry bird has both of its birdy parents!! How's your mom? Oh that's right, she is not here anymore ooooops, my bad!"* Mikay said, responding back. At this point, the juniors in the class started to crowd around the two including Mikay's friends.

Jay looked down, then he looked up. *"Keep talking, gonna get kicked in the face."* Jay said under his breath. He remembered his years of martial arts training, how he learned self control and his Mother taught him to always watch his mouth.

*"Well, I'm right here... Haha, kick me in my face"* Mikay said laughing with his friends. Mr. Hines observed this and said nothing.

*"Alright, keep talking,"* Jay said, clenching his fist. Jay thought about his right foot, he didn't lift it up because if he did, he knew that he could drop Mikay to the ground with it. He thought about the consequences of his desired actions, the thought of getting kicked out of camp and the disappointment his father would have would not be worth it. *"I swear just wait..."* Jay said, walking away from the group. Mr. Hines walked up to the group.

*"Mr. Mikay, all you proved is that he has more self control than you,"* Mr. Hines said.

*"Well, this little twat should be in jail!"* Mikay said, speaking over the top of Mr. Hines. This comment made Jay turn around. Jay quickly started speed walking towards Mikay *"ALRIGHT SAY IT AGAIN"* Jay said. Jay lifted his leg. Kye flew in, running in front of Jay while Jay was beaming at Mikay with his eyes.

*"Bro, c'mon. It's not worth it... Let it go."* Kye said. He saw a look in Jay's eyes that he has never seen before.

*"C'mon, lets go"* Kye said

*"SELF CONTROL!!!" Mr. Cruz"* Hines said.

*"EVERYONE GATHER AROUND!!"* Mr. Hines said. The students all came in a close huddle, things had simmered down but some eyes were still landing on Jay and Mikay. Jay's face read an unpredictable mind set, at this moment he was channeling his alter ego, ruthless they called his other side.

Mr. Hines put his shades on because despite the lack of sun the sky was still a little bright. *"OKAY, annyyyyyway. Its life, you two squash the beef or I will squash it for you. You better become a vegetarian real quick. It's like this, in life. There is too much pulling at you and you have far more things to worry about than the people at your opposition, if anything that should fuel you. You have a backpack, yes that's right. A backpack everywhere you go and in this backpack are dreams, and on top of those dreams is stress, anxiety, past failures, doubt, self doubt, low self esteem, I can go all day. All of the emotions that we allow ourselves to feel. And you have to make a decision to either travel light or travel heavy. You see, there is a difference between an emotion and a feeling. An emotion is something temporary. It's with you for a second, then it's gone. A feeling lasts for a longer period of time. To be emotionless at times is healthy, see the more you go through in life, the more you know how to handle things and if you're wise you let these things make you stronger. After all, life is 10% what happens to you and 90% how you respond. You begin to learn how to put your emotions aside and focus on the task at hand. I don't know and frankly I don't care what that little scuffle was just about but I do know this, you along with this generation allow things to get to you too easy. You will learn the art of silence, the art of warfare, the art of patience and the art of becoming the best you. Are we clear?"* Mr. Hines said, asking the class.

*"YES SIR"* The class responded, Jay said nothing.

*"Alright, we are going to seperate you into three groups and three different pools located on the edge of camp, at these stations are different skill sets for possible careers, this is the main focus of camp choice choosing a career. The first station over here to my right is a lifeguard and tactical safety station, we focus on things such as timed response, water rescue, completion of the camp allows you to enter the coast guard. If that is the career you choose. That is the level that our training is at."*

*"This next station directly behind me is the swim coach and swim lesson mastery career station. The last station is for those of you that want to become a skilled master of swimming itself. Olympic style*

*professional career team swimming. The NSA. The national swimming Association For those of you that thought I might have meant the government organization that used to spy on people."*

*Every week, we will discover 3 new career options. The first day is designed to be a demo day before you start actually learning and perfecting the craft. Does everyone understand?* Everyone nodded.

"Alright Jay, you will be in the first group for lifeguards, pool protection along with Mikay, Tammy..." Mr. Hines continued to name the names of the students that were in his group. Jay temporarily phased out for a moment, his mind gravitated towards the pool on the other side of the campus. The one with the octopus emblem, there was something about this pool that was drawing him. Something that attracted him to a different sense of himself. He could not quite put a thumb on it. Before he knew it the groups were separated and Jay was headed for his pool station.

At Jay's first station, there were dummies set up, lifeguard tubes and CPR masks everywhere. On the side of the pool. Jay observed a sign that read 12" Feet. Jay had never been to a 12 foot pool before this experience was completely foreign to him.

"Alright, class goes ahead and line up at the edge of the pool. Give me one second." Mr. Hines left to the shack that was located on the shack of the building. He brought on one more red tube that read LIFEGUARD on the top of it. Jay looked around to possibly try and locate the rest of the 3-legged stool but they were nowhere in sight.

He heard the other instructors speaking loudly and some even yelling seeming to believe that they had already started at their station. When Jay reverted his head back to the pool, he stared down at the crystal clear pool in front of him. His heart began to race a little and drills or skills haven't even started yet.

Mr. Hines jogged back to the top of the pool, he stood on a big diving board with the guard tube high across his chest. Jay took one large deep breath in.

"OK, you're probably wondering why I am here out of all three stations. Two reasons, one. Lifeguarding and pool safety is my favorite and two... well two I have to be somewhere" a few students giggled.

"Ok, who here has ever seen a lifeguard jump in the water to save a life?" Mr. Hines asked, looking around. Jay's hand was the only one that raised. Well, when you saw this you probably saw that they had urgency, yes? Well being a lifeguard is not about waiting for somethin to happen naw, this is the business... the business of saving lives aaaaannd guess what, you're IN IT! Yes, you're in it to win it. One of the most important things about being a lifeguard is that there is very minimal room for error. As a lifeguard, because ya gotta think. You're in charge of an entire pool. This is why I said accountability is a very important life skill. Because you can't have an off day as a lifeguard. If you're pissed off because your girlfriend or your boyfriend dumped you, you better get over it. Those people in that pool come first, the objective is to be proactive versus reactive. Well Mr. Hines, what do you mean by that? For example, you see someone running, the ground is wet, slippery and it's on concrete. You're trying to prevent an injury so you tell them STOP RUNNING! Right? That is just the very basic surface of being a pool protector. But that is what being a lifeguard all is about. Through this course, you will learn how to conduct rescues, make entries and be fully equipped in everything first aid, CPR, AED and using an oxygen tank. We are going to touch most of those today for a sample. Alright everyone hop in, 300 yard swim, lets go!" Mr. Hines said, jumping off of the block, landing on the ground.

"Uh, sir, do you want us to change out?" Jay asked. Looking at everyone else crazy for hoping in the pool with their regular workout attire on.

"Uh, Jay... No?" Mr. Hines said.

"But isnt cotton heavier in the pool," Jay said.

"Alright, everyone hop in!" he yelled. He stepped closer to Jay about a foot away and took off his shades.

"Son, see here is the thing about being smart. It doesn't always guarantee that you're right. Did I say to change out? This isnt P.E. IF you can rescue someone while they are wearing heavier clothes than normal swim attire then you can rescue them when they have on swim attire" Hines said. He leaned forward and lowered his voice to where only Jay could hear what he was saying.

"Look, I have a prophecy for you kid, you are meant to be a LIFE-guard in and out of the water. Your mission is to save lives in and out of the water. You, my friend, are going to be a symbol of hope, and a beacon for those who are lost." Hines said. He began to walk away, to retrieve something from the shack when he noticed that the class was keening in on the conversation, trying to ease drop.

"Jay, you're really testing my patience today. Get in the pool." MR. Hines said. Jay got in the pool with the rest of his classmates, he decided not to think too much about what was just prophesied to him but he remembered those words and kept them in the back of his mind.

Over in Sokki's station, the students were learning techniques to teach students how to swim. There was a woman instructor in the pool with blonde hair that resembled Yammy, Ironically they were in the same group. In Sokki's mind, having Yammy as a friend was a full time job and just like any relationship, she felt she needed space. But with the two of them it was a bit more complicated than that, their past reached back not a great distance but a memorable one.

"In this industry, we always want to use the tell show do method. We want to tell them what skill they are going to learn and give them a brief description then we want to show and demonstrate the skill correctly, and this is important especially with little kids because the first time you *show the skill, they could possibly, more than likely be seeing the skill for the very first time. Then after that we want to have them do or practice the skill."* As much as Sokki seemed focused on the seminar, she couldn't stop thinking about the fact that Yammy somehow could not leave her side. She felt trapped.

Yammy and Sokki met each other back in freshman year at legion. Sokki was using the restroom when all of a sudden she heard tears coming from the stall next to hers. Sokki being her true self, said *"Are you alright?"*

"Yes, Im fine…. Well, no i'm not fine. Me and my boyfriend just broke up". Yammy said. "I'M sorry… I know heart breaks are tough" Sokki said.

"Yes, well… I broke up with him. HE was only dating me so he could get something for himself out of the relationship" Yammy said.

"Wow, these boys, always using the wrong body part to think with." Sokki said because she truly had never said anything like that before and she didn't know what else to say. Sokki had never experienced anything sexual.

"No, not like that, he just wanted me to take him to Texas. That is the only reason he was dating me." Yammy said.

"Well, me and my friends are going to get ice cream after school. Do you want to come?" Sokki asked.

"Well, I have to let my brother know oh wait. It's fine he just told me." Yammy said.

"Really? That quick, you two must read each other's mind! HAha" Sokki said.

"Oh.. You have no idea" Yammy said. They both exited the stall at the same time and when they came out the stall they saw each other for the first time. They both washed their hands in silence. After they dried their hands they looked at eachother.

"Im Sokki by the way," She said. She reached out to shake her hand

"Hi... I'm Yammy, nice to meet you." She said as she reached her hand out shaking Sokki's hand. Sokki's phone started vibrating.

"Up, looks like they are waiting on me. C'mon I think you will like them" Sokki said.

Sokki stood there observing the seminar, having a flashback and thinking about where her and Yammy's relationship is now. The unexpected turn it took but she was glad they were back on speaking terms. This flashback made Sokki think of Jay and Kye which made her look over to Kye, luckily Kye happened to be looking over and Sokki right after he had just finished a lap and placed his goggles above his head. Back at his camp, the instructors were teaching the racers how to make their stroke faster for stronger finishes.

Kye was always a natural born swimmer, from the time that he was born he was just very attracted to water but he never knew why. He heard his father was a swimmer but never knew the extent of the talent. Oftentimes he would think back to when he was racing on the junior high swim team. Always faster than all of the other kids, but his mother would still make it to all of the swim meets. This was huge for Kye coming from a single parent household.

The death of Kye's father remained a partial mystery for him. The extent he understood was that his father died of an illness he got for traveling overseas on a business mission. Days would drift by that Kye would think about his Dad and what his Dad was like. How they would bond if he were still here. What they would do together but more importantly Kye thought about how much happier his mother would be and what effect it would have on her.

For Kye, at the end of the day when all the swimming medals are won Kye just wanted to see his Mother happy.

# CHAPTER 17

The clouds seem to become more and more impairment of the skies leading the students to believe that it might actually rain, Jay could smell the precipitation in the air causing the fresh smell of rain to prepare to sing to the skies and make its grand entrance.

*"Good, sink the tube! Lean back, Lean Back! Good! All the way under GOOOOD! Bring him to the wall."* Coach Hines said, talking to Jay.

*"Alright, hop out! Ok, it's time to run a real scenario. My professional lifeguards that I brought with me to camp will be your additional responders. We are only doing the rescue, if you choose this career you will learn how we incorporate CPR in the same scenario later. Alright Sam, your victim. Steven, you're secondary. Jay your primary."* Said Mr. Hines.

Jay began to feel a little strange, partially due to the fact the name Steven sounded extremely familiar. Then it dawned on Jay, this is what Jay's dream was about. He was about to experience the exact same scene from his dream that he had on the morning of the last day of school. Jay's body became covered in goosebumps. And he began to sweat even over the water that was already dripping down his skin.

His heart began to beat really fast. Jay had never had a dream that actually happened in real time. Jay didn't know what to do. His mind went completely blank, like someone just erased a white board that Einstein was using to draw up his complex equations. *"Calm down Jay, calm down"* Jay he said to himself as he tried to take really massive deep breaths in but in reality he was breathing short quick breaths. Then, his breathing slowed all... the way... down.

*"Alright Jay when you recognize the emergency, activate your EAP like we talked about and make the appropriate rescue. All of you have already had your turn so Jay is the only one in the scenario with my team*

so that means all of you are the patrons in the pool. OK, victim, are you ready?" Mr. Hines said looking at Sam,

"Yes sir!" Sam said,

"Secondly, are you ready?" Mr. Hines asked, looking over at Steven. Steven nodded.

"Primary, are you ready?" Mr. Hines asked. Jay said nothing, he stood there with his guard tube high across his chest standing there shaking and shivering with a complete blank look across his face like he had seen a ghost. He was peering into the forest of trees that was 500 yards away. The class stared at him.

"Hello earth to Jay, are you ready?! Are you going to get on the stand?" Mr. Hines asked with intensity raging through his voice.

"Yah" Jay said with the same look but reverting his eyes into the crystal clear water, in this moment, for some odd reason, he thought about how this water was crystal clear but the pool near the entrance with the octopus emblem was even clearer. But that thought was secondary to the thought of what Mr. Worthy told the class on the last day of school. Those words replayed back in his head *"Always remember this in life…..It is in the moment of your greatest struggles and triumphs that you will discover who you really are."*

Sam started walking wobbly on the pool deck resembling intoxication. He soon grabbed his chest and collapsed into the pool.

*BEEP! BEEP! BEEP!* "Clear the pool, everyone out of the pool!" Everyone stops and stares in shock as Jay blew his whistle and jumped off an extremely high chair near the pools edge.

"Steven, grab the board he's going down!" Jay yells as he sprints vigorously towards the end of the pool. *BEEEEEEEEEEEEEP!*

# SPLASH

"Everyone out of the pool... All MOD's and Directors to the pool deck immediately" Reported Steven over the radio. As he heard the response

"We are on our way" He grabbed a bright orange bag labeled "AED" off of a hook located at the front pool entrance and continued his sprint towards the lifeguard. Just as Steven grabbed the board Jay jumped off of one leg into the water... ***SPLASHHHHHHHHHHHHHHHHHH!!!***

Jay's mind went blank again, this time he felt completely different, as he looked around he realised that he could see very clearly under the water with his eyes open, it was 20/20 clear vision which is not supposed to happen. For a human. He felt like his eyes were huge and he could see everything. He felt bigger than he ever has before. As he looked down he realized that he could not see his feet, not because the water was murky, it was because he didn't have any from his eyesight. Instead he focused his eyes on what was there... a tale.

This made him start panicking, he then looked at his hands and realized that they were fins and no fingers. He felt his mouth was significantly wide. He raised one of what he thought was his hands and put it to his teeth. They were very large and sharp. Jay began to freak out, and began to look all around. He emerged from the water to see everyone staring at him. He quickly checked his teeth. When he did this he realized that his hand was an actual hand and he had normal sized teeth.

Relieved, Jay dove back down to the bottom of the pool. On his way down he realized that his fins and tail came back as soon as he submerged again. Not desiring to fail the drill and worse to let one of Hines' staff drown. He quickly wrapped one arm around Sam's chest and jumped up from the bottom of the pool, getting him to the surface of the water and placing him on the red lifeguard tube. Jay looked at Coach Hines, the coach nodded.

"Alright, let's do some review," Hines said. Leading everyone to the front end of the pool.

# SPLASH

Jay, still panicking on the inside, looked down as half of his body was submerged under water. He still saw his tale but the rest of his body was normal. *"Am I ...... a shark? Maybe it was the french toast... I knew that tasted too good. But if that's the case then wouldnt everybody be turning into animals?"* Mr. Worthy's words appeared in his head again. It is in the moment of your greatest struggles and triumphs that you will discover who you really are."

***

Meanwhile, back at Kye's camp Kye was getting ready to run a very competitive race. The instructor was timing them aiming to improve times on the 10,000 Freeflow swim. As Kye stepped up on the racing block he began to feel a little strange as he was experiencing a strong case of Deja Vu.

Whenever Kye felt like this, he always started talking to himself out loud, murmuring things to himself to try and figure out why he is experiencing that particular feeling. Mr. Hines had even done his due diligence with setting up the camp to go as far as hiring announcers, extra racers to create a real race environment. The announcer walked over and sat down at the white table with the speaker phone in front of her.

"OK, for our first race we have the 10,000 freeflow swim. For this race we have: JY, GR, ST, and KN.

All racers swimming please step up! All swimmers take your mark, Get set...." All the swimmers bent down, crouched and leaned forward. *BEEP!* The swimmers jumped off of the long starting block. Kye dove into the pool, as he approached the surface of the water the pool seemed to open up, the water began to get darker, and darker. The water began to split to the side. *AHHHHHHHHHHHHHHHHHHH! *SPLAAAAAAASSSSSHHHHHHHH.*

Kye's mind seemed to go completely blank. He felt like his body was growing extremely small, but he felt strong. He began to swim up to the surface in a diagonal motion, he stopped swimming upward towards the surface when he realized that his arms that he was using to swim weren't arms at all. Well they were but they were not human, instead they were short and stubby, about half of the size of his normal arm length.

They had little mini spikes on them and his fingers were more like claws. For some strange reason, Kye kept swimming more than likely due to the adrenaline. He really wanted to improve his time. Kye continued to keep swimming, finishing his time at 53 minutes and 32 seconds. When the race was over he put his hands on the deck in a tiresome fashion and rested his head on them relieved to know that they were actually hands.

*"Good job! You shaved an entire two minutes off of your record. Wow! that was... Incredible. Kye, how did you do that?"* The coach asked, looking at him, she was blushing red. Her face read that she was impressed.

*"I have no idea, how did I do that?"* Mumbled Kye under his breath.

*Kye took off his goggles off of the top of his head and intentionally let them go under water eventually sinking to the bottom of the pool. C'mon, man hop out. We're gonna switch soon a swimmer said to him while he hopped out the pool himself.*

*"Hold on, I dropped my goggles."* Kye said.

Kye swam down under water and realized that he was back to this claw creature again, this is just weird. He thought to himself. He looked at his hands and clenched them multiple times and felt his head, he could feel that his head also had spikes on it.

He looked down at the bottom of the pool at his goggles that were about 15 feet down. He looked up at the clock from inside of the water and saw that the swim clock read 2:03:03. He took a deep breath and swam down to the bottom of the pool, picked up the goggles and bounced up from the bottom of the pool like a rocket ship. Woosh!! He came flying out of the water and landed on the deck on his feet "Wooooah!" Kye said, looking around with really wide eyes.

Luckily the rest of his group was away on one of the far corners of the pool going over review and looking at times. He looked at the clock and saw that it read 2:03:05. On average the fastest swimmer including the fast Olympic gold medalist himself could only travel down to the bottom of a 15 foot pool and all the way back up in the matter 7-9 seconds or so but somehow Kye had managed to do it in 2. He looked down at his hands as he was standing there on the pool deck. They were completely human.

The sky seemed to have gained its darker shade as the sky lessoned its channels of light. The students' switched stations three times so all of the students would have a chance at all of the career practices for the day. *DOOM*!! The thunder raced the lighting around the surrounding mountains in a derby but for some reason the thunder could never seem to catch the lighting. It is more on the good side that it didn't because that would mean bad news and the race would be over. Violent rain began to pour down on the students' one drop after another.

Mr. Hines blew his whistle very loud to get all of the students and instructors attention. Somehow, he was mildly successful over the wind and the loud sounds of thunder (the thunder still losing). He motioned for the class to come over to the main section of the campus which was a big open area that had a big concrete entry near the main doors next to the Olympic sized swimming pool that had the octopus emblem. The class came over to Mr. Hines soaking wet and they gathered around him.

*"Ok, Listen up. I know you are all soaking wet but after all this sunny Cedorport. You shall be fiiiine. How was career practice? We will all talk about it shortly, along with the question of the day I have for you...*

*Mongoose VS. A Snake, who wins in that fight? Think about it, we talk about it in our closing discussion. Buuuut for right now, remember when*

*I said that we would have a life skills session in camp... Here it is. "Mike and Mikay please step forward. You two are first. Everyone else please take 5 steps back. There stood Mike, Mikay and Mr. Hines all stood in the middle of the dirt walkway, the class stood in a circle around them. A sliding hard grey brick wall that the class didn't even know was present opened up to the Los Aqui dessert retracting into the wall adjacent to it. A jeep-like vehicle with no roof or doors came strolling in like some kind of extradition wild nature tour.*

*Your scenario is this: You are a manager at a wild animal nature resort. The resort has just closed for the day. You get alerted that the last vehicle tour vehicle is just returning from filling up from the gas station that is across the desert. You open up the gate but before you can close the gate, the button on your remote is stuck. I have the remote right here. You do not have an extra remote, you do not have extra batteries because your next shipment isn't here till Tuesday.*

*OH, and by the way. Everyone say Hi Tachi"* He said looking up at the girl in the driver's seat of the vehicle.

*"HIIIIIII TAAACHII"* The class said loudly.

*"THIS is my daughter, my daughter Tachi. She is 12, but studies abroad at a university in Mexico."* Ms. Till's jaw dropped hearing the information.

 *"She is home for the summer, she will be our tour driver who is just returning from grabbing gas from the station.... There's more... her tour vehicle has just lost its power. Your objective is to solve the issue someway somehow..... Ready. To give you guys a little bit more encouragement, every week or two... We will run one scenario, I call these impossible scenarios. If you successfully solve the scenario for the week then you automatically get chosen as one of the five to come work for me during the school year. It's a valuable opportunity to have a prestigious employment position that you can hold on to during your college years. OK, I'm done talking... GO."*

# SPLASH

Mike and Mikay started looking for some clues, they tried to manually close the gate but it wouldn't budge. When they went back to the vehicle to lift the hood. A sound that sounded distantly familiar made them pause what they were doing. They turned around and began peering through the droplets of rain.

As the figure became closer they realized that their notion of their current reality was now haunted by their past. The evil war wolves of the Aqui desert were now upon them. Two of them. They came strolling in as the class began to get frightened. Everyone became quiet as a mouse. The panic that compared to the bus scene was terrifically lessened due to the fact that they were now out in the open and not trapped on a confined bus.

"Here... is your other variable..." Mr. Hines said as he eyeballed one of the wolves as they walked right past him.

"I will tell you this, my daughter is a first degree black Belt in taekwondo, aikido and wing Chun, she is highly capable of defending herself. And yes. That includes against wolves but nevertheless if you let one of these crazy wolves even lay a piece of fur on her then you will be removed from my camp, no exceptions." Mr. Hines said. As important as his last statement was, a great amount of uncertainty of comprehension from the students was at play. Especially when wild starving wolves are at play.

Mike and Mikay stood there confused and afraid. They came close together to game plan. When they broke from the two person huddle they began to creep slowly towards the vehicle. When they got right up on the vehicle the two began to push the vehicle in reverse back towards the gate. The look on Mr. Hines face was priceless confusion.

"Ok, so push my daughter out of the gate where there are more wolves. Very clever" Mr. Hines said very low in a voice where only he could hear himself.

Mike and Mikay left the vehicle sitting outside of the open gate along with the rain. The two of them picked up sticks that they saw on the ground. They looked at each other to signal their readiness. They then charged at the wolves swinging their sticks, the wolves' contered the attack, grabbed the two sticks and snapped them in half with their teeth.

Two huddled up again, they then walked around to gain a vantage point behind the wolves. For some odd reason, the wolves didn't turn around; they kept sniffing the ground. Although sniffing was less threatening than snarling, the wolves did not appear to be any less frightening. Mikay was getting frustrated, he ran up on the wolf and grabbed his tail from behind. *"Ouch!!"* Mikay yelled loud enough for Texas to hear him. The wolf had turned around with a blink of an eye and slashed Key in the eye with one of its claws.

Mikay began to bleed covering up his eye and he started to walk away stumbling through the rain with 20/0 vision.

*"Medic!"* Mr. Hines yelled.

A lady wearing all white scrubs walked out from behind the group. Unbenounced to them, she was there the entire time. She ran towards Mikay leading him off towards the healing station back inside the building. *"Ok, scenario over"* Mr. Hines clicked a button on a remote that he had behind his back. The wolves ran out of the gate down the road that they originally arrived. The vehicle stayed where it was sitting. The gate then closed after.

*"He will be okay, I promise... Mike, this is a two person scenario only son, so please step back with your peers. NOW, understand this, this scenario is a newly designed scenario to ensure that you don't magically reach out to a CC alumni to try and figure it out. But even with that being said, I have tested this scenario 100 times, and it is safe proof. There are many many ways to attempt the scenario, 5 of those ways include getting hurt, or worse. Of course those 5 lead to a failure. Out of the rest of the 95. There is only one way possible to solve this, to solve this you*

*must secure the resort, extract danger and secure staff members. That is all I will tell you, if I tell you all five ways to get yourself hurt, then you are surely not going to do those things. So, that is why I say that this is a LIFE lesson. Sometimes in life, you must go through things and either suffer the consequences or achieve victory and oftentimes one comes before the other. Well…. Actually, there are two possible ways to beat the scenario buuuuuuuuut I don't think anyone will go that far."*

*Okay up next we have Tammy and……. Donald"* Stated Mr. Hines.

Donald and Yammy stepped forward. Donald was a short stubby boy with a mullet, forget bringing sexy back, he was bringing Mullets back.

"*Ready, go!*" Mr. Hines said.

The two of them ran to both sides of the gate stomping their feet in the mud. As soon as the gate finished opening, the two of them ran and closed the fenced gate that their bus originally came in. They ran back to the middle of the walkway where the vehicle was sitting and started staring at Mr. Hines with a slight smirk on their faces. Mr. Hines smiled back but said nothing.

Donald looked back and forth between Mr. Hines and the gate, waiting for him to say something, but still Hines said nothing. Donald kept up the awkward staring contest until his eyes stopped on the gate. He saw 4 more dots. Even though he expected this, he couldn't take his eyes off of what was about to happen next. The wolves came sprinting towards the gate, but that was the issue. They kept sprinting, and unlike the last time, they didn't slow down.

The mud that they were kicking up from the rain was a non factor. The wolves sprinted up to about five feet away from the gate, they then jumped up really high, then landed over the gate. The gate was at least 6 feet. The students starred in amazement, although this made the wolves look even scarier. A jumping war wolf is far scarier than a grounded one.

The two students momentarily stood still. After they talked they decided to go outside of the gate. At this moment, Mr. Hines stopped them. *"STOP! I do have to let you know, if you go outside of this gate, I can't necessarily help you because you are not inside the campgrounds."*

Mr. Hines said yelling at them over the loud rain. Although Tammy found this response very weird. He also did not take a chance because he knew that he should not take a chance due to the fact that he thought about what would happen to Yammy if something happened to him. After all, they lived by themselves.

Their parents stayed in Texas but they sent money to the twins every month for their living expenses. Tammy backed away, and thought of a different plan.

*"How about we use our same plan but do it inside of the gates."* Tammy said, looking at Donald.

*"Then we... Brilliant!"* Donald said. They both ran in opposite sections against the walls of the camp, Tammy was on the side near the pool and Donald was on the opposite side. They signaled to each other by nodding.

*"Hooooooooowllll!!"* They put their hands on the side of their mouths and started howling like wolves. The wolves then started creeping up on them slowly. They both climbed the wall that they were near the gate entry. Surprisingly, they both made it up to the top of the wall but after Donald reached the top he lost his footing while he was busy focusing on the wolf that was at the bottom of his wall chomping his jaws.

Apparently these kind creatures did not appreciate being fooled or mocked. Donald lost his footing then slipped off the wall... ***CRACK!!!*** Donald hit the bottom extremely hard.

*"Ooooooch!"* Donald yelled. *"Scenario over!"* Mr. Hines yelled. He pressed the button and the wolves ran back outside the gate and his daughter along with them and the gate began to close. Tammy saw

this very incident happen right in front of his eyes and he hopped down landing in mud which felt like quick sand, he sprinted towards Donald. He helped him up and the two of them walked over to Mr. Hines

"Hold on son, let me see, is it... oh yeah, it's broken, Tammy can you walk him to the other nurse, you will see she is inside helping Mrs. Sacrude" Mr. Hines said.

"BROKKEN!!??" Donald said. The two of them walked towards the building. Let me just say, that is NOT one of the ways I calculated that you can get hurt. BUUUT we learn something new everyday don't we.

"OK Next up!" Mr. Hines yelled.

A few more unsuccessful attempts were made until Mr. Hines decided to end the scenario for the night.

"Ok, let's head over for discussion, we will pick this up monday, you have until the end of the week to try and figure this out... and trust me, you will need that long." Mr. Hines said. Miraculously, there was a giant tent that Mr. Sidious set up near the field that they were headed to. Once everyone gathered underneath the tent. The smell of wet cotton and wet hair was everywhere. No one seemed to comment on it though.

"Ok, tomorrow is a little different schedule wise so we will have a little discussion of what we thought about career practice, but for now. Let's talk about the question of the day. Mongoose or a snake, who wins in that fight?" Mr. Hines said lighting the fire identical to the fre from the previous day.

"I'm gonna say a snake because sake is so quick and venomous." Tammy said.

"Ok, I like your thinking, anyone else?" Hines said.

"Yeah, snake" a bunch of other students blurted out.

# SPLASH

"So everyone thinks a snake would win huh? Ok, not bad. It's a common sense answer. Let's do this, we are going to try a little something different, a change in scenario if you will. Here we have two creatures. One has the ability to produce poison and unleash it into its victim's skin and pathway, it is also lightning fast and can swallow an entire human being and it kills 5 human adults. It also listens with its tongue and can weigh up to 550 pounds. ON the other side we have a creature that is lightning quick, has cells that are capable of rejecting poison. Can only weigh up to eight pounds, giggles at a high pitch tone when they sense danger, and they have non retractable claws... Who wins this battle?" Mr. Hines asked

The class started to murmer to themselves. *"That is a pretty good match up!"* Someone said,

The class became quiet. *"Well, I think that the second one because it can reject the poison that the first can deliver... Yeah i mean, it may be smaller and a little on the weak side but because of the fact that it's so quick and agile, all it has to do to win this fight is to move around like a boxer, don't get bit and attack when the first one least expects it."* Yammy said. *"Like Ali!"* Someone yelled out. Jay turned around and stuck his hand out.

*"Ok! Do we all agree on option number two?"* Hines said.

The class agreed. Mr. Hines put his hands up in the air, the palms of his hands facing himself. He flipped his right hand, option *1 was the snake, he then flipped his other hand. Option 2 was the mongoose."* Hines said.

The class was in shock, laughter and signs of disbelief went off in the group.

*"See that? See what we did there? We took to facts about two different creatures and we compared them without knowing what they were and we made a decision using facts on the information given to us. This is called objective thinking. This is also a critical skill in life. We will*

practice this because you can apply this in everything, and sometimes it's just better to hear the facts than to simply know what the cover is because it's hard to be objective when you know what or who the variables are. You heard snake and mongoose and you immediately thought how dangerous a snake is and how cute and small a mongoose is. Well that cute little mongoose is a cold blooded killer, stone cold. Mongooses kill hundreds of snakes per year. Think I'm playin'? I'm not. A mongoose is one of the snakes' only predators, so what he does, you will all see... The mongoose he goes from being all cute and cuddly to this savage of a monster, he gets serious, his eyebrows get really low and he waits for the snake to attack then he zooms in there really quick and goes for the kill. We will watch the video tomorrow then we talk about how that battle plays into life at the beginning of the week. But for now, class good job today, way to give 100% today, I saw beast mode come out in all of you ladies and gentlemen."

Alright, enough said class dismissed. Go get some rest." Mr. Hines said

The class walked out of the tent and began to head towards the main entrance, the rain was still present. The pitter-patter gave it away for the students.

Sokki began to feel a very familiar feeling in her stomach. She couldn't quite pinpoint what the feeling was. The skies in sunny Cedar Point were still throwing down rain. The sun had just gone down...

"Hey Sokki come on," a voice said from afar.

"I'm coming, one second. I'm just going to put this stuff away then text my mom" She said.

She grabbed the two bright yellow kickboards that were sitting on the pool deck. And placed them in the shack near the building. She walked back to the pool deck. Unplugged the time clock that was sitting on the edge of the pool deck, walked over to the edge of the deck and picked it up. She pulled out her phone and began texting my mother. *"Hey Mom, the first few... At that moment I felt two hands on each of my shoulders and all of a sudden she started to tilt, she lost her balance and fell into the water. **SLASH!!!***

Sokki was extremely confused. The moment she hit the water she felt like her body became electrocuted, she felt a pulsing shock that seemed to continue. She looked down at the bottom of the pool and she saw her legs but only they weren't her legs. It resembled a tail. There were electro waves traveling up and down her. Did I just get electrocuted? If that's the case then why do I feel so calm... wait a second, this is from my dream.

These thoughts crept in Sokki's mind, she quickly swam to the surface, when she did the entire pool was raving with electricity pulses scattering throughout it. She swam to the side of the pool, lifted herself out, when she looked down at her legs, they had returned to human form but her veins had not. They were blue, as the crystal clear pool water.

# CHAPTER 18

The skies had completely darkened and the thunderstorm seemed to have taken its place among the city, striking the fields all around camp. Almost as if it were waiting for the students to go inside. The grand ball festival continued along the mountains. Well they did exactly that, everyone went inside along with the staff, and Mr. Hines himself.

"Dad, I'm fine! Really! I have done it before, your way too over protective" Tachi said as she stormed off.

Ms. Till was standing around the corner from them unharmful eavesdropping.

"I'm so... Sorry, I couldn't help but overhear" She said as she stepped out from behind the wall

"I don't know what it's like to have a daughter, but I imagine the work life balance must be a little tough, but from looking at her I can tell you and your wife must have done a good job." Ms. Till said with a slight smirk on her face.

"Wife? No... I'm not married, me and her mother separated when she was 5 years old" he said.

"Oh my goodness... I'm so sorry, I didn't know".

"Don't be sorry, It's ok you didn't know....But yeah it has been a crazy uphill battle since then, I will say though, I think one of the hardest parts about raising a child from a split household is the truth that you involve the child in... I mean that's something that I struggled with and still do till this day because in all reality you wanna protect your child from getting hurt but at the same time you want them to know the truth. We were a little fortunate because she just came to us one day and told us, she goes mommy and daddy, I know you two are getting a divorce.. I just wanna say it's ok, i'm not mad at either of you. I love you both equally.

*Seriously, it was like something outta a movie. I never thought I would raise a daughter like this but I mean look how she turned out. I am truly blessed because it could have turned out worse. That's why I don't know what is worse, to grow up in a household where your parents are separated or to have had both of your parents but one passes away. That's why I say, man that Jay kid is really special because HE is truly remarkable, he is going to be something one day. I mean look at his circumstances, his mother died in a terrible accident and he is still one of the top students in his school. And his father, geesh! I can't even imagine what he has gone through, not only raising his son but raising his sister's son too... Those kids, Jay, Kye and Sokki are all special"* Mr. Hines said, staring at Ms. TIll.

*"Oh, trust me. You have no idea! We are just waiting for them to realize their full potential"* She said, smiling at him. Mr. Hines, smiled back looking at her with a clarity in his eyes, for a moment the two of them connected until the silent stare was interrupted.

*"Hey you two comin? It's coffee time!"* Mr. Worthy said, looking at the two.

*"Yeah, c'mon let's go..."* Mr. Hines said he held his elbow out in hopes that Ms. Till would take it. *"We shall".* She said as she hooked elbows with him. They walked into the coffee room that was located near the front entrance on the left when you entered the building. Inside the room all of the instructors and trainers that Mr. Hines hired were in there with lounge chairs, TV and most importantly... Coffee.

Mrs. Noble looked at Ms. Till with an excited look as the two came strolling, linking elbows. They soon let go, splitting to opposite sides of the room to converse with their colleagues. This was all manifesting itself while the students in their respective halls, getting ready for bed.

*"Hey, um... do you know where Sokki went??"* Jay asked Yammy, all schizophrenic like looking around like the fins were trying to find him. He was scratching his neck with his eyes really big.

"Ok, why does everyone keep asking me where Sokki is? I know she is my roommate but dang?? She is your best friend. Look darlin, all I know is that I saw her put her head down, and speed walk upstairs like she was trying to be in the genius world record book for speed walking or somethin. Do YOOOU know where Kye is? AHA! Until then, I don't want to hear it." Yammy said with her chin high and her arms crossed.

"Whatever, hey look if you see her can you tell her I need to speak to her ASAP MRN. She'll know what that means." Jay said, still bug eyed.

"Ok, ok, geeesh. Dude you ok? Because uh ya look like you're strung out on a... That stuff that those boys do in texas, the white stuff. They put it on these dirty tables, get a straw and sniff it...yeah that stuff." Yammy said.

"Drugs are stupid, did you never take D.A.R.E?" Jay said, looking at Yammy which had a confusing face on. "D stands for DON'T question Jay if he has done drugs because he has not, and he never will, A stands for stop with your nasty Yammy, wammy, flammy, ATTITUDE and N stands for.. Oh wait no R stands for I will RESPECT those who are smarter than me like Jay and E stands for I will EDUCATE myself on Crack cocaine before I ask Jay if he is taking it. All of which you. Are. Not. Doing..."Jay said whispering on the side of Yammy's ear.

Yammy's jaw was near the floor, or at least it felt like it to her because of how shocked she was to hear it come out of Jay's mouth, she could see Sokki, maybe even Kye, even though she didn't know Kye well but Jay is the last person she expected to lash out like that.

"Okay, I don't know what or who crawled into your bacon this morning but you're looking at me like you either want to stand here and keep yelling at me or like you want to eat me because for some reason, your teeth look sharper today and omg I feel like they're growing... i'm gonna go find ya friend and deliver your message sir vampire." Yammy said, she look frightened, she turned around and started skipping stairs just to get to the top faster.

Jay knew that Yammy was someone who got scared easily but he remembered what happened to him in the pool earlier so he ran to the restroom to look at his teeth. He looked at his teeth in the mirror and they seemed to have become really narrow and pointy almost…. Sharp. Jay stood there examining his teeth until he reminded himself of the fact that he didn't know where either of his two best friends were when normally they would be together.

He walked out of the bathroom, his mouth closed shut, as he passed other stranglers in the hallway he did his best not to make eye contact with anyone. He ran up the stairs to the boys' corridor of the house and zoomed inside his room 05 and closed the door. He put his back to the inside of the door and he let himself slide down hitting the ground with a thump. He put his head down in his hands with his elbows on his knees. What in the world is going on?? He thought to himself, I must have been drugged maybe Yammy was right, why me though? This is some kind of hallucinogenic of some sort.

When he opened his eyes, his vision was blurry but he still thought that his eyes were playing tricks on him. To his surprise he saw something moving up and down, he soon realized that it was Kye. Kye was doing push ups but he was doing them one handed. He was counting them.

"82…83…84….85….86….87" he said.

"Kye?" Jay said, assuring himself that is actually Kye and not an imposter.

"99,100!" Kye said. He looked over at Jay

"Hey buddy! Finally something that makes sense, how are you? You don't look so good".

"I've been drugged," Jay said.

"What no you haven't, stop, you're being silly..." Kye said then he paused, he had a flashback to what happened to him in the water earlier.

"...WAAAAIT! Hold up, why are you saying that? Like Jay I need to know now because if you have been drugged then I might have been drugged as well." Kye said.

Jay's head along with his attention shot up quickly. *"Wait what? Why what happened to you?"* Jay said.

*"I feel so weird, I mean well I feel great but I feel weird"* Kye Said.

*"Go on......"* Jay said

*"Well.... Why in the world am I able to do one handed push ups, you know for as long as you've known me I have always wanted to do one handed push ups. I've tried them before but I have never been able to do them and I just did one hundred! Like straight without stopping... and that's freaky"* Kye said.

*"That's true,"* Jay said while scratching his head.

*"But something else also happened earlier... in the water,"* Kye said.

*"Ok, wait what the heck happened?"* Jay said anxiously.

*"Geesh! So I was getting ready to race, and it was so weird because I felt like I had been through this exact same scenario before... in a dream. I was getting ready to do the ten thousand freestyle flow to shave off some of my time. I got on the starting block, they blew the horn and I dove in like normal but when I actually got closer to the water it seemed to have opened up a little and it just kept getting darker, and darker and Darker. But this is where my dream stopped. When I actually became submerged under the water, I just felt really strong but I felt like five times smaller. I looked at my hands and they looked like they were CLAWS instead of my actual hands. I really didn't know what to do, so I kept swimming without paying attention. I finished my race and I ended*

up shaving like two minutes off of my record. C'mon bro you know that's hard to do. SO when I went back under to retrieve my goggles I realized that my entire body was covered in like these spikes of some sort. Jay, bro it was so weird. Like I felt my face and it wasn't my face almost... like I was a... Animal. When I tell you it was weird it was weird I don't know if it's because I didn't get much sleep or what but the whole thing was just really freaky." Kye said, pacing back and forth in the room near the door.

Jay's mouth was wide open and his eyes were incredibly wide, Jay appeared to almost be a little frozen.

"Dude, what's up? You ok?" Kye asked.

Jay's face became covered in relief. *"Thank goodness I am not alone!!"* Jay said.

"Uhhh, what do you mean?" Kye said.

*"A very similar thing happened to me!!"* Jay said, staring up at Kye.

Kye froze from hearing this and he immediately sat down on the wall that ran on the outside of the bathroom. He began looking at Jay with an intense stare in his eye.

"WHAAAAAT???" Kye said.

"Yeah, so I was in the lifeguard training and it was tough mind you, so we go through all of the skills and drills then we finally get to the point where we are all testing scenarios by putting it all together. And that's why this is crazy, because you just said that you had a dream that was similar to this. Bro, I kid you not. I had a dream on the last day of school before I woke up. That's why when I was daydreaming in school, I remember because you tried to snap me out of it. I told you that I had a dream that I was a lifeguard? Well..... the dream must have been about camp because right before we were about to run the scenario I knew what was going to happen and it almost made my stomach feel a little sick. The victim, he fell in the pool and started sinking. When I jumped *into the pool and submerged I felt really big and strong, but my eyesight was like dialed in to Thirty-Thirty it felt like, I looked down and I saw a fin. Not legs, not arms but fins! Then I tried to feel my face and it felt pointy. It was literally the strangest thing that has happened to me yet."* Jay said,

"Ok, now I am a little freaked out because it happened to you too. Have we been drugged? Nooo.... There's no way." Kye said, looking around on the floor as if it had the answers that he was looking for.

"You're right, that would be silly, oh my gosh!" Jay said.

"What?" Kye said

"I snapped on Yammy, I should probably apologize, I just feel this... like adrenaline. Man, if this is what it's like to have anxiety, no thankyou don't sign me up". Jay said laughing.

"I was thinking like maybe it was something that we ate!" Jay said.

"I thought that exact same thing earlier. Because I mean what else could it be, especially if it's just me and you. I know everyone is not going through this, because SOMEONE would've said something when we were on the field" Kye said. And we all ate the same thing, I mean no wonder that french toast tasted so good" Kye replied laughing back.

"Knock, knock, knock!" Let me in, it's Sokki" she said from outside the door. Jay stood up and opened the door. Kye still sat there on the floor. Sokki came in the room and slammed the door, she had on a hoodie and shades on. This appearance made Jay and Kye look at each other in confusion.

She began pacing back and forth with her head down, Kye stood up and proceeded to look back and forth at her and Jay. Jay stood in Sokki's walkway and stopped her from her pacing. She then looked up at Jay.

"Tell us what's going on?" Jay said to Sokki, looking at her in her shades. He lifted her shades up and took them off of her head simultaneously pulling her hood off of her head. She looked at him in his eyes...

"Dannng, what happened to your hair girl?!" Kye said, looking at Sokki's hair in agreement. Jay set the shades on the desk that was in the corner of the room.

Kye knew something was wrong because Sokki didn't reply to him with some kinda rude remark.

"Everything I touch I end up shocking! Mostly water. Why am I electrifying the water?? That doesn't make sense. Then I turned into some kind of crazy creature underwater! I was practically sparking in the shower! By my calculations, that is not supposed to happen in any way. Not according to the natural laws of motion." She said.

Jay and Kye looked at each other with a shocked expression on their faces. Everything else that Sokki was saying did not connect to their brain.

"Wait, stop!" Jay said to interrupt Sokki's rambling,

"What??" Sokki said.

"What did you say about turning into a creature?" Jay asked.

"You're probably not going to believe me if I told you... I was putting some stuff up from the pool deck then I fell in the water, when I did, I felt like my entire body was electrocuted but the electromagnetic pulses didn't affect me. Almost as if I shocked the pool then when I looked down, I didn't have my normal body. It was long and slippery. Ugh!!" She said.

She observed the two staring at each other once again.

"What?? You think I'm crazy??" She asked them while she brushed her hair to the back of her head.

"Umm, something strange is going on" Jay said while he walked to the door to lock it.

"Sokki, similar things happened to both me AND Kye today, that's why we have these crazy looks on our faces," he said.

Sokki cocked her head back in shock.

They could tell that she thought that she was the only one who had strange events today. Jay and Kye explained to her their experiences and how they both thought that something strange was happening to them.

"So, you're meaning to tell that we all had something weird all happen to us in one day, yeah somethings up... Do you think it has something to do with that Octopus thingy by the front pool?" Sokki asked.

"No, I don't think so. I mean we weren't swimming in that pool." Kye said.

Ok, and you had no headache right?" Sokki asked Kye,

"No," Kye said.

"And your hand wasn't shaking today?" Sokki asked Jay.

"No," Jay responded.

"And I didn't really have a crazy anxiety attack and I wasn't sweating like crazy. Something is really weird."

"I think we need to go and see if we are still turning into these animals and two, we need to see what we are turning into.... What?" Jay said as he noticed Kye and Sokki looking at him.

"Umm uh dude, your teeth are freaking pointy" Kye said

*Yeah, you ok?"* Sokki asked him.

"*Uh, not again!*" Jay said. Frustrated, he ran to the bathroom to examine his teeth. Afterwards, he then walked out of the bathroom and looked at Kye and Sokki that were still standing in the middle of the floor.

"*It's been happening so much ever since I left the pool and I turned into whatever the heck I turned into!!!*" Jay said.

"*Same here, Sokk*i said, I *literally have been shocking everything I touch until I came to your room. I don't know what in the world is going on."* Sokki said.

"*Kye did one-hundred one handed pushups without stopping!!"* Jay said

"*Thank you, because if you didn't say it, I would have!"* Kye laughed.

"*I know that's why I beat you to the punch*" Jay replied chukling.

"*Whaaaat?!! One hundred pushups with one hand, I am pretty sure there is a word for that and it's called steroids*" Sokki said.

"*But that is just it, everything in my body just feels ridiculously strong. I broke the door handle when I went into the bathroom earlier*" Kye said. They all stood there and looked at each other for a moment in silence without a word.

Finally Jay broke the silence. *"What about if we asked if we could go out into the pool a little early and practice our skills that we learned yesterday before anybody gets in the pool? That way we dont look suspicious and we could finally get to the bottom of this.*

"*That is actually a pretty good idea,*" Sokki said.

"*Yes, it is! I'm down!"* Kye said.

"Let's figure this out together!" Jay said. He put his hand up high in the middle of them

"Together!" Kye said as he put his hand on Jay's looking him and Sokki in the eye

"Together!" Sokki said as she did the same as the other two.

Together standing there in their infamous huddle with their hands connected they stood there ... 1....2...3 "Us!" They all said in unison.

"...I'm sorry Sokki, your hair does look like J-Lo's on monster in law!" Kye said, anticipating that she was going to retaliate.

"You know what?!" Sokki said she grabbed a pillow and wacked Kye with it. *WHACK!*

Jay came to his rescue and returned a pillow to Sokki's head. Starting a full blown pillow fight, Laughing all night in their room like they were back in Los Aqui.

The students soon fell asleep in their dorms after a loud night of tired excitement. The Thunderstorm continued to bear louder and louder around the camp. At moments waking a few students up at times. One could suppose that the thunder buddy system did not apply to Los Aqui students

***

Soon morning came to the camp and awoke the students out of their accoma, similar to the previous day. The smell of freshly made food came creeping through the halls like a burglar. Noise seemed to have filled the halls, but Jay's room was quiet. There slept the three amigos, they slept like they worked, hard. It wasn't until they heard a knock that they awoke from their luxurious sleeping session.

*KNOCK, KNOCK, KNOCK!*

"Wake up time for breakfast!" Mr. Worthy said as he went strolling through the halls.

Sokki was the first to move, she raised her head up with sleepy squinty eyes and messy hair. She began looking around all confused. She saw Jay sleeping on the floor while she was the one sleeping in his bed. She took her two pillows from behind her and chucked one at Kye and one at Jay, to her surprise they both raised their heads up and sat up matching the tired squinting that Sokki had.

"Breakfast is ready," She said. Sokki quickly put her hair in a ponytail and stood up from the bed, and walked out of the room.

Jay and Kye were a tad slower than Sokki getting out of the bed. Once they did, they traveled downstairs to find everyone sitting and enjoying their meal. The tiresome mood in the room was sensible. Jay and Kye looked around to find Sokki already sitting down at the table eating.

They walked over to her and sat down across from her.

"Ok, how did you get here so fast!?" Jay asked.

"I walked here," Sokki said, sipping her orange juice.

"I mean... you had to get dressed then come here, and you came from our room so I'm just wondering how you beat us." Jay said.

"Well, you know that common stigma about women taking a long time to get ready?" Sokki asked. They both nodded.

'Well, Im changing that." Sokki said. I'm the exception to that rule. You two should be embarrassed" She said, still sipping her orange juice.

"So how did everyone sleep?" Kye asked, ignoring her comment.

"Good, I'm still a little tired," Jay said.

"*Same, I wish I had some coffee.*" Sokki said. A chef reached in front of Jay and Kye and set their plate filled with yummy foods in front of them. The plate had oatmeal with raisins and brown sugar. There was a banana on the side of their bowl. Jay and Kye began to dig into their much needed breakfast.

The three sat there and ate in silence for a while along with their peers.

"*On a side note, we need to ask Mr. Hines if we can practice after we eat.*"

"*Im done*" Sokki said,

"*You must just be racing us today,*" Jay said.

Soon after, the three of them finished eating and located Mr. Hines standing at the end of the table with the rest of the teachers. They placed their garbage in the trash and headed towards the teachers with Jay leading the pack. "*Mr. Hines, we were wondering if the three of us could go practice in the pool today and work on some skills and techniques, we won't be long. We really just need a few minutes, a half hour maybe at the max if that*" Jay asked.

Mr. Hines was quiet for a moment as were the rest of the teachers that were looking and listening to what Jay was proposing.

Mr. Worthy looked and Ms. Till and Ms. Till looked back at him then looked behind her to make sure the other teachers were listening.

"*Mr. Cruz, I designed this camp with lifestyle choices in mind. I believe that one should never work on Sunday because it is a day of spiritual reflection, peace and rest.... What do you think?*" He asked, looking at the other teachers.

"*I think that would be good, it is probably wise to let the young lads practice, after all, in doing this they may find something new about themselves that they have never known before.*" Mr. Worthy said with a strange face. The rest of the teachers began to nod and Ms. Noble put her hand on the front of her face and smirked.

Mr. Hines found his response a little strange.

*"Well... I suppose sacrifices have to be made, after all to be great demands everything from you. Very well!"* Mr. Hines said.

*"Yes!"* the three said excitedly.

*"BUT after you go through the tour, we have the camp tour today. Then after you will be allowed to go out there for a little, I don't believe I need a lifeguard for you three, you seemed to have it together in the water pretty well."* Mr. Hines said.

*"Thank you sir!"* Jay said.

*"Alright, everyone outside!"* Mr. Hines yelled. The students all piled to the doors that led outside the front of the dining hall.

After everyone was outside, the class realized that Mr. Hines was not wearing his normal running attire, instead he was wearing jogger sweatpants and a shirt with a hood attached presenting a very comfortable look.

*"Goodmorning!"* Mr. Hines said

*"Goodmorning!"* The class responded.

*"Alright, today will be a little different. We will do our normal PT, we won't have our skills practice. Instead we will have a rest day, from this point forward I will use Sunday as a day of rest and reflection. My hope is that you all take that you all take that into your personal lives. After all, I have done it and it has really helped me with my development, not only spiritually but mentally as well. The way the brain operates, it needs a rest period, and when you take 24 hours to rest it recharges you mentally and physically and prepares you for the next week. So ideally your week really should be starting on Sunday not Monday. Start your*

*week off right, reflect so you can respond to the upcoming challenges of the week and not react to them. We'll be a little more loose on Sunday mornings so when you wake up, and come down for breakfast on Sunday, you don't need to start eating at a certain time but I do expect you to make call time for PT, so which means be out here at 9:15 AM. The latest. Anyways, back to today... We have our normal PT, then we will have a tour of the facility, show you where the library is, XYZ then you will have the rest of the day to do like i said, explore, relax and reflect. Just make sure you don't leave campus, everyone understood?"* He asked the class.

"*Yes!*" The class responded.

"*Alright, 10 laps. Jog it out, nice and easy... WAIT!*" Coach said.

The class was now staring at Mr. Hines.

"*Who decided to mess with the pool last night?*" he was in shock staring at the pool with the octopus emblem on it.

The class stared back at him in confusion unsure of what he was babbling about.

"*Why are you all acting like you have no idea what I'm talking about? Look at the pool, does anyone else notice that the water is nearly completely black, when yesterday it was nearly the cleanest pool in the state?*"

The class walked over to Mr. Hines to get a better view, the pool was foggy black with black chucks floating to the top. *"Ewww" "that's gross"* and many more disgusting remarks came from the teens.

"*So, ha-ha, who was it? If you tell me now, I will lessen your punishment*". Mr Hines remarked.

No one said a word.

"No one wants to confess, alright! We will run 20 laps every day until someone comes clean"

"Yeah no pun intended", a student blurted out.

"Very funny Mikay, now it's 25 laps for everyone, do we need to go for thirty?" Hines said as his face began to glow bright red as his chest became inflated. Beneath his big black bulky shades, his students could read his demeanor.

"GO!" he yelled

The class began jogging around the course. Meanwhile, all four teachers were sitting in a row in front of the building. In front of Mr. Hines who sat down with them.

"Jay, call it out." He yelled back at the group.

"... One!" Jay yelled.

The teachers were performing some kind of stretching routine with Mr. Hines, he was leading them in a series of different stretches. Los Aqui had its way of having its effect on the cities around it. The birds would come around and chirp their songs just like they would back in the city. Although, the chirping didn't sound like music to the people who heard it. It made sense to the birds.

"Did your daughter leave out yet?" Ms. TIll asked

"Yeah, she flew out early this morning," He responded.

"Switch" He said. The teachers switched over to the other leg they were stretching to and leaned forward.

"Seven!" Jay said, panting a little.

After three more laps, the class stopped running then they went over to the wall in the field and began leaning against it. All of the students seemed to skip the cups of water this morning. Especially Jay.

Mr. Hines left the teachers to finish stretching then headed over to the field where the students were standing.

*"Good job, let's have some MOS."*

The students squatted down against the wall with their arms out. For some odd reason, this was Jay's favorite part of PT. probably because everything and everyone was still. He began thinking about home again. He liked the idea of being away, while most students would get a little homesick, Jay loved the excitement of being independent in his own little world. Jay thought about relaxing today then something interrupted his thought process abruptly. It was the image of the kid that was standing in front of the Camp choice gates. Peering out looking at something.

This visual made Jay gain goosebumps all along his arms.

After the minutes of silence were up, the students followed Mr. Hines into the main building, grabbing some water on their way inside. They traveled into the main entrance and went around the stairs where they would pass the dining hall on the left and meet two double doors that read *"Study halls"*. Mr. Hines opened both doors and the fresh smell of books came rushing the students.

Inside, there was a hardwood floor and bookshelves were tall and matched the color of the floor. Straight ahead was a sky window that shone in on the center of the floor. At the end of the room was a theatrical stage without curtains equipped with three steps led up to the platform. On the side, there was a check out station for student's book checkout. In the middle of the floor, there were chairs and beanbags and tables for sitting and studying.

Mr. Hines turned around and walked backwards looking at the class.

"Alright class, this is the library, where you can study and read, this is not school by all means, but a lot of these books are written on topics from experts in their field, whether it was lifeguarding, national swimming champions that didn't use steroids to get ahead in their sport and many more, over there is the checkout. I do not care how many books you checkout as long as you bring it back before the end of camp. You all will be allowed to take one book home before you leave." He said.

He went over to a computer and pressed a button on the keyboard. A big projector screen came out rolling down from a base in the ceiling. When it finished retracting down a still picture of a snake and mongoose appeared on the screen.

"So, a little bit about what we were talking about yesterday. That is a black Mamba killer snake and a little mongoose. Like that mongoose is about to go up against the Kobe Bryant of snakes. The black mamba. Watch." Mr. Hines said.

The video on the screen began to play, the mongoose stood up, started circling around the killer snake quickly. The killer snake striked and tried to bite the mongoose with his fangs. The mongoose moved out of the way, and continued circling quickly. The snake tried again, and the mongoose moved out of the way again. Mr. Hines paused the video.

"You see that? What's the mongoose doing? He is moving out of the way so he can focus," he said. The video resumed.

The mongoose got really low towards the ground and started creeping; he then lunged forward and quickly bit the snake and then backed up quickly. It was so quick that the students didn't observe it.

The snake laid down out of its rising up position. The mongoose crept back to the snake looking at its limp body. Then he approached the body cautiously and grabbed it by its neck close to its face and dragged it off into the forest. The screen went black.

"Remember what I was saying about being like the mongoose when life attacks? That snake is your problem, that snake triumphs, that snake is hardship. Be tactical, then attack. Everyone understand?" Hines said.

*"Yes sir!"* the class responded back.

*"Alright, let's move on"* Mr. Hines said as he began to walk to the left of the stage inside a room that was filled with tables and bottles...

*"This here is the applied science mixing room. We have different animal species fluids in here, oxidizes and everything you need to make the complete table of elements including carbon dioxide sulfate. Also, we make aero grade equipment in here. Take a good look around because some of you will be spending a lot of extra time here"* Mr. Hines said.

Sokki began to get extremely jumpy with excitement. Hines moved his way through the crowd of students and got out of the science room. He then went around to the right side of the stage and entered into a different room that was right near the library checkout. He flicked on the lights and the room lit up. When it did, the students observed three big globes sitting in the middle of the room and maps plastered along the walls of the room.

*"This is our location district. We have state of the art equipment that allows world class knowledge of this world's location and prevents you from being directionally challenged like Mr. Cruz who thought that Cederport was next to Vegas"* Mr. Hines said. The class laughed. Jay just smirked.

*"Ok, we have one more stop before I let you all enjoy the rest of your day, follow me"* Mr. Hines said. He left the door shut and began to walk back towards the entrance of the library and proceeded up the staircase. When Mr. Hines got to the middle section where the two staircases split off there was a door. It had an electronic number pad on it. He looked behind him to make sure no one was looking then he put in a combination, *CLICK!* The sound the door made gave an

unsettling vibe to the students. ***CRRREEEEEEEEEK*** the door went as it opened fully and minds of dust brushed out.

*"Well looks like no one has been here in awhile"* Tammy said looking at the cobwebs on the side of the door henge...

"The entry of the room was completely dark, the students couldn't see a single thing. Mr. Hines still walked through the doorway expecting the students to follow. ***HSSSSSSS!*** A sound came from inside the room.

*"Woah! Uh uhhh!"* A student said jumping back terrified.

*"It's just an effect the room makes whenever you enter the room. C-mon"* Mr. Hines said...

The students followed him up a very steep staircase that led to curtains at the top. He pushed them open and light shined through. *"This is your lounge, equipped with bean bags, foosball, arcade games, board games. Something for you all to wind down when you have free time"* Hines said. The students marveled in amazement with chatter sounds and enthusiasm.

Mr. Hines walked back downstairs just before he left the exit he looked up at a ladder that was practically invisible due to the lack of light in the room.

*"Everyone hear me clearly please... None of you are allowed up there. For what's up there is not for your eyes, do I make myself crystal clear??"* Mr. Hines said.

*"Yes sir!"* The class said.

Jay stood there and stared at the staircase until someone accidentally nudged him causing his focus to shift. Mr. Hines led the students out to the middle of the house.

# SPLASH

"Alright, well that's your tour. You are free to use any part of the facility today. Enjoy the rest of the day. I and the other instructors will be wandering around. Let us know if you have any questions or need anything" Mr Hines said.

He nodded at Jay, Sokki and Kye. They knew what this meant, this meant that they were finally able to go to the pool, the thing they had been craving to do all morning.

The three of them waited until the students settled into their choice of lounge then discreetly walked outside one by one to the pool deck. The sun was shining but wasn't beating on them, there was a slight breeze, and some leaves were blowing around on the deck and around the grassy field. They looked at eachother then started taking off their running gear which had their swimsuits underneath. They walked to the edge of the pool and stared down into the sparkling blue water.

"Alright ready..." Sokki said, anticipating as though she was going to jump.

"Wait! Hold on..." Jay stood in the middle of Kye and Sokki and grabbed their hands.

"I don't know what this is or what we are going to see but whatever this is, we are going to figure this out together." He said looking back and forth at the two.

"Together," Kye said.

"Together," Sokki said. The three of them stared into the water not knowing what awaited them beyond the deep darkest part of the water, the uncertainties tainted the reality and the reality revealed itself as the white knight honoring his sword.

"1...2...3" Jay said...

Linking arms, they jumped up high in a cannon ball motion into the water ... *SPLAAAAASSSSHHH!*

# SPLASH

\*\*\*

An extreme amount of bubbles covered the three of them in the water, the water seemed to have come alive and taken on a personality of its own. There were three lights that appeared in the water, a green, blue and white light all made themselves known. Where Jay was, there was a white light aura surrounding him while a green ora surrounded Kye and a blue ora covered Sokki. The three observed this light and began to look all around wondering where such a source was coming from. After a while the ora's from the three seemed to dissipate away and the three of them could see each other clearly.

Kye immediately shot back up towards the surface of the water, the other two followed. The faces were out of the water treading on the middle of the pool. *"You ok?!"* Jay questioned looking at Kye.

*"DUDE, am I ok? Aaaam I ok? Dude, you are freaking SHAR-"* Kye was interrupted due to Jay rushing to cover his hand with his mouth.

*"Kye, brother, we must stay quiet, careful. We don't have the entire camp to hear us. We don't know what this is yet.... Sokki, are you good?"* Jay asked her as he took his hand off Kye's mouth.

*"Yeah! I am good, I feel that electricity again, and you both... You both look so different"* She said.

*"I know, that's why we are going to figure this out. You ready?"* Jay said looking at the both of them. They nodded in agreement.

*"Alright, let's go,"* Jay said. Simultaneously they all submerged again when they did, the ora's reappeared glowing the same colors.

The four teachers had snuck in the student lounging area and locked the keypad before anyone could get in. They walked around to a window that was peering over the main entrance of camp. The four teachers observed this from a little tiny window that one can barely make out from the front entrance. From a vantage, the four of them could see them going under water.

"What on earth are they doing?" Ms. Till asked in hopes of creating a discussion or at least seeking an answer.

"That is a good question," Mr. Sidious responded. The teachers observed from the window like highschool cheerleaders trying to look in the football player's locker room from a cracked door.

"Um, what are you doing?" a voice said from behind. Frightened, they turned around and saw Mr. Hines standing there scratching his hair.

They were revealed to discover it was Hines but one mastermind of the group had to come up with a response that was better than we were spying on our students to see what they were up to. *"Well, we have uh... Never noticed this window before. We saw it earlier and we were wondering what viewpoint it has to offer us in the city."* Mr. Worthy said

*"Okaaaay"*, Mr. Hines said,

"Fair enough. Hey, well I need your help with a special lesson for the last week, can you help?" Mr. Hines said to the four. No one said anything for a brief moment until Mr. Sidious responded *"Yes, that would be perfect!"* He said.

They left the longue and followed Mr. Hines to the Coffee room. *"Really? Wanting to see what view we have for the city?"* Mrs. Noble said, mocking him whispering. Mr. Worthy heard the comment but said nothing. They soon went inside the coffee room and shut the door.

At the pool, the Ora's seemed to have faded out again and the water was now clear again.

Jay, looked towards Kye's direction and saw what almost looked like a lizard with dull spikes on its body.

When he reverted towards Sokki's direction he saw what looked like a water snake, but a huge one. There were blue pulses traveling to its tail which seemed to be a little bit more blue.

"This is... Unbelievable" Jay said to himself in his mind, so he thought.

"Wait what!!!?" A voice said.

"Who was that?" Jay said, frightened he looked around in the water to see if anyone or anything else was in the water with them, there was no one. Only those three.

"Jay, it's me Kye, Over here the voice said.

Jay looked over and the voice was coming from the lizard, it was moving its mouth. Despite these incredibly strange circumstances Jay had to come to the conclusion that the lizard was talking to him.

"Kye, is that you?? I am sorry, did you just say what you can hear me? I can hear you???" Jay responded.

"Yeah, buddy!! It's me!!" Kye said.

"Yes, wait, yes. Jay we can hear you!! I don't know how??!" A voice said.

"Ok, if im me, you're you then that voice has to be Sokki's!!!" Jay said she looked at the water snake. That was moving its mouth.

"Woah, we can hear each other, and talk to each other? This is just AMAZING!! Ok, so guys I can see you but I can't see me" Jay said.

"First umm tell us we are!!" Sokki said.

"*Ok, Kye help me out here…. Sokki You have a long slithery body*" Jay said.

"*You are black, well navy dark blue I suppose!*" Kye said,

"*You really look like a water snake… Oh duh!!! Sokki…*" Jay said.

"*WHAT?*" Sokki said.

"*You are an electric Eel!*" Jay said.

Sokki's skin glowed with electricity even brighter. "*Wow!!! This is so strange, I could literally shock this entire pool right now, I can feel it!*" Sokki said. She looked down to the bottom of the pool, she slithered down to the bottom and swam back up

"*Ok, what am I!!*" Jay said.

"*Jay, this will be easy, you're…. y-y-your a great white shark*" Sokki said.

"*WAHHHAT??? I'm sorry, did you just say shark??!*" Jay said, incredibly shocked. He opened his mouth to try and smile but all his friends saw was a great white shark with incredibly sharp teeth with its mouth wide open.

Sokki, and Kye swam back a couple feet. "*What's wrong??*" Jay asked.

"*Well, dude!! You look very scary and intimidating, it's really hard to look at you right now because I feel like you are going to eat me! And honestly, I don't know if electric eels are your cup of tea but I also don't know if I am in your line of the food chain because I don't even know what I am??!*" Kye said, frightened.

"*I'm not going to eat you two!*" Jay said,

"How do you know that, you don't know if you have full control of this new found body of yours...? So I am keeping my distance, Plus if you come too close, I'll zap ya into next week soooooo stay back big fella!!" Sokki said.

"I feel like I have control which is weird...." Jay said.

"GUYYS, uh HELLO, did you forget about your old pal?? Kye, your best friend. Yeah that guy, did ya forget about him??!" Kye said, putting his lizard arms on his hips.

"Right, Sorry! Well you look like a lizard, and you have some spikes.... And claws my goodness." Jay said.

"You almost look like a gecko or chameleon or something." Sokki said.

"What color are my eyes?" Kye asked

"Uhhhh, grrrrreen, yeah green" Jay said as he got closer.

"Ok, first of all, back up! Second of all..... Oh my goodness" Kye said

"What!!"Sokki said.

"Guys, I know exactly what I am, I am a marine iguana," Kye said.

"How do you-" jay started

"My mom, is a marine Biologist remember? It's what she does for a living. She loves the Marine Iguana, she tells me about it all the time, and she LOVES them. She said there are not that many around... That will explain why I feel super strong. Marine iguanas are one of the strongest lizards and creatures in the entire ocean of its kind." Kye said.

"Guys, that is not the only way we know this!!!" Sokki yelled. She zoomed up to the surface of the water. And her normal human head appeared out of the water. Jay and Kye followed. Along with Sokki, their faces were back to humans out of the water. The three of them were treading in the middle of the pool.

"Wait, what?? What are we missing?" Kye asked Sokki.

"After we broke into the school, I did some research on the lizard or what we thought was a lizard, I learned that the scientific name is a marine Iguana. But you guys.,..."In the classroom, the tanks and in the pictures that we found....she took a deep swallow there was... a Marine Iguana, an electric eel and a Great white shark... Guys, unless im mistaken or blind... That's US!"

# CHAPTER 19

*Hey Davidson. Did you get anywhere on the legion case?"* Captain Sting said.

*"So I checked with our videographer tech and he tried tracing where the glitch came from and he could not find any source, there is definitely a glitch but we don't know who the source is."* Davidson said.

*"That's strange, keep searching,"* Captain Sting said as he continued walking past Davidson's desk. He took a few steps then stopped. He then turned around and looked at Davidson.

*"Oh, by the way, since we know what class room he went into, do we know what was in the classroom or what he might have taken, who he is? Do we know any of this?"* Captain Sting said.

*"No, but I'll get to the bottom of it".* Davidson said.

***

Sokki came walking into Jay's room with a towel wrapped around her hair for drying. Followed by Jay and Kye. *"I reaaallly want some coffee right now, not because I'm tired but more so I just want the taste of it,"* Kye said.

*"What is with you and coffee?"* Jay said, walking in right behind Kye and closing the door.

*"I don't know, I have been craving some ever since Mr. Hines was drinking some on the bus right before we got attacked by wolves,"* Kye said.

*"Ok you two, we really have to figure out what is happening to us"* Sokki said plopping down on the floor near the front of the bed joining the other two.

"Let's go back to that night in the classroom…. So we saw those three animals and now we are "those three animals," Jay said

"Jay you're a scary looking shark, great white to be exact, Kye you're a Marine Iguana and I am an electric eel? As far as I'm concerned, those three animals have absolutely nothing to do with each other minus the fact that they live underwater and they can all swim…….OH! Yes, and Jay! While you were rummaging through the teachers desk looking for the envelope Kye and I saw all three animals in the same tank! Alive and not attacking each other!" Sokki said

"So the weird thing is… That's the reason it's called a Marine Iguana is because of its uncanny ability to adapt to both land and water. It can live on both. It's really interesting considering the fact that I'm not turning spikey right now" Kye said, feeling his skin to see if his statement was true.

"Ok, what else do we know… wait duh… That's what we have a library for, Jay could you go down to the library and see what you can find on the relation of these three animals?" Sokki said.

"Ok, would you like me to cite my sources?" Jay asked, kidding around.

Sokki giggled.

"Wait, we are also missing one key variable…The octopus," Jay said. Immediately Sokki's hands started to glow light blue underneath her skin which had goosebumps, Kye's skin began to get bumpy and Jay's teeth started to get sharper and his hand began to shake.

"What in the world is happening to us?" Sokki said.

"That's true, we DID also see an octopus in those papers and there was one in the tank that practically charged at me. He just looked angry" Kye said.

"Annnnd there is an octopus on the emblem on the side of that pool that is near the entrance… Why though?" Jay asked.

"Because we have not used that pool since we have been here," Sokki said.

"But that's JUST it, there doesn't seem like there is anything wrong with that pool. So im wondering why we haven't used it."Kye said

"Uh, I wouldn't say that. That fracking thing is covered in black stuff, Ink maybe?" Sokki asked.

"We have to figure out what is wrong with that pool," Jay said. The three of them stared at each other in confusion and silence for a brief moment. Goosebumps attacked the three of them in one instance covering their skin.

"Ok…. So I think we know what we need to do… Kye you're good at being sneaky, no offense but can you find out what is so special or not about that pool? Sokki you're the science genius, can you find out what would cause our bodies to do this? Pull resources if you have to, do whatever you need to do. In the meantime, I will find out how these three slash four animals are linked."

"…I never thought Camp choice would be like this" Jay said staring out of the window.

"I will also continue running that sample that I pulled from your shirt, the black stuff." Sokki mumbled looking down

"What?" Jay asked, snapping out of his gaze.

"Uh nothing, talking to myself sorry!" Sokki replied.

"Yeah, I just didn't think camp would be like this at all" He said again this time with an even more depressed tone.

# SPLASH

"Hey, I don't think any of us would. It's going to be ok" Sokki said as she laid her hand on Jay's shoulder ***ZAAAAP!***

"Ouch!! You shocked me!" Jay said

"Oops! I'm sorry! Are you ok? .... Well I told you I would zap you if you got too close! Haha" Sokki laughed but was still concerned for Jay.

The other two laughed along with her while staring at the window watching the Cederport Sun set.

Later on as the day began to wind down the students began to head up to their dorms and get ready for bed. Jay went downstairs to drink some water from the water fountain. After drinking, while walking back to his side of the staircase he noticed the pictures on the wall again, the pictures of the alumni from camp choice. He began to stare at the wall thoroughly.

Looking at all of the faces and names, he read them to himself **"Ridrough N, Donald I, Stephon S, Timothy R...**

He then stared at the picture that was missing, it was a frame with no picture in it and the name tag on the bottom of the picture was not present like the others.

Mr. Worthy noticed this, when he did he then walked over to Jay

"Don't stare too hard" He said to him quietly stirring his coffee with a spoon inside of a blue mug.

"Why is there one missing?" Jay asked

"Well, I'm afraid that question is not for your knowledge yet Mr. Cruz, but let's just say that that person had taken place in something monumental to Los Aqui's city and because of that some very bad people were looking for him to seek revenge". Mr. Worthy said, staring at the empty frame together with Jay.

"Well, whatever this person did… was it a bad thing?" Jay said.

"No, let's call it a disagreement," Mr. Worthy said.

"So why are the two sides split?" Jay asked

"Well…" Mr. Worthy paused.

"Was the disagreement between the two sides?" Jay asked.

"Go to bed young lad, seriously before I must answer questions that I probably shouldn't answer." Mr. Worthy said.

Jay stood there, took a few steps to walk away back upstairs then he stopped, He looked back at Mr. Worthy with a glare.

"Fine, yes, your answer is yes" Mr. Worthy said, now seriously go to bed before I ask Mr. Hines to wake your entire class to run laps." Mr. Worthy said.

"Goodnight" Jay said as he walked back upstairs.

That night, Jay must have thought about nearly every single scenario as if why would the people on the left want to attack the missing picture person or better yet, the left side must have not along with the right side, Jay thought back to how Mr. Worthy told him, everybody has to make a decision. It stuck out to him because it reminded him of something his Grandpa said to him when talking about politics. At the present time, politics seemed to have been the most peaceful that it has been in some decades. Everyone was understanding of each other's values and viewpoints.

Back in 2020, the United States changed their name from the United States to the united. Besides the catchy shortened name, it was changed in large part due to the effect of the country not having any president. They formed an alternative to the dilemma, in which every state seemed to agree on. The states will govern themselves. Ever since 2020, The States would have a meeting of the minds. Which involved the leaders or captains as they would call them from the States forming together, and discussing what policies to implement for their people.

Everything seemed simpler, and fairer. They concluded that it was far more productive than someone shouting out orders from a big white house.

Jay's Grandpa was really big into politics and he would often share his viewpoints with his grandchildren even though at the time, they might have been too young to understand. Sometimes he would look down on them and say *"You're either on one side or the other"* All of these thoughts brought him back to the pictures in the lobby.

Typically an extensive thought process would make Jay fall asleep, especially if he was laying down. Which he was at the moment. He stayed up all night thinking about who was against who… he could barely close his eyes, the detective in him was kicking in full effect, unlike Kye it didn't derive from a paranoid sense. It came from just wanting to solve puzzles, and this was a puzzle that he could not solve alone.

When the next morning came Jay awoke before everyone else by default, with no sleep he went straight to the library around 6AM. He began looking in the city history section where all of the ancient artifact books were. He skimmed through the books but he halted abruptly. He turned around slowly and his eyes landed on a book titled the Making of Los Aqui. Sokki must be rubbing off on me, he thought.

He picked up the book and went straight to the table of contents. 1. How Los Aqui became a city…. 2. The early stages of Aui. He read, he opened to the first chapter but when he did all he saw was the second chapter. He realized that the first chapter was entirely ripped out of the book. Something about the missing chapter didn't sit right with him. He quickly looked around then tucked the book behind the regular placed books ensuring it was out of sight for reasons he planned on going back to retrieve it.

Jay walked through the quiet library practically tip-toeing around the bookshelves to reach the other side of the library into an aile titled animals. He began looking through books about Sharks, Eel's, and Iguana's but he did not examine any books detailing octopuses. About an hour and a half later he began to hear chatter from around the corner in the main hallway. This caused him to speed up his research. On his way out of the library, standing right outside of the door leaning against the wall was Mr. Worthy.

Jay paused for a moment, not knowing what to say he just said *"Good Morning"*. He found it odd that Mr. Worthy didn't return the gesture. Jay continued to walk towards the dining hall

*"Cruz... you know if you go looking for answers that you seek to find, you will soon have questions that you do not wish to be answered,"* Mr. Worthy said.

Jay did not turn around, because he did not want to see the look on Mr. Worthy's face and he also didn't want to strike up some conversation about why he was in the library at 6AM. Instead he just said *"Yes sir"* and kept walking into the dining hall.

When he sat down, he was the only student there, he was so sleepy that he didn't even realize that fact until he sat down. After all the commotion he heard he thought to himself that there would be students in there for sure. This actually played to his benefit, he rubbed his eyes, put his head down into his arms on the table and closed his eyes.

This oddly was one of the first times that Jay wasn't dreaming about some strange looking kid in the newspaper or worrying about studying, in his mind at this very moment he just wanted to rest.

*"JAY?? Wake up... You ok?"* Kye said, shaking his arm.

"Yeah, I'm ok, I'm just resting my eyes" He said, still muffled under his arms with his head still down.

"Well, your food is right there," Kye said.

Jay raised his head up from the table and smiled and took a big sniff in. *"ahhhhh french toast!"* Jay said.

"You addict," Sokki said.

*"Ya knoooooow some obsessions are a good thing"* Jay said, taking a huge bite into his french toast.

*"Ya well not when it's a buttery piece of bread drenched in syrup. Just saying"* Sokki said.

*"Geeesh, who coughed in your cheerios?"* Jay said. Kye laughed, almost spitting out his juice.

"Well, I'm eating right..." Sokki was cut off.

*"Let me guess, you were about to say I'm eating right in front of you, no one is coughing and they are not cheerios"* Jay said in his best Elmo impersonation.

*"Ok, wait until later... I'm going to zap you!"* Sokki said. Her eyes sparkled blue for a quick second as she winked at Jay.

*"Ok, we will see if you still say that when we take this into the water"* Jay said. As he smiled his teeth got really sharp and large. He tilted his head slightly to the side still holding his smile waiting for a response. Sokki sat there looking at his really long sharp teeth and said nothing.

"Yeah, didn't think so," Jay said as he continued eating his food as his teeth shrunk back to their normal size.

*"Man, I will say this is kinda funny to not be the one in the fire, normally he wouldn't say something like that!"* Kye laughed.

*"Kye, you can get zapped too!"* Sokki said.

*"If you can catch me,"* Kye said underneath his breath.

*"Jay, I hope you choke on those things,"* Sokki said, looking at Jay devouring one piece of French toast after the next.

Jay looked up from his plate *"My bread?"* He said looking at her with a silly face

*"No... your teeth,"* she said as she winked at him. Stood up and went to throw her plate away and prepared to get ready for PT. Her best friends did the same and headed for the door. The three of them ventured outside of the house.

The 3 of them Walked over to the pool and stared at it in despair. *"What do you think is with that pool?"* Jay asked.

*"I'm not sure but we will find out,"* Kye said.

*"Hey, let's make sure we stay low, we don't want to attract any attention. As hard as it sounds, we have to try to blend in."* Jay said.

*"Aye aye captain!"* Kye said

*"Roger!"* Sokki said

The students began to pile outside of the dining hall and they walked to the front of the building.

Mr. Hines came walking out behind them with a clipboard in his hand. *"Ok! Good Morning!"* He said.

*"Good Morning!* The class said.

*"Day three of camp. Ok, first things first. We will do some PT then we will break off into our stations then finish with our scenario. You all only have until the end of this week to solve it, at the end of the day I will

choose a few of you to try and see if you can solve the impossible scenario.... We will continue to introduce new careers to you all until Friday at that point, you are required to choose a career, Let alone in the aquatic industry there are fifty two. Which is pretty awesome, plentiful right? Ok, so for those of you that have already found a career that you like, can always stay with that or spend time getting introduced to something else. If you already know, why waste your time right. But at the same time I encourage you to try something new as well."

"Alright, with that being said 50 laps, stay together. Let's go. But wait! You all have now graduated, you will be running laps around the green field. Matt, your counting... GO!" Mr. Hines commanded.

The students started running *"Wait, wait, wait! Question of the day... What is self awareness? And is having self awareness more or less important than having confidence... Ok, now go"* Mr. Hines said.

The students continued running around the field while Mr. Hines met with the instructors from various camps that were featured. The three pools were divided into sections for the different career choices. The day took its course with no interruptions, just hard work and dedication from the students.

After various failed attempts of the impossible scenario Mr. Hines brought the students over for another campfire. This time, the students all sat down on the grass in the field surrounded by the fire with the smell of sweat and the outside air. The sky turned dark blue and the stars looked down upon them

*"So who wants to answer the question of the day?"* Coach Hines said from behind the fire

Tommy, an African-American transfer student from Vegas began to speak

*"Well, look at it like this. Self awareness is knowing yourself and honestly it's hard because I sing... I never knew how good I was at singing until someone recorded me and now my video has over a million*

views. Sometimes with these hidden talents we still lack the confidence, that's the other part of the equation. But Jay, I'm sure you can attest to this, like your video went up and you had tons and tons of views and people loved it because that is one thing, i mean i've only known you for a little while now but that is one thing that you can do is speak. But no one really knew so sometimes we lack confidence. But with Self awareness i just feel like you have to know yourself. You have to trust yourself as well. If I had to say which one is more important than I would say that it is definitely confidence because sometimes even if you know yourself you still may lack the confidence to chase your dreams" He said.

"Excellent, I like that. Using real world examples that are right in front of us. Very good... anyone else want to counter?" Hines asked. Kye raised his hand

"Yeah, I completely understand that and I definitely agree that confidence is key but I think self awareness is being more knowledgeable, so for example, let's take that Phelps guy from the Olympics. He is very good, but if he didn't sit in his pool and say you know what? I can be the best in the world at this, I mean he took swimming competitively to a whole nother level with his dedication to the craft but I think most of that came from his self awareness and ability to realize that, the confidence probably came a little later or along the way through the process. If you suck, you suck, if not then believe you can be great. Kye said

"Awesome! I also like that viewpoint, remember team, oftentimes when I present you with these questions it's not because there is a right or wrong answer but I want you to think outside of the box like those two just did. Let's look at self awareness for a moment. When we are self aware, like Tommy said we are very keen on knowing ourselves. But the flip side to that is knowing who you are and where you are at. What is the reality and what can you do to make your situation better because if we stay blind to the problem then it will never get fixed and what self awareness is.... It's realizing that there is a problem and taking steps to fix it. Confidence has nothing to do with that or maybe very little to do with that. Since we are using examples tonight, take when you are young for example. If we have a toy truck and this toy truck has four wheels. If one of these wheels falls off, we either will have two different responses depending on the personality type. Either we sit there and cry because our toy is broken or we pick up the broken wheel and try and fix it. And that is how life is, sometimes our wheels fall off but when something happens to us in life, you can sit there and complain to your peers how x,y, and z happened to you oooorrr you can tackle the problem head on and try to fix it. Get back in your truck and keep riding option two is ALWAYS better one hundred percent of the time. Never forget that......Any questions? Alright, Goodnight!" Mr. Hines said. He threw a big bucket of water on the fire, the area was now pitch dark and the students left to the main building.

"Hey Yammy, I think I know how to solve the scenario but I will need your help, I'll talk to you about it in the room tonight" Sokki said while walking next to Yammy.

"I'm actually pretty intrigued to hear since you and your little boy toys are literally the smartest people here." Yammy said.

"I appreciate that but there are alot of top ten students in this house," Sokki said.

"Reaaaally?" Yammy siad.

"Yup! Remember, I work in the counselor's office at school so I get to see where everyone is at ranking wise.

"Well that's fancy, what am I?" Yammy said.

"I have no idea, I'm sorry, I don't study them. I just glance at them every blue moon when Mrs. Morris tells me to file something away for one of the students, she will identify them by ranking, not by student number. Because the list is in order so it's very easy to just look at the number and see what each student is" Sokki said as she opened the door to the main building for Yammy.

The students all piled into their side stairway and made their way to their dorm rooms. Sokki let Yammy go ahead so she could wait for Jay and Kye. While she was waiting, she made the conclusion that she was so tired that she didn't even correct the incorrect statement Yammy made about Jay and Kye being her boy toys. She saw the two walk in from outside into the main lobby.

"Hey, you know our little project?" She said to them

Jay seemed to get the hint but Kye responded with

"Huh?"

"It's kind of weird how no one is noticing our fun underwater waves that we make," Sokki said...

"Water waves, is that code for something?" Kye asked. She smacked her lips and crossed her arms. Our little project??" Sokki said, looking around at the various students passing by.

Kye stood there for a moment frozen...

"Hey, I know I am super sleepy and tired but I swear I thought I saw a shark today?" A student said to another as they walked past the three.

"Duuuuude! Me too, I thought I was trippin... I mean I know there are no sharks but geesh!" The other said.

"Way to stay discreet fellas!" Sokki said.

"Fellas? They didn't say a lizard, they said a shark" Kye said

"I'm sorry! I can't exactly control this thing" Jay said whispering and looking around him to make sure no one was listening.

"Well... you're the one who told us to lay low... So blend yourself in captain!" She said back

"Blend in... I... am.. a FR-EAK-ING shark!! That's like me giving a submarine to hide in your pocket and me telling you to blend in" Jay siad.

"*Blahh*!" Sokki teased him.

"*Bleeeh*!" Jay said.

"*Haha, you two ok today?*" Kye asked.

"*Anyways! Our project?? That's what we discussed yesterday?*" Sokki asked

"*Oooooooohhhhhh, our project uh huh yeah whats up, you have something?*" Kye asked, finally getting the picture.

"*No, let's meet Sunday after breakfast and PT in your room,*" Sokki said.

"*Sounds good to me,*" He said.

Jay drifted off from the conversation and his eyes were fixated on something... Sokki began waving her arms in front of him in a tired motion.

"*Yeah, sorry.*" Jay said regaining focus.

"*Sunday? Does that work for you?*" Sokki as if they were in the city but nevertheless they were in a house with 60 people and plans had to be made.

"*Yeah, that works perfect,*"Jay said.

"*Goodnight you two,*" She said.

"*Seriously, are you two ok?*" Kye chuckled

"*Yeah, tell your giant friend here to go sharpen his teeth!*" Sokki said

"Yeah? Need some energy? How about you go wet your hand with water then stick it into the outlet" Jay said, giving her a bow.

"I freaking swear, I can't with this kid right now," Sokki said. She gave them both a hug and went upstairs to the girls section.

Jay's sleepless night was now catching up to him. He wanted to lay down right where he was in the middle of the lobby and close his eyes. Instead, he and Kye walked towards the stairs that led up. On his way there he glanced at the frame with the alumni of camp choice and saw something different.

From his eyesight, there was an image in the blank empty spot of the frame in the spot of the missing picture. Due to the fact of him being really sleepy and his eyes being blurry, he thought that his mind was just playing sleepy tricks on him. Kye helped him up the stairs, when Jay got in his room he laid straight down on his bed and fell asleep within 60 seconds.

Later on that night when the teachers had finished their coffee meeting a noise caught Mr. Hines's attention coming from outside of the main building

"You ok?" Ms. Till asked?

"Yeah, hold on. I'll be back" Mr. Hines said. He walked to the front door and poked his head out then walked outside. He looked around the courtyard when his head swiveled to the right side he saw a wolf lurking around the pool with the emblem staring into it with its red eyes.

The other teachers became curious and they followed Mr. Hines outside and they then saw the same thing that he saw. Hines went over to a big stone that was on the ground. He picked it up and chugged it directly at the wolf. The wolf didn't give the bolder a chance to try and make its mark. Instead the wolf scurried over to the wall and climbed up it. Then ran out into the desert.

*"How did that thing get in here?"* Ms. Till said.

*"That is a very good question and one that I am trying to figure out,"* Mr. Hines said.

The teachers then went inside and proceeded to go to their dorm section to sleep. Once again, the house of Camp choice was silent again.

***

Meanwhile, the atmosphere of the police station was a more complicated one, all was silent except that of Captain Stings office.

*"Davidson, we got anything yet?"* he asked, looking up from his computer.

*"Umm, we do actually sir"*, he said finishing his fourth cup of coffee for the day.

"Well,"

*"So, I talked to Frank over in Ramport, at first he was having quite some trouble figuring out the video but he confirmed our suspicion. The video has been manipulated to create a tiny loop causing a gap in the authentic version of the recording,"*

*"So what are you saying?"*

*"Someone fixed the video to take something out"*

*"Darn it! This is the last thing I wanted to hear, can we trace it?"* Sting asked.

*"Unfortunately sir... the encryption is untraceable"* Davidson said nervously anticipating his bosses' next reaction

*"Great! Just what I needed"*

"But, there is something, he gave me a copy of the encryption code, Here. He said you might know the source" Davidson said as he gave him a folder.

The captain snatched the folder out of his hand and then froze.

"What is it sir?" Davidson asked.

"Alien Technology, Damn it, this is exactly what I feared" He said under his breath

The captain stood up from behind his desk and started pacing back and forth

"I'm sorry did you just say alien?"

"Yes, well Los really... That kid, Jay. He is a Los, I should have known."

"A Los? What is that?"

"Something I hope you never encounter, a highly dangerous creature. Look son there is not much time to explain, I need you to go home, get some sleep because we will have to do a raid tomorrow morning, that's an order"

"Yes sir, but what are we raiding?" He asked. The captain was silent for a moment preoccupied.

"The Cruz residence" He responded.

# CHAPTER 20

Morning came and the students followed the same routine, by now the students were used to it.

Throughout the week, Jay continued snooping for answers in the library. Sokki practically slept in the science lab and Kye poked at the teachers as to why the students were not using the pool near the entrance. Most of the teachers gave him the same answer except Ms. Till.

Shocked at her response, he was eager to tell the group. Come Saturday evening, the students returned to their normal tiring state of exhaustion. Mr. Hines was in the middle of running the last of the attempts at the impossible scenario as this was the last day to solve it.

After two students had tried to solve the scenario. Mr. Hines took off his watch and set it on the floor.

"Alright!! It's Saturday night! We will be out here all night until we get this thing right! Like it, love or hate it" Mr. Hines said

Sokki and Yammy both raised their hands for an attempt.

"Ahhh... the roommates. Well then, very well why not?" Mr. Hines said. Everyone knew how intelligent Sokki was so naturally everyone's attention doubled. The scenario began to reset and Sokki began whispering to Yammy.

Mr. Hines stood in his normal spot in front of the pool waiting patiently. Once the scenario was reset he looked over at Yammy and Sokki.

"Ok, go!" He said. The gate began to open and this time sitting in the vehicle was one of his many assistants since his daughter had returned home. After the vehicle was stopped, the wolves came lurking in from the fields, slowly prowling this time and not running.

Sokki and Yammy ran over to the shed behind the building and grabbed two shovels and came back to the scenario.

Since no one has seen this idea before, everyone thought that they were going to start hitting the wolves with the shovels which they all concluded was a bad idea. But that is not what they did, instead they walked over to the spot in which the wolves were standing and started digging. Everyone was confused except Mr. Hines. He knew exactly what they were doing. They kept digging until they hit some plastic with their shovel.

Sokki reached down and began pulling the plastic bag out of the dirt. This of course made the wolves anxious, one began pulling Tammy's leggings with their teeth, pulling her leggings down a slight bit. "**WHACK!!**" Yammy took her shovel and smacked the wolf with a great deal of force.

"*OOO!*" the classed reacted

"*Yeah, bet ya seeing stars now buddy!*" She said.

The wolf that had just been smacked began seeing stars and walking like he had just drank some angry orchard beer. The other wolf slowly put his mouth around Sokki's arm. This made her angry but more nervous. Panicking, as the wolf's teeth were sinking into her arm. She closed her eyes and concentrated a great amount.

The wolf started vibrating at high frequency then he let go and let out a little yelp. Sokki was finally able to get the bag out of the dirt, when she did everyone observed that there was a bloody piece of meat in the bag. This made her peers react in an oooh ahhh fashion. She walked over to the gate. Yammy was behind her walking backwards with a shovel watching the wolves very closely. The wolves seemed to have changed their behavior due to the fact that one had just got smacked with a metal shovel and the other one just got electrocuted.

# SPLASH

Sokki threw the bag past the gate and to the right of the entrance. The wolves saw this, they ran after it. Sokki and Yammy quickly ran to the gates and closed them in a hurry. The two walked back to the middle of the circle of everyone. Mr. Hines began clapping, the rest of the students followed in applause.

*"Well well, congratulations, looks like I have my first two employees, Sokki and Yammy!"* he said. He shook their hand and then gave Sokki a towel with alcohol on it for her arm. Sokki took the towel but when she looked down at her arm, the marks were blue and not red like she expected. This made her think but her thought process was thrown off because Jay and Kye came rushing up to her. While everyone was walking to the field.

*"Woah, you ok?"* Jay asked, staring at her arm.

*"Yeah, I'm good,"* Sokki said.

*"Did you just..."* Jay stopped

*"Yes I did, I shocked that wolf, i-i- I don't know how I did that, honestly. That was really weird"* she said.

*"Well ladies and gentlemen, like I said, whoever solves the impossible scenarios instantly gets a spot in my team and let's clap it up for the newest members of Hines incorporated!"* Mr. Hines said.

The class began to clap with authentic joy for the two.

*"Oh my... It feels like I just won the beauty pagent back home or somethin"* Yammy said to Sokki

*"You won the beauty pagent?"* Sokki whispered

*"No darlin but let's just pretend"* Yammy whispered back.

"So, let's talk for a moment Sokki and Yammy, how in the world did you know to do that?" Mr. Hines asked, the group all looked at the two waiting for a response.

"Well, I have been watching every scenario carefully, and I realized that everytime the wolves came into the gate, they would stand in one exact spot. Like every single time so, it made me ask why... Like you said on Monday.. Self awareness and confidence play hand in hand. I had the awareness I guess on a more micro scale but I had the awareness to take a step back and look at everything then I mustered up the confidence to actually test my theory. Sokki said.

"Yep, I mean you gave us the library so I decided to use it, I did some of that... What do you call that here in Aqui? Ah yes research, I did some of that then I learned that the only thing that Los Aqui war wolves are attracted to is meat, and when they are hungry they look at humans as meat. But I and Sokki stood there, and we studied the character traits. They never attacked any of the students first, only if you messed with it. So we wanted to know why they were standing in that spot" Yammy said

"So on Monday we marked it and every single time they came in they went to that same spot, there is nothing there but dirt so the only way to know for sure is to dig and find out." Sokki said.

"Surroundings guys, sometimes, it is as simple as that. Sometimes things are not as hard or difficult as they seem. You were all stuck on the fact that there were wolves and that they wouldn't leave. Sokki and Yammy.. Well done. OK, next order of business, as of right now, we only have a little over four weeks left of CAMP. I am very impressed with your progress thus far but we still have a long way to go until we get you where you should be. Ok, with that being said, go enjoy dinner. See you in the morning for breakfast." Mr. Hines said

The students all slothed into the dinning hall for dinner and ate quietly, they were too exhausted to carry on conversations including the three amigos. Jay, Sokki and Kye. Instead everyone just ate in silence, it was amazing to see a group of juniors all in one place and not converse. Last time this happened was back in 2001 when some crazy guy crashed a big plane into two towers in New York killing many people. These days were of course better but the students were just really exhausted. After Jay, Kye and Sokki finished eating they headed to their separate staircases to go to their dorm.

"*Goodnight you two*" Sokki said as she gave them both a group hug. *Hey don't forget, we meet after PT tomorrow.*" She said.

She went upstairs to her dorm room. When she did she saw Yammy doing yoga. She decided it was better not to question her. Sokki proceeded to take a shower and wind her mind down from such a taxing week. Yammy thought it would be funny to sneak into the bathroom, so she grabbed a cub. Filled up with cold water and threw it over the shower curtain.

"*REALLY!?*" Sokki yelled.

Yammy hurried out of the bathroom and closed the door and she started giggling. Yammy had already taken a shower, somehow she wasn't sleepy so this made her bored. Plus she wasn't really into TV a whole lot.

When Yammy heard Sokki getting ready to exit the shower she quickly turned off all of the lights and jumped in her covers and pretended like she was sleeping. Sokki ignored this, set her clothes on her bag and climbed in her bed across the room.

"*Yammy, I know you're still awake, goodnight. I forgive you for splashing cold water on me, I kinda needed it*" Sokki said.

"*How did you know?*" Yammy asked.

"*I just did, now to go to bed*" Sokki said with a softened voice.

"*Goodnight darlin, don't choke me out in my sleep*" Yammy said.

Meanwhile, Kye and Jay were chatting with Tammy about swim meets and lifeguarding. As they started to head upstairs. Jay stopped walking with the two. *"Hey go ahead Kye, I'll see you up there"* Jay said. He walked back down stairs and stood directly in front of the frame. The picture was still missing, he knew he was seeing things the other night, but depending on how tired he was there appeared to be a picture in the blank spot.

He started looking around for Mr. Worthy but he was nowhere in sight. He heard some thumping in the coffee room so he went to the door and knocked on it. ***KNOCK, KNOCK, KNOCK!***

The door opened, it was Mr. Worthy and Mrs. Noble. Jay could see that all of the teachers were in there, but they were just very quiet, which was odd.

*"Yeeees Mr. Cruz?"* Mr. Worthy said.

*"I'm sorry, Can I speak to you outside really quick?"* Jay asked

*"Why yes of course"* Mr. Worthy said as he stepped out of the room and closed the door.

*"To what do I owe the pleasure Mr. Cruz?"* Mr. Worthy said.

*"Well, I need to know something, I must be seeing things but the other day I thought I saw a face in that picture in the missing spot… Mr. Worthy, I need to know who that is… I know you said you can't tell me, but I am absolutely dying to know, could you ple-"*

Jay, I told you to leave this alone, PLEASE!

*"I can't, i've tried!"* Jay raised his voice not daring to let one eye blink, staring into the soul of Mr. Worthy.

*"David Cruz"* Mr. Worthy said. He looked down, then looked back at Jay.

SPLASH

*"The man in the picture, his name is David Cruz."*

# CHAPTER 21

A moment in time seemed to freeze as he heard the words come out of Mr. Worthy's mouth in slow motion. Everything seemed to move slower around him. He did not even realize that Mr.Worthy had started to walk away.

He felt this heaviness that began to consume him, a sense of confusion, betrayal and a sprinkle of anger. Even though he did not know where the anger was coming from. He eventually regained his presence in the current time.

*"Hey wait, why are they after my father??"* Jay asked Mr. Worthy as he was now at the door to the coffee room.

*"I think I have said enough,* Mr. Worthy said scruffeling his beard. He went into the room and closed the door.

Jay stood there, very confused. He ran to the library but the library was locked. He was hoping to seek and find some answers there. ***BANG! BANG! BANG!*** Jay knocked on the door in the hopes that someone was on the other side, hoping that someone, just someone would let him. *"Let me in!"* He cried, *"I know you're in there!!"* Jay banged on the door some more but still there was no answer. In tears Jay wept as he kneeled facing the door, there crying on the floor Jay felt very afraid.

This triggered his deepest emotions. *What if those people found his dad while he was away at camp and Jay wasn't there to protect him? What about his cousin Zeke?* All of these thoughts crept in Jay's mind swirling back and forth.

***

*"Jay, wake up man, get your slides, let's go"* Kye said, shaking his foot.

Jay began to rub his eyes. *"Slides, what the heck are slides, and I don't even remember how I got up here."* Jay mumbled.

*"What are you talking about? And slides are sandals, where have you been?"* Kye said.

*"You have been hanging around Vegas people too much,"* Jay mumbled.

Everything that occurred after training last night was a blur to Jay, for him the question still remained as to how he got up the stairs to his dorm.

*"You comin?"* Kye said.

*"Yeah, I'll meet you down there,"* Jay said. He waited for Kye to leave the room, then he rolled over to his side and closed his eyes, his mind still trembling on the fact that his dad was wanted by unknown people. He picked up his phone and tried to send messages to his Dad but he realized that his phone didn't work in Cederport.

He scratched his head, rolled out of bed, put on some sandals and walked down stairs. In the dining hall, the mood seemed to present as it did the previous Sunday, tiresome. Sunday morning, one of Jay's favorite days of the week. Sitting from her vantage point, Sokki observed a ghost walk in the dining hall but it was really just Jay.

*"Oh my God is he ok?"* Sokki asked

*"Honestly, I'm not too sure, that's exactly how he looked earlier when I tried to wake him up."* Kye said.

Jay came wobbling over to the table.

*"Are you ok?"* Sokki asked concerned

*"Yuuuup!"* Jay said in sarcastic enthusiasm as one of the chefs put a fresh bowl of fruit and an egg burrito on the table.

*"Cause you dont look like it. Just saying"* Sokki added.

*"I'm fine. Thanks for your concern though"* Jay said with a fake smile on his face.

*"Hey well I was telling Kye that we should ask Mr. Hines if we can hop in the water again today before we head up the stairs,"* Sokki said.

*"Sure,"* Jay said.

*"Are you..."* Sokki stopped in the middle of her sentence because of the look Jay was giving her.

*"Ok, I'm sorry, I know the rule, don't ask twice"* Sokki stabbing a piece of watermelon.

*"Oh shoot! We better hurry, we only have ten minutes,* Kye said.

After the students finished eating they all piled outside for PT.

*"Alright, listen up, I will introduce the next impossible scenario to you tomorrow, I suggest you prepare yourself, I really want you all to take today and enjoy it, you all have been working really hard. Even you, with the broken arm"* Mr. Hines said looking at Donald

The class chuckled.

Mr. Sidious ran over to Mr. Hines whispered into his ear.

*"However, I had troubling news"* He said, the mood changed.

*"Someone is missing, while there are supposed to be 60 of you and we are counting 59, we will get to the bottom of this, he probably just overslept, we will check all of the dorms, please do not panic."*

The students began to whisper to each other in secrecy.

*"This makes no sense, do you think it was Johnny Silver?"* Jay asked Kye and Sokki

*"SHHH! Do not say that name here, you almost just gave me a heart attack, I've had nightmares! We will talk about it later.*

*"I'm sorry, did you ask him about practice?"* Jay asked Sokki

*"Not yet, I will ask him after PT"* She said back.

*"OK, you all know the deal, 10 laps. Yammy, you're counting GO!"* Mr. Hines said.

The students began to jog around the field, groans were heard from the students dealing with the aches and pains from their previous training.

*"Camp is almost over,"* Mr. Hines said to the group of teachers standing right behind him.

*"Yes, yes it is,"* Ms. Till responded. She had her shades on, she tilted them downwards as he was walking towards her.

*"This is by far the most intense camp that I have ever seen,"* Mr. Sidious said.

*"Thank you, Legion is one of the best schools around, so I had to upgrade my criteria and the way I structured camp,"* Mr. Hines said.

*"Well, we really appreciate it,"* Mr. Sidious said.

After a while passed the students finished jogging and went over to the wall.

*"MOS"* Mr. Hines said. The students squatted with their backs against the wall.

During the two minutes Jay closed his eyes and thought about his Dad, for a brief moment until his focus shifted from thinking about that to the pool that was across the yard with the octopus emblem on it. His craving desire to get to the bottom of this odd occurance with him and his friends turning into animals underwater. Soon the two minutes were up. And the students all went their separate ways.

*"Hey Mr. Hines! I was wondering if myself, Jay and Kye could practice some more today."* Sokki said.

Mr. Hines looked and Mr. Worthy who was nodding his head yes.

*"Well, there you have it! Be careful!"* Mr. Hines said.

*"Thank you, thank you both"* Sokki said.

She ran off to Jay and Kye who were standing at the water fountain drinking water.

She gave them a thumbs up as she was running towards them. When she finally reached them Kye handed her a cup of water.

*Ok, let's wait for everyone to go inside and do their thing then we will hop in"* Sokki said in excitement.

*"I know your abilities are awesome but you are SUPER excited!"* Jay said.

*"You'll see why,"* Sokki said as she got close to his face and winked at him.

*"Why are y'all staying out here??"* Yammy asked as she walked by.

*"I don't know, we just want some extra sun"* Sokki said

*"Oh... ok, well I mean, Sokki you could use some, Jay please don't bother because you will look like a pop tart and Kye, you could probably use it but okaayyy sun birds see you inside I guess"* Yammy said as she

turned around and walked to the building, switching from one hip to another

The three of them stood there laughing on their way to the practice pools. "*Hey poptart, oops I mean Jay*" Sokk said.

"*That's funny huh?*" Jay said walking towards her

"*No, no that means I'm sorry,*" Sokki said, still snickering.

Jay took one foot forward and pushed her in the pool... ***SPLAAAAASH*!!***

Jay and Kye then jumped in the pool as well... ***SPLAAASSSHHHH!****Bubbles surrounded and danced around the three of them. With no ora this time, they were able to see each other immediately.*

"*I am still not used to this,*" the shark said to them.

"*How could you be?*" It's not exactly something that you just wake up with, well... I guess we did. But you get my point, we have had this incredible ability for a week and it's still unbelievable to me still" The eel said to the shark.

The eel, shark, and Iguana all stared at each other in amazement, trying to get closer and swim around each other to examine the incredible life forms they saw in front of their eyes.

The eal was a lighter shade of blue with light pulses of electricity flowing through its veins. It had a dark blue tail on the top of its head.

The Iguana had bumpy rough skin the color of a sandy desert and claws sharp enough to penetrate a sub.

The shark was big with a white belly and teeth sharper than any animal in the sea.

*"How did we get like this?"* They asked each other

*"This is not just a dream or some spiked orange juice and french toast, this is us, this is now real life"* Jay said.

*"Dude, I'm sorry I know…. but I must say, I can tell we all love having this ability but I think the burning question remains, which is why.."* The Iguana said

*"And that's exactly what we are going to figure out. We are going to determine how this happened to us, I promise. In the meantime, we're gonna play catch!"* Sokki said.

*"Catch? With what?"* Jay asked, confused.

*"With THIS!"* Sokki said as she charged her tail creating an electronic ball of electricity which somehow left Sokki's tail and traveled over to Jay in a ball shaped form. Jay, not knowing what action to take, thought quickly and came to the conclusion that the ball could not harm him, after all he was a shark.

Instead of dodging the ball like his first instinct told him to do, he stuck his fin out and hit it towards Kye's direction. To his surprise it worked. The ball-shaped form of electricity traveled towards Kye without breaking form. The iguana put his eyebrows down and hit the ball towards Sokki, Sokki caught it with her nose then tilted it to the shark. This time when the ball came to him. He held one of his fins out to try and catch it. When he did he was shocked. *"Look! I caught the ball, how in the world am I holding a ball of electricity?"* The shark said to the Iguana and the Eel. The Shark stared at the ball for a brief moment, *\*ZZZZZAAAAP!\** The ball exploded with electricity then shocked the shark *"Ouch!"* Jay said.

*"Sorry!"* Sokki said. The shark looked at her as he rolled over onto his back, floating upside down pointing his belly to the surface of the water.

"*Now that's creepy,*" Kye said. The Iguana swam closer and landed on the shark's belly.

"*C'mon! Come over here*" Kye said to Sokki.

The Eel swam to the iguana and also landed on the shark's stomach.

"*Woah, it's squishy!*" Sokki said.

"*Watch it!*" Jay said in response to Sokki's remark.

The eel and the iguana continued to play on the shark's belly. The shark began to roll in circles like a barrel around and around. The eel and the Iguana began to run on the shark like a treadmill. The shark suddenly stopped with his belly facing upwards.

"*Why did you stop? I was getting a workout haha*" Sokki laughed. The three of them chuckled,

"*Hey, do you want to try something? You trust me?*" Jay said.

"*Sure, you always seem to have bad ideas... But what the heck!*" Sokki said.

Normally, although Sokki has never consumed an alcoholic beverage. The only way she would be this enthusiastic about one of Jay's many crazy ideas is to be intoxicated.

"*Hey! I support his decisions %100 percent!*" Kye said. The iguana crossed his arms and began blinking really fast leaning towards the eel.

"*Eww! Dont do that!*" Sokki said.

"*Ok... Hold on*" Jay said.

"*Uhh... Woah.. what is he doing?!*" Sokki asked Kye. The Eel wrapped her long body around the Iguana. The shark's stomach began to cave in really deep, almost swallowing the two animals.

"*Jay!!!! Stop swallowing us with your stomach!*" A voice came from the sharks caved in stomach.

The shark then uncaved his stomach and pushed it out really big and fast creating a trampoline effect. The iguana and eel came flying out of the shark's stomach which had pushed them so hard that they were now zooming to the surface of the water. They broke the surface of the water flying high enough to converse with an eagle that was flying by if they had any interest. Now in their human form the two of them were flying outside of the water with their course projected for the pool that was next to them gapping the concrete floor between. As they started descending they both began to scream.

"*Oh no, oh no, oh no!*" Sokki yelled.

Racing to the water like a diver from a skyscraper.

**SSSSPLLLLLASH**!!!* Underwater the bubbles began to take over as they normally do when you infiltrate their home. The two of them returned to their water form.

The eel and the iguana looked around and did not see their shark friend. After a while, through all of the rushing adrenaline, they had realized that the shark had pushed them so hard from his stomach that they flew and gaped into the pool that was next to them.

'*Woah!! What in the world? That is freaking crazy!*" Kye said to Sokki.

"*Yeah! Especially considering that we are still alive... hey what are you - what are you doing?*" Sokki asked, looking at Kye while he was coming near her with his arms open and a big smile.

"*I'm going to throw you into the other pool,*" Kye said.

"HA! What do you think you are? A whale? I think this whole strength thing has gone to your head honestly, I would like to see you try" she said still glowing blue.

"Okay, you asked for it," Kye said with a determined look on his face. He swims over to the Eel and grabs it by its tail. He swam all the way to the bottom of the pool. When he reached the bottom he began spinning in circles with the tail still in his hand similar to a discus competition. He continued spinning then he let the iguana go mid spin. The iguana flew towards the surface of the water again and gapped into the pool where she and the iguana had originally launched from.

*SPLLLAASH!!*

"What the? Where's Kye?" Jay said.

The Shark swam up to the iguana quickly

"Uh uh! Back up!" Sokki said.

"Oh yeah, sorry!" Jay said,

"That... was... freaking... awesome!! I was super scared then we flew up in the air then landed in the other pool" Sokki said

"Then she underestimated my strength so I threw her from the other pool into this one," Kye said, swimming up to the two.

"Woah, where did you come from?" Jay said.

"The other pool haha!" Kye laughed.

"Yeah, I know but I meant where... Nevermind!" Jay said.

"We should probably go inside now, we have probably been out here for an hour or close to it" Kye said.

The group agreed and the sea creatures began to swim towards the edge of the pool.

***ZZAPPP!*

"*Ouch! What was that for?!*" Jay said as he turned around looking at the eel.

"*Tag!*" She said, the eel then swam over to the iguana to tag zap him as well but he swam away and three of them began chasing each other around for a one way game of tag, mildly unfair, they did not mind the slightest. After tiring themselves out, the three of them agreed to leave the pool. Sokki stopped them before their exit.

"*Hold on, wait... I want to try something... It's just a theory but I think it will work*" Sokki said.

"*Jay come here, Kye come next to him, Ok good.*" Sokki began charging her tail up

"*Wait, wait, wait, what are we doing?*" Jay said.

"*We're playing tag, with a spin on it... Ok, I'm going to zap you, well I'm not going to zap you exactly, I'm going to send you an electric current shockwave, from there I want you to try to send it to Kye without shocking either of you. Now this is kinda like catch. You have to focus. Ready?*" Sokki asked.

The Iguana took one big deep swallow, becoming a little nervous.

"*Ready,*" Jay said.

Sokki put her body vertical. She charged up her tail which began vibrating with electricity. She landed it on Jay's fin. Jay began to vibrate and lose control then the shock faded.

"*You have to focus, c'mon you got this,*" Sokki said.

This time she charged up her tail and placed it on Jay's fin and Jay closed his eyes and reached out to Kye slowly opening his eyes. The lighting traveled through Jay's left fin to his right fin and it continued to Kye. Kye reached out his arm, letting the lightning travel through to his other hand and then shooting off to the bottom of the pool.

"Woah..." Jay and Kye both said breathing hard.

"How did... how did we just do that?" Kye said, looking at the other two.

The shark, Iguana and eel all swam up to the surface and got out of the pool returning to their normal human self.

The three of them went to Jay's room with a water bottle in hand, they closed the door and sat on Jay's bed. The light from the sun was beaming through the blinds of the window and providing light throughout the room.

"Ok, so it's time for a little discussion, what did y'all find out?" Jay asked.

"Ohhh me first!" Sokki said, raising her hand, simulating as if she was in school.

"Yes, you with the red hair!" Jay said.

"Ok, so this week I had to do some crazy research. I've had like no sleep trying to figure this out. Ok, so do you two remember back to bio chem freshman year where we had to deconstructulize the molecules to match the DNA of the original host?"

"Yeeeeah, I think," Jay said.

"Nooope," Kye said.

"Ok, so we had this lab we were doing after that, we found out that we couldn't match the DNA to the host or even to a normal functioning human because we found that the offspring didn't have enough chromosomes" Sokki said.

"Chromo what?" Kye asked, scratching his head.

"Chromosomes, you don't remember? Threadlike structures of Nucleic acids and protein found in the nucleus of most living cells, carrying genetic information in the form of genes? Any who, yeah so the chromosomes" Sokki said.

"English please" Jay said

"DNA threads that hold protein in order to determine our genes," Sokki said.

"That was still more like Spanish but ok, I follow" Kye said.

"Well, every human is supposed to only have two copies of DNA strands aka Chromosomes. After taking a sample of all of our blood, we all have one hundred copies of chromosomes" Jay and Kye's face went into shock.

"Yeah... There's more. Those types of numbers for Chromosomes are only found in type C species, guess what they are?" Sokki asked.

"Very large beast?" Jay said.

"No, but close.. Sea creatures.. Except, we look completely normal on the outside, for crying out loud Jay you could be a model. Kye you won homecoming king last year and I was Ms. Sophomore. It's the strangest thing I have ever seen, when I looked at the DNA, they seemed to be moving normally compared to a regular DNA set but when I diluted the sample with water, the cells completely transformed and developed into these hard forms of Molecules, it seems that our cells transform and freeze when we enter the water... but with all that being said, I don't even know why this is happening to us, I barely know the how" Sokki said.

The room was silent, no one said a word. Until Jay broke the silence.

"*You are brilliant... good work*" Jay said.

"*Thank you*" Sokki said with a peculiar smile looking at Jay.

"*Speaking of, I did some research of my own, I spent all week in the library and I think I know why we are feeling what we are feeling,*" Jay said.

"*What do you mean?*" Kye asked.

"*Well, like you with your headache, Sokki with her anxiety and me with my crazy hand shaking.*"

"*So Kye, I'm sure you already know this but you are what they call an Amblyrhynchus Cristatus. What that means, which it took me forever to find out that you are amongst the smartest creatures which allows for your adaptability on land and in water. All of this is coming from your prefrontal cortex which is sped up by 10*" Jay said.

"*I'm not sure I follow*" Kye said, Well, look at it like this, your prefrontal cortex is what allows you to make decisions, to reason, and it is pretty much the control center for your brain, there are pulses that travel through it, pulses that feed information. Your pulses are extremely sped up which allows you to have more adaptability in return makes your head very important. There is only one reason Marine Iguanas get a headache*" Jay said.

"*What?*" Kye said

"*When they are scared,*" Jay said.

"*That's weird... When I experienced these headachesI I didn't feel scared...*" Kye said with a concerned look on his face.

"*Yeah, but your Iguana self did. I feel like somehow, our two different bodies are separated when it pertains to certain emotions. I don't necessarily think it is always the case though. Ok like Sokki with your anxiety at random times. With Eels their pulses in their body become stronger when they have feelings of apprehension. But the sharks are different, here is why, with a shark's hand or its fin is used to guide them, it gives them a sense of direction. Kind of like their GPS. Their hands only shake when they sense danger or they are nervous" Jay said.

"This is all starting to come full circle..." Sokki said

"Why? How come?" Jay asked.

"Well, it's obvious... when was the first time you two were having your symptoms?" Sokki asked.

"When we first got to camp and we went near the pool when we were running" Jay siad.

"Same," Kye said.

"Wait, so you two didn't feel anything when we were being attacked by crazy wolves?" Sokki asked.

"Yeah, um that is a little weird, I have no idea why not." Jay said, looking back and forth at the two. This notion puzzled him so he got up from his bed and began pacing back and forth, it always helped him think.

"Well, maybe our animal selves are not afraid of wolves?" Kye questioned.

"You know, that almost makes perfect sense," Jay said.

"Haha, What how?" Sokki laughed

"Well because think about it, a Marine Iguana is probably stronger than a wolf. I mean he threw you from one pool to another, I'm not calling your eel self chubby but you have some weight to you, for crying out loud you are a sea creature." Jay said. Kye covered his mouth knowing that something was coming.

***WHAACK!***

Sokki took a pillow off of Jay's bed and chucked at him.

"*And there it is... wait, bro I thought it was you who was the one who told me never to comment on a woman's weight*" Kye asked looking at Jay who was still pacing back and forth.

"*She is a sea creature with credible abilities! All Eels are probably heavy!*" Jay said.

Sokki stood up from the bed and stared at Jay. "*Don't you dare comment on my kind like that?*" Sokki said glaring at Jay as she sat back down, this time on the love seat near the window as she walked past Jay she punched him in the arm.

"*Your kind?*" Jay asked, laughing.

"*Yes! My people*" Sokki said.

"*You don't even know your people but whatever*" Jay said still laughing.

"*Here is the thing, like I was saying... before I was rudely interrupted... An Iguana could take a wolf, even if wolves could breathe underwater. And an eel could shock one of those things into next week. And obviously I'm a shark sooo you know how that goes*" Jay said.

Sokki sat on the chair with her legs crossed.

"*Ok, so this is all starting to come full circle like I said, we all started feeling our symptoms when we got around that pool. And ... somehow, at the school. I knew something was up, I could almost sense him coming*" Sokki said.

"There's more, so these animals, these extra forms of ourselves whatever you want to call them... They don't exist together in the ocean. Like you are never going to find any two of our animals together at one time in the ocean. Matter of fact sharks prefer not to be around eels and vice versa" Jay said.

"That's why we weren't getting along and nagging each other!" Sokki said.

"Exactly..." Jay replied

"WAIT!" both Sokki and Kye said at the

"What??" Jay said

Kye and Sokki looked at each other at the same time.

"Whales... That's why you're afraid of them!" Kye said.

"Oh... because sharks are afraid of whales duh. Why didn't I think of that?" Jay said.

"Oh wait a second. The whale that my neighbor just bought tried to attack me! He backed up then rammed the glass, almost breaking it!" Jay said.

"Your neighbors have a whale?" Kye asked.

"Yes. They just got one, it was kinda random in a way then they asked each other if they knew what it meant... They are a little on the strange side" Jay said.

"Your neighbors have a whale?" Kye asked.

"They just bought a little tiny whale in a tank. It's probably huge by know" Jay said laughing.

"Now thinking about it... on the bus. Those wolves, they ran away from you! But is that because they knew you were a shark?" Sokki asked.

"Yeah, then that gigantic thing just looked at you and walked away," Kye said.

"I'm not sure... We have a lot of questions that need answering. We ... speaking of questions. Kye, did you find anything out about that pool?" Jay asked.

"Unfortunately," Kye said.

"Wait, what why?" Jay asked as he stopped pacing and sat down on Kye's bed. Sokki then rushed off of her love seat then sat near the two beds on the floor.

"That pool where the octopus emblem is the same pool that all of the drownings were in," Kye said, looking down at the bed.

The room was silent. The group did not know what to say.

"So the drowning that we read about in the paper... those, those all happened in the same pool that is sitting right outside...." Kye said.

"You know... the thing is we have to figure out what is causing the drownings and why our cells are like this.... we need to attack this strategically though because as far as we know. The teachers do not know that we know about the drownings. They must have kept this under wraps. We need to find old news specials. Articles, books, anything we can find about the drownings.... So what do you say team, are you in?" Jay asked with determination.

Kye and Sokki appeared to be shaken up a bit after hearing the information that was just given. They stood there, Jay always trusted his circle but the silence in the room presented fear of the fact that something could be set out to ensure that these entities, these creatures collide. Sokki's radar was ringing off of the charts.

"We have always stuck together and we have always had each other's back and we are not about to stop now" Sokki said.

"Agree to that!" Kye said with enthusiasm racing through his voice.

They huddled in a circle and put their hands in the middle. In this particular huddle, they stayed there, and stared at each other.

"I think that it's time to recommit ourselves in our pack" Jay said.

The other two nodded in agreement. The three of them stood there in silence

"Repeat after me... We are JSK."

**"We are JSK."**

"We will always stick together."

"We will honor God with our heart."

"We acknowledge the pursuit of freedom is a must, not an option for there is no success without sacrifice."

"We will not let the fact that we only have one parent stop us."

"We will not let the place we are from stop us in the same instance."

"We will always remember where we are from."

"We don't conform to social norms because our standards are much higher."

"We will be relentless."

"The good for the ones around us outway our personal needs."

"We will be here for eachother always, no matter what until the end."

"Now let's begin."

The three of them stood there in their circle with their hands piled on top of each other

"1...2....3... US!" They shouted. As the uncertainty covered the room, the three of them stood there in anguish remaining silent. They embraced each other in a hug for a moment.

Later on, towards bed time, the students began to travel to their dorms and get ready to go to sleep. Kye came walking down the stairs slowly, following Jay and Sokki Jay and sokki walked towards the front entrance. Kye stopped walking behind them.

"Are you coming?" Sokki asked

"Yeah, I'll be right there" Kye said as he was pretending to look at the pictures on the wall that was next to him.

After Jay and Sokki went outside Kye quickly walked into the dining hall and went to the side where the teacher's room was on and put his ear against the wall so he could listen.

"Look, its taking them too long to figure this out" Mr. Worthy said from behind the wall

"Ok, but how do we know that they haven't figured this out already?"

"We don't, that's the thing... Hold on I feel something"

Kye heard the door of the teachers room open from the hallway. Kye ran towards the janitor's closet and hid inside.

Meanwhile, outside of the building in the front courtyard. Jay and Sokki were on the grass conversing with each other.

"Jay?" Sokki asked as she stared up at the sky, laying on a lounge chair.

"Yes?" Jay responded doing the same in a chair next to her.

"Why are we sea creatures?" Sokki asked very bluntly.

"That is a good question... but you know, this is sort of a good thing. I like it, it's scary, yes but I like it" Jay said.

"It feels so weird... It's almost as if I feel free, like I have been unleashed from myself..." Sokki said.

"Yes, definitely agree, I feel like... I have become a different version of myself. I think... it's a better version of myself" Jay said, still staring up into the sky.

Sokki looked over at him in disarray, she looked at him, with such conviction, such curiosity. This statement from Jay made her go into a very curious state. It was at this moment that she had a mini debate with herself on what to say and how to respond to such an odd statement from her best friend.

"I think.. this version of Jay. This one right here, the one that I am staring at is a pretty amazing version, he is the version that smiles but makes others smile. He laughs and makes others laugh. He cares and by that he causes others to care. Not to mention he is smart, and handsome, a cute sight for sore eyes. This is the same Jay that I met in the aquarium on our school field trip. The same Jay that helped me through the toughest times after my dad passed away. I think this Jay is an amazing version. Anything more is a plus" Sokki said.

In Jay's mind, he was blushing. "I ummm, I have never heard you talk about me like that. That was very kind of you" he said after he turned towards her.

They laid there under the stars In the cold night time air staring at one another. Sokki had a different sparkle in her eye, one that Jay had never witnessed before.

*"Your welcome"* Sokki said

*"Thank you, thank you very much,"* Jay said.

*"Speaking of, if you don't mind me asking… What are you all doing for the anniversary this year?"* Jay asked.

*"Well, my mom wants to continue honoring him the same way we have always honored him and the same way that he would want…. All get together, spend time with family and eat a meal. My father was a big believer in family. He was a simple man"* Sokki said. She took a deep sigh

*"What about you?"* Sokki said, reverting to gazing back up at the stars.

*"The same……every October. That is crazy how all three of our parents died in the same month, practically the same day, my mom, your dad and Kye's dad"* Jay said.

*"Yeah, it is pretty unbelievable. At one point it almost drove me so crazy that I researched it but I know that the three incidents were completely unrelated"* Sokki said.

*"Jay,"* Sokki said.

*"Yes Sokki"* Jay said.

*"I am about to say something that I have never said before to anyone in my life"* Sokki said.

This made Jay's mind began to race fast as he started to think of all the different possible things she was about to say.

"*Ok*" he said back.

She took a deep sigh and then exhaled. This gave Jay chills. Or was it the cold air? Who could really tell?

"*Loosing my father was one of the hardest things that I ever endured... it took a lot from me, I'm sure you can say the same for your mom. I was depressed for many years. It took me a long time to cope with the fact that he was gone, the last words were I love you. But it was still incredibly hard but what it bought in return was immeasurable on a very high level. I guess what I am trying to say... is something that I have been wanting to tell you for the last year now. Yeah, losing my father was tough, BUT if someone came to me and told me that I had to choose between getting my father back and never meeting you, or to have things how they are now with you in my life... I would choose to have you in my life. I could never lose you. I realized that truly when the fins got you and you were in jail a few weeks ago.... I heard about this in a movie, it's called collateral beauty. You know the term collateral damage? Well collateral beauty is when something detrimental happens in your life, let's say the death of a loved one. The beauty from that tragic death is what you gain in return, and if my dad would have never died I would not have met you and so many other things. My scholarship, my awards... When I didn't have you to call... Honesty, knowing that I couldn't talk to you started to destroy me on the inside. I began to feel that emptiness, a similar emptiness that I felt years after I lost my dad. But it was different because something told me...* " Sokki said.

"*Told you what?*" Jay asked. He now sat up from his lying position and began gazing at her from his seat.

"*Something told me that I would get you back*". Sokki said.

They both stared at each other for a moment, Jay stood up along with Sokki and they embraced each other. Jay wrapped his arms around her neck and Sokki wrapped her arms around his back squeezing him tight. It was at this moment that they expressed great appreciation for one another.

"Wait a second, I just now thought of something..." Jay said.

"What?" Sokki said, still hugging him.

"The aquarium, freshman year, remember the jellyfish that practically embraced your touch of the glass?" Jay asked

Sokki stepped back from their long embracing hug.

"Yeah, oh wait! We definitely know why I and the stunning fish felt so attached! Get it, stunning. No pun intended haha!" Sokki laughed

"Hahahah!" Jay laughed along with her as they laid back down in their chairs.

"Hey can I borrow your red shirt? The one you wore the first day of camp?" Sokki asked Jay.

"Suuuuure, I suppose. For what though?" Jay asked, looking at her with one eyebrow raised.

"I need it for something in the lab," She said.

"Haha ok"

From the entrance Kye observed the two of them laughing with joy in their chairs. He smirked, then closed the front door and went upstairs to his room.

Two weeks flew by with various attempts from the students at the impossible scenario. Camp seemed to have taken its course, just like with anything. Hines believed that if you build on something and do it consistently for 21 days straight then it will truly become a strong habit, one that is really hard to break. There was not a single leaf that flew by for the intense winds of Cedorport had come to a halt drying up everything in its path.

There is a Cedeport saying that goes: to understand what tomorrow holds, look at the weather. Many different interpretations of the saying but the common knowledge of the saying was the meaning of the unpredictable weather of Cederport. Sometimes the weather in Cedorport would change from Sunny and thriving to scary thunderstorms in a matter of a few hours or typically it would change from day to day.

If one were to pose the question of what another had planned, they would say, they are not sure until they know what they will be wearing. Jay has known about Cederport for a long time and could never understand how one could live in such a dull city full of such nothingness. Jay believed that the only thing in town was camp. He believed that the citizens of the city had to travel to get to the supermarket or to a restaurant or to watch a movie.

The movie that premiered at camp was the movie of the impossible scenario starring Mr. Hines and tons of failed attempts including, Jay, Sokki, and Kye. The scenario presented itself as a simple but challenging one.

There were seven holes that didn't connect to each other. 6 of the holes had mini snakes that would bite one's hand if an attempt was made into a hole. 1 of the holes had a cute adorable rabbit. The objective was to grab the rabbit and the egg that the rabbit was protecting.

Each time an attempt was made, Mr. Hines would have his assistants hold up a thick cover sheet that the students couldn't see through so he then could move the rabbit and the egg to a different hole. The bite that the snakes delivered created no amount of pain, it only left a little indented mark on the hand of the one that reached in the hole. Possibly, one could feel some pain.

This was the last day of the attempts of this particular impossible scenario. The students were tired and the assumption of not completing the scenario peered in the students.

"And with the last attempt of this scenario before I give you an entirely new scenario next week..... Tammy, you're up son." Mr. Hines said.

Tammy stepped forward and looked at the holes for a brief moment. He walked slowly around them, he examined inside the holes even though he couldn't see inside the holes. He looked at the holes even more closely, he began feeling around the holes with his feet. He went to each hole and did this about 3 times each hole. This confused the students as they watched him walk around and around the holes.

He stopped at a hole that was near the edge of the rest. He bent down and reached inside of it, wiggled his hand around a little bit. He first pulled out a little blue egg and set it on the ground. Then he put his hand back in the hole and grabbed a little white rabbit and cradled it. The class oohed and ahhed, he brought the white rabbit to Mr. Hines and then grabbed the egg and placed it in a basket that Mr. Hines was holding. Mr. Hines placed the rabbit in the basket as well.

"Well, give him a round of applause," Mr. Hines said to the class. The class began to clap in applause as they walked to the field for their afternoon discussion. Miraculously, the sky was still light outside with promises of becoming dark at a later time. After everyone huddled around in the field Mr. Hines opened up the group to discussion.

"Ok, I do have just one question right now. How did you know what hole to choose?" Mr. Hines asked, looking at Tammy. The rest of his classmates looked at him as well.

"Well, I thought about it, snakes technically don't have hands.. So they can't really dig. But bunnies can dig. So I thought about it. I learned that the animals in Cederport are a little weird. They don't really like to go outside when the sun is out, which is the strangest thing to me. I sat back and watched all of these attempts and not once did the rabbit or snakes come out. So I figured that the bunnies will probably dig further into their hole in a sideways fashion. If they were digging then the ground below would be more hollow than the other holes, all I really had to do is figure out which hole was hollow, that's why I took the extra second to make sure that it was the correct hole" Tammy said.

"Wow, there was more than one way to solve this scenario, and until now. I did not realize that way. Good job Mr. Tammy. See that y'all? Just reasoning, sometimes. Some reason and a little extra caution and certainty is really all we need. But, too many of you are reasoning in the wrong areas of your life. Your reasoning with your dreams, don't gamble with your dreams. Those are your dreams. No one else's, your body tells you you're tired so what do you do? You go to sleep? No see that really all depends on how bad you want your dreams. Others will gladly support someone else until you make it there, then all of a sudden everyone is on your team. This is why you must tap yourself on the chest and say, I am doing this for me, no one else. At the same time, you must have something that's stronger than the distraction. What do I mean by that, too many of us are getting distracted by TV, by video games, shopping for things that you don't even need. Watching movies... when you truly want to become successful. None of that will truly matter in the long run. You're not focused, that's the issue. Here is the thing... You can say you want your dreams SO bad but your actions need to be predicated on your words. You have to deal with the reality that pondering and hoping for your dreams is not going to do anything. Focus, that's what it's all about. What's interesting is that you all are in a field that requires your very best everyday. You can't have an off day. As a lifeguard you have an off day and someone drowns, this person loses their life because you were on stand thinking about the fight you just had in your relationship or you were thinking about the fact that you failed that test. Compartmentalize, structure and discipline yourself to understand that there are different compartments in your life and you must separate them. You will soon know what I mean as you grow in maturity. The last two scenarios will be given to you differently, we only have two weeks left so I will give one each week but the last one I will wait until the very last day so you all have to think on your feet....... with *that being said, if no one has any questions. Please go eat, have a good night."* Mr. Hines said.

Another weekend finished and the students just had two weeks left of camp and the anticipation of returning to their awaited kingdom haunted the students. One week later Kye ended up solving a crazy scenario that involved covering the surface of one of the three pools with flames, minus the wolves the students agreed that the third scenario was by far the most intense.

Kye had to find out exactly where to place the fire that he lit. As the water had flames ranging from it Jay stood there, and stared into the orange light raging and roaring loud right into his soul.

# CHAPTER 22

***KNOCK, KNOCK, KNOCK***

"Um, hello? It's 6:30 am how may I help you officers?" Mr. Cruz mumbled half awake

"We are aware of the time Cruz" The officer said

"Again, what do you want? I don't have time for this"

"We need to bring Jay in for questioning" Captain Sting said

"WHAT? He is already innocent" Mr. Hines said

"So we thought, we have a development in the case that may affirm his affiliation with unknown creatures"

"What in the hell are you talking about officer?"

"Captain, and what I'm referring to... you see has Jay ever seemed a little odd to you?"

"Odd, how so? What's this about, cut to the chase?"

"Just trying to have a conversation that's all sir, is Jay available?" Sting said, trying to peer over Mr. Cruz's shoulder into the house. Mr. Cruz stepped in the way of his eyesight

"Tell me what this is about" Mr. Hines said firmly

"We have new evidence that directly links your son to the Los race" The Captain said while his partner cleared his throat

"The What?"

"The Los, you know... Like the ancient creatures who formed this city"

"You have GOT to be kidding me, this is a prank right?"

"I wish we were kidding"

"Wait, so you think my son is some mistakenly ancient being because he got mixed up with some documents? How stupid do you think I am?"

"Look, we want to speak to Jay, Where is he?"

"He is not here, I am not sure, that's honest. I really am not sure"

"You don't know where your own son is?"

"Don't insult me!" Mr. Cruz snarled

"We need you to cooperate-"

"He is at camp Choice no?" Zeke blurted out from behind the door

Mr. Cruz quickly stepped all the way outside and closed the door in hoped that that the officers did not hear the outburst.

"Ah, that's right. He went to camp, I don't know how we missed that, C'mon Davidson we have to get on the road" He said with a smirk on his face glancing at Mr. Cruz once more with a devilish grin on his face.

Mr. Cruz went back in the house and slammed the door.

"BOY! What the hell is wrong with you?" He asked Zeke who was standing there in the living room motionless.

"I'm sorry, I don't know what I was thinking, I was just trying to help"

"Help? Know what?"

There was a long pause in the house that ended with a slam of a door. Mr. Cruz's bedroom door.

***

On the dawn of the last week an uneasy flow seemed to take over the camp in full effect. After discovering the results of Kye's ease dropping, the group decided on a more tactical approach to try and discover what the teachers were not telling the students. Thursday night after a hard day's work of drills and skills the three of them snuck out to the pool and began swimming around.

*"I dunno about you three but I am finding out that swimming regularly is far more boring!"* Kye said as he was spinning around on the surface of the pool. The three of them were on the surface of the water in their normal bodies, at least above the water. Swimming back and forth and splashing each other.

*"I can't believe camp is almost over!"* Sokki said.

*"Yep, tomorrow is the last day,"* Jay said.

*"I wonder what our parents are going to say about our abilities,"* Sokki said.

*"Our parents? I have no idea if I am going to tell my dad"* Jay said.

*"Sorry, Maybe I am just speaking for myself. I tell mom everything"* Sokki said.

*"You know, I have thought about it and I am not entirely sure if I will tell my mom, at least not right away,"* Kye said. The three of them swam to the edge of the pool and put their arms on the pool deck letting their sea creature bodies hang in the water.

*"You know what?"* Kye asked.

"*Whhhhat?*" Jay and Sokki asked

"*I will say confidently that I feel like I can beat both of you in a race*" Kye said with an evil smirk on.

"*In a race? In what dream?!*" Sokki asked

"*Wait, wait, wait, wait.. Hold on, are we talking about on the water regularly or below the water?*" Jay asked, perking up with a smile on".

"*Either one, you two just don't want this heat!*" Kye said.

"*Time out, now we have to find out,*" Sokki said.

"*I GUESS WE DO,*" Kye said.

"*Just for kickers, we will race regularly first,*" Kye said.

"*I wouldn't be so cocky if I were you Kye, I have gotten faster since we first raced a while ago*" Jay said,

"*Agreed, I'm sure but you're still not faster than I,*" Kye said.

"*Incorrect grammar sir, maybe after I school you in this race I'll also school you in some proper english*" Jay said.

"*Yeah? You beat me? Ok, sure and two plus two equals seven*" Kye said.

"*Ok, and two MC squared equals pie. Now can we race please so I can beat you BOTH!*" Sokki asked.

"*Hold your horses static shock, we need stakes on this so you two can't say you let me win on purpose... ah got it! The two people that lose will have to wear a pink shirt that says Kye is the best swimmer in the world! Or whoever ultimately wins the race,*" Kye said.

"*That's fine with me!*" Jay said.

*"Me too!" Sokki said.*

*"Alright, I will count it off," Kye said.*

*"The three of them put one hand on the wall and got ready to launch."*

Kye changed his voice to that of an announcer.

*"Swimmers! Please take your mark… get ready…"*

*"HOW ABOUT DON'T GO!?"* A voice said from their right. Startled, the three of them jumped back in a frightened fashion.

They saw that it was Ms. Till and the rest of the teachers

*"I'm sorry to break up your little Olympic race here, as curious as I am to know who would win that race. Did we approve you to be out here?"* Ms. Till asked.

*"No ma'am"* Jay responded

*"Then why are you out here?"* She responded

The group was silent.

*"Please get out of the pool and report to the teachers lounge immediately!"* Ms. Till said angrily

*"Yes ma'am"* The three of them said together. As the teachers began walking away to the building the three students started looking at each other.

*"Oh my! Do you think she saw us?"* Sokki asked whispering

*"OF COOOURSE she saw us, she was looking right at us.. She SPOKE to us"* Kye said whispering loudly while the three of them began leaving the pool and walking to the building.

"Uh, no you idiot! Not like that, I mean, do you think she saw our sea creature legs under water??" Sokki said pointing down.

"Oh, I don't know, but what I do know is she sure did save you two from getting beat pretty bad!" Kye said.

"Ohhhh, shut up!" Sokki said. The teachers had already planted themselves in the teacher's room and the students were walking towards the building almost at the entrance.

"How about both of you chill for a moment, we need to figure out what our response is if we get asked" Jay said.

"Uhh... Deny, deny, deny" Kye said.

"It doesn't happen often but unfortunately, I have to agree with him," Sokki said.

"Who knows what could happen if the teachers find out? They may shoot us with tranq guns and have us shipped away so they run tests on us. I am not spending the rest of my life sedated in some tank screamin Jay, you should've listened to us". Kye said.

"Dude, what movie were you watching last night?" Jay said.

"Yeah, seriously, and what are we ANIMALS??" Sokki asked, moving her head sideways and crossing her arms. Kye took one hand and shot it up in the air.

"Umm DUHHHHHH?!! Yes, that is EXACTLY what we are" Kye said.

Sokki scratched her head, the first time she almost made no sense in her reasoning.

'Sokki, I need your antennae up for this, if something seems off you should say something about sleep. That will be our clue. I know you two want to deny it if asked but please, im asking. Follow my lead on this one,"Jay said.

"*Copy that*" They said together.

The three of them walked into the teacher's room to see all four teachers standing there and not sitting.

"*Close the door and lock it please,*" Mr. Sidious said.

There was a tense silence in the room, Jay hated this. This awkward moment of who is going to say what next, or who is going to do what, Jay just wanted to attack the issue head on. Something about this particular transaction seemed different. This didn't seem like a harsh punishment or engagement.

"*We are really sorry for going outside, I mean we knew we only had one day left. So we had to spend one last night in the water!*" Jay said standing next to his two partners in crime.

"*Cruz, that is not why you are here*," Mr. Sidious said.

"*It's not... then why we are here?*" He responded.

"*You are here because of the extraordinary gift you three have been given*" Mr. Sidious said.

"*Yes, we are very smart. Man it took a lot of...*" Jay started. Mr. Sidious cut him off.

"*That is not what I am referring to either, yes you are incredibly intellectual but your brain power is only merely a smudge on the surface of you three..... Let me guess, Shark... something electric, a jellyfish maybe? And. hmmmmm oh, oh definitely a marine animal of some sort. How close am I?*" Mr. Sidious said excitedly.

"*I am sorry, what are you talking about?*" Jay asked.

Umm, Sarah. Can you please?" Mr. Sidious said, looking over at her to his left.

"*Really, first name huh right in front of the students. Thanks*" She said.

"*It's on our grade report that you send home every two weeks,*" Kye said.

"*It is? What?*" Ms. Till asked, the entire room looked at her. *Is it just mine?*" She asked. The other teachers nodded at her.

"*Oh no! I must get that fixed*" She said.

"*Im, Sorry so why are you calling us animals again?*" Jay blurted out

"*Ms. Till if you would please,*" Sidious said again.

Ms. Till began filling up a red bucket in the sink next to the coffee maker. Mr. Sidious turned off the lights in the room. The room was completely dark without a trace of light anywhere. The water in the sink stopped.

"*Sokki hun are you dry from the pool?*" Ms. Till asked

"*Yes ma'am*" She responded

"*Ok, good,*" Ms. Till said. She then took the bucket of water and splashed it on Sokki, Sokki's viens lit up blue and her skin was giving off sparks with addition to her hair glowing blue which made the room glow. The room glowed blue from Sokki for a moment, Mr. Sidious then flicked the light switch and the room lit up again.

"*Do you still want to pretend like we are not knowledgeable?*" Mr. Sidious said.

"*Yeah, you do know that we are four smartest teachers in Los Aqui right?*" Ms. Till said while looking at the students. While handing Sokki a towel to dry off with.

"*I got it, thanks though*" Mr. Sidious said to Ms. Till

"*So, you want to uh talk to us now or what's up?*" Mr. Sidious asked.

Jay took a deep breath. "*How did you know?*" Jay asked

"*Well, we didn't really until we just confirmed it, and you just double confirmed it right now. But however, we did have our suspicions, you three are very clever. I will give you that but your little buddy Kye here gave it away when he tried to eavesdrop on us. We were eating breakfast last week and I realized that there was an indentation on the wall, a fairly large one, it just so happens to be the same wall that is connected to this room on the outside. Well it just so happens to be that the only camera that is in this building is above the ledge in the dining hall in the corner. After reviewing the footage, I saw that Kye was ear hustling on the opposite wall leaning in that exact same spot. Kye, you are so strong that you made a dent in the wall*" Mr. Sidious said.

"*So what? Are you here to capture us or something?*" Kye asked.

"*No, we never harm our own kind*" Mrs. Noble said.

"*I'm sorry, did she just say our own kind!?*" Sokki asked, looking around at everyone.

"*Yes she did, you are what we are. Ever since you woke up a few weeks ago you have become an Aqui*" Mr. Sidious said.

"*What do you mean like the city?*" Jay asked.

"*Yes, like the city, but you three are now AQUI, the city's full name is LOS AQUI. Back in 1912 when this city was founded. The world was at war, but back here in the states, a different war was taking place. Between the Los and the Aqui, equipped with the same powers and abilities that you and your two friends have. The Aqui are noble heroes, those sought to defend against the Los, it's Somalian for* **"The Lost".** *They represent evil serpents aiming to do wrong to this city. In 1912 the Los lived on the eastern hemisphere and the Aqui lived on the western hemisphere. The two lived in harmony away from each other until the third month of the year came and it was time to send out their* messengers out into the unknown parts to find new land. One messenger from the Los tribe and one messenger from the Aqui tribe found a new land that was new and untouched. Surrounded by water like our city is, it was a dream for the Los and the Aqui. Having abilities like we do, living near a body of water, preferably an ocean is a strong desire. After the messengers returned to their respective villages. The Aqui tribe returned to take their place on the new found soil and claimed their land but when they arrived the Los came shortly after to claim the land. With the two tribes living in opposition they could not live on the same land. The elder of the Aqui tribe and the elder of the Los tribe agreed that whoever would win in a duel amongst tribes would claim the land. So the two tribes engaged in battle, in our element of water right under the city of Los Aqui... Forever known as the battle of Los Aqui. Blood was shed and many lives were lost. Both sides becoming relentless and unwilling to surrender, the two elders eventually agreed to share the land. So the name became Los Aqui" Mr. Sidious said.

By now, the students were sitting down and Kye managed to get his hands on some popcorn, Sokki was sipping coffee with Ms. Till. Jay was still, listening in shock.

"What happened to the Aqui elder?" Asked Jay

"We know where the elder is but we don't know where his brother is. He disappeared, no one has found him, because Aqui and Los do not phase on land we truly have no way of finding him. Aqui and Los age differently than normal people" Mr. Sidious said.

"I'm sorry, did you just say phase? What's that?" Sokki asked.

"Phase, it's what you have already done. It is when you truly become the full version of your Aqui. For example, when you enter the water, you change from your human body into your Aqui animal, yes?" Mr. Sidious asked, the three of them nodded.

"That, my friends, is called phasing" Mr. Sidious said.

"Can you control it?" Jay asked

"No, well, not technically, I have been studying how this could even be possible for many years but phasing on land is something that we have never seen. You see... Phasing is meant to be activated through destiny, uh uh, alignment if you will. You see one can only phase when they are activated in their true element which for Aqui and Los is the water. However, there was one time that I have seen someone phase on land for a brief moment. The elders brother, ah yes... but however he is lost so my research is limited." Mr. Worthy said, looking down in despair.

"BUT you three... you are interesting, you three seem to still be showing symptoms of phasing on land." Mr. Worthy said.

"But wait, what do you mean? I thought you said we can't phase on land" Sokki said

"Yes, yes, you can't, however. When you first wake up to your Aqui body, you show early symptoms of your body aiming to adjust, meaning. Your body has to make room for the new chromosomes and in order for that to happen certain walls in your cell structure have to grow, on a... multi molecular level. When that happens your genetic structure is modified and sometimes even compromised... I suppose in English that means that your body responds to the change rather hmmm irregularly. You may experience, let's say uhh anger or frustration and yes, you may see signs of phasing... Jay, I've noticed your sharp teeth, Kye we know how strong you are... And Sokki... Could probably electrify an entire 500 gallon pool if she wanted to. But all of this we are seeing on land. For an extended amount of time... we usually never see this but we have strong suspicion of why" Mr. Worthy said.

"David, stop, they are not ready for that yet!" Mr. Sidious said sharply

"Ready for what?" Sokki asked

"Wait, wait, so you're telling me that we are not the only Aqui?" Jay said.

"No, you are it... Son, we haven't seen an Aqui in over 20 years. This is why we are shocked that you three even exist." Mr. Sidious said.

"No... so what happened to the others?" Jay asked. The four teachers were really quiet...Mrs. Noble cleared her throat.

"They umm, they were killed," She said.

"What?! By who?" Jay asked.

"By Los im assuming!" Sokki said.

"See, I told you she was smart" Ms. Till said.

"I don't understand. You said that we made peace over the land?" Jay asked in a confused tone.

"No, I never said that our tribe made peace with the Los, we will never be at peace with them. It's just not possible. The Los and Aqui agreed to share the land that is it. For a slight moment in the early days of Los Aqui, things seemed as if they could be completely peaceful until one day, shortly after the war. The Los began hunting the Aqui in our city, we recently decided to wage full war on the Los almost five years ago when two of our own and one innocent by standard were kidnapped and killed by the Los. However, the Aqui have gone into hiding to protect themselves, their true identity and most importantly...The ones around them" Mr. Sidious said.

"We have to be frank with you... A war is coming and you all three need to be ready" Mr. Worthy said staring at the three.

"A war? But hold on, Since we have the same abilities.. How do we know who is Los and who is Aqui?" Jay said.

"It's a feeling, you can feel it," Mr. Sidious said. Jay gave him a funny look as if Mr. Sidious just told him that he is a Jedi.

*"No, seriously when you are with your family. You can tell"* Mr. Sidious said.

*"Ok, close your eyes ….. What do you feel"* Mr. Sidious said.

*"I feel fine, kinda strong actually,"* Jay said.

*"Ok then, you see that? That's because you are around Aqui. Trust me, if you weren't then your senses would be ringing off of the charts. You would know, have you three been experiencing anything weird happen to you lately? And tingles? Twitches? This is more important for us to know than you think"* Mr. Sidious said.

The three students together made a unanimous decision together to gesture no. even though this wasn't the case. Jay immediately thought about his shaking, Kye about his headache and Sokki about her anxiety.

*"Ok, but why us? Why were we just randomly chosen to receive this gift?"* Sokki asked.

*"Well hun, there is only one way that you can become an Aqui…"* Ms. Noble chimed in. Then and there another silence was born in the room, a strange one and an oddly placed one that made Sokki uncomfortable.

*"Ummm"* Sokki said fishing for answers

Mr. Sidious gave the nod to his teachers similar to king lion signaling to baby cubs that it's okay to talk to his new found friends.

*"Minus the elders, you have to be born from an Aqui".* Mrs. Noble said.

**"KNOCK, KNOCK, KNOCK!"**

To the students, the knock didn't seem to present itself as completely real, maybe a symbolic nature of a drumming beating down an empty street with only hollow buildings to echo off of. This was all a component of their heart at the moment.

Beating at a rate of 120 beats per minute, faster than one would typically administer CPR on an unconscious person. Their souls dropped to their feet only to be picked up back again when they realized that it was an actual knock on the door of the room and not realty knocking for them to let it in.

***KNOCK, KNOCK, KNOCK!*_**

*"GUYS, I NEED YOUR HELP TO PACK UP SOME STUFF, DO YOU MIND GIVING ME A HAND SINCE YOUR STILL UP?"* A voice said from outside.

*"Um, why yet of course. We will meet you there!"* Mr. Worthy said.

The room remained quiet, the students due to a state of shock from the last words Mrs. Noble uttered and the teachers to mask the silence to hear when Mr. Hines had stepped away.

*"Ok, you three need to leave. We will discuss this more in the morning... Congratulations, you are now Aqui!"* Mr. Sidious said as he was escorting them out of the room, once the students left Mr. Sisious sighed a relieved breath.

*"Well, how do you think that went?"* Mr. Worthy asked

*"Fairly well considering that they are some of the strongest Aqui that we have ever seen,"* Mr. Sidious said.

Back in Jay's room, Jay and Kye were sitting on their respective beds and Sokki was pacing back and forth.

*"Our parents? That means that we were all being lied to for 17 years. GREAT!"* Sokki said.

*"You heard him, our kind is being hunted so they have to remain quiet about their identity,"* Jay said.

"*Guys, so we are Aqui,*" Kye said.

"*Sokki, stop! Please stop pacing back and forth. We are all in the same position here... Calm down*" Jay said.

"*I doubt that*" she trembled underneath her breath.

"*What?*" Jay asked.

"*Nothing, I was just saying that this has all been a little overwhelming for me... For us all really i am going to try and get some sleep, you two should do the same*" She said.

She gave them both a hug then left the room. Jay turned off his light, causing the room to go pitch black. Then he laid down and one phrase haunted Jay in his sleep *"A war is coming".*

# CHAPTER 23

The next morning, business continued as normal with the students eating breakfast and continuing outside to conduct PT. After PT Mr. Hines gave his closing remarks to the class and the students instructions were to pack for the trip back home.

*"Sokki you comin?"* Yammy said, waving at her from on top of the staircase.

*"Yeah, I'll be right there I just need to finish checking something really quick,"* she said.

Sokki went into the science lab and reached in the freezer and pulled out a test kit that had a vial of blac fluid in it along with a red shirt that was propped up on a clamp. On the mini screen underneath the vial, it read: **"Test 98% complete."**

Meanwhile, Jay was walking outside on the pool deck with Mr. Worthy.

*"What is that you wanted to talk to me about?"* Jay said.

*"Well, it all makes sense now why my father is the photo that is missing and now I know who is hunting him..."* Jay said standing next to Mr. Worthy next to the forbidden pool.

*"And you figured this out all by yourself?"* Continue Mr. Worthy said.

*"There is something else I have to tell you, I wanted to tell you last night CAMP CHOICE DNE..."* Yes, we do know, we were the kids that snuck into the school that night.

Meanwhile, in the lab, the vial that Sokki was testing now read 100%. The light on the screen flashed green. She stared intensely at the screen. *"OH MY GOODNESS IT'S A MATCH"* She shrieked. She jumped back from the vial knocking over a table causing glass to shatter on the ground. She ran out of the lab and sprinted up the stairs to Jay's room to find Kye packing. She ran inside.

"Where's Jay??!!!" She asked.

"Woah, woah woah! Calm down, he is downstairs talking to Mr. Worthy by the pool" Kye said.

"WHAT??! What POOL??" She screamed and ran towards the window banging on it begging for Jay to hear her but she was unsuccessful. Looking through that window down on him, she felt hopeless.

"SOKKI, what is wrong?" Kye said, grabbing Sokki by the shoulders, staring at her in her eye.

"I-i-i-i-i- I finished my test, th-th-the test!! From Jay's shirt, you know the black stuff that landed on his shirt?? I tested against octopus INK and it is a direct match. Jay is in trouble!!" She said stuttering out breath barely able to get her words out.

"Ok, umm we have to go, c'mon!!' Kye took her hand and they rushed downstairs as fast as they could, swinging their way through students.

***

"Ok, but Jay if you were at that school then the cameras would have caught you and since you're not on the... SO you're telling me that someone erased the cameras but who?" Mr. Worthy asked.

"IIIT WASSSSS MEEEEE!!!!!!" A deep horrendous terrifying voice came from behind Jay. A big black gigantic figure emerged from the water. Jay felt a slimy rope wrapped around his neck extremely tight and picked him up in the air.

"NOOOOO!" Mr. Worthy yelled at the top of his lungs.

# SPLASH

Jay was being choked, panicking and strangling his legs as he turned around to see what got a hold of him.

When he did, he saw a ginormous black octopus with purple spots with big white eyes. Jay realized that he was being choked out by one of his tentacles. The deck began to get foggy, Jay could barely see Mr. Worthy

"HELLOO YOUNGSTER!!" The octopus said. Staring into Jay's eyes

"WELL, IF IT ISN'T MR. WORTHY. REMEMBER ME? JOHNNY SILVER?! THE KID THAT YOU LET DROWN IN A THUNDERSTORM? I REMEMBER IT LIKE IT WAS YESTERDAY!!

It was the last week before camp. It was raining outside, I had just completed one of the impossible scenarios, I wanted to show you that I have been working on my backstroke, I was the only one in the pool when all of a sudden, **"BOOOOOM!"** Lightning struck the edge of the pool right THERE! *"Where my emblem is"* The octopus said while he shoved Jay right in front of his emblem. Then he raised him back up high in the air

"SO WHERE WAS I...? AH YES, SOMETHING STRANGE ABOUT ME AT THE TIME, OH I DON'T KNOW... MAYBE I WASN'T THAT GOOD OF A SWIMMER...

"So what did you do, you stood there, on the edge of the pool deck, it was windy, and it was raining, we were in the middle of a storm!! And you stood there like a coward and watched me drown!!! For what?? You could've easily saved me but NO!! YOU DIDN'T you sent a dive rescue team to come and rescue me but they didn't find a body. BECAUSE by then I had already become what you see now. So yes, when all of those schools thought it was a briiiiight idea to bring more students into CAMP CHOICE which is my home I decided to show them what happened to ME!! So I drowned them! Six in counting. Yoooouuuu want to be number seven??" The octopus said as he brung Jay closer to his own face.

*"Something feels off about you kid! Anywhoooo when I heard that you had the sheer audacity to come back to my pool, my home. I said that's it! I have had it! It just so happened this meidling student interfered with my plan so I erased the tape to a degree to ensure that you would be here and NOT IN JAIL. SO YES you little kid you. YOU'RE WELCOME!!"* The octopus said.

*"Johnny, your quarrel is with me, not HIM! He is just an innocent boy!!"* Mr. Worthy yelled.

*'PLEASE, I'm BEGGING you, put him down!"* Mr. Worthy said.

*'OK!! YOU ASKED!!"* The octopus said as he began to shove Jay under the water. At this moment, Sokki came running out of the building with Kye and the other three teachers to a pool deck full of fog. Through the fog Sokki felt like she was moving in slow motion as her heart began to pound, she felt as if her life flashed before eyes as she saw Jay being nearly choked to death and being shoved under water... *"**SPLAAASH**!!!"* Everyone froze, then Sokki ran towards the water, Kye grabbed her and held her back. She began fighting Kye, struggling to get out of his grip when she finally got loose she ran to the pool, just as she approached the edge she saw a great white shark swimming towards the surface of the water *"**WOOOOSH**!"* Jay emerged in his human form flying towards the pool deck, until a tentacle caught his neck again and began holding an even tighter grip this time around.

*"JAAAAY!"* Sokki cried

*"PUT HIM DOWN!!!"* She yelled in tears on her knees near the surface of the pool.

*"WAIT, NO THIS CAN'T BE POSSIBLE!!??? AN AQUI... ONE HASN'T BEEN SEEN IN OVER 20 YEARS... AND YOU'RE A SHARK?!! THAT CAN ONLY MEAN ONE THING, THERE IS ONLY ONE SHARK AQUI FAMILY, AND DID YOU SAY JAY?? AS IN JAY CRUZ?? THAT MUST MEAN THAT*

YOU'RE.... OH BOY THIS NIGHT JUST GOT EVEN BETTER. HAHAHAHAHAHAHAH!"

"Jay Cruz, what a pleasure it is to meet you! You know? I and you are destined to meet, we have A LOT in common ya know being the son of an elder and all!" The octopus said.

Jay's eyes became big from hearing the information as he struggled to get air.

"What? You didn't hear?? Yes, your father and my father are the reason your precious little city of Los Aqui exists. OUCH!!" The octopus said. Kye and Sokki were throwing boulders at the octopus.

'OK, looks like things are happening in threes!" The octopus said has he grabbed the two of them each with a tentacle and began choking them

"You see? That's the good thing about having 8 arms, I never run out of space!!"

Meanwhile, Jay was losing color in his face, struggling even less progressively.

Mrs. Noble began sprinting towards the water. She dove into the water, she got to the bottom of the pool, there was a red light coming from the bottom,

"AHH!" The octopus yelled as he sank back under water releasing the three of them. They fell into the water, as they did they phased until they swam back up to the surface of the water.

"What is she doing??" Jay yelled from inside the water.

"She is holding him, and she won't be able to hold him for long!! Ok, Sarah go inside and make sure not a single student comes outside don't worry about the windows because this fog is giving us the perfect cover.

*Sokki, can you create enough shock to generate a volt through a natural source?"* Mr. Worthy asked her.

Ms. Till ran towards the building. *"I think so! But why??"* Sokki asked

At this moment, Jay had an epiphany. *"Because! We need to recreate that night that Johnny Silver drowned!"* Jay said

*"How do… You know that?"* Sokki asked curiously.

*"I will tell you later, right now there is no time!"* Jay said.

'*Uh, yeah! I should be able to!"* Sokki yelled behind her to Mr. Worthy.

*"Ok, I am going to cut this wire on this volt box and throw it in the pool, when I do. I want you to generate your shock then send it down towards Johnny got it?"* Mr. Worthy asked.

*"Got it,"* She said.

Mr. Worthy cut the wire and threw it in the pool but Sokki could not generate from it.

*"I think we need something stronger!"* Jay said.

*"Where do we find that??!"* He asked.

*"THERE!"* Jay pointed to the electricity poll right near the main gate. He remembered that poll from the picture in the file.

*"JAY, in order for that to work we would need-"*

*"All of us to transfer the shock YES I know!"* Jay said.

*"OK but…. Since you can absorb the most impact, Jay you are going to have to deliver the shock and Sokki will initiate it. With a shock like*

that, it could kill you the moment it touches your body!!" Mr. Worthy said.

"Great whites can absorb over two hundred volts of shock at a time, Sokki how much is the poll?" Jay asked.

"Seven hundred!" Sokki said,

"Ok, let's try it!" Jay said.

"Jay' Are you crazy?? You COULD DIE!!" Sokki said.

"Yeah Jay, that is pretty risky!" Kye said.

"Guys!! Either I try or she dies!! This is no time to be Skeptical!" Jay said.

"Ok, you over here" Mr. Worthy said to Sokki and Kye.

"Ok, here is how this is going to work. Sokki I am going to pull this wire from the box, and throw it to you in the pool then from there you channel an electromagnetic current from it then transfer it to Kye, then Kye you transfer it to Jay. Is everyone ready?" Mr. Worthy said.

"YES!" Jay and Kye said.

"I can't!! What if you two die??" Sokki said.

"Sokki, remember what I said to you a week ago? Trust me!" Jay said.

Sokki began to panic

"SOKKI!! WE DON'T HAVE TIME… Do you remember? Just like tag, you must have FAITH, Faith right now is the strongest weapon we have." Jay uttered peering into Sokki's soul

Sokki remembered that she had said those exact words to Jay and Kye. She closed her eyes and took a deep breath in. The three of them submerged under water. The Eel began to charge her body, her eyes opened glowing blue. The Shark and Iguana viewed in amazement as they have never seen this before from her. The wire got thrown in the water, the eel absorbed the electrical current from the wire creating an initial shock effect in the pool.

She swam towards the iguana, the iguana reached his hand out touching the Eel's nose. When he did, his eyes and veins also became blue, still connected with the eel.

He swam towards the shark and placed his hand on the shark's fin transfering the shock. The shark's eyes became blue pulsing with electricity. At this time the Octopus observed a bright light coming from the surface of the pool. He pushed the sword fish to the bottom of the pool and swam up towards the surface.

The shark then detached from the iguana and swam faster up towards the surface. The Eel and Iguana looked in shock. The shark broke the surface at the same time as the evil octopus, Jay remained in his Aqui form out of the water, glowing blue in mid air looking at the octopus the shark turned his fin towards the octopus releasing a great shock lightning bolt. *"BOOOOOOOOOOOM!!!!"* There was a big flash of black and blue light in the air, fog began to thicken in the midst of the explosion, the air was eerie and calm with no voice to be heard.

# CHAPTER 24

The three students and teacher climbed out of the water, all out of breath. On the ground panting. The fog in the air began to clear.

*"Did we get him?"* Mrs. Noble said out of breath.

*"Yeah, I think you did…. There are only two times when you will see ora from a Los or Aqui, when they wake up or when they die. His ora just shined for the last time"* Mr. Worthy said.

Mr. Sidious came and helped everyone up from the ground.

*"Is everyone ok?"* He asked.

No one said anything but he observed that no one seriously hurt due to their tiresome body posture on the floor. Jay looked at Sokki and Kye barely squinting his eyes through the smoke. He was laying on the ground using his elbow as a kickstand to hold him up.

*"Jay, Jay. Jay!"* Sokki said running over to where he was

*"Are you ok? Are you hurt?!"* Sokki yelled as she finally ran over to where Jay was. Kye was shortly behind her.

Jay made a grunting noise as he got pushed himself up

*"Ah you scared me! I don't know why you did that! You could have gotten yourself killed!"* Sokki said as she gave him a big hug and embraced him

*"To say the least!"* Kye said while he held his hand out to help Jay to get up from the ground.

*"I don't... Know, I just felt it"* Jay said. The three of them looked over at the teachers standing a few feet away in a huddle.

# SPLASH

"Was that a swordfish I saw Mrs. Noble?" Jay asked

"Haha, Let's take a walk" Mrs. Noble said with a slight smirk on.

The seven of them walked outside of the gate a few yards away from camp.

"Yes, I am, or my Aqui if you will, is a Siberian Swordfish". Mrs Noble said.

"So, the Los or the Aqui, their underwater creatures... that's... Another version of themselves?" Jay asked while limping out towards the forbidden lands of the desert although just about everything in Centerport was considered forbidden.

"Yes, but you are also it, meaning you and your Aqui are one when you have phased, you have your own instincts plus that of that of your Aqui" Mr. Sidious said.

"So that's Johnny silver?" Jay asked, looking around at Kye and Sokki then looking back up at the teachers.

"Yes, Jonny Silver, son of Zach Silver, who is the Los Elder. Jonny has been in that pool for a very long time, that is probably why he is able to remain phased when he is out of the water..." Mr. Worthy said.

"So, you three were the one who took the documents from the school that night?" Mr. Sidious asked.

"No, no, no, no! We didn't, we promise, we did sneak into the school to look at the documents. I saw that envelope that said do not enter camp choice. And I wanted to know why... I'm sorry" Jay said.

"I can't tell if it was Jay's instincts or your Aqui's instincts that kicked in that night" Ms. Till said.

"Wait... So our instincts are like double?" Kye said.

"Yes, but remember this, gaining full control over your phasing abilities does take some time to get used to... which leads me to think. Jay how were you still phased when you dove out of the water to throw the electricity at Silver?" Mr. Worthy asked

"I... don't know" Jay said

"Well, that was remarkable... I haven't seen a phase out of the water like that since... your Father, well your uncle really" Mr. Worthy said.

"WAIT WHAT??" Kye asked, looking at Jay.

"Your father is the Aqui elder from the battle of Los Aqui??" Sokki asked, confused.

"Yes, David Cruz, the elder of the Aqui" Mr. Worthy said.

Kye and Sokki stared at Jay in disbelief with their mouths wide open, Sokki was covering her mouth with her hand with big eyes. The two of them began to bow.

"My apologies my Majesty" Kye said the group laughed at his comment

The elder and his brother were the only two of known location and contact until the elders brother disappeared and we haven't heard from him or seen him since. We are under the assumption that the Los has captured them" Mr. Worthy said.

"Wait... You said that you must be born from Aqui to become an Aqui... So that means that my parents..." Sokki was interrupted.

"Sokki, hun imma stop you there. We have decided that we are going to let you have that conversation on your own with your mother" Ms. Till said.

"Wait, but how come Jay doesn't get that chance?" Sokki asked with her hands on her hips.

*"Well, because Silver ruined that for Jay"* Worthy said.

*"So we really just defeated a Los!"* Jay said

*"Yes, well to be quite honest we were lucky, there is a much greater threat coming. This could have gone extremely terrible, but that is neither here nor there"* Mr. Sidious said.

*"And plus, it's time for your ceremony!"* Ms. Till said in tired excitement.

*"Ceremony?"* Kye asked

*"Yes, your Aqui ceremony. It is mandatory that we do this for each Aqui that eventually wakes up."*

*"We hereby dub you officially Aqui"* Mr. Sidious said as he touched each one of them with a sword on the shoulders. Thank you for being noble heroes today, you shall now be noble heroes for the rest of your life. There are 4 four rules for being an AQUI.

- *"Never take a life without just cause."*
- *"Always use your powers for good."*
- *"Never turn your back on Aqui."*
- *"You must never tell anyone that you are Aqui."*

The teachers began to clap with enthusiasm and excitement. Then the group began walking back to the camp along the long dusty road.

*"Mr. Sidious?"* Jay asked

*"Yes Jay?"* he responded

*"Why can't we tell people that we are Aqui?"* Jay asked

*"Well, there are two types of people in this city, first there are…"*

*"Ones who believe in God and those who don't?"* Jay interrupted.

"Yes, but what I was going to say is there are those who believe that the Los and Aqui's are an ancient myth, a folktale if you will. And then there are those who believe that the Los and Aqui war happened thousands of years ago and they are extinct like dinosaurs". Mr. Sidious said.

"So why don't they have a museum for us? …. Yall… us. You know what I mean" Jay asked.

"We still have some pull in this city and I won't let that happen," Mr. Worthy said.

The group eventually returned to camp, shortly after the same bus that had brought them to their destination had returned to take them home still hosting the cracked windows. Mr. Hines gathered everyone around in front of the bus.

"Ok, LISTEN UP. After I announce to you who will be working for me this off season, I will do a quick roll call then we will go home. First and foremost, I just want to say that I am extremely proud of you and all that you have accomplished over this summer. You all have worked really hard and I am grateful for that. More importantly, you should be proud of yourselves. Do not, I repeat, do not let anything or anyone in this world stop you from reaching your fullest potential. From what you all have exhibited this summer, you now have no excuse, no excuse to not reaching your fullest potential. Now… The new team members of HR tactical are….. SOKKI, YAMMY, TAMMY, KYE AND……… JAY!" Mr. Hines said. The group began to clap and cheer for their fellow classmates. This was one of the only times that Jay felt appreciated by his peers.

The students all piled on the bus with hopes of returning home safely. The trip seemed to warrant a shorter distance than that of its previous wearabouts. Throughout the trip, Jay thought about what returning to their parents would present. He thought about his time in Jail and how glad he was to be released. The entire trip, he didn't doze off. He stayed awake anxious for their return.

When the bus parked, the three students waited for all of the students to exit the bus before they did themselves. After everyone was gone, the teachers walked up to Sokki, Jay and Kye and gave them a hug,

*"Remember, you are family now,"* Ms. Till said.

The three left their Aqui family and began walking home to their neighborhoods. During this hike back home with their luggage, not much was said to each other, silence was the majority. When it was time for them to split ways they gave each other a ginormous hug, they could agree that they became even closer than they already were.

*"Love you"* Sokki said to the boys.

*"Hey wait... we need a name"* Sokki said just as she was about to walk away.

*"For what?"* Kye asked

*"Well, we are kinda like heroes... water heroes!"* She said with enthusiasm.

*"JSK?"* Kye asked.

*".... How about....... SPLASH!"* Jay said.

*"I like it!"* Sokki said.

*"Yeah me too! But why splash?"* Kye said.

*"Huh, I don't know yet, but that is the sound we make when we jump in the water... I guess we will have to come up with an acronym for that later"* Jay said.

*"You know? I guess we will"* Sokki said smiling.

*"Bye guys"* Jay said, going his separate way.

The three of them went their separate ways, Sokki reached her house first.

Before Sokki walked into her house, she took a deep breath. Then lugged her bags up the steps that led to her front door.

Sokki walked into her house distraught.

"Hey honey, your home!" Her mother said as she rushed to her to give her a hug.

"Uh huh, don't hug me" Sokki said to her mother.

"Excuse me?" Ms. Sioso said, shocked at Sokki's response trying to figure out why her daughter was telling her not to hug after not seeing her all summer. The house was quiet and an unsettling tension rose to the occasion.

"You freaking liar!! How could you mom?? You have been lying to me about the way dad died, lion accident huh?! Real convenient, you lied to me about who he really was. How could you? AND you kept this from me, my abilities?? You didn't even have the decency to tell me the truth. Instead, you let me sit here… FATHERLESS from a lie?? Really?? YEP! GREAT! Team Sioso ALRIGHT! What a load of B.S. I am what I am and you couldn't tell me that I have these abilities?" Sokki said, yelling with her voice trembling, red eyes and tears running down into her mouth.

"Honey, I have no idea what your" Her mom paused, getting cut off by her daughter.

"Oh NO?? More lies, when will your lying stop?! You… are … so… full… of crap" Sokki said.

Breathing heavy in between her words. At that moment, a multitude of tears came traveling down Sokki's face.

Sokki walked over to the sink and slammed up the sink faucet nozzle nearly breaking it, she let the water run then she stuck her hand in the water. Blue pulses of electricity began vibrating from her hands.

*"I'm so sorry"* Ms. Sioso said with tears running down her face.

Meanwhile back at Kye's house, the mood was a little less harsh.

Kye walked into his house and his mom was sitting at the dining table.

*"How was camp son?"* She asked.

*"GOOD! Hey mom, hey we needa talk… dad is not the person we thought he was."*

*"But son, what do you mean?"* Ms. Nacksworth asked.

*"I'll explain everything,"* Kye said.

Finally, Jay had reached his home to return to his beloved bed soon. He walked into his house and set his bag down. His dad and his cousin rushed up to him to give him a hug.

*"How was it?"* they asked him after hugging him.

*"CRAZY, but good. Hey dad, me and you need to sit down and talk later"* Jay said.

*"Ok son, I would like that. I have been waiting to have this talk for 17 years."* He said.

The two of them made eye contact, Jay's eyes were filled with disappointed curiosity and the hint of frustration for his father but from his comment he knew that his father knew the contents of the discussion.

Zeke walked up to Jay after taking his bags upstairs.

"Hey Jay, your friend from camp just called like 5 minutes before you walked in. He told me to tell you that he had a great time and he is looking forward to getting to know you better, he said he will see you soon.. His name... Let me see I wrote it down. Oh! John wait, uhhh Johnny……….. Oh yah………….. Johnny Silver."

*...to be continued*

**THE END**

Made in United States
Troutdale, OR
09/08/2025